First published 2020

First printed edition published 2024 by Drollery Ltd.

Copyright © Alice Coldbreath, 2020

ISBN 978-1-916736-07-8

More books available by Alice Coldbreath:

The Vawdrey Brothers Series:

Book 1: Her Baseborn Bridegroom

Book 2: His Forsaken Bride

Book 3: An Ill-Made Match

The Brides of Karadok Series:

Book 1: Wed By Proxy

Book 2: The Unlovely Bride

Book 3: The Consolation Prize

Book 4: Her Bridegroom, Bought and Paid For

Book 5: An Inconvenient Vow

Book 6: The Favourite

The Victorian Prizefighter Series:

Book 1: A Bride for the Prizefighter

Book 2: A Substitute Wife for the Prizefighter

Book 3: A Contracted Spouse for the Prizefighter

The Royal Palace at Caer-Lyoness

Lenora's shoulder twitched. Did they really imagine she could not hear them?

"'Twould be better," her father's voice said heavily, "if she'd died, rather than suffer this cruel fate."

"That face—it's a mockery of her former self," her mother sobbed dramatically. "Whatever will become of her?"

"Oh, my poor lady." Lenora heard someone weep. She guessed it was Hannah, her maidservant. "Her face, her lovely face. It's quite ruined."

Unable to bear much more of their caterwauling, Lenora stirred, letting them see she was conscious. After all, she supposed she would have to speak to them at some point.

"She wakens!" her mother screeched and fell against her husband in a swoon.

Trust Mother, thought Lenora sourly, *to make it all about her.*

"Thirsty," Lenora murmured. She noticed it was the old crone, who had been attending her since she had been afflicted, who came forward now to pour water for her. Her solicitous parents stayed pinned against the door for fear the pox was still catching even though it must be well over two months now since she'd been truly ill.

Thank goodness she was on a bed now. For weeks she had lain on a filthy straw mattress in the crypts below the royal palace, with the other afflicted, waiting for death. But the raging fever, aches, pains, and vomiting had passed. Then the rash had come with a profusion of small red pustules that had covered her face entirely in bumps. In lucid moments, Lenora had felt them beneath her fingertips, marring her skin and making her own face feel like that of a stranger's.

At the time, of course, she had been more worried about the spots that had filled her raw throat, making it difficult even to breathe. Many a time she had woken in the night, choking and gasping for breath. Even her tongue had been swollen with spots. She had forced herself to swallow each mouthful of water down her throat, so sore it had felt like she had blades embedded in it.

The worse part though, to Lenora's mind, was when the pustules had erupted their noxious fluid all over her face and down her throat. She had retched as her mouth was filled with its taste and her raw face was bathed from the weeping open sores. She even felt it run into her greasy, crusted hair. Her sweaty, dirty body had squirmed. She hated even to breathe the foul air that surrounded her.

The crypt had been manned with ghoulish-looking attendants, their faces covered with scarves. They nudged you with booted feet to check if you were still alive and grudgingly brought you water. Lenora heard them railing and threatening those who piteously wept for aid, so when the time came that she realized she was not actually going to die, she had not begged. She had demanded in a loud, imperious voice.

2

She had threatened and she had bribed until they had brought her watery soup to drink, so she could grow strong enough to lift herself off the squalid pallet she lay on. She had insisted, too, on washing water and a clean mattress and a shift once her sores had scabbed over. When she could not get a comb through her matted mess of blond hair, she had called for shears and cut it herself to her shoulders where once it had hung down so low she could sit upon it. She had cut it blindly, refusing a looking glass. She was not that brave. Not yet.

Finally, she had been permitted to ascend from the fetid cellars to empty quarters in the south wing of the castle. The bare walls and broken furniture had seemed like luxury after the dark, dank crypts, and there she had set about her long road to recovery. She slept on a bed, she had clean clothes, and she had Berta, an old washerwoman, to attend her. It was now getting on three months since she had collapsed. In truth, she was well again and quite free now from all infection.

There was just one area that would never recover naturally and that was her former looks. She had shied away from demanding a looking glass. She could feel the rough, uneven skin along her jaw, the puckered texture across her cheekbones. Even the smallest thing, like closing her eyes, made her realize how tight and crinkled the skin on her eyelids felt. She must truly be hideous now. Her parents' words now confirmed it like a knife to the heart. But she still wanted to live.

She wanted to live so badly. Hearing her father say that it would have been better for her to have died filled her with a hot, bubbling anger. Of course, he did not know how she had fought even to breathe that musty, diseased air down in the vaults, surrounded by the bones of the dead. How would he? He had not been to visit her even once.

"Where are my cats?" she said aloud. "I want my cats to be brought to me."

They met her words with a stunned silence. "Your cats?" her father asked at last.

Lenora nodded. "I am quite well now and would appreciate their company." When no one spoke, she turned to Hannah. "You will have them brought to me, forthwith."

"Aye, milady," she gasped and bobbed a curtsey, though she could not meet Lenora's gaze.

"And you will send me a looking glass," Lenora forced herself to say. Her mother emitted a low moan. "It would be as well for me to know the worst," she added with quiet dignity.

"My child…" her father started, but when Lenora looked at him enquiringly, his eyes swiveled away, avoiding hers. "We will send the cats and your personal things," he said lamely.

"Thank you," Lenora said briskly. "Berta, will you bring me my mantle? For I mean to rise now and sit awhile. I must have a letter from Eden to read somewhere." Her cousin Eden was the one member of her family who Lenora prized above all others. Eden wrote to her once a month without fail.

Her father cleared his throat, and Lenora looked up sharply. "Here it is," he said, reaching into his doublet. He held it out toward Berta, who stepped forward to take it from him. "It was delivered by hand this time," he added. "Doubtless you have lost track of time, daughter, but the Autumn Tournament is upon us."

"Eden is here?" Lenora burst out. Her cousin was now married to the King's champion, Roland Vawdrey, and often toured the country with him whilst competing.

4

"Nay," her father said, clearing his throat. "Eden has not long discovered she is with child. Sir Roland did not permit her to accompany him to Caer-Lyoness this time, when so many have fallen prey to the speckled pox."

Lenora relaxed slightly against her pillows. "No, of course not," she said quickly. "He is right to be cautious with her health." She took the note from Berta with hands that slightly shook. So, her cousin knew what had befallen her. Indeed, Eden must have wondered why Lenora had not written to her all this while. Though not as regular in her habits as Eden, Lenora did write— dutifully to her grandmother and fondly to Eden.

Lenora twisted the letter between her fingers. A feeling of strange nameless panic washed over her. She had been living in a sort of dreamlike state while she convalesced, concentrating only on getting better. Thinking about it now and watching her parents awkwardly take their leave of her, shuffling backward through the door, she wondered if she had purposely shied away from all thoughts of what people's reactions to her would be.

Yes, she thought with detachment as Berta bundled her woolen mantle around her shoulders. She rather thought she had. The older woman held out a scrawny arm to steady her as Lenora levered herself out of the bed. She still felt washed out and lacking in energy, though not quite as weak as she had been.

Tottering across the floor, she dropped into a high-backed chair and sat patiently as Berta plied her with cushions and jammed slippers onto her bare feet. Tearing open Eden's letter, she found her eyes filling with tears as she read:

Darling Lenora,

You will have to excuse my appalling scrawl, but I have written so many letters these last few days that my hand is quite incapable of elegance.

5

My dear, I cannot tell you how dismayed I am that Uncle has only recently apprised me of what has happened at the summer court. I am greatly relieved to hear of your resilience and recovery and am determined to have you here at Vawdrey Keep for the duration of the year. Roland quite agrees with me, and as he will be at Caer-Lyoness for the Autumn Tournament, we have made arrangements for him to bring you back here with him.

What a happy family party we will have! I am not sure if you have heard, but I am expecting our first child in the spring, and Roland has become extremely overprotective, else I would have journeyed with him to watch him compete at the Autumn Tournament. Forgive me for not being there in your time of need. I am determined to make it up to you when you accompany Roland back to Sitchmarsh where I will endeavor to make you most comfortable.

I am beside myself with anticipation to introduce you to our home with its surroundings which are of great natural beauty. It is true that presently we are in the midst of building work for expansion of the Keep, but I know you will appreciate our vision and I am convinced we can make you comfortable here.

I am sure you have suffered terribly, Lenora, and I look forward to having you here with me at last, and I might add that our grandmother quite agrees with the plan. We neither of us think that the convent idea is a good one for your future. I beg you, please do not make any hasty decisions before you have had a chance to fully consider your position and to recoup after your illness. Things can appear overwhelming when you do not have enough distance from them. I am convinced that Vawdrey Keep is the ideal place for you to fortify your good health and I await your arrival with keen affection.

Your ever-loving cousin,

Eden

Lenora lowered the letter and stared blankly at the wall opposite. There was a convent plan? Strangely enough, her father had not seen fit to raise it with her just now. The cynical thought flashed into her mind that her parents' visit might have been prompted by Eden's flurry of letters. She had no doubt her cousin's letter-writing campaign had been about her. Eden would have been writing to her grandmother at Hallam Hall as well as Lenora's mother and father here at court. *If Eden had not written, would my parents have stayed away even longer?* she wondered. On the whole, she thought it more likely than not. They had evinced no pleasure at the sight of her. Quite the opposite, in fact.

A convent? Would she even be allowed to keep her precious cats there? Many was the time Lenora had heard her own father extoll that joining a religious order was a "waste of a life." Yet now, he was more than happy for Lenora to disappear behind some abbey walls. Her loss of beauty apparently meant her life no longer held any value whatsoever.

Her gaze flickered to the window and the view of the kitchen gardens. Her current quarters were not exactly high-status ones. Indeed, she strongly suspected this part of the palace housed mostly servants. Still, the view was a pleasant one as the afternoon sun shed its golden rays over the neat herb and vegetable squares. *Could it really be the time of the Autumn Tournament?* she wondered with mild surprise. It had been early July when she been struck down with her illness. The castle had been almost suffocating in the heat. It was still warm, but the leaves were rapidly turning golden. She sighed and closed her eyes. The interview with her parents had been strangely draining, considering she had not set one foot out of her bed.

7

The chair was comfortable, and she must have dozed off, for the next thing she knew she was back in the darkness of the crypt with the sound of labored breathing all around her. Not again. Mercifully a knock on the door startled her into wakefulness. She jolted upright in her chair. Berta, who was laying the fire for that evening, hurried to answer it. For a moment, Lenora felt a sort of sick dread as to who it might be. She felt frankly ill prepared for visitors. However, she did not recognize the voice at the door, and the next thing she saw was a basket being thrust into Berta's hands. Lenora almost cried out. Surely that was a faint meow she heard.

"Oh, bring them to me, Berta!" The older woman muttered under her breath but shut the door and carried the basket over to her gingerly. "Unfasten it! Oh, never mind, you're too slow," Lenora said, shuffling forward in her seat. "Set it here." She patted her lap. Her eager fingers fumbled with the straps and she flung back the lid. There lay Lady Grizelda, her own dear beloved cat, and next to her, three adolescent males who were not yet fully grown. "Oh, my darlings!" Lenora crooned. Purcel opened his mouth in a soundless meow; Tybalt sprang to his feet and then jumped down to the floor, and Fendrel blinked at her and yawned. "You're so much bigger!" Lenora lamented. She had missed three whole months of their kittenhood! Lady G uncurled herself and then swarmed out of the basket and onto Lenora's chest. She stretched her face up toward her mistress, and Lenora lowered her own and they touched brows. Lenora felt her eyes swim, and she realized she had been afraid even her pets would recoil from her altered appearance. As if to allay her fears, Grizelda immediately started to loudly purr. "I've missed you so!" Lenora told her, embracing her pet and feeling her cheeks turn wet as the tears streamed down unchecked. At least the cats could be relied on for constancy in their affections, if no one else.

8

It was not until after her supper of simple pottage and bread that Lenora noticed the other item she had sent for. Her hand, which had been stroking the youngest of the kittens, Fendrel, stilled. Her looking glass lay facedown on the side table. Lenora stretched out one arm but could not quite reach it from her seated position. She glanced down at the gray kitten who was stretched out on her lap with an expression of sleepy bliss on his face. She would not disturb him. His comfort was too precious, and besides, she needed to rebond with the three boys. They were almost fully grown and had been forced to do without her for so long. She glanced over at the bed where Grizelda had settled herself with her eldest son, Purcel. His black coat shone in direct contrast to his mother's gleaming white. Tybalt, the ginger, was sat on the window ledge, washing his paw. Lenora sighed with relief. Their return to her was a blessing she could be thankful for.

Berta shuffled into the room and removed the tray of food. She scanned the remains in the bowl with disfavor. "Will we put the leftovers down for the cats?" she asked doubtfully.

"I doubt they'd eat it."

"Beggars can't be choosers," Berta sniffed.

"They're not beggars," Lenora answered. "But you can try by all means."

Berta pulled a face and plunked the bowl down in the corner and set about lighting the small fire. Lenora glanced in the direction of the hand mirror again before looking away. She would wait until Berta left her for the night. "Berta," she said impulsively. "Have the knights arrived yet for the tourney?"

Berta jerked her chin aggressively. "Oh aye," she said bitterly. "Flooding in like a swarm of locusts. Nasty, brawling brutes!"

9

It seemed that Berta was not an admirer of knights. "Apparently my cousin's husband has already arrived. Sir Roland Vawdrey."

"I don't know one from t'other." Berta scowled. "And what's more, I don't want to know!"

"His standard is a black panther on a red field," Lenora elaborated, but Berta made no reply. "Has the tournament begun? The jousting, I mean."

"I wouldn't know." Berta huffed. "I got better things to be going on with."

"Well, perhaps you could ask some of the other palace staff," Lenora said pointedly. "It would be useful for me to know."

Berta looked sullen and straightened up from the fire. "Anything else?"

"Some fish, for the cats." Berta drew a scandalized breath, but Lenora forestalled her before she could make her retort. "Tell the kitchen staff it is for me."

The door slammed shut as the curmudgeonly Berta retreated. Fendrel was startled from his slumber and shot an accusing look at his mistress. "There, there," Lenora murmured, but he refused to be pacified and jumped down, making his way to join his sibling at the window.

Lenora stood up slowly from her chair, stretched her stiff body, and went to retrieve the looking glass. Taking a deep breath, she turned it over and held it in front of her face.

Oh.

Despite the shock of her own reflection, Lenora slept the best that night that she had in a long time. She attributed it to the familiar weight of the cats curled up on her bed. It was strangely soothing somehow, and even though she was plagued with the usual bad dreams, the cats' presence made sure she was *aware* it was only a dream and not her present reality. She gritted her teeth until she could surface into wakefulness, and when she did, she lay there a moment, dazed and blinking as she heard Berta bustling around in the adjoining room. Presently the old woman entered carrying a jug of warm washing water.

"Black with a white gate, yellow with a black stag, and blue with a white hart," she chanted like an incantation.

Lenora rubbed her eyes, sitting up. "Good morning, Berta," she murmured. "What did you say?" Then she realized it had been a recitation of knights' crests. "Blue with a white hart?" she repeated slowly. She knew that design. That would be Sir Lionel Emworth, heretofore one of her most devoted admirers. She threw back the covers. "Yellow with a black stag," she said thoughtfully as she slid from the bed, her feet hitting the floor. Surely, she knew that one too. She rather thought that was Sir Edward Bevan, who was a friend and companion of Roland Vawdrey's.

She crossed the room and poured water from the jug into the ewer. Lenora had always rather enjoyed the lists. She liked how you faded into the crowd as everyone watched the knights with bated breath, united in the spectacle. *What was the first one Berta had said?* Black with a white gate. *Oh.* She pulled a face. She knew who that was of course. Sir Garman Orde. Oh well, they couldn't all be crowd favorites.

"'Tis the first day today," Berta told her, setting down some drying cloths.

Lenora felt a flicker of something. The first day! She thought of the crowds, the fluttering pennants and standards, the banners, the hawkers, the pageantry. "Have you never been, Berta?" she asked, turning to the servant.

"Always been respectable, I have," the old woman said sourly. "They got no call for respectable women at those places," she added. "Or ugly ones."

Lenora stiffened, then realized the maidservant was not referring to her. She looked sidelong at Berta a moment, trying to imagine her as a young woman, and failing miserably.

"It's different for noble folk," the old woman said with a sniff. "You sits in a box away from the common rabble. Untouchable."

But was it? wondered Lenora. She doubted she would ever fade into a crowd now. Not with her face. *They've got no use for ugly women.* "Berta," she said, "I need you to make some purchases for me. Do you mean to go to the marketplace today?"

"I could do." Berta shrugged. "What are you after? Your people said they would send more of your clothing now you're up and about—"

"I need new head veils," Lenora interrupted her. "Opaque ones that cover your face."

The old woman squinted at her. "Is that so?"

"I want a good deal of them," said Lenora, lifting her chin. "One for every day of the week. Of all different lengths and sizes."

She felt strangely restless for the rest of the day. Berta returned in the afternoon with a bundle of veils for her to try out. Lenora found she could only achieve the level of opacity she desired by layering three veils of differing lengths on top of one another. She started with the shortest which extended over her face, then placed one over that which reached to her décolletage, and then another that extended down to her waist over that. Rolling her blond hair into a bun at her nape, she fitted a toque decorated with pearls to the top of her head, and then pinned another veil to the back of that and stood back to get the full effect. "Berta," she said, turning.

The old woman straightened up from the hearth she had been scraping out. She took one look at Lenora and fell back. "Lord's sake!" she squawked. "You look like a faceless specter!"

"Can you pass me my rose damask gown?"

"Where you be off to in that getup?" the old woman asked suspiciously as she helped lace her into the dress. It was the first time Lenora had been fully dressed since her illness.

"Nowhere," she answered lightly. "But I don't mean to lie in the sickbed all day long, now I have started on the road to recovery."

"Humph!" Berta shot her a suspicious look.

Lenora ate her supper of vegetable stew sat upright in her chair. Tybalt and Fendrel played at her feet with a loose thread from the unravelling chair upholstery. It was a castoff after all. Looking down, she noticed her dress was rather loose in the bodice. She supposed she could recover her figure at least, if she put her mind to it—if not her face.

A knock at the door was answered by Berta, and she heard the fretful tones of her father, Sir Leofric Montmayne. She wasn't really all that surprised. Her father had always been fonder of her than her mother. And Mother's presence always meant there could be no real exchange of conversation as she insisted everything revolved around herself. Indeed, Lenora had been surprised to see her mother at all as Lady Montmayne rarely bothered to come to court these days. Lenora supposed she should be flattered, really, that she had thought her daughter's illness warranted her presence.

Without thinking, Lenora drew down her veils and covered her face as her father approached.

"Lenora." He cleared his throat.

"Can we offer you any refreshment, Father?"

"Er—no," he said, retrieving a chair from against the wall. He whipped a handkerchief over it fussily before being seated and sat there in silence, looking about him. "We will have to see about having you moved from these apartments, Lenora," he started uncomfortably. "Now 'tis plain your life has been spared."

For a moment, she considered pointing out these rooms felt like luxury after being left to rot in the crypt for weeks, but thought the better of it and held her tongue. "And that attendant," he continued fretfully, "belongs at a deathbed, or a laying out, not serving the living." Lenora could think of no response to that either. Her father eyed her headdress approvingly. "A very good notion, that," he said, gesturing. "Though I think you should leave your hair loose, daughter. Your hair is still bountiful? It did not fall out?"

Lenora shook her head. "Though I was forced to cut some of its length."

"It is still of a good golden hue," he pointed out. "You must needs make the most of what is left to you. Especially if you—er—mean to resume public life."

"Public life?" Lenora was startled by the turn the conversation was taking.

Her father cleared his throat. "People are starting to ask after you. The Viscountess of Morpington, Lady Helen Cecil, indeed, the Queen herself has expressed an interest in your well-being."

"That is very good of them," Lenora replied in a wooden voice. Of course, she thought without rancor, they would be curious. They would all be vastly interested to see if she was still the most beauteous in all the land, or if another could now lay claim to that title. Lady Helen Cecil, the King's mistress, was the pretender to the role and was no doubt invested in the outcome. The thought of people appraising what was left of her looks made her feel a little sick.

"Your cousin Eden has offered for you to stay with her at Vawdrey Keep for a few months, until the—er—color returns to your cheeks," her father said weakly.

Lenora's lips twisted. There was now a permanent red discoloration to her face, she thought listlessly. A patchy dry redness which mottled her skin and probably would till the end of her days.

"I had thought," Sir Leofric blustered, "that you might wish to withdraw from—well, things," he said lamely. "But your grandmother is strongly averse to the idea." *Ah, finally the convent*, thought Lenora. *Here it comes.* She readied herself to trot out her objections. He took a deep breath. "She suggests accepting Sir Lionel Emworth's suit forthwith."

Lenora caught her breath. *Marriage?* Her mind went blank. She most assuredly had not been expecting that! "Sir Lionel Emworth?" *Blue shield with a white hart*, she thought.

"He is one of your many admirers, is he not?" her father said bracingly. "My mother writes he is young and idealistic and that moreover, he had an epic poem written in your honor." Lenora was silent. "The preface of which contained a dedication swearing his undying devotion to your pure soul," her father continued doggedly. "Your soul which remains unaltered despite your outward appearance."

Lenora gave a choked laugh. "He may have sworn devotion to my soul, Father, but we both know it was my face he was enamored of."

Sir Leofric looked exasperated. "He could scarcely cry off now, Lenora, if you accept his suit. Not without looking exceedingly unchivalrous."

"There are worse things to look than unchivalrous," murmured Lenora. *One of which would be a pox victim.*

"Your grandmother thinks—"

"No, Father," said Lenora quietly.

Her father gave a huff of exasperation. "If young Emworth is as tenderhearted as people say, then it may well be—"

"You mean," Lenora interrupted him, "that he might be induced to wed me out of pity?"

Her father reddened, but lowered his eyes, unable to deny it. "Beggars cannot be choosers, Lenora," he snapped waspishly. It was the second time she had heard that saying today. "You seem to forget your current predicament, daughter. You are no longer in the position to pick and choose from an army of

16

suitors." He drummed his fingers on the arm of the chair. "My child, I am trying to provide for you. We need to be realistic about the future now available to you."

"I realize that, Father, and appreciate the plain speech," Lenora answered steadily. "But I will not have someone marry me because they feel sorry for me or fear the judgment of others."

What she wanted, thought Lenora suddenly, was the very opposite of that. Someone who never felt sorry for anyone and did not care two pins for the opinion of others. That was when one of the other sigils Berta had mentioned earlier sprang suddenly to mind. The black field with the white gate. Of course. Sir *Garman Orde*.

3

Garman Orde groaned and rolled onto his side. Everything ached from where that bastard Roland Vawdrey had attacked him in the melee. Plus, he needed a piss. He never should have drunk that last flagon of ale. He rolled off the mattress and maneuvered the chamber pot from under his bed using his feet. Then, after freeing himself from his braies, he relieved himself whilst staring out of the window at the still night, until his full bladder was empty. He had a feeling sleep would not return now. Perhaps, after all, he should have brought a wench back to while away some hours, but something about the women who hung around the tourneys depressed him. They were so desperate for something special in their life—a winner, anything that elevated them from the drab monotony of their everyday drudgery. It grated on him. They would find nothing like that underneath him for a night. He'd rather pay a whore than have to brag about his victories to keep them happy. It left a bitter taste in his mouth. He was just pulling his linen braies up over his bare arse and tying the drawstring when his chamber door blew in as if on some invisible breeze. But there was no breeze in Caer-Lyoness tonight. It was still and silent. Then he saw it, the pale hand at the latch. The slender body clad in shadows who drifted through his door, the shrouded head and shoulders. Stronger men than he would have quailed at such a spectacle, but Garman Orde was made of stern stuff. He simply took a step back and uttered an oath strong enough to make the specter flinch.

"Oh," said the faceless wraith with relief. "You're already awake. Thank goodness, I thought I'd have to try and rouse you."

"Who the—what the hells—?"

She seemed to notice his discomfiture and sat promptly down on a chair in the corner of his room, holding up her hands. "Did I frighten you? I'm sorry."

He rallied himself, fixing her with a stern gaze. "Who the hells are you, woman? Why are you here?"

He watched the direction of her head go from the chamber pot to him and then back again. "Oh!" she said belatedly. "I never meant—"

"To interrupt me midstream?" he asked sarcastically. "If you'd been a fraction earlier, you'd have seen the whole show."

Her head tipped back at that, and one hand rose to her breast in agitation. "I do apologize," said the faceless specter, sounding mortified. "I thought you'd be asleep at this hour."

"You thought waking me from my sleep in that getup would be a good notion?" he asked in disbelief. "What's your game? Did de Bussell set you up to do this?" He already knew the answer. This wasn't some female for hire. She was a lady, through and through. But he was rattled and letting off steam. "What if I'd been sporting with a couple of wenches in the bed with me? What then?"

"A couple?" she echoed faintly.

Yes, a real lady. He rolled his eyes, plunking his hands on his hips. "Get to the meat of the matter," he said irritably and sat down on the bed opposite her, glancing at the door.

"No one's going to burst in," she said calmly, following the direction of his gaze. "I'm not trying to entrap you. My name is Lenora Montmayne. You know of me, I think?"

He snorted. "It would take more than the likes of your kinsmen to trap me," he said, casually insulting the men of her family.

19

"What do you want from me?" he asked. "That you come to my bedchamber in the middle of the night." He cast a look over her slender body. Her face was swathed in so many veils he couldn't make out a single feature. "How do I even know it's you?"

"You've heard what has befallen me?" she asked quietly. She was sat eerily still now.

He looked at her, then gave a brief nod. *The pox*. Everyone was talking of its most famous victim.

"I don't want to remain at court," she said. "To become an object of pity. I want to leave Caer-Lyoness."

He shrugged. "What's this to me? You want a paid escort?"

"It is said"—she began speaking a little less confidently—"that you are in pursuit of your own fortune." Her words were breathless now, hesitant. "To make your way in the world."

He sat stock-still. "And?" he rasped.

"My circumstances are not what they were," she said haltingly. "My prospects are quite altered."

His eyebrows rose. The only thing of note about Lenora Montmayne was her exceeding fairness. Without that, he supposed she no longer had a claim to her fame or position at court as resident beauty. But what was that to him? Then it hit him. She was talking about her marital prospects. His lip curled. Her clamoring suitors must have all cried off once she lost her looks. And now she had come to him, *crawling*. "And?" he asked. He wanted to hear the haughty bitch say it. That she was offering herself to him, now her face was ravaged and her beauty gone. Her veil seemed to flutter, as if her breathing grew labored, and just as suddenly he found he didn't want to make

20

her say it after all. "Let me see your face," he said gruffly instead.

She sat very still. Then, just when he thought she'd refuse, her hands rose to lift the veils to show him. His eyes widened. The rumors hadn't lied. Lenora Montmayne's legendary beauty was quite gone. Where once her complexion had a bloom like a flower, it was marred with pockmarks and an uneven redness was spread across her skin. She tilted her face first one way and then the other, so he could see the full extent of the damage. Oddly enough, that impressed him. That, and how slowly she moved, to give him the chance to examine the ravages the pox had wrought on her once-fair face. When she closed her eyes, he thought she was finally showing distress, but then realized she was letting him see the crinkled, misshapen eyelids. She kept her head tilted up, waiting for him to tell her he'd looked his fill.

"How far down does it extend?" he heard himself ask.

She gave a slight start. "Just my face."

"Nowhere else?"

She shook her head. When he didn't speak further, she seemed to rally herself. "My cousin Kit inherits my father's estate, as it's entailed, but he has a sizable private fortune and always swore to give a handsome bride-gift with me."

"I'm guessing there's a reason Sir Leofric's not approaching me with this offer?" he asked dryly. "One that doesn't involve my popularity at court." *Or lack of it*, he thought.

Her face flushed, the areas of it not already red. "There is a reason," she agreed.

"Which is?" he pressed.

21

"We would need to elope."

He pursed his lips. "So, I would be taking you without your father's consent," he ruminated. She nodded. "Who's to say I'd see a penny of this famous dowry?"

"My father is fond of me. He would be angry, yes, at first, very angry. But then he would relent. He would want me happy."

He wondered at the grim determination in her tone. Was she saying what she wanted to believe?

He frowned. "Then why not set him the task of finding you a groom?"

Lenora licked her dry lips. "Because…" she started lamely.

"Yes?"

"Because, he'd have to bribe someone to marry me," she said, her voice rising. "Someone who would be kind to me—" She broke off. When she spoke again, her voice was low, but no less impassioned. "Someone who would feel sorry for me for the rest of my days. And everyone would know it… and that he'd paid them a fortune to do it." She clasped her hands together; he suspected to hide the fact they were shaking.

"What's the difference with me?" he asked bluntly. "My reason for wedding you would be no less mercenary."

"But you are quite pitiless, my lord, are you not?" she said simply. "You will not be kind, and I need not feel guilty about you making any kind of sacrifice on my behalf. I have no doubt you would lead whatever woman you married a dog's life."

He gave a short laugh at that. He had no idea she was so gutsy. When she reached up a hand to pull down her veil, his own shot out to forestall her, catching her wrist. Lenora froze.

"I heard you had pockmarks the size of pennies and a hole where your nose should be," he said bluntly.

"Who said so?" she gasped.

He shrugged and let his eyes roam over her face. "You're not beautiful anymore, but it's not so bad as all that." The oddest look crossed over her face. "What?" he found himself asking.

"'Tis nothing," she said, avoiding his eyes.

He considered her. "When?" he asked abruptly. "When do you envisage us running off into the night together?" He spoke dryly, but to his own surprise was clearly contemplating the idea.

She stared at him a moment, then gulped. "Before the tournament is ended would be better for me."

He frowned at that. "I'm competing," he pointed out heavily.

"I'm aware, but there is someone here I do not wish to see."

"Who?" His voice was sharp, surprising him.

"Family," she answered promptly. "How long would it take you to get your affairs in order?"

He shrugged. "A day."

"Have you...someplace we could go? Just until my father relents?"

He was silent while he pondered this. Then he gave a short nod. "I've a place."

"Where?" He stared back at her stony-faced. "What I meant was," she elaborated slowly when she realized nothing was forthcoming, "how many days' ride is it from Caer-Lyoness?"

Oh. "Three days." Then feeling he had been ungracious, he added, "It's near a village called Cofton Warren. I've a farm there." He narrowed his eyes in anticipation of her response to this, but she made no reaction to the fact he was proposing to take her, the daughter of a noble family, to a mere farmhouse.

"Then, this time tomorrow night?" she suggested, her voice high, betraying her nerves. "I could meet you in the courtyard by the west gate."

He looked her over again. Was he really going to do this? It would mean withdrawing from the Challenge to Arms, which was a blow. He had a good chance of winning in that event. Still, at least he could participate in tomorrow's jousting. He nodded swiftly and released her wrist. For a moment he thought she would topple off the chair; she looked so suddenly drained. Then she seemed to collect herself, pulled the veils down over her face, and tottered from the room. A nobler man than he would have seen she made her way back safely, but she had made it plain that she expected no better from him. He smiled grimly to himself. Well, well, well. The Flower of all Karadok, begging for his hand. Even if the flower was now quite spoiled and had lost its bloom.

"Berta?" It was the third time she had called for the servant's attention, only to lose her nerve when she looked up and give some lame excuse for her interruption.

The old woman looked up and eyed Lenora with faint impatience. She was busily picking yarn from her distaff and did not appreciate the distraction. "Whatever is it, miss?" she huffed. She never had got used to calling Lenora *my lady*. In truth, she'd never even tried.

Lenora bit her lip. "Have you any ties here in Caer-Lyoness?"

"Ties?"

"Family or…people you're fond of." Lenora frowned. "Do you live here in the servants' quarters or in the city center?" She should really know the answer to these things. *Being ill made you self-centered*, she thought uneasily, but knew deep down that was just an excuse. Many a time, her cousin Eden had urged Lenora to take more interest in the people around her, and still she struggled to take that advice on board. She needed to try harder.

Berta eyed her beadily. "Well, you're definitely on the road to recovery," she muttered sourly. "You're that restless today, you're giving me the twitches!"

Lenora hid a smile. "Well, have you?"

"None," Berta snapped. "Three sons and none of them with a consideration for their poor old mother! The last one moved out—leaving me for some redheaded trollop," she muttered. "And now I've to shoulder the burden of the rent by myself!

I'm working two jobs these days, just to keep a roof over my head and food in my belly."

Lenora nodded thoughtfully. Without fail, Berta disappeared for a few hours at midday to undertake her washer-woman duties. "You should have had daughters," Lenora told her impulsively.

"Daughters?" Berta squawked. "What's the good of daughters? They belongs to their husbands as soon as they marries them. No, it's sons that's supposed to provide for their old mothers." She shook her head, her jaw working angrily. "Only there's some as neglects their duty!"

"You have a house in Caer-Lyoness?"

"A house? Chance would be a fine thing! I rents two rooms," Berta admitted grudgingly. "At an outrageous price. Goes up every year it do. And that scoundrel Will Bilford is waiting on this month's rent like a vulture. I told him I'd give it him," she complained bitterly, "as soon as it was in my hand."

Lenora took a deep breath. "How do you feel about skipping out on Bilford? And throwing your lot in with mine?"

Berta's jaw slackened. "Do what?" she uttered in astonishment.

"I'm eloping," Lenora told her calmly. "Tonight."

"Eloping?" Berta stared at her. "Where you off to?"

"Some place called Cofton Warren."

"Never heard of it!"

"No more have I," admitted Lenora. "Apparently it lies three days from here."

"Who you going with?"

Lenora hesitated. "You would not betray me, Berta?" she asked.

26

Berta stared back at her blankly. "Who would I betray you to?"

"My father."

Berta snorted. "He made it plain last night that my services wouldn't be needed for much longer," she said grimly. "I'm not grand enough to wait on his living daughter, only his half-dead one!" She darted a sharp look at Lenora, who gazed back at her.

"So then, you owe him nothing."

"No, but he owes me!" Berta fired up. "He ain't paid me yet for this week!"

Lenora pondered this a moment. "Perhaps you should ask him for it," she suggested. "Tell him you've found other employment."

Berta looked uncertain at this. "What if you takes a worse turn?"

"Well, if I do, I shan't be here for you to nurse me, Berta. I shall be at Cofton Warren. As I say, you are very welcome to accompany me."

"In whose employ?"

"Mine," said Lenora. "And my husband's." *How odd it sounded to say that!* Her voice wavered slightly over it. It was somehow vastly disquieting to think of Garman Orde in those terms, for Lenora harbored no illusions about what manner of man he was. A surly, quarrelsome brute with a nasty temper. Certainly, that was the impression he left you with after seeing him compete in the tournaments. Still, she thought, brightening up, he would not press her hand and sigh over her lost beauty.

She doubted very much she had ever been the sort of woman he admired. Her suitors had agreed she had the face of an angel. She fancied Orde would have little use for anything angelic.

27

She remembered how casually he had spoken of sporting with not one but *two* wenches in his bedchamber. *What was the surplus wench supposed to do while he copulated with the other?* she wondered vaguely. *Sit on a chair and wait her turn?* Lenora frowned. Sadly, she didn't have anyone to ask. Maybe she could ask him when they were married? No, that was silly, she admonished herself. They weren't to have that sort of marriage. The sort where they shared confidences.

She had every expectation that Garman would abandon her as soon as her father paid over her dowry. And that was exactly what Lenora wanted. To be settled on a small estate that would be bought with her father's coin—that she could run as its mistress. Her husband she would barely see hide nor hair of, she was confident of that. He would be off fighting in the tournaments, she thought contentedly. And sporting with wenches, two at a time. When he turned up, mayhap on feast days, they would be perfectly civil to one another, only rather distant.

In this instance, she thought her ruined face would be the card up her sleeve. It ensured she would not be troubled with unwanted attentions from a boorish husband. Garman Orde might not be overly fastidious in his tastes, but she was sure that he did not lack prospective partners to fill that bed of his to capacity. For starters, he was a winner, and she had seen how the victors were lauded at tournaments, treated as gods to be fawned over and lavished with attention. She had seen Orde lift the cup on enough occasions to know he was a lethal competitor in the field and more than competent in all areas of the tourney.

Then, she thought, there was the fact that though not conventionally handsome, there was *something* about him. His dark blond hair was too close-cropped for current fashion, and his muscles far too pronounced. Those light blue eyes were cold and hard, no warmth whatsoever lay in their depths. His lips

28

were full and firm, but almost permanently curled into an unpleasant sneer. He was not so much pleasant to look at as, well, *startling*. She remembered the spectacle of his naked torso she had been subjected to earlier. He had shown no shame whatsoever at being bared and on display to her. His chest and shoulders were wide, his hips narrow and the muscle and sinew around them strangely delineated. She realized she had never really seen an unclothed man at such close quarters before. The muscles on his stomach had been shockingly defined and there had been a strange trail of dark gold hair that disappeared into braies that Lenora had been forced to drag her astonished gaze from for decency's sake.

No, she would find no piteous solicitude in this bridegroom. He would soon be shunning her company for bonnie wenches with come-hither smiles, she thought with satisfaction. Then she noticed the old woman eyeing her sourly.

"Sweet on him, aren't you?" Berta snorted.

Had she been smiling? Hastily, Lenora rearranged her expression to one of sober reflection. "You don't understand, Berta."

"Oh, don't I?" Berta said loftily. "I'm guessing that's why you insisted on getting all dressed up last night. Am I right?" A knowing glint flashed in her eye.

"Well…yes," Lenora admitted after a moment's pause. "But it's not what you think."

"You…er…let him see your face, did you?" Berta asked with feigned casualness.

"Of course," Lenora replied coolly. "It would hardly be fair not to."

"Not fair?" The older woman's eyebrows rose. "All's fair in love and war, least that's what I'm told."

"Neither apply in this case," Lenora hastened to assure her with some amusement.

"Humph! Why did you bother putting all those layers over your face, then?" asked a clearly skeptical Berta.

"Oh, that wasn't for his benefit," Lenora explained. "But for casual onlookers. I don't see why I should be expected to provide a sideshow for them." Even she could hear the bitterness in the last few words. She strove for a lighter tone. "You see, Berta, before the pox, my face used to be quite a sight to behold." The words came out rather dryer than she intended.

Berta shrugged. "I gathered that much from the way your kin carried on," she admitted. She set her yarn down. "And?" she asked pointedly.

"And?"

"What did he say?" Berta demanded curiously.

"He?" Lenora was momentarily thrown.

"Your sweetheart," Berta said with clear exasperation.

"Oh!" Lenora struggled a moment with her impulse to protest the term. "He...er...he said my face isn't so bad."

"Did he indeed?" Berta spluttered. "That must be that courtly chivalry they talk so much about."

Lenora shot a suspicious look at the old woman's bland expression. Was she being sarcastic? "Oh, yes," she agreed smoothly. It probably wouldn't do to explain that Garman was marrying her purely for mercenary reasons. After all, what if

30

Berta didn't come with them and repeated the tale for the ears of others? "He—um—said he could live perfectly well with it."

"Good of him," sniffed Berta.

"Yes," Lenora murmured in agreement. "I thought so."

5

It was the next night when Lenora emerged from the shadows in the dark courtyard for her assignation with Garman Orde. She easily made out his bulk as he moved stealthily along the stables, though he moved with remarkable quiet and a sort of grace which surprised her. He halted on catching sight of her, and she saw he was now leading his massive charger and her own palfrey behind him. She had seen him dip in and out of the stalls but had not realized he had saddled and collected their horses en route. She was impressed, though of course, they could not ride on two horses. Not when she had Berta and her cats to think of.

"I'm afraid," she assured him in a loud whisper, "that two horses won't be enough. I have my things with me and my servant, Berta."

"And I don't ride," Berta cut in mutinously. "So, you needn't think I'm climbing atop one of those brutes!"

Lenora watched his gaze flicker over the basket Berta bore with ill-concealed annoyance. And he hadn't even seen the two sacks of clothes and things that Lenora had dragged down with her yet.

"Are all these sundries strictly necessary to you?" he asked scathingly. "We've a three-day ride and will be slowed down considerably by taking a cart." He spoke the last word with deepest contempt.

Lenora lifted her veils to stress her point. "*Strictly* necessary, yes," she said with emphasis. "And once we are outside the capital, the speed of our progress will not matter overmuch." She lowered her voice conspiratorially. "I do not anticipate we will be pursued. I have left my father a letter saying I have eloped but giving no clue as to my destination or betrothed."

Garman's gaze snapped to hers. "A letter?" he repeated with disgust, shaking his head. "I might have known! *Women*. You can never have enough fuss made, can you?"

"I could hardly disappear without leaving word for my family," Lenora pointed out reasonably. "That would have caused great perturbation indeed. This way, Father will be alarmed, but will not find it necessary to send out soldiers looking for me. I said I would send him word as soon as I was settled."

A scornful look still on his face, Garman turned on his heel and marched back to the stables. Lenora watching him, noticed his gait was a little stiff. *Of course, he had been competing today.* She wondered if his mood had been affected by a crushing defeat, or if he was simply bad-tempered. She suspected the latter.

"Huh!" muttered Berta. "Vastly pretty manners, ain't he?"

Now that, thought Lenora, was definitely sarcasm. She did not reply, but instead fussed with her headdress, pulling her veils back down again to conceal her face.

When Orde emerged some ten minutes later, he led a plodding horse and cart behind him. Waiting until they drew level, Lenora turned to take the basket from Berta. "You climb up first, Berta, and then I'll pass the cats up to you."

Berta picked up the two sacks of clothes and belongings and flung them into the back of the wagon. Then she clambered up into the seat. Lenora waited until she was comfortable and then passed the basket up.

Berta placed it on the floor at her feet. "Safer down there," she explained.

Lenora turned to find Garman stood directly behind her. "Oh," she said in startled tones. He was very light on his feet for such a large male.

"I can't speak to you," he said irritably, "when your face is covered like that."

Lenora whisked up the veils. "What is it?" she asked, surprised that he should desire speech with her at all.

"You intend to take your horse?" he asked, glancing toward Brunnhilde.

"Yes, I'm going to ride her. I'm a fair horsewoman."

He shook his head. "You're not thinking this through. The west gate is guarded, same as all the other gates to the palace. You need to be up on the cart beside your servant. We can secure your horse to mine and it can follow along behind me."

"Why?" asked Lenora in startled accents.

"If a lady rides out of the castle at dead of night, on a fine horse like that, wearing a fine dress like yours and a veil, the guards are going to remember it. They may even challenge your leaving."

Lenora chewed her lip, considering this. "I see," she said after a moment's pause. "Then what do you suggest? About my dress, I mean. And my"—she hesitated—"veil." He was looking at her now in a speculative fashion, she realized. Now why was that?

"I say your servant gives you her cloak to cover up your gown, and you take off the headdress." With an effort, Lenora managed to bite back the objections that sprang to her lips. "If challenged, I tell the guards you're my servants," Garman said with a shrug. "Accompanying me back home after the tournament."

34

"Servants?" Lenora repeated blankly.

"Aye."

Lenora swiveled around to look up at Berta. "What say you, Berta?" Her servant grimaced but started unfastening her drab wool cloak. Lenora reached up to unfasten her headdress. Luckily her hair was simply coiled at her nape instead of worn in any of the elaborate styles she had favored before her illness. She removed her coif and unpinned the many veils. "Where shall I put these?"

Garman took them from her and crammed them unceremoniously into one of the saddlebags. Berta passed down her dark gray cloak and Lenora swathed herself in it. She looked uncertainly at Garman.

"It'll have to do," he said, and, to her surprise, seized her by the waist and hefted her up onto the seat beside Berta with little apparent effort.

Lenora straightened herself. "Thank you," she said. He did not acknowledge the pleasantry, but instead moved back to his own horse, secured her mount to his, then swung up into the saddle. Seeing Berta had made no move to, Lenora took up the reins and urged the cart horse to follow along behind him as he moved forward. "Do you think we will be challenged at the gate?" Lenora murmured to Berta as the horse hooves struck against the stones in the courtyard.

"Don't know that I've ever tried to pass through 'em at this hour," Berta said doubtfully.

"Neither have I." Lenora grimaced. "I can't help but think it might look a little strange. Still"—she brightened—"perhaps he lost today." At Berta's blank look, she added, "And did not want to hang around to compete on the third day."

"Even if that were so," Berta said heavily, "would he not have left before all the celebrations, while it was still light?"

Lenora's face fell. That was probably true enough. Dead of night was hardly ideal traveling conditions. "Or mayhap he was a victor?" she ventured.

"If he'd won, what would be his reason for sneaking away under cover of night?" Berta asked wryly.

"Maybe..." Lenora hesitated, waiting for a plausible reason. "He has a sick relative on his deathbed?" she ventured.

Berta snorted. "You see him rushing to hold their hand?" she asked. "*Him?*"

Lenora flushed. "Maybe he's their heir?" she suggested. "And wishes to ensure there is no last-minute change to the will."

"What an imagination you do have," Berta retorted. The way she said it was not complimentary.

"Do you think so?" asked Lenora. She spotted lit torches ahead and her heart sank. The gate was manned, and the guards milling there looked up with interest at their approach. *Oh damn*, thought Lenora. She did not imagine that Sir Garman would be at all good at thinking up plausible stories. He looked far too tight-lipped and grim to possess a silver tongue. She steeled herself for a confrontation, watching anxiously as the guards exchanged a few words with Orde. She definitely picked out the word *servants* as he gestured toward them. Lenora watched as one of the guards detached himself from the others and strolled over to their cart. She felt his keen gaze pass over her as he held up a lit torch so he could peer into the back of the cart.

"Where you off to then, so late, ladies?" he asked in a faintly mocking tone. He was a good-looking young man, and rather

36

pleased with himself, thought Lenora. Not to mention officious. None of the other guards seemed remotely curious about them after listening to Orde's explanation.

"We be off to the country," she supplied, doing her best imitation of Berta's accent. "To my master's estate at Cofton Warren."

He made no comment, peering into one of the hessian sacks. "Who's that?" he asked, glancing up at Berta. "Cat got her tongue?"

"This is my old mum," Lenora told him confidingly. "But she's quite deaf, poor old thing. Did you want her to speak?" She turned to Berta. "Mum?" she said loudly. "Tell the nice guard how we're going back home to the country."

Berta started. "That's right, dearie," she said loudly. "And don't you be bothering my girl. She's a good girl, she is, not one of your city slatterns!" She eyed the soldier cantankerously.

He snorted, glancing back at Lenora. "Why in the midst of night? Seems a funny sort of time to be setting off."

Lenora leaned forward. "Well, we thought so too," she said, lowering her voice. "I reckon the master had a bad day in the lists. Gone into a proper fit of the sulks, he has."

The guard's gaze flickered over to Garman, who sat stony-faced and glaring at them, though Lenora didn't think it likely he could hear a word of their exchange.

"These knights and the notions they do get," she added with a sigh. "Some days a poor maid doesn't know her own arse from her elbow!" She winked and to her surprise watched a faint blush cover the soldier's cheeks.

He cleared his throat. "Yes, I—er—can imagine."

"What the hell is this delay?" Garman barked. "I fail to see why I'm stood waiting here while you importune my servant!"

The guard stood back smartly, his face flaming now. "Carry on," he said in a hoarse voice. Lenora beamed at him, but he seemed unable now to meet her eye.

6

Five hours later, they sat outside a small inn at a backwater village, having left the main road out of Caer-Lyoness as soon as was possible. Garman had put in an order for ale and oatcakes and now joined Lenora and Berta, who were sat at a rough-hewn wooden table. The old servant shifted to the far end of the bench and turned her face in contemplation of the fields opposite in what he could only surmise was a tactful retreat to give them some privacy. He wondered briefly if Lenora had confided in the old woman that he had been bribed to run away with her? He fancied she had not, as the servant seemed to think they might desire private speech with one another. He found himself lowering his voice accordingly.

"For your information," he started grimly. "I was successful yesterday in the joust." For some reason, he had been smarting the entire journey at her ridiculous sallies with that impudent guard.

"Oh, you heard that, did you?" she responded without, Garman thought, any noticeable discomfort.

"Yes, I did. Unlike 'your old mum,' I'm not deaf." His tone was biting, but whatever reason his words tickled Lenora Montmayne's fancy and she went off into a peal of laughter. He stared at her.

"What did you think of my accent?" she asked.

"It was execrable," he answered bluntly. "I couldn't tell if it was meant to be Aphranian or Somerlow."

Her eyes widened. "Oh, but that's good!" she said. "For Berta was originally from Aphrany but has lived these past twenty years in Caer-Lyoness! And I was doing an impression of her, you see. So, it must have been pretty accurate."

He grunted. The delight she clearly took in this surprised him. Watching her through narrowed lids, he began slowly revising his impression of Lenora Montmayne. From his glimpses of her about court these past three years, he had thought her a bloodless, limpid type, pure of feature, and somewhat dim.

Then there was the fact he had never heard even a smidgeon of scandal about her fair name. He had thought her virtuous but very likely vacuous with it. Her favored suitors permitted to squire her to events usually had one foot in the grave or else were pompous bores like Colfax, whose favorite topic of conversation was himself. Either that, or wet dishrags like Emworth, who wanted to simply sit and gaze at her in silent worship. He supposed he had assumed that, at the end of the day, she had very little to say for herself. It appeared that was not the case.

Which was probably why seeing the way she had flirted with that guard had shocked the holy hells out of him! Could it be that Lenora Montmayne was not the blameless bore he had always imagined her? He stole another sideways look at her. She was leaning back against the table, her elbows resting on its surface as she lifted her face to the late September sun. She had a smile on her lips that he could swear he had never seen her wear before. It was not the usual vacant simper at all. Her eyes were closed to the sun. Her eyelids looked pink and mottled; he wondered if they were sore.

"Who did you award the tourney crown to?" she asked suddenly, surprising him as her eyes were still shut.

"What?"

"You said you won the joust," she reminded him. "So, I wondered which lady you bestowed the crown on."

He cast his mind back. "Lady Helen Cecil," he said abruptly, naming the King's current paramour.

"Oh, of course you did."

"What do you mean by that?" he asked, feeling unaccountably annoyed.

She opened her eyes, looking mildly surprised. "Just that it was the obvious choice."

"Now you're out of the running, you mean?" he said sharply.

She nodded. "Yes," she agreed without rancor, and he felt a prickle of something he could not quite identify. "I did not mean anything particularly by it. Just that most knights give very little thought to who they bestow the honor." She smiled at him. "They just plump for the prettiest girl present."

Which means you will never receive the crown again, he thought, but for some reason did not voice. He was not usually so reticent.

"I expect Lady Helen will receive all the tributes now," she continued.

"It doesn't hurt her cause that she's the King's current whore," he found himself adding gruffly. "Doubtless some mean to curry favor with the King by flattering her."

Lenora arched a brow at him. "I doubt that was why you picked her," she said mildly.

"Well, no," he conceded grudgingly.

"Then let us just say that she is extremely beautiful."

41

"I don't think she is beautiful," he admitted unexpectedly. He felt Lenora turn her surprised gaze on him. "I just think she's comely. I always preferred comeliness to beauty."

"I see," she said. Then after a moment, she asked curiously, "Did you...?" Then hesitated.

"What?"

"Did you think I was beautiful? Before"—she made a gesture, twirling her fingers before her face—"this befell me, I mean."

"Yes," he said promptly. "Beautiful and dull as ditchwater."

Instead of protesting or flouncing off, Lenora merely nodded thoughtfully. Silence fell over them a moment, Lenora lost in her thoughts and Garman staring hard at her profile.

"You're not what I thought you were," he said after a moment.

"No?"

"Not at all," he said heavily.

"You mean, because I'm neither beautiful, nor boring?" she asked lightly.

Which *was* what he meant, but he found himself flushing all the same. He cleared his throat. "You could put it like that." *But only if you wanted bluntness to the point of pain*, he thought. Was that what she wanted? She certainly wasn't flinching away from any hard truths.

Her servant chose that moment to interrupt. "They're bringing the food over," she said, shifting down the bench to sit closer to her mistress. Garman felt her eyes on him and looking up saw Berta regarding him with frank animosity. *Devoted to her mistress*, he thought wryly, *and probably served her for years*. Still, she did not look the type of lady's attendant he would

42

expect for the likes of a court beauty, and neither did she look like a bygone relic of the nursery. If anything, she looked the sort of sour old crone one saw hanging around the gallows, hawking cheap cures or picking pockets. Remembering how readily Lenora had identified her as her mother almost had him choking on his dry biscuit.

"I think we should find a priest as soon as we are able," Lenora told him once she had drained her cup of ale and plunked it down on the tabletop. "We must be married before nightfall. Do you suppose there will be a church anywhere in the vicinity?"

Garman glanced around at the small hamlet they currently found themselves in. A cluster of cottages and a duck pond was all his eye could see. "I highly doubt it," he said, taking stock of surroundings.

"No matter, we'll find somewhere on the road, I'm sure," Lenora said optimistically, helping herself to an oatcake.

"You think so? On these back roads?" Berta interrupted sharply.

It struck Garman that Berta did not trust him one whit. "We'll find somewhere," he said, narrowing his eyes at her.

"Before nightfall?"

Perhaps the old woman had been used to thinking herself defender of her mistress's virtue, Garman thought, but it seemed a little redundant now. After all, he was hardly likely to be overtaken with lust. "Either today or tomorrow." He shrugged.

"Tomorrow won't do," Berta insisted. "My lady has her reputation to consider!"

"Berta," Lenora murmured mildly and laid a hand on the agitated woman's arm. "All will be well; you must not fret." Garman watched their exchange with raised brows. Lenora turned back to him. "I feel sure we will happen upon somewhere." She crossed her fingers in a superstitious gesture Garman recognized meant *if the fates will it.* He rolled his eyes. Superstitious too, that was all he needed.

Seeing a weak-chinned youth trailing out with a tray of ale, Lenora turned impulsively to hail him with her most friendly smile. Garman stared as she cajoled him into bringing her out some fish—any fish, she assured him winningly. His Adam's apple bobbing, the youth disappeared stammering that he would see what they had in the kitchen.

Garman stared. As far as he could recall, Lenora Montmayne had never been remotely flirtatious in her manner heretofore. His own impression of her demeanor was that it had been bland in the extreme and somewhat remote. Even her most ardent admirers were known to lament her cool lack of familiarity. Where the hells had all this coaxing and coquetry coming from? he wondered in frowning bewilderment. And why the fuck was it annoying him so much? He gritted his teeth as she exclaimed over the plate of whitebait the fellow presented, as though for all the world he had given her a dish of roasted swan.

"As the price of the fish will be added to my bill," he said coldly, "I fail to see why you have to gush over him so much." As soon as the words had left his mouth, he wished he could recall them. Both Berta and Lenora appeared surprised by them, but he fancied Berta's gaze held a malicious gleam of satisfaction.

"I'm just being polite," Lenora told him reproachfully, and carried off her prize to the cart. What the hells was she doing? He craned his neck to watch her gracefully climb onto the wagon and stoop over a wicker case there. Was she feeding something? he wondered with misgiving. He shot a look at her maid. "What's in the basket?"

The old woman gave a humorless smile. "Cats," she said with malevolent enjoyment.

Cats. Garman turned away from her in disgust. He might have known.

7

It wasn't until midday that a likely solution came their way. Set up at a sort of crossroads, was a holy shrine and to the side of it, a makeshift sort of hut such as religious hermits used as a retreat. Garman reined in and turned to look over his shoulder at Lenora, who was following on along behind. "Perhaps Fate has provided after all," he said ironically, and nodded toward the hut.

She leaned forward in her saddle, her eyes widening. "Is it inhabited?" she asked eagerly. For a moment he was surprised. He had expected her to balk at the idea of being married by some grubby hedge-preacher. You'd think, he thought wryly, that he would have realized by now that Lenora Montmayne would overturn his every preconception. "Wait here and I'll see," he said, dismounting.

Pushing aside the strung-up bit of fabric that served as a door, he stood still while his eyes adjusted to the gloom. After a few seconds, he made out an austere figure knelt in prayer. For a moment he had thought it a graven image, it sat so still. Certainly, it gave no acknowledgment of his presence. Garman cleared his throat. The slight figure stirred, sighed, and then rose stiffly to its feet. When it turned around, Garman found himself surveyed sharply by a pair of watery blue eyes under a thin aquiline nose.

"My son, you have come to worship at the shrine of St. Valmunda?" the hermit asked, sounding aloof and faintly annoyed at the interruption. His gaze was shrewd and swept Garman in a coolly assessing fashion.

"I have not," Garman told him bluntly. "I come to offer coin for a service I want performed."

"Prayers for your everlasting soul?" the hermit suggested wryly. "Why, what have you done, I wonder?" He eyed the sword at Garman's hip. "Run some poor wretch through, more than likely," he muttered with disapproval.

Garman narrowed his eyes at him. For two pins he'd tell the old fool what he really thought of him.

"Nothing like that," he answered in curt tones. "I want marrying."

"Marrying?" For the first time the hermit seemed taken aback. He peered into the gloom of the small space he inhabited as if to seek out the mysterious female. "To whom?"

"She waits outside."

The old man tutted as he brushed past Garman to make his way out of the hut. "Highly irregular," he muttered.

Garman followed him outside, his expression grim. He halted abruptly when he saw that Lenora had donned the wretched headdress again and was completely swathed in veils. He was not the only one taken aback by her appearance, he thought grimly. The hermit was peering at her in some concern.

"This is your bride?" he asked in an uncertain voice. "What is the reason for all this concealment?" Garman rolled his eyes at the querulous note of suspicion in the old man's voice. He was as fussy and nitpicking as any priest. So much for thinking a wayside ceremony would be less troublesome.

"There's no secrecy," he answered swiftly. "Only the lady is somewhat…shy," he pronounced dryly.

The old man's eyes narrowed shrewdly. "I must have some speech with her alone," he said, drawing himself up stiffly. "To assure myself she has not been coerced into this."

47

"Coerced?" Garman repeated, feeling more irritated by the minute.

"But of course, Father," Lenora said, seeming to realize the hermit was within a hair's breadth of refusing to oblige them. She threw up her veils and hurried forward to take the hermit's arm. "Allow me to reassure you on that score."

Garman watched the old buzzard thaw as Lenora dragged him over to the other side of the shrine and spoke to him in low, urgent tones. He watched the quick gestures she made with her hands as she talked. Periodically, she threw quick glances over at him, and more than once, the old man turned his hawklike profile to gaze frigidly at Garman. What the hells was she telling him? he wondered. Whatever it was, it was not softening the old man's cantankerous attitude toward him one whit!

As he drew closer, the look the holy man favored him with was so blighting that Garman almost took a step back. "What the hells did you say to him?" he hissed at Lenora as the hermit swept past them back into the hut.

"What was necessary to enlist his aid," she replied serenely. "He was inclined to be unhelpful, so I was forced to be extremely frank about our circumstances." She smoothed down her skirts.

"Circumstances? What circumstances?" Garman frowned.

"That I could not hold you off," Lenora told him sadly. "And have been performing the duties of wife to you for several weeks now. I begged him to make an honest woman of me before I am utterly disgraced." Garman stared at her a moment in open astonishment. "At that, he saw his remonstrances were quite useless and he is now willing to perform the ceremony for us."

"Oh, he is, is he?" Garman glowered at her as his ideas about gently born women underwent a rapid revision. "How fortunate for your honor."

The hermit reappeared, carrying a quill and a large book. His bearing was stiff with outrage and the eyes he bent on Garman were glacial with disapproval. "I will require your names," he said. "And those of your parents and your birthplaces," he said, opening the pages and scratching away with a quill.

It occurred dimly to Garman that this was rather more formal than the roadside handfasting he had imagined. In truth, the hermit looked more like a senior cleric than a holy man or lay-preacher. He eyed the sparse iron-gray hair and the hawklike features with grudging curiosity. "And your name?" Garman asked abruptly, interrupting proceedings. "What is it?"

The hermit fixed a stern eye on him. "My name is Father Udolphus," he answered in clipped tones and returned to covering his page in spidery writing.

Garman opened his mouth again to pursue his line of questioning, but Lenora chose that moment to reach across and clasp his hand tightly.

"Beloved," she said in a sweet, syrupy voice that immediately put Garman's teeth on edge. "Let us remain focused on the task at hand," she urged. "And not interrupt the dear father with needless questions."

Garman narrowed his eyes at her, but if anything, she merely tightened her grip on his fingers until he relapsed into silence, snatching back his hand with an ill grace that had Father Udolphus pursing his lips tight. He ascertained in a few terse questions that both were willing and at liberty to give their vows to one another before taking down their details in ink.

"It is done," Father Udolphus said crisply, mere moments later.

Garman was so surprised that he stared down at his empty hand a moment, before reaching across and grabbing Lenora's. She looked up in surprise.

"Is that it? No blessing?" he asked gruffly.

"Do you want a blessing?" The old man sounded skeptical. "I understood this was a mere formality to follow on from the fact you have already been living as man and wife."

Garman met Father Udolphus's severe gaze squarely. "Men like me need to be bound tightly," he said. "Lest we find a way to wriggle out of our obligations."

Father Udophus's eyes flashed. "Indeed?" He tutted under his breath. "The old ways still abide!"

"Use this, Father," Berta said, coming forward with a piece of green string. She passed it to him, and after a moment of resistance, the hermit grudgingly took it.

Garman lifted their clasped hands and Father Udolphus, his lips still grimly pressed into a thin line, wound the string about their wrists, an expression of distaste upon his face. Garman glanced across at Lenora, who looked suddenly pensive now. Instead of relaxing his hold on her, he tightened it. Her eyes darted to meet his, wide and questioning. Instead of speaking, he gazed steadily back at her. It seemed to him that she had not really considered the prospect of being owned before, body and soul by a man. He watched it occur to her now as the color rushed to her face. For some reason, this pleased him.

She could not withdraw her hand now even if she wanted to, as Father Udolphus made the last few passes with the twine. The holy man made a quick gesture with his fingers over theirs and then stepped back. "You are now bound as tightly as one such as I can achieve," he intoned grimly.

Garman gave a sharp nod. "Good," he simply said and dropped a purse into the old man's hand. He turned to leave, but Lenora did not. The twine cut into his wrist as she tarried to thank Father Udolphus, and he was forced to step sharply back to accommodate her. She gave no sign of discomfort when she finally turned to accompany him out of the shack.

"You will need to cut me loose," she murmured as they emerged into the sunlight. Berta was already clambering into the cart.

"The old woman can take the reins for the cart," he told her, compelling her to accompany him to his horse. "You'll ride up before me."

"Why?"

"Custom," he said shortly, and at her surprised glance, he added, "You're not supposed to cut the bond directly in case it doesn't take."

"Superstitious? You?" she said as he seized her waist and hefted her up into the saddle. He swung himself up behind her, adjusting their position to work around their bindings. Lenora held her arm out at an awkward angle. "This might have worked better if we had sat side by side in the cart."

He gave a short laugh. "You think your crone could ride a horse like this?"

"You could have tethered him up behind us."

"Don't insult my horse. He won't be slighted." He saw the puzzled look she shot him from the corner of her eye.

"You are whimsical, Sir Garman?" she said, tipping her head. "That is not your reputation."

"Whimsical?" He gave a short, hard laugh. "No. I am not...whimsical."

"It's good you like pets, at any rate," she commented.

"Pets? I thought I told you not to insult Bria'ag."

He watched a faint smile touch her lips. "What would you call a horse, then? Your companion?"

"Closer to companion than pet."

She appeared to consider that a moment, then nodded. "I feel the same way about my cats."

"Cats?" Garman repeated, startled. He remembered the basket. "How many do you have?" he asked with some misgiving.

"Four."

He grunted. He would have thought one cat was more than ample.

"Grizelda, Fendrel, Tybalt, and Purcel," she continued brightly as if he had expressed an interest in their names. As far as Garman was concerned, the less said about them the better. A silence fell between them, and after a while, Garman noticed her give up trying to hold herself aloof. She slumped back against him, pulling down the veils over her face with her free hand.

"You draw considerably more attention to yourself in that getup, you do realize?" he asked dryly.

She did not answer, merely shifted slightly against him as if trying to get comfortable, and it occurred to Garman with some amusement that she was going to try to take a nap. *Good luck with that, sweetheart.* He doubted very much that Bria'ag's saddle provided the same level of comfort as the feather-filled mattresses she was used to.

When some moments later she started to list to one side, he wound an arm about her waist, pulling her in tight against him. She made no objection, and glancing down at the way her head lolled to one side, he could only conclude that against all odds, she had managed to nod off to sleep. His eyebrows rose. Mind you, she had been ill, he thought to himself. She was probably exhausted.

A swift glance toward the cart showed her servant was grimly absorbed in directing the horse before her. He took the opportunity to use his unbound hand to press Lenora's head to his shoulder. She curled further into him and he rested his hand at her shapely hip. She was a surprisingly pleasing armful, he thought, all things considered. That bloody headdress though, the gods alone knew why she insisted on wearing it. He could see the slight rise and fall of the veils with her steady breath but could see next to nothing of her face. The aftereffects of the pox really weren't as bad as she made out. His lip curled. So much fuss over a few pockmarks and some reddened skin. It would be laughable if the whole royal court wasn't buzzing with the news that the beauteous Flower of all Karadok had been blighted. *Bloody fools.* He smiled grimly to himself. Their loss was his gain. He was starting to suspect the famous flower was far more resilient than they had all guessed and possessed a lot more useful properties than mere beauty.

To his surprise, they did hit upon a remote inn early evening time. He would have pressed on for a couple more hours but felt the burning gaze of the old crone boring into his shoulder blades. "We'll stop here for the night," he said grudgingly and called for a stable lad to unfasten and store the wagon securely.

Lenora stirred and gave a start finding herself plastered to his chest. "We've found an inn," he told her as she straightened herself, fussing with her headdress which had slipped down one side.

"How fortuitous," she said, clearing her throat. "I think I nodded off there for a while." She gazed down at their bound wrists in bewilderment. "Oh! We're still joined?"

"Till death us do part," he answered ironically, and she gave a splutter. He wanted to see if she'd blushed, but the damn veils were in the way.

"I hope it wasn't too uncomfortable for you to ride with," she said suddenly. He merely shrugged. "We shall have to disentangle now," she pointed out.

"It can wait till after supper," he said mildly. "After all, the old tradition was not until the following morning." He cut her a sharp glance at that but was frustrated by the head veils once again.

"Well," she said after a moment's pause. "After supper, then."

They had made their way around the back of the inn to where the stables and outhouses lay. "I want all three horses rubbed down, fed, and watered," he instructed as he caught her up in his arms and swiftly dismounted. Lenora gave a suppressed yelp, finding herself swung down so precipitously. "I have you," he pointed out as an aside.

"Could you kindly—" she started with dignity, but he was already setting her on her feet.

"Keep up with me," he said with a frown, and started toward the inn. Lenora huffed, but made haste to keep pace with him.

"It might be more convenient—" she puffed, but he did not let her finish, instead propelling her through the low inn door by jostling her through with a hand at her hip.

"Sir Garman!"

"I can't make out your words through that mass of veils," he lied. "Speak up."

"I don't—"

"Good day, good day, good sir and lady both!" a jocular voice hailed them. A round, ruddy-faced man beamed at them as he rubbed his hands with a cloth. "Will you be wanting a room for the night?"

"Two rooms," Garman clarified and saw Lenora relax slightly out of the corner of his eye.

"A handfasting!" the innkeeper exclaimed, catching sight of their wrists. "Felicitations!" He gave a quick bow. "You honor my humble abode; I will have your rooms readied forthwith." Garman saw his gaze wander back to Lenora's heavy veils with confused unease.

"And supper," Garman growled.

"Immediately, good sir," the innkeeper assured them, turning to look back over his shoulder. "Brigid!" he yelled. "Kate!" He turned back with an unctuous expression. "The main room is through here, good sir." He gestured to the right of the entrance. "Where you and your lady can take your ease."

Garman looked pointedly at Lenora, and she slipped past him into the room with him following on her heels. The landlord's hand on his forearm stopped him. He froze and Lenora was also forced to come to a halt.

"Your pardon, good sir," said the landlord hoarsely. He licked his lips. "I am but a humble man trying to make an honest living—"

"Spare me the spiel," Garman cut across his words harshly. "What do you want?"

"Your assurance, good sir," he said, wringing his pudgy fingers, "that the lady is not afflicted with the plague."

"The plague?" Garman repeated. "Nay, she is not—"

"I do not have the plague," Lenora interrupted them, flinging back her veils. "As you can see, I am in perfect health with a few simple aftereffects of the pox. I am long recovered from the actual illness." She held up her face for the innkeeper's perusal, and Garman felt a stab in his gut that bewildered him. Evidently, his expression so terrified the landlord that he fell to bowing and scraping again.

"Your pardon, good sir, good lady," he said hastily, his words tumbling over each other. "I meant no offence, I assure you!"

"None taken," Lenora said sweetly, and turned on her heel, their bound wrists necessitating Garman follow into the room after her. "I'm starting to think you may have a point about the veils," she muttered as they made their way to a table.

"Don't do that again," he said, just about managing to keep his tone even.

"Do what again?" asked Lenora. "You mean wear the headdress?"

"I mean," he gritted the words out, "present your face like that, for others to—" He broke off. "Look at," he finished grimly.

Lenora looked at him with surprise as she dropped down into a seat. "You'll have to sit opposite," she said, "if our wrists are to remain bound through supper."

He ignored her, sitting down beside her, forcing her to move up the bench. "I don't like it," he scowled.

"Yes, but he would not have let us stay if he thought I had the plague," she pointed out reasonably.

"Oh yes he would have," he said grimly and clapped his free hand to his sword hilt. "He would have accepted my word."

"But what is the point in terrorizing the poor man when I could so easily reassure him?"

He took a deep breath in and out. "Presumably, you're wearing that veil because you don't want people seeing your face."

She appeared to consider this. "Well, yes, but..." She frowned. "In truth, it was more the scrutiny of people who knew me before that bothered me. They would be contrasting how I looked previously with how I look now. But mere strangers or new acquaintances don't really make me feel the same need to hide."

His gaze flickered to the headdress perched atop her head. "Why don't you leave it off altogether, then?" he suggested. "No one we meet on the road or at Cofton Warren will have known you before." Lenora sat stock-still, and for a moment he thought she would refuse. Then suddenly she reached up and plucked it from her head, setting it down on the table before them. She turned and looked at Garman wordlessly. "Better," he growled. Then a servant approached with an ale jug, distracting them.

They ate what Garman considered to be a light supper of bread, cold meats, vegetable pottage, and cheese, although his own trencher had to be refilled several times before he considered his needs adequately met. He watched covertly as Lenora picked over her food. He ate four bowls in the time it took her to eat one, and even then, she did not fully empty it, but left at least a quarter of it unfinished. She smothered a yawn once or twice and eyed their bound wrists which lay on the table between them with an unfathomable expression. As for himself, he was strangely aware of the touch of her smooth, pale skin against his own rough and tanned forearm.

"I need a bath," she said at last as he drained his ale to the dregs. "Did you order one?"

"Aye," he admitted, slamming his cup back on the table.

"Oh good." She glanced significantly at their bound wrists. He lifted an eyebrow. "If it hasn't taken by now, it likely never will," she said with a small smile.

He gave her a long, considering look as he reached down for a dagger in his boot and then cut through the cords with a deft flick of the blade. "I believe it'll hold," he said.

He watched a look of surprise flit across her face before she rubbed absent-mindedly at her freed wrist. "Should we drink a toast?" she said as a servant obligingly refilled their cups with frothing ale. Instead of shooting such a suggestion down, as was his first impulse, he found himself raising his cup and waiting for her to do the same. "To our bargain?" she said with a trace of uncertainty.

For some reason, it seemed to Garman the toast was lacking, but he could not have said why. "Aye," he rumbled, but still paused, his cup hovering in the air.

As if aware of his dissatisfaction, she added, "A long life and happiness!" and looked across at him for agreement. He shrugged and swigged his ale. It would have to do.

8

Lenora heard the door open and close behind her and carried on dragging the wet cloth up and down her limbs. "Are there any more soap leaves, Berta?" she asked over her shoulder. "These ones don't seem to work up a lather."

"Likely the quality is not what you're used to," a deep voice rumbled, making Lenora drop the cloth with a yelp and a splash. She craned her head back to find Garman Orde stripping the clothes off his big, hard body. Lenora's jaw dropped. "Wha—?"

"I'll climb in the tub after you," he said, ignoring her obvious shock at his appearance.

"You could have waited," Lenora told him primly once she managed to catch her breath. "Until it was carried into your bedchamber."

"This *is* my bedchamber," he countered swiftly.

"*Your* bedchamber?" Lenora repeated. Her gaze swept the room, taking in her belongings strewn all about. "But—"

"Did you imagine I meant to sleep alone on my wedding night?" he asked dryly, stalking around the tub to face her.

"Frankly, yes!" Lenora spluttered, her face flaming. He did not wear so much as a stitch of clothing, and his muscular bulk was disconcerting to say the least. She dipped down into the water until she was submerged to her shoulders, folding her arms across her bare breasts. She wished there were more soap suds to impede his view.

He quirked an eyebrow at her. "And leave our marriage unconsummated?"

Lenora stared at him. "But…" She took a deep breath. "M-my face?" she asked in disbelief.

"What about it?" His gaze challenged her. "If I'd thought I couldn't perform, I wouldn't have married you."

"Couldn't—? Oh!" She bit off her words as comprehension dawned, her gaze drifting down to where his manhood curved away from his thighs in illustration of his point. Lenora stared, then gulped, snapping her gaze up to meet his. "Could you kindly turn your back?" she asked with dignity. "So that I may climb out of the water?"

"No," he answered promptly. "You're getting an eyeful, so why shouldn't I?"

Lenora's jaw dropped. "But I don't want to get an eyeful!" she told him with a note of shrillness to her voice that startled her.

He gave a short laugh. "You'll be getting up close and personal with it before this night's through," he promised, gesturing to his manhood. "So, you may as well get acquainted with it now."

Lenora shut her eyes a minute before opening them again. "Are you having a joke with me, Sir Garman?" she asked.

"A joke?" he said, quirking his eyebrows at her.

"You can't possibly want to—to do anything of that nature with me," she retorted with spirit. "So kindly cease from this pointless teasing."

"Teasing?" Garman repeated blankly, his gaze roaming over the parts of her on view in a manner that Lenora found extremely disconcerting. Maybe he wasn't teasing? She bit her lip and shot an uncertain look at his face.

As if guessing her thoughts, he said with deliberation, "I'm in deadly earnest, Lenora." Her eyes widened at his use of her

61

name, though in truth he was now entitled to far more familiarities than that. "I not only want to do those things, but I am going to. Make no mistake about it. We are husband and wife after all."

Lenora's head spun. How could he possibly want to? And why? She could hardly credit such a thing. Unless? "You want children!" she breathed in sudden dismay, sitting straight up. Damn, she had not thought of that! "You should have told me!" But when she looked up, she saw he was not attending to her words at all. Instead, his gaze was riveted on her bared breasts. Lenora made an exasperated sound and sank back into the water. His eyes snapped to meet hers. "You have no title to pass on, so it simply did not occur to me that you might want them! That's it, isn't it?" she persisted when he made no reply.

"Children?" he uttered, a look of undisguised revulsion crossing his face. "Gods no!" He shuddered.

"No?" Lenora stared at him. "But—then why? I'm *hideous*!"

He looked at her a moment, then gave a short laugh. "Plenty of worse-looking women than you have to suffer their husband's attentions, I assure you!"

"Sir Garman—"

"Just call me Garman," he interrupted her, his voice thick and strange sounding. Lenora tensed, sensing that his mood had undergone some kind of change. He stalked closer to the bath and her eyes were drawn irresistibly to the alarming part of him that seemed to point toward her with intent. "If you're getting out, do it now."

For some reason, his tone filled her with renewed alarm. She sank down further into the water. "Why?" She wished her voice didn't sound quite so panic-stricken.

"Well, it won't bother me to share." He shrugged and lifted a foot as if to climb in.

"Wait!" Lenora squeaked.

"Too late." He was up and over the side, lowering himself into the water opposite her before Lenora even had the chance to scramble to her feet.

Lenora gaped at him. "You're in my bath!" she pointed out.

"Have you never shared a tub before?" he asked, holding his hand out. Lenora stared at it blankly. "Soap," he prompted.

"Oh!" Flushing, she placed the leaves into his palm, careful to avoid touching his fingers. "And of course I have. When I was a *child*!"

He stretched his legs out, and Lenora drew her own in sharply, bringing her knees up to her chin.

"Did you honestly believe I would forego my husbandly rights?" he asked, eyeing her frankly.

Lenora spluttered. "Of course! It didn't even occur to me for a moment that you might want them!"

He smirked at her as he rubbed the soap leaves over his shoulders. "Not very well acquainted with men are you, for all you've so many suitors."

"*Had* so many suitors," she corrected him automatically.

"Mmm," he agreed in a low rumble.

She huffed, staring at his massive upper body until his eyes lifted to meet hers, then hurriedly adjusted her gaze to stare over his left shoulder.

"And you never granted any of those poor bastards *any* liberties?" he asked.

"Of course not!"

"Not even a kiss?"

"Certainly not," she shot back primly and felt his hard stare on her face. "I'm not fond of being cornered or fawned on," she said, lifting her chin. "And I certainly don't like people breathing all over me or trying to grab me, rumpling my gowns."

His mocking gaze made her color flame. Doubtless he thought her a spoiled madam and probably coldly frigid as well, she thought, but it was no good lying to him about her disinclination for being fondled. She had always hated it.

"I see," he said dryly. "So, you had no favorites among your legions of admirers."

"Of course I had favorites," she answered, slightly startled.

"It doesn't sound like it."

"Sir Lionel Emworth could always be relied on to be very courteous and proper," she said defensively. "Either he or Sir Winston Colfax were my preferred escorts."

"Sir Winston Colfax!" he echoed derisively.

"Sir Winston is a very cultured and gentlemanlike man."

"He's sixty-five if he's a day!"

"A very cultured and mature gentleman," she amended conscientiously. "I enjoyed his company very much."

"Then why not ask one of them?"

"Pardon?" Lenora dragged her gaze away from where he was now propping a foot on one knee and scrubbing a sponge over a muscular calf.

"To elope with you," he elucidated.

Lenora drew herself up. "Is it not obvious?" she asked with dignity.

"Not to me." He shrugged.

"The reason I liked them," she explained carefully, "was because they did not demand anything from my company, save the opportunity to savor my beauty." When he looked as though he expected more, she was forced to add, "They did not trouble me overly for conversation and they did not press wet lips onto my fingers or attempt to maul me in dark corners."

"How considerate," he commented dryly.

"Yes." Lenora nodded. "I always thought so. But now my face is quite ruined, I could hardly expect them to step into the breach when the appeal I held from them is now quite gone, could I?"

"I suppose not," he agreed. "Did you even try?"

"Try what?"

"To see if their regard ran any deeper than an appreciation of your face."

She blinked at him. "Of course not. What else could they possibly like about me? There is nothing else."

He lowered the soap. "You've a pretty pair of tits in all events," he said with a shrug, taking Lenora's breath away.

She regarded him indignantly. "So that is what it means to be held in true regard by a gentleman," she said when the power of speech returned to her. "I did not realize it ran quite so deep as all that."

He smirked. "It's the only inventory of your charms I've been able to take so far."

She regarded him in silence, and then on impulse came abruptly to her feet, staring straight ahead of her as she stood naked before him. The only sounds in the room were the droplets of water running down her wet form into the tub. She gazed resolutely at the door, her head held high as she let him gaze at her, until she felt herself begin to turn to gooseflesh. "Have you looked your fill?" she asked quietly.

He was silent a moment. "Aye, for now," he said gruffly.

She gave a curt nod and clambered over the side of the tub, her cheeks burning at the indecent view she must be affording him of her backside. If there was one thing Lenora had always been insecure about, it was her somewhat ample rear. Luckily, flowing gowns concealed the fact she was somewhat fleshier in that area than she felt she ought to be. Her cousin and childhood playmate Eden had always been slender and perfectly proportioned to Lenora's eye. Eden had an even distribution, whereas her own frame was decidedly broad in the beam.

Clothed, it was undetectable, for she had a trim waist and a high, perky bosom. But naked was a different matter altogether. Naked, you could see her shamefully fleshy buttocks. She hurried across the room, intent on covering herself as soon as possible. Hopefully it was only her imagination that told her Garman's eyes were fixed on the twin globes of her abundant rear. She thought she heard a sharply indrawn breath. Doubtless he would be greatly amused to find the great beauty so universally admired had always had a concealed flaw!

When she whipped around after dragging a large drying cloth about her, she found his eyes still trained on her, but the sardonic gleam she had dreaded was not present. If anything, his gaze seemed hot and devouring. Finding this equally disturbing, she turned away and dived behind a conveniently placed screen to don her shift. To her dismay, she found she was trembling all over from the confrontation. Her hands shook as she pulled the voluminous white shift over her head. For all her best-laid plans, she had not anticipated this turn of events. But then how could she have ever guessed that Garman Orde would want to bed her? Once she was covered head to toe, she reemerged from her hiding place and cleared her throat. She certainly did not want Orde thinking her cowed and terrified by his advances. A quick glance in his direction showed him fully absorbed in his ablutions, scrubbing his shoulders.

Thankful of the reprieve, Lenora wrapped the drying cloth around her wet hair and picked up a comb as she made her way to the fireplace. Two of the cats, Grizelda and Tybalt, were lying in front of it on a rug. A quick scan of the room showed her Purcel was curled up in one of the two chairs set before the fire while Fendrel sat washing himself in the window seat. Quickly, Lenora crossed over to check the window was securely fastened. She could not lose one of her precious cats en route to her new home. Then she returned to the fire and sat in the empty chair, turning her back resolutely to the bathtub. She dragged the cloth from her hair and began finger combing through its tangles until she could get a comb through her damp locks.

The warmth of the blaze began to seep through her, and Lenora relaxed her muscles, letting exhaustion overtake her. The journey had been draining and her fitness and stamina were at a low ebb after her illness. Her eyes started drifting closed, and the comb fell from her fingers with a clatter. She needed to braid her hair, she told herself, even as she drew her legs up and tucked her feet under her. She was so tired though, bone-weary. If she just let herself take a quick nap, that would energize her, she thought, curling around the arm of the chair. Garman would just have to wait unless he liked his women unconscious. Her lips twisted. Who even knew how he liked his women? Apparently, he did not care if they were pretty. She ought to be grateful of that, she supposed. Was she grateful? She thought of his large, hard body and shivered. It wasn't exactly gratitude she felt. In truth, she wasn't sure what it was. She yawned, dragged a cushion under her cheek, and lapsed into a deep sleep.

*

When next Lenora woke, it was with a scream in her throat. She had been in the crypt again with its foul stench, surrounded by corpses. Everyone was rotting about her, and she had been left for dead, the entrance sealed up, trapping her in there. The horror of it left her breathless and frozen with terror.

"I have you," rumbled a deep voice by her ear, and to her astonishment, she found herself in someone's lap, with big, strong arms wrapped tightly about her. Far from feeling alarmed at this unexpected situation, Lenora's overwhelming response was one of relief. She was not alone. A warm and vital body was wrapped around her, though all was in darkness. Catching her breath, she burst into noisy, shameful sobs as her rescuer rocked her silently to and fro. After a few moments of this, she managed to relax her rigid limbs and take in her surroundings.

"We're at the inn," she mumbled, gathering her wits. "I'm not dead."

"Not yet," he agreed calmly.

She took a deep and shuddering breath. "I didn't mention, did I?" she said haltingly. "That if we share a bedchamber, I will invariably wake you screaming in the dead of night."

He paused slightly in the steady rocking of their bodies. "This is a nightly occurrence?" Lenora just nodded wearily. "You were sleeping soundly when I put you to bed."

"I always do at first." That explained why she remembered falling asleep in the chair and no more. Garman must have carried her there. Then what had he done? Climbed in after her? She glanced at him, trying to make out his expression in the dark, but the light was too faded. "I'm sorry," she said dully. He gave no acknowledgment of her apology. "You can release me now."

Unhurriedly, he withdrew the comfort of his embrace, and Lenora shuffled sideways off his lap until she lay on the mattress beside him, making sure there were no points of actual contact. The bed protested when Garman followed suit and stretched out his far bigger body.

She would not sleep now, she never did after being racked with nightmares, but she would lie as still and quiet as a mouse so he could drift back off. She nearly jumped when he spoke.

"You need to gain some flesh," he said casually, and from the rustle of the pillows, Lenora thought he put his hands behind his head. "A roll in the sheets with me at present would likely snap you in half," he added.

Lenora blinked. "Are you so rough, then, that I need to be more robust?" she asked with some acerbity. She felt sensitive about the changes illness had wrought upon her and answered without any thought of delicacy, despite her relief that she was to have a reprieve from the wedding night consummation.

"At present, you've only flesh in one place enough to please me," he answered with a note of relish to his tone, as though he enjoyed pursuing such a shocking topic of conversation. "You've seen me compete in the field?"

Lenora's face grew scarlet, and her brain scrambled as she realized he was likely talking about her ample rear. She tamped down the mortification to try to focus on his question. "I have," she admitted, wondering where he was going with this.

"Then you'll know I give it my all," he answered coolly. "I'm the same with bed sport. I expect the same level of exertion and abandon from all participants."

Lenora was so astonished by this she lay a moment in complete silence as she absorbed his words, her breath coming fast. Sir Garman was brutal and uncompromising in the field. What was he saying exactly? "It seems a strange analogy," she said a hoarse voice. "You would compare the act of lovers to those of combatants?"

"Lovers?" he echoed with a short, derisive laugh. Then he seemed to consider her words. "And yes, I do compare them. For me it is a physical act, much like any other exercise. It's only worth doing if you go all in." She heard a rustle, as though he turned his head to look at her. "You should probably put everything your mother ever told you about beddings out of your head. When I take you, you'll be on all fours. I like it rough and I like it loud. If there must be words, then they won't be sweet."

Lenora clutched the bedsheet, her eyes opening wide in the dark. "My mother never spoke to me of beddings," she heard herself say and was glad to hear she sounded calm if a little out of breath.

"Good," he answered coolly. "Then you won't have any preconceived notions about it."

"And what about your preconceived notions?" she heard herself ask. "To my knowledge, you've never bedded a wife before. At least not your own," she added tartly.

"You think it would be any different?" he asked skeptically after a slight pause.

"I wouldn't know," she replied coolly. "But *I* shall endeavor to approach it with an open mind."

"Will you indeed?" he muttered, and again she could hear the amusement in his voice. "I won't give a damn about crumpling your dress, Lenora. And if you don't like wet kisses then we should probably dispense with them altogether."

Lenora's color flared. She wished she had not told him that about her suitors. She had not expected him to turn her words back against her. "Noted," she said stiffly. Her suitors had never dared to press their lips to anywhere but her fingers, she thought, staring up at the shadowy ceiling. But she would not tell him that. What did he mean by wet kisses? she wondered. She thought of his full, firm mouth and swallowed. And her being on all fours?

"So, from the morrow," he carried on with a casual arrogance that quite took her breath away, "we need to start fattening you up."

"To fortify myself for your attentions, yes, so I gather." Her tone was rather dry, but he didn't pay that any attention.

"Good," he said, then yawned. To Lenora's surprise, she found herself suppressing an answering yawn of her own.

The absurd notion occurred to her that Garman had initiated this shocking conversation simply to distract her from her horrific nightmares. She dismissed it almost at once. He just wasn't made that way, she thought as her eyes drifted shut. She did not doubt he was being frank about his tastes. Indeed, it was hard to imagine him ever sugarcoating his desires to make them more palatable. She doubted very much he would ever take that trouble.

The mattress dipped as he rolled onto his side, and Lenora tensed, though he did not reach for her. Why would he? After all, he had made it perfectly clear that he found her body scrawny and unappetizing. Yet for some reason, she *had* expected him to drag her back against him. She wondered briefly if they had been sleeping in that position before she woke up, then told herself she was being foolish. Something niggled away at the corner of her memory, but she was too tired to focus on whatever it was. To her surprise, sleep was overtaking her again. She welcomed it, for they had another day's travel ahead of them, and when next she woke, it was morning.

*

Lenora made a good breakfast. Doubtless the previous day's traveling and the fresh air had done her some good, for it had sparked her sleeping appetite. Berta joined them at the table, but sat further down the bench to give them some privacy.

Garman pushed every platter toward her after first helping himself. Consequently, she found herself with a loaded plate of smoked trout, salted cod, and preserved herring. To accompany this were two kinds of bread: a brown barley and a white loaf which smelt pleasantly of herbs. Garman eschewed this one, helping himself instead to a large hunk of the barley, but Lenora was intrigued. Sniffing it, she could discern both parsley and rosemary and something else she could not quite identify.

"You're supposed to eat it," Garman rumbled, glancing up from the plate of food he was decimating.

"I will," Lenora replied with dignity. "I just wondered about the herbs in this bread."

"They won't do you any good unless they're in your stomach."

As she started to saw herself off a slice, Lenora pondered if Garman was especially churlish in the mornings, or if he was always this bad-tempered. She wasn't sure. It came to her that she had never yet seen him spontaneously smile, let alone laugh, though she had seen him victorious in the lists on several occasions. She shot a look at his face only to find him watching her progress with disgust.

"Pass it to me," he said impatiently and flung down his knife and spoon, gesturing with his hands for the bread knife.

"I can do it," Lenora protested, but found it taken out of her hands. Immediately he began cutting her a large wedge of bread. "That's rather a large piece."

He lifted his brows at her. "Have you forgotten your new resolve already?"

Lenora flushed. "No, but—" She broke off when she saw him start to slather it with a thick coat of butter. "I do not like it spread so generously!"

"For now, this is how you will take it until I'm satisfied you fill out your bodice well enough," he answered brusquely. Involuntarily, Lenora found herself glancing down at her rather loose gown. He had no manners at all, she thought as he thrust it back at her, and then recommenced shoveling his own meal down.

She had to admit, it was strangely fascinating to see how much food he could consume; she watched wonderingly as the bowls and trenchers emptied at a dizzying rate. When they had first taken their seats, she had thought the landlord had vastly overestimated how much food they would need on their table, but now she could see he had gauged it almost perfectly.

As if becoming aware of her scrutiny, Garman paused and looked pointedly across at her. Seeing as she was making good progress with the contents of her plate, she wondered what he could possibly find fault with now. "Something interests you?" he asked, mopping up some of the juices on his plate with a chunk of bread.

Lenora colored, realizing her surprise had not gone unnoticed. "My father never breaks his fast until noon," she said by way of explanation, not adding that he ate only sparingly then.

"You'll find I'm a man of large appetites, Lenora."

She met his gaze and reddened. He wasn't just talking about his stomach, she realized, and let the subject drop. His glance mocked her for a faintheart, but Lenora cleared her throat, refusing to be drawn on such an indelicate subject. Did the man think no subject was off the table?

Finally, when every scrap of food was demolished, Garman sat back in his seat and stretched his long legs out before him. Lenora could feel his eyes on her face as she swallowed the last morsel of the herb bread, and almost wished she had not left off her face veil this morn—though t'would be difficult indeed to try to smuggle pieces of food under it.

"Who's the knight you particularly did not want to see?" he asked suddenly, catching her off guard.

Lenora lowered the cup of weak ale she had raised to her lips to wash down her food. "Pardon?"

"At the royal tournament."

"When did I ever suggest—?"

"In my bedchamber at the palace," he interrupted her. Lenora shot an embarrassed look in Berta's direction. The old woman was absorbed still in finishing her herrings. Lenora frowned at Garman, who looked back at her blankly. Clearly, he thought a servant beneath consideration. "You said there was a knight in particular you wished to avoid," he repeated.

"I'm not sure—oh," she said, her frown clearing. "I meant Sir Roland Vawdrey."

Garman's expression grew grim. "And why was that?" he asked in a low voice with a sharp edge to it.

"Oh, well…" Lenora said awkwardly. "He's family now, and they were all making various plans for me and I wanted to choose my own path." He was silent, but Lenora saw he was displeased by her response. "My cousin Eden wrote, inviting me to convalesce with them at Vawdrey Keep, and I did not want that," she elaborated. "Her plan was that I should accompany Sir Roland back there after the tournament, which I wanted to avoid."

Garman gave her a hard look before asking tonelessly, "He was your betrothed at one time, wasn't he?"

She gave a startled laugh. "Hardly that. It was all a misunderstanding." His skeptical look forced her to add firmly,

"He married my cousin and I supported their match from the outset."

"If you say so," he answered, clearly not convinced, and Lenora felt a flicker of annoyance.

She plunked her cup down and stared at him. "What are you implying? That I had some alternative reason for avoiding Sir Roland's presence at court?" He looked startled, as if not anticipating she would go on the offensive. When he said nothing, she said, "You do! You think I had some motivation for fleeing from Sir Roland!" His continued silence proclaimed the truth of her words. "What earthly reason could I have?" she asked. "If there was anything betwixt us, my cousin would hardly invite me to stay with them for months on end, or offer her husband as escort," she pointed out reasonably. When he continued silent, she grew irritated. "What? What are you thinking?" she asked abruptly. He just shook his head. "Out with it!"

"That maybe your pride could not withstand his beholding your face now," he admitted harshly.

Lenora gasped at the brutality of his words. Here then, was plain speaking. She forced herself to relax and think before flinging out the hot words of denial that sprang to her lips. Once she had caught her breath, she said, "If my pride could withstand being jilted in favor of my cousin, as you seem to think, then I'm sure it could withstand Sir Roland seeing my ruined face."

He grunted, and Lenora felt the strangest impulse to throw something at his head. Her gaze fell on the dish of butter between them, but instead she took a steadying breath. "Sir Roland and I never exchanged more than a handful of words together in our lives—" she began, but he held up a hand.

76

"I don't want to hear his name on your lips," he said in a warning voice. "I won't say it again."

Lenora's jaw dropped. She stared at him in astonishment. He was the one who had brought Sir Roland up, was he not? She frowned, going back over their words. Or at least, he had raised the subject. When he stood abruptly from the table and strode from the room without another word, she transferred her incredulous gaze to Berta, who met it with a dry cackle.

"Feeling proprietary this morn, ain't he?" she said, smacking her lips over the last of her own meal.

"I don't remotely understand what that was about!" Lenora admitted shakily. "It made no sense and seemed to spring up out of nowhere!"

"It's called jealousy, my girl," Berta said dryly.

"But that's ridiculous!" Lenora was pretty sure men did not get jealous over women as disfigured as she.

"Is it? He's got a bee in his bonnet about your ex-suitor, and no mistake."

Lenora puffed out a frustrated breath. "But Sir Roland and I were never really—"

"Best not speak his name, miss," the old woman recommended heartily. "I'd get out of the habit of saying it if I were you. I wouldn't put it past his kind to put you over his knee if you go against his word."

"I am not in the habit of speaking Sir Roland's name above any other!" Lenora said hotly. Then she registered the rest of Berta's sage advice and her eyes widened. "He wouldn't dare!"

"Oh, wouldn't he?" The old woman sounded grimly amused. "Seems like something I could imagine this fine husband of yours doing quite readily."

Lenora rallied herself. "He may appear rough and uncouth at times, Berta," she said huffily. "But I assure you, he is a knight of this realm!"

Berta gave a chuckle. "Seems to me you've led a sheltered life, miss, as befits a girl of your station. I've seen those same knights spilling out onto the streets of Aphrany of an evenin'. Seen 'em brawling, seen 'em whoring and let me tell you, them precious knights of yours don't seem no better to my mind than any other men. Some of 'em far worse!"

And just like that, the tension went out of Lenora's bearing. She slumped forward onto her elbows, resting them on the table. Truth to tell, Berta likely had far more knowledge of life than the cossetted daughter of a nobleman such as she. "You're probably right," she admitted frankly and saw a surprised look cross Berta's face. "You think I should curb my tongue around him, and very likely you have a point. Only I'm not used to—" She broke off. "It beggars belief that he could feel jealousy about…me," she finished flatly.

Berta rolled her eyes. "You're in his bed now, miss. He made no bones about the fact he wanted you there." When Lenora opened her mouth to protest, she forestalled her. "Nay, don't come that with me. I know very well you thought to have your own quarters last night, but he was having none of it."

Lenora blushed. "Well, no," she admitted. "But even so—"

"Most men ain't so particular in their tastes that they'll balk at anything but a flawless face," Berta said pragmatically.

"I understand that," Lenora answered without rancor. "What I don't understand is his suddenly getting high-handed about past suitors. After all, when first I—" She had to break off hastily. She had been going to say *approached him*, but she did not want Berta to know how she had been forced to proposition her husband. "I mean, when first he paid me his addresses, he showed precious little interest in them."

Berta sniffed. "Likely they never bothered him, before he began to think of you as his," she said with a shrug. "You may have been contracted," she continued, "but men are practical creatures in the main. He wouldn't have considered you truly his till he'd bedded you."

Lenora opened her mouth, but the words did not come out. Instead she closed it smartly again. That didn't explain it either, but she could hardly tell Berta as such. "Maybe," she agreed instead, rather lamely.

"We'd best get our things packed up," Berta told her, clambering to her feet. "I got a feeling he wouldn't care to be kept waiting."

"Very likely," Lenora agreed, following her servant to the narrow staircase.

"If they could all see me now," boasted Berta in a sudden change of subject. "With my very own bedchamber at an inn!"

"Where would you normally be expected to sleep?" Lenora asked, for in truth, she had thought her maid would sleep in with her the previous night.

"There's usually communal rooms for common folk or else you can doze on a bench downstairs by the fire."

"That all sounds extremely uncomfortable. I'm not sure which would be worse!"

They were climbing the stairs now, and Berta rolled her eyes. "Your father's servants all had their own rooms did they, when your family traveled abroad?"

Lenora bit her lip. She had never really thought about where the servants slept before. Her own maid, Hannah, would usually be in with her, but her parents' servants would not have shared her mother and father's room. It had never occurred to her before to wonder.

"You needn't answer," Berta said mildly. "And your husband only got me my own room last night to lull you into a false sense of security, and well I knows it!" Lenora nearly missed her footing. Berta gave a cackle of laughter. "He's a downy one and no mistake."

Which was also probably true, Lenora reflected as she hurried to her room and began gathering up the cats. Yet for all his blunt words about beddings, he had allowed her to sleep on last night instead of forcing his attentions on her. She lowered Tybalt into the basket alongside his siblings and then closed and fastened the basket lid over their indignant meows. "We'll soon be in our new home, my darlings," she soothed them.

That was another thing, she thought. He had not insisted that the cats were relocated into Berta's room on the previous night. If anything could have encouraged her to look at him in a favorable light, it was that. Of course, she was thankful that none of them had ventured onto the bed—that might have been a step too far. She had not missed his disapproving tone when she had compared his steed to her dear cats on the previous day. Still, he had forborne from comments she would find hard to forgive, so she had to acknowledge that his conduct, apart from forcing her to share her bath with him, had been really quite beyond reproach.

While it was true his speech was both shocking and crude, he had not actually acted on his words, and after all, she had known what manner of man he was from the outset. She remembered how he had spoken of his sporting with more than one wench at a time, on the occasion of their very first conversation. He had not made any secret of the fact he had large and unnatural appetites. Of course, she had not thought he meant to slake them on her at the time, but oh well, whatever husband you plumped for would probably have undesirable facets, she thought with a shrug. Marriage was a gamble and women were frequently dealt a losing hand. You had to make the most of what you were given. As she hurriedly stowed the rest of her few things away into a sack, she reflected optimistically that things could have been a good deal worse.

9

They rested briefly at midday, but other than that pushed on until long after the sun had set. Then there was another inn, far less congenial than the previous nights. There were no baths to be had or generous suppers at this place. They had to make do with bread and cheese and a small, dark room with a hard, narrow bed. Berta elbowed her way onto a long low bench by the fire in the main chamber downstairs and professed herself comfortable. Lenora followed Garman up to their room and had to make do with a strip wash and no fire. While she was preparing for bed, her husband went back out to the stable to see to the horses himself, not trusting them to the weaselly looking grooms. While he was gone, Lenora let the cats out of their basket and encouraged them to settle on a blanket in the far corner of the room. None of the cats were impressed with the lack of a fire, and Tybalt showed a tendency to make for the bed whenever she took her eye off him.

"No," Lenora reproached him for the third time, snatching him up and depositing him gently on the blanket. "You must remain here with your brothers." Purcel scratched forlornly at the blanket with his claws and mewed. "I'm sorry, but this is the best we can manage for this evening. Look at your mother," she implored. "Grizelda is perfectly content. Can you not emulate her in this respect?" She was pleased to see the remaining kitten, Fendel, was curled up next to his mother. "At least you're being good," she sighed. Hearing a footfall on the stairs, she hurriedly retreated to tip the dirty washing water out of the window and comb her hair. Sure enough, three raps were heard on the door, and Lenora made haste to unlock it as prearranged. Garman came through the door wordlessly and removed his tunic, making his way to the basin and pouring the clean jug of water into it. Lenora plaited her fair hair as she listened to the sounds of water swishing about as he washed. When she had secured her thick braid, she tossed it over her shoulder and made for the narrow bed.

"There won't be much room, I fear," she said critically as she climbed onto the hard mattress. Garman made no reply but glanced back over his shoulder at her. For a brief moment, she wondered if he could be induced to take half the blankets and sleep on the floor. Or could she sleep on a chair? she wondered, glancing at the two rickety wooden objects that were the only other furniture in the room. The idea rapidly paled, besides she actually felt cold in these sheets. She was sure the room was damp. Scanning the ceiling, she fancied she could see damp spots in the flickering candlelight. "Hurry," she said, her teeth chattering. "I'm cold." She heard him moving about, then the thud of one boot, then the other being removed. Lenora shuffled to the edge of the mattress, facing the wall as she heard his bare footsteps cross the room. Then the bed dipped behind her and a far bigger body joined her, crowding up against her own.

If there had been room, she might have flinched away from the press of warm, hard flesh, but she had nowhere to retreat to. His solid bulk was flush against her back, the fronts of his legs coming to rest against the backs of hers. For some reason, she had thought they would lie back to back, but clearly that was not the case. One of the flat pillows rustled overhead as he adjusted it; Lenora wondered what it could be stuffed with. It felt like straw. When he did not speak but just exhaled a noisy breath, Lenora realized she had not heard him speak for several hours.

"Comfortable?" she found herself asking over her shoulder. There was a heavy silence, then he replied grudgingly.

"I've had worse."

Clearly, he did not want conversation, but perversely Lenora found herself craving it. She already knew sleep was not going to come easily to her tonight. She tried to concentrate instead on the warmth seeping slowly from his limbs to hers, but it was too gradual for her liking. "I think these sheets are likely damp," she ventured.

He huffed again in the darkness. "Go to sleep, Lenora."

"This room certainly is. Damp, I mean."

Silence. Lenora bit her lip. "Did you see Berta in the taproom?" She peered back over her shoulder again, but he had blown out the candle. "I only wondered if she was comfortable," she explained. He shifted irritably, but clearly had no room to escape from her either. For some reason, the idea of his wanting to flee from their marital bed struck her as funny and she had to suppress a laugh. She heard his head turn toward her in the dark.

"What's so funny?" he asked grudgingly.

"Just the two of us, crammed on this mattress," she admitted with a chortle. "Both of us heartily longing to be elsewhere."

He was silent, and Lenora found herself worrying she had offended him. Which was absurd. "I only meant—" she started hesitantly, but he didn't let her finish.

"Are you always this solicitous of your servants?" he asked grouchily.

"What?" She was thrown for a moment.

"The old woman. She may have been with you since you were a child, but that hardly—"

"Oh, she hasn't," Lenora interrupted him. "She has only been with me these last three months."

"Three months?" His tone was frankly disbelieving.

"Yes," Lenora said. "But it was a rather *intense* three months. You see, I nearly died." He was silent, and for some reason, Lenora couldn't abide the silence and found she had to fill it. "Berta nursed me back from the brink," she carried on blithely.

"She doesn't look much like a healer." His tone was dry, skeptical even.

"She's not," Lenora said. "She's a laundress by trade, but to earn some extra coin she lays out the dead."

His pillow rustled. "What do you mean?"

She could hear the frown in his voice. Lenora was careful to keep her tone light. "We were all put down in the crypt," she said. "The afflicted. We—we had attendants. They identified which of us needed to be dragged out. They had their faces covered with scarves and they used to nudge us with sticks. Sometimes they brought us water." When her voice wavered, she stopped and took a breath in and out. She carried on again and was pleased to hear her voice was steady. "When I was certain I was going to live, I caught hold of Berta's skirt and refused to let go. I told her I was rich, that if she fetched me water and food, I would see she was rewarded."

Garman was silent a moment. "You're lucky she believed you."

"Oh, she didn't at first. I think most were dying servants. The pox really swept through their quarters. But no matter how many times she kicked me off, I would not leave give her any peace."

"Seems a characteristic of yours."

Lenora turned her head to peer at him. Did she see the slight gleam of his eyes? "Persistence?" she asked, oddly flattered.

"That pleases you?" he grunted.

She nodded, then remembered he could not see her. "Yes. I don't think—" She broke off.

"What?"

"That I've been much described, in terms of my personality."

"You didn't exactly encourage it," Garman told her bluntly. "As you never seemed to have one."

Lenora fell silent. After all, what could she say in her defense? He spoke nothing but the truth. She remembered all the times she had not troubled herself to make conversation or cultivate friends among her fellow courtiers. It had all seemed like a pointless exercise when she could simply drift through her charmed life, troubling herself about nothing. Her cheeks burned.

She remembered, too, the words her cousin had spoken to her months ago, encouraging her to connect more with the world around her, to have compassion and interest in her fellow creatures. But all Lenora had cared about was her cats and having her fortune told by the latest soothsayer to appear at court. She smiled bitterly in the dark. They had flattered her, everyone, from the lame beggar at the cathedral entrance to the famous seer from across the seas. All had hinted at a glittering future, she remembered, and not a single one had hinted at her spectacular fall from grace.

How funny, she thought, that absorption with such things should come crashing down around her ears so spectacularly like everything else in her life. She no longer believed in fate or fortunes. How could she? And yet, it had been something she had clung to from such a young age.

How well she remembered her very first encounter with a fortune teller in Bonbartle on a feast day as a child of eleven. She and Eden had wandered from their attendants and been importuned for coin by a fellow dressed in multicolored rags. *I'll tell you of your true loves, my pretties*, he had wheedled.

Eden had scoffed even as a child, sticking her nose in the air, but Lenora had been entranced. After parting with her copper, which had been intended for the cathedral alms box, he had seized her hand in his and predicted a mighty lord whose emblem was that of a bleeding heart.

Lenora had tottered through the rest of the day oblivious both to her cousin's scandalized reaction and her nurse's scolding for straying. A mighty lord with the emblem of a bleeding heart was her true love. In the dark, a tear tracked down Lenora's cheek, quickly followed by another. That had been a lie too. That foolish dream she had clung to for all these years. She had no true love. She had nothing.

"Lenora?" Garman's voice startled her, coming out of the dark. Had she made any noise? She'd rather die a thousand deaths than let him know she was crying like the spoilt, silly idiot they both knew she was. Keeping very still, she squeezed her wet eyes tight, feigning sleep.

It's not too late, Eden had urged her. But was that still the case? For a woman with a ruined face? Lenora swallowed. Only Eden had ever believed there was more to her than her superficial appearance. But her cousin was the person she loved best in all the world. Should she not trust Eden's opinion, over that of people who did not really know her? Even her own father had always thought her no more than a pretty fool. *Your looks will bring the suitors flocking*, he had predicted sagely, and he had been right. Only her grandmother had thought she should apply herself more to studies and music lessons, advice Lenora had blithely ignored. She had been lazy and self-indulgent, she acknowledged now with bitter self-reproach. If she had studied her books and her lessons, she would have inner resources to fall back on now, after losing her beauty. She would have more *substance.*

She thought of her cousin. Eden was so strong and proud and clever. No one would ever describe Eden as wishy-washy or lacking in personality. Lenora knew deep down inside that she would never be strong or clever, but in her own small way, could she not carve out a life for herself now? Surreptitiously, she wiped the back of her hand across her eyes.

I will change, she vowed. *While I will never have a really decent character, true love, or even much by way of brains, I can still seek out some semblance of happiness.* Plenty of wretched creatures were forced to eke out a life with far less good fortune than her own. She thought of Berta, who had never owned her own home and was forced to labor away at two jobs to even keep a roof over her head in her old age.

She had no right to wallow in self-pity like this. She had her beloved cats and was on her way to a new home, away from the prying royal court, where she could lick her wounds and recover. And recover she would, she vowed silently into her tearstained pillow. She would prove her naysayers wrong, her parents included. Far from being better off dead, who knows, maybe this new version of herself would lead to much-needed improvement in her character? Stranger things happened, or so people said.

This new resolve brought some relief from her scalding self-reproach and she felt her limbs relax as her eyelids drooped. Whoever would have thought that a spot of honest soul-searching would be so exhausting? She would have to write to Eden as soon as they arrived at Cofton Warren and let her know of her new resolutions. She knew her cousin would approve of the resolve, if not her choice of groom. A faint smile touched her lips. No, Eden would not approve of Garman Orde, she thought wryly. Far from it. For some reason that thought fortified her as she drifted off to sleep.

10

Garman paced the courtyard and glanced up at the small window in the eaves. Where the hells was she? He had half a mind to go barging up there and drag her down. He wanted to be off. If he pushed hard today, they could reach Cofton Warren by nightfall. And he intended to push hard. He'd had enough of being slowed down by a pair of women. He had already hooked up the cart and saddled his horse first thing. There was not a bite of food to be had in the place to send them on their way, so he wanted to clear out at first light. Shambling footsteps heralded Berta's arrival. She squinted evilly at Garman before making for the cart.

It crossed his mind that Lenora might have told the old crone about how he'd made her cry the night before. He didn't doubt that she would make much of it this morning, looking tragical and making a great play with wet eyelashes and hurt feelings. She was a spoilt court beauty after all, he thought with a scowl. He had spoken naught but the truth, and he stood by every word. If she expected him to start pussyfooting about her, she was in for a big disappointment. It would be a cold day in hell before he started that game.

He turned his head sharply at a footfall in the doorway, then saw Lenora maneuvering the basket she kept the cats in through the narrow opening. "Sorry," she called out cheerfully. "I had a bit of a trouble rounding them up this morning." She headed straight for the cart and swung it up before her. Garman could make out the faint mew of indignant cats. Berta thrust out a hand and Lenora seized it and climbed into the wagon. Once she had settled into the bench, she looked over at him brightly. "Are we ready to depart?"

He grunted and swung into the saddle, steering Bria'ag back out onto the open road and away from the dismal inn. He was surprised. And Garman Orde was seldom surprised. He had been grimly certain that he was in for a scene of female play-acting and hysterics. It seemed he was wrong.

As the morning wore on, he found for some reason he could not tune out the women's conversation. Snatches of it drifted over to him despite him being several yards in front. Lenora's tone was bright and breezy; he heard her rippling laugh and Berta chiming in sourly at intervals. It slowly sank in that Lenora was not bearing tales about her husband's brutality. Far from it. She seemed to be putting on a determinedly bright front this morn. He wondered at that, considering she had not much sleep the night before.

He had not been taken in for a minute by her unconvincing semblance of sleep. She had been stiff as a board and even he, not finely attuned to the moods of others, could tell she was upset and faking it. Then, when she finally had managed to drop off to sleep, it had been a mere couple of hours before her night terrors had roused her screaming from whatever it was that haunted her dreams. *Whatever it was*. He hunched a shoulder in irritation. No point in feigning ignorance to himself. He knew full well what that was about now. Lovely Lenora Montmayne, the Flower of all Karadok, had been left to rot down in the crypt with the rest of the condemned.

He couldn't even imagine how she must have felt. The spoilt court darling, suddenly finding herself cast onto a fetid human rubbish tip. No matter how much he tried to tell himself she'd had it no worse than the other pox-ridden beggars, it rang hollow. What were her family thinking leaving her to fester and die down in the palace crypt? He really couldn't fathom it.

Of course, Lenora Montmayne had been spared from a mass grave, but how much of that had been due to her own merit? She'd had the presence of mind to call on her privilege when she needed to and a surprising amount of dogged determination not to give up the fight for survival. He himself had recognized these qualities in her after only one day in her company. Yet she said no one else had ever drawn any such conclusions as to her character? Her family must be a bunch of fucking idiots and callous ones at that.

At the end of the day, she had clawed her way out of a pile of dead and dying to find her beauty and her suitors fled. Instead of descending into maudlin despair, she had cast about her for a way out of court where she would be an object of curiosity and pity. She had struck on him. Only one conclusion could be drawn from that. Lenora Montmayne was brave as fuck or foolhardy as hell. He wasn't sure yet which it was.

Suddenly, the image of her arose in his mind of her standing up naked in that damned bathtub, letting him look his fill. Again, brave or foolhardy, one or the other. A bold move that filled him with grudging admiration as well as lust. It could have gone either way. That backside, *fuck*. Who cared about her face when she had an ass like that?

Glancing over his shoulder, he found her debating with Berta about the qualities of household cats. The old woman seemed to think they should be booted out of doors come nightfall. Lenora was strongly against such action as it meant a pile of dead birds on the doorstep come morning. Neither woman seemed to notice his scrutiny. He found himself once more wondering at their closeness. In spite of himself, he had been shocked by Lenora's account of their meeting.

The crone Berta was a far from endearing character. Her face was withered as a rotten apple and she had a voice that could curdle milk. By all accounts, she had been far from solicitous in her care of her mistress in the early days. Yet Lenora treated her now as if she were…what? A trusted member of her household. She had even identified Berta to that soldier as her own mother, something he would never have believed if he had not heard it with his own ears.

Of course, he knew in his own experience that family could be forged from extreme circumstances and near death. He thought of his own point in case, the Hainfroys. He had been squire to old Bernhard Hainfroy from the age of twelve, but he had become another son to him through the hardships of the war. His sons, Huw and Ivo, had become his brothers, although they shared no blood. They had shed plenty of it in defense of one another.

It had been four years since he had seen them, since he had returned home. And now he was returning to Cofton Warren with a wife in tow. He smiled grimly to himself. He had amassed quite a fortune from his success in the tourneys, and at some point, in the near future, he could finally achieve his heart's content—Matchings Halt. The handsome manor house and its fruitful acres had long been the object of his boyhood admiration and one day very soon, would be his. If Lenora's father, Sir Leofric, actually did hand over her dowry, then he could possibly achieve it even sooner than he'd hoped.

For now, he would have to stash Lenora at Matchings Farm with his grandfather Sutton, he thought with a grimace. His grandfather had run the farm for some twenty years now and ran it with the same calm efficiency he applied to everything. Garman had no doubt it would be turning a good profit, though he only ever received letters few and far between from his grandfather, sometimes several in one go would catch him up as his travels took him far and wide to compete.

His maternal grandfather was a conscientious man, and though he and his grandson had very little in common, there was a blood bond between them. His bride would be assured a punctilious welcome at Matchings Farm, even if not overly warm. He could have taken her to Cofton Grange, of course, as when he'd left, he'd been promised a perpetual seat at Huw's table, but who even knew how things fared with the Hainfroys. He had not kept in touch with them any better than he had with his own grandfather, and neither Huw nor Ivo were known for their letter-writing skills. It was hard to think of either of his quarrelsome friends faring well in times of peace. No, on reflection, it was better to take Lenora on to his grandfather's farm. They were making good progress and looked set to reach there by nightfall.

11

It started to rain at midday. At first Lenora hoped it was only a passing shower, but it kept on and on until by late afternoon, her raised hood and closely wrapped cloak were drenched through.

"We can't go on like this," Berta grumbled beside her, but in truth Lenora had not seen much sign of shelter along the stretch of road they had been traveling. Almost as if he had heard, Garman slowed ahead of them and dropped back.

"Detour!" he shouted above the rumble of thunder.

"Where to?" Lenora shouted, and he pointed to a lane approaching on the left.

"Man of few words, ain't he?" Berta huffed. "I thought he said we would reach his precious Cofton Warren by nightfall."

Lenora glanced up at the darkening sky, but it was thunderclouds rather than nightfall that had caused it. She judged the hour no more advanced than five o'clock. Pulling on the reins, she urged the horse to take the bend in the road and hoped he had somewhere dry and safe in mind. After a half a mile or so, she saw a low gray-stone building looming in the distance and nudged Berta.

"Looks a ramshackle sort of place!" Berta sniffed.

In truth, it did look rather abandoned with a trail of outbuildings leading up to it, all in varying states of dilapidation. Creeping vines had taken root and were spreading over the walls as if nature was trying to reclaim the place. Could this be his grandfather's farm? Lenora wondered. And if so, it seemed like his grandfather had frankly given up the struggle.

She followed where he led, to the largest of the outbuildings which turned out to be a large stable, well equipped and dry with clean hay and housing two large brown horses every bit as big as Garman's own beast. He climbed down and immediately set to unhooking the wagon and rubbing the horses down. Lenora's cats mewed pitifully, and she was tempted to let them out in this large, well-appointed barn, which she was starting to suspect was in better repair than the house itself would be.

Draping her cloak over a nearby stall to dry out, she picked her way around to where Garman was feeding the cart horse. "Are we sleeping in this barn?" she asked forthrightly.

He spared her a glance. "We should find a welcome up at the house."

"I could not see any lights, and it looks half-abandoned."

He did not answer this, and Lenora wandered over to where the two large horses eyed her curiously. One pawed the ground while the other tossed his head. "I suppose these fine horses must belong to someone. They at least are well cared for."

Again, he made no answer, turning back to his own beast and leading Bria'ag into a spare stall.

"I cannot decide whether to let my cats out in this stable," she said, swinging back to face him.

"Why wouldn't you?" he asked. "It's dry and warm and there's plenty of straw."

"What if they wander off or go astray?"

He snorted. "In this weather?"

Lenora glanced out of one of the narrow window openings. "I could not depart on the morn if one of them were missing," she warned him.

"They will not wander in this rain," he replied confidently.

Lenora rounded the cart and lifted down the basket. By the time she had installed the cats in a warm spot and given them the last of her scraps, they were huddled together and purring. Berta was shaking out their wet things and Garman had settled the horses for the night. He nodded meaningfully toward the exit, and Lenora reluctantly donned her wet cloak. "Come along, Berta," she prompted her maidservant, who seemed to be making herself comfortable on a bale of hay.

"I'll remain here," said the old woman. "I can keep an eye on the cats."

Lenora was touched. "I would not expect you to sleep out here though." She frowned.

"Nay, I'd prefer it." The old woman yawned. "I likes me own space and I saw a pile of blankets in the corner."

"Those will be horse blankets," Lenora pointed out.

"Makes no odds to me."

"Well, if you're sure." Lenora faltered, seeing Garman was growing impatient by the door.

"Quite sure."

"Very well then, I'll bid you good night."

The old woman nodded. "If you finds a welcome within, perhaps you'd send me out a bit of bread and cheese."

"Of course," Lenora assured her and hurried out after Garman into a cobbled courtyard filled with puddles of rain. "Whose house is this?" she asked with some misgiving, wondering if she should have retrieved her veils from his saddlebag. They

97

would doubtless be badly creased after being stuffed in there these last two days.

"Friends," he grunted. "Old friends." On reaching the dark, gray house, he hammered on the studded door and drew her under the overhanging masonry of the elaborate doorway. It looked, she thought, rather like an abbot's grange. A badly kept one whose brotherhood had abandoned it. Heavy drops of rain dripped onto her from an overhanging stone griffin's beak.

"Who be it without?" called a countrywoman's voice doubtfully. "We're not expecting anyone."

"Ask if they've brought cakes and ale," Lenora heard a man's voice yell within. "Or they'll find no welcome here!"

The maid giggled. "Oh sir," she remonstrated, and Lenora glanced at Garman to find him looking irritable.

"It's Garman Orde," he bellowed. "One who was ever assured a welcome in this house."

There was a stunned silence, followed by the noise of furniture being overturned. Lenora steeled herself as the door was wrenched open and two well-built men with dark hair came tumbling out. They seized Garman about the shoulders and neck, and for a moment Lenora thought they were assaulting him as they wrestled him to his knees, rubbed his head, slapped his cheeks, and rained light blows about his person. Then she realized it was just an excess of male affection.

"Cease!" Garman boomed, grabbing one of them in a headlock. "Let us in out of the rain, you bloody fools!" She wasn't mistaken though, she thought as she watched one of them slap him heartily on the back. There was affection here.

Garman reached back for her and, grabbing her wrist, pulled her into the dark low-beamed room after him. She saw the brothers, for brothers they must be they were so alike, notice her for the first time. Their gazes flickered over her without much interest before returning to Garman. Lenora took the opportunity to divest herself of her sodden cloak, as the idea did not seem to occur to the black-haired maidservant who was agog and staring at Garman.

"Orde, you bastard! Finally, you've come home," said the first with satisfaction. "And not a day too soon! We've looked for you any time these past four years!"

"Sit ye down, brother, sit ye down!" urged the other, dragging out a seat. "You need not stand on ceremony here. Our home is your home. Martha!" he said, turning to the buxom maid. "Fetch another tankard, for Sir Garman is come home at last."

"Two cups," Garman interposed, holding up two fingers. Instead of taking the proffered chair, he led Lenora to it and saw her seated. "My wife, Lenora," he said by way of introduction.

Again, both brothers turned to look at her blankly. The idea of bowing did not seem to occur to them, and after sitting down it seemed rather foolish again to stand for an unwarranted curtsey. Instead she looked at Garman.

"These are Huw and Ivo Hainfroy, my sworn brothers," he said, catching her unspoken question.

"I am pleased to meet you," she said, but they had already turned away and were exclaiming over their long-lost friend once more.

"You have eaten? No?"

Garman shook his head. "Not since this morning, and I must ask a bed of you this night."

Both brothers seemed dumbfounded at his request. "Ask? You've had a bed here since you were twelve!" one of them boomed. "Don't be daft, man!"

"We hope you'll stay more than a night at least!" the other rejoined. The remains of a large meal were on the table, and he began dragging any unemptied plates toward Garman. "Martha, fetch more bread and another wheel of cheese!"

Lenora noticed that Martha made no haste to follow any directions and still lingered, throwing admiring glances at Garman.

"I mean to travel on to my grandfather Sutton's on the morn," Garman admitted grudgingly.

This announcement was met with great resistance from the Hainfroys.

"Your grandfather's? What the devil for?"

"You've no ambition to be a farmer after all these years?"

Garman brushed off their exclamations. "We need to wash off our travel dirt before we can eat," he said. "If a room can be made ready." He spared a glance for Martha. "Have you no other servant? If not, I can boil us some water."

"Nay," said the one starting out of his seat. "I can do it. Martha, fetch those goblets I say!"

Martha pouted, but left the room closely followed by one of the brothers.

"I'd let you have your old room," the remaining Hainfroy said, "but it is a little small for two." He hesitated. "Perhaps Isabeau's room?"

"It makes no odds to me." Garman shrugged.

"I'll fetch blankets for you," he said decisively and, picking up a candlestick, strode from the room.

Only one measly candle remained in the long, narrow room, plunging them almost into darkness. Outside a streak of lightning lit up the sky illuminating them briefly. Garman reached for one of the two tankards of ale already on the table and passed it to Lenora. He took the other and toasted her silently before draining it. Lenora sipped from the other. Absently, he fetched two candlesticks down from over the mantel and knelt down to light them from the flames in the hearth before placing them at strategic points. Lenora shivered, and he threw three more logs on the fire.

"Do you think Berta will be warm enough?" she asked quietly, but a returning Hainfroy drowned out his response.

"The back bedroom is now set up for you, and there is a basin of water," he said with a nod. "You know where it is. I'll go and fetch more food and ale."

Garman held out a hand for her. "Come and wash," he said. "And get out of your wet clothes."

Lenora followed him up the steep staircase and he helped to peel her out of her wet dress and into a dry one with an efficiency that impressed her. She had half a mind to climb into the big bed covered in red draperies and forget anything else, but Garman was already shepherding her back down the dark narrow staircase.

"You need to eat, remember?" he rumbled at her, and she flushed, wondering if he had caught a few glimpses of her damp body in the darkened room after all.

When they reached the dining hall once more, they found the table replenished and a sulky Martha pouring out wine. Lenora set about wrapping a warm woolen mantle about her shoulders as Garman started piling a plate with bread, cheese, and meat. Lenora was just about to ask if she could prepare a plate for Berta, when he disappeared out of doors with it.

"Where's he gone now?" a Hainfroy demanded, coming in as the door banged shut.

"I believe he has taken our servant some food," Lenora answered. "She is sleeping out in the barn this night."

He grunted, but made no other response, though he did pass her some wine which Lenora took with thanks. His brother entered moments later, and Lenora observed that their brotherly resemblance was strong. Both were tall and muscular, though not as powerfully built as Garman. They had dark chestnut-brown hair which waved from their brows, high cheekbones, and rather patrician noses. They did not bother with her presence, which Lenora found strangely relaxing. She sat back in her seat and sipped her wine as the warmth from the fire seeped into her chilled bones.

Both sprang up as Garman reentered the room, but his first words were for her ears. "The cats are fine," he murmured as he shook himself off like a dog.

"Good. And Berta?"

"Fine as she'll ever be." He frowned. "Why do you not eat?"

Lenora sat forward, not troubling to point out that no one had provided her with a plate. Garman seized one for her and began carving at the meat.

"Not too much," she admonished. "I'm tired and soon for my bed."

"You'll retire to bed when I do," he corrected her firmly. "And not before."

Lenora eyed him. What was this about? Noticing the Hainfroys were following their exchange with interest, she took the plate from him and picked up a knife.

"You've married money, Garman?" one of them asked curiously.

"How much did she bring you?" The other grinned. "A pretty penny, I'll warrant."

Lenora suspected they assumed her fortune must be pretty, as her face was not. She ignored the slight pang this caused her and steeled herself for his response.

"Not a single coin," Garman admitted blandly. He sliced a pear and placed half of it on her plate. "As we wed without her father's consent."

The brothers were speechless for a minute. Lenora felt her face burn as she speared a piece of pear. More than ever she wished she had her face covered as she felt their incredulous stares burn into her. Looking up, she could see one of them had a question trembling on his lips, but seeing her eyes trained on him, he bit it back. Lenora held his gaze and felt rather proud of herself.

"Which one are you?" she asked directly and saw him start in his seat. If they did not stand on ceremony, then she did not see why she should. And she had resolved to have an interest in her fellow creatures, had she not?

The other one gave a bark of laughter. "His name is Huw Hainfroy and I am Ivo." He inclined his head and she saw that his eyes were very green, whereas his brother's were more of a blue green. He also had a scar that ran from his cheekbone all the way down and right through his top lip. Although it had healed and faded, it must have been deep.

Lenora turned to look at the speaker. "And you are my husband's sworn brothers?"

"That is so," he agreed cautiously.

"Which makes me a sister of sorts, I suppose."

He leaned back in his seat and regarded her thoughtfully. "We have not had a sister for some two years now." His brother, Huw, stiffened at his words and shot a look in Garman's direction.

"Have you heard from Isabeau?" Garman asked after the smallest of pauses. *Oh, then she had not died*, thought Lenora. For a moment she thought she had stumbled on some family tragedy. Isabeau's room, she remembered, was the room they were staying in.

Both brothers looked affronted by his question. "Of course not!" scoffed Ivo.

"We would not acknowledge her if we had!" swore Huw angrily. "What do you take us for?"

"Her brothers," Garman answered dryly.

"Not anymore! Not after what she did to you…!" Huw's words trailed off, and he glanced furtively in Lenora's direction.

How interesting! Lenora swallowed her mouthful and reflected that the conversation would likely flow far easier without her presence. She wondered at Garman's refusal to let her retire early. As their conversation turned to the tournaments, Lenora let her gaze wander over the parts of the room that she could see through the gloom. A large portrait hung on the wall of a tall, gaunt man in a suit of armor. His eyes were sharp and flinty and his large bony hands grasped the pommel of his sword tight.

"Our father," Ivo said suddenly, seeing the direction of her stare. "Sir Bernhard Hainfroy. Garman was his squire."

Huw broke off from questioning Garman to glare in their direction. "What's that you say, Ivo?"

"Mind your own conversation," Ivo retorted rudely. "You don't get to dictate ours."

Huw scowled at him. "Garman says he's made a fortune in the tournaments, you should be attending to what he says, not gossiping with his wife."

"Mayhap you should listen to him," Ivo snorted. "For he told you he would succeed, and you did not believe him four years ago."

"No more did you!" Huw snapped. "He asked you to go with him too, did he not?"

"Don't start your quarrelling!" Garman growled. "The truth is that both of you should have come with me, though neither one of you did!"

Both brothers lapsed moodily into silence at this.

"Your horses certainly look like destriers," said Lenora. "Have you never jousted?"

Huw twitched a shoulder irritably, but Ivo rumbled back with the negative.

"They could turn a hand to it easy enough," Garman predicted. "If they were willing."

After this exchange, the conversation seemed to hit a lull, and Lenora hastily finished up the last of her meal. Almost as if he had been waiting for her to finish, Garman pushed his own empty plate away and held out a hand for her.

"You're not retiring already?" Huw Hainfroy asked in surprise.

"We've been journeying for three days," Garman pointed out.

"What's that to you? We journeyed for weeks on end during the campaigns," Ivo snorted.

"Lenora's been ill. She needs her rest."

"Then send her up to bed and you follow on later," Huw suggested rudely. "We'll drink another flagon."

An imp of devilment whispered in Lenora's ear. "We're newlyweds," she sighed by way of explanation. "He cannot bear to be parted from me come bedtime. Isn't that right, beloved?" She angled a look at Garman from the corner of her eye, but if she had meant to embarrass or annoy him, she had apparently missed the mark.

"Aye," Garman agreed straight-faced. "And I find you're at your most appealing flat on your back."

12

The rain continued to drum against the windowpane. Garman began to undress as Lenora climbed into the bed.

"I hope the stable roof doesn't leak," she murmured.

"Trust me," he answered dryly. "If there's one thing the Hainfroys prize, it's their horses. That roof won't leak."

She yawned and turned onto her side, showing him her back. He stripped off the last of his undergarments, blew out the candle, and climbed in beside her. It was a moment or two before she spoke.

"Who is Isabeau and how did she serve you ill?"

He stiffened. *Bloody hells.* "You don't believe in holding back, do you?" he asked grimly. He heard a rustling sound as though she was turning to face him. Really what was the point? It was pitch black in the bedchamber.

"You only have to answer half that question since I've already deduced she was a Hainfroy, before they disowned her that is."

"I don't have to answer any of it, Lenora," he pointed out dryly, propping his hands behind his head. For some reason her chatter wasn't annoying him as much as it should. And why was that? He frowned into the darkness. He had the strangest suspicion he had been waiting for her talk to him as soon as he'd blown the candle out.

"What did she do, I wonder," she mused aloud. "Break your heart?"

He gave a short laugh. "Don't be ridiculous."

"That's almost a pity."

He turned his head, then remembered he couldn't see her expression. "A pity?" he echoed sharply.

"It would give you a vastly romantic reason for why you are…the way you are."

Little wretch. "Has anyone ever put you over their knee, Lenora?" he asked mildly.

"No, would you like to?" Her tone wasn't teasing at all; it was surprised, curious.

He almost caught his breath. "I believe I would." The tone of his voice gave him away. He didn't sound angry. He sounded gravelly and aroused. He could almost hear her puzzling it out. Then she shrugged it off. He felt strangely disappointed they were not going to pursue the subject.

"If you won't tell me, doubtless I could induce Martha to," she said breezily.

Garman frowned. "Who?"

"The maidservant." She sounded faintly exasperated.

"Oh." He dredged the image of the unhelpful wench up in his mind. "I think she must be after my time. I doubt she'd know."

"Why, because you don't remember her?" She sounded skeptical. "I don't think you're very good at noticing people."

"What makes you think that?"

"She was far too interested in your appearance not to know who you are."

Garman huffed out a breath. "This is a provincial backwater. She'd behave the same toward any stranger that turned up."

"She wasn't very interested in me," Lenora pointed out.

"You're not a virile male."

That shut her up for a moment. Then she gave a gurgle of mirth.

"What?"

"Nothing. Just…virile male."

Garman stared irritably at where he imagined her face might be. Why the hells was she always laughing when she was in his bed? he wondered. He couldn't remember it ever happening to him before. Mind you, he never usually permitted women to sleep there let alone ramble on with words. "You doubt my virility?" he asked. "Maybe I should prove it to you." He was already half-hard after entertaining the notion of spanking that luscious rear of hers.

"You should probably let me get a little fatter first," she said and had the cheek to reach out and pat him indulgently on the chest.

He jumped at her touch. It entered his mind that she might actually think he could not get the job done with her at present. Reaching out, he caught her hand and slid it down the sheets so she could feel his hardening cock beneath them. It flexed impressively under her fingers and he heard her smothered gasp.

"I'm being considerate, Lenora. Not incapable." He let that sink in before he let go of her hand. She snatched it back as though he'd burnt it. "Let me know if it's not appreciated and I'll happily remedy the situation."

She was silent for a minute or two, her breathing shallow. Suddenly, he found himself worried that he might have upset her again. *Shit. What was it she'd said before?* She didn't like men pressing wet kisses to her hand? She probably thought hard cocks was far worse. "Lenora?"

"Um, no, no," she said rather breathlessly. "I appreciate you're being considerate," she assured him.

He relaxed in spite of himself. "Go to sleep," he said gruffly. A rustle of sheets again and she turned quiet, but he wasn't fooled that she had fallen asleep. He waited until he heard her breathing even out and the tension leave her body. Then, gingerly, he shuffled closer. It would not be long now until she woke again in the grip of her nightmares. He wanted to be close at hand when she did. He heard the muffled sob just as his own eyes were closing and reached out, dragging her firmly against him. "Shhhhh, you're here at Cofton Grange. With me," he murmured, closing his arms around her tight. She floundered a moment and he waited for her to surface from the confusion.

"Where?" she gasped.

"Cofton Grange, the home of my old master, Sir Bernhard Hainfroy." He kept his voice low but reassuring.

"I don't—?"

"His sons live here now and are letting the place go to rack and ruin."

"S-sons?"

"Huw and Ivo Hainfroy. You met them at dinner, remember?"

He felt her relax as she became aware of her surroundings. If she recognized what was poking into her backside right now, she gave no indication.

She huffed out a big sigh. "I'm awake now," she said in a small voice.

110

He grunted but did not release her. "Then go back to sleep." He'd let her go when he was good and ready and not before.

For some reason, he was not ready, even when sleep took him under some half hour later.

13

He woke early next morning and found Lenora wide awake and lying very still under him. "What the—?"

"Oh good, you're awake," she said with relief. "I'm half crushed to death!"

Garman promptly rolled off her and sat up to hide his obvious state of arousal. He glanced over at her, clearing his throat. "I didn't—?" He broke off his words to rake her appearance. Thankfully there were no tears in her eyes or others sign he had done aught amiss. She still wore her shift and looked quite calm.

"I tried to get up and you rolled atop of me," she explained with an upward quirk of her lips. "Any attempt to remonstrate with you met with resistance." She yawned and then stretched.

Garman had to avert his eyes as her shift was fine and thin. He realized that whatever aversion he'd had to her too-slender frame had now passed. He cleared his throat and turned his back to her as he rose carefully from the bed.

"The rain's stopped," she commented, turning her attention to the window.

He grunted, pulling his braies over his hips and tying the strings.

"How far is it from here to your grandfather's farm?"

"Not far. An hour at the most." He glanced over his shoulder to find her hugging her knees and gazing out of the window. The thick braid of her blond curling hair had half unraveled in the night. She looked disheveled, and for some reason, he enjoyed the sight almost as much as if it had been his own handiwork.

His still-hard cock twitched, and he frowned. Had he named a specific amount of time for this reprieve he had given her? Just how long did it take to fatten a woman up anyway? Lenora Montmayne had never been plump, just not scrawny from illness. He just wanted to fill out a few of those hollows, not change her shape altogether.

She turned her head toward him. "You know you've told me nothing about your grandfather," she said, pulling him out of his thoughts.

He dragged his tunic over his head. "What did you want to know?"

"Which side of your family is he from?"

Garman took a deep breath. "His name's Sutton and he's my mother's father. He was a steward all his life. Now he runs a farm." Surely that's enough for her to be going on with.

"Are you close to him?"

Garman paused. Apparently, he had not told her enough. "He raised me from the age of four, until I came to be Sir Bernhard's squire."

She nodded slowly. "And you were only twelve when you came here?"

"Aye."

"When did you last see your grandfather Sutton?"

He considered this as he tied the lacings at the front of his tunic. "Some three years ago or thereabouts."

"How do you know that all continues well with him?"

"He writes to me," Garman said abruptly. Damn long prosy letters giving him a scrupulous account of how he had spent all the monies Garman ever sent him. Every penny was invested in the farm, and he gave detailed updates on their returns, their crops, the labor he employed, everything. As if Garman was his damned employer rather than his own kin.

"And do you write to him?"

Garman opened and closed his mouth. He usually sent some couple of lines of scrawl with the purses of gold he sent to his grandfather after his wins, but you could hardly call them letters. "I'm not much of a writer," he said shortly and made for the door. Her voice halted him as he reached for the latch.

"Will he be disappointed?" she pursued. "About your marrying without his consent?"

Garman gave a short, dry laugh. "Hardly."

"Should I—?"

He turned about impatiently when she did not finish. "What?"

She lifted her chin. "Should I wear my veil when I meet him, do you think?"

The faint hint of uncertainty in her eyes stopped him from snapping back a harsh, instinctive negative. Instead he forced himself to look her over a moment impartially. What would his grandfather think of this woman he had married? He considered the question, but in truth he hardly knew. He bore not the slightest resemblance to his mother's people and never had. It was the Hainfroys with whom he had found kinship and not his blood relatives.

Old Sir Bernhard had been the only father figure he had ever known. He knew what he would have said. *If the wench takes your fancy, then the opinions of others be damned!* And against all the odds, Lenora Montmayne did take his fancy. "You don't need it, Lenora." She gave a faint start and colored at his words, but he held her gaze.

"Very well."

Garman continued downstairs but found all was in confusion. The remains of last night's supper were strewn across the table with no attempt having been made to clear it. He suspected Huw and Ivo must have stayed up drinking until the early hours and would not stir before noon. The serving wench must surely be warming one of the brothers' beds or else her slovenly ways would not be tolerated even at Cofton Grange.

Back in Isabeau's time, she would soon have been slung out on her ear. Though apparently done for his sake, Garman could not help but think the brother's decision to disown their sister had been a poor one. Without a mistress, the place was clearly going to the dogs.

He wanted water for washing, so he made his way to the back of the building to where the kitchen fire lay a pile of cold ash. With a scowl, Garman set about lighting it. Ten minutes later, he was outside fetching water from the well when he saw Berta stumping up the path from the barn toward him. Wordlessly, she followed him into the kitchen and took over the preparation of the water, setting a large pot in the hearth as he went back out to fetch more wood for the fire.

"Your mistress is in the room at the top of the stairs and needs water for washing when that is heated," he told her as he set down an armful of logs in one corner. She grunted and Garman went through to the hall where he set about clearing the table. He had just taken the last of the supper remains through to the kitchen when Berta finally addressed him.

"There's rats in this kitchen," she said, fixing her gaze on him challengingly.

"I don't doubt it," Garman responded. He had been about to take the cats down a plate of leftover mutton, but now he changed his mind. "Wait here." He made his way down to the barn where he found Lenora's cat Grizelda still curled in the hay, watching her offspring indulgently. He was somewhat alarmed to find one of the young males sat up on the stall partitions being nuzzled by Ivo Hainfroy's horse. The cat's eyes were shut as though he was savoring the sensation of the horse's velvety muzzle.

"When did you get a hankering for cats?" he asked Pollux, who tossed his head and struck his large hooves against the barn floor. Garman eyed him warily as he removed the foolhardy cat from his position of danger. Neither the cat nor the horse seemed impressed at his intervening in their budding friendship. The cat craned his head over his shoulder to glare at Garman as he went in search of his siblings.

The other two overgrown kittens were chasing one another through the barn, but their curiosity led them Garman's way and he scooped them up without too much bother and bore all three back to the house. Grizelda, he left to enjoy her leisure. Once relieved of her charges, she sprang up into the cart and made herself comfortable on the wooden seat, washing her white face.

Once set down on the flagstone floor of the kitchen, the young cats immediately set about darting and leaping under the benches and tables in pursuit of unseen quarry.

"I wasn't sure such pampered pets would take to ratting," Berta admitted with a short laugh.

"They haven't caught anything yet," Garman responded dryly.

"Cats is cats," Berta muttered, then shook her head as one of them skittered into the wall with a thud. "That water will be ready about now." She pointed to the top of a dresser at a large jug and basin. Catching her meaning, Garman wordlessly lifted them down for her and grimaced at the liberal coating of cobwebs and dust.

"I'll see to the water," he said. Feeling the old woman's eyes on him as he cleaned off the jug, he looked up. "What is it?"

"Handy, ain't you? For a knight, I mean."

Garman grunted. "My old master didn't hold with idleness."

Berta's eyebrows rose. Then one of the cats darted forward, laying a dead rat at Berta's feet. He meowed loudly. "That's a fine big one," she acknowledged. He meowed again.

"Give him some milk," Garman recommended.

"Milk?" Berta looked around.

"The pantry's through there," Garman said with a nod in the direction of a low doorway. Berta went in search of milk for the cats as he swung the pot from the fire and filled the jug with steaming warm water. A footfall in the doorway made him look up, and he found Lenora there, gazing about in astonishment as one of her cats jumped down off the bench, oversetting a basket of apples, and the other ran across the floor before diving behind the log pile.

"What on earth—?"

"We're overrun with rats," he told her shortly. "Here's water for washing. Shall I take it upstairs?"

Lenora shook her head and started rolling up her sleeves. "I'll wash here."

Which was eminently sensible as she had already dressed, but for some reason Garman found himself displeased. "Why did you not wait? I was fetching it up to you."

She looked up as he passed her a clean cloth and soap flakes. "You did not say," she pointed out mildly. "And I was not sure any would be forthcoming. It is of no matter."

Garman frowned, watching her covertly as she set about washing her face and neck. He would not be happy, he realized, if either Ivo or Huw were to show up right now and see her at her ablutions and this confused him, for she was decently arrayed in a modest gown of mauve wool and he was far from prudish.

Berta reappeared, sniffing doubtfully at the contents of a jug. "It's soured, I think," she grimaced.

"Good morning, Berta," Lenora greeted her. "Did you sleep well?"

"Aye, well enough," her servant admitted grudgingly. "Though this ginger one," she said, pointing to the largest of the three cats, "would not leave the horses be and insisted on cozying up to the fiercest one for the remainder of the night."

"Tybalt?" asked Lenora with surprise. "I do not think he has ever met a horse before."

Garman cleared his throat. "He was still at it this morn when I fetched him."

Berta gave a crack of laughter. "They always land on their feet, cats."

"He's a fancy to be a stable cat, has he?" asked Lenora, drying off her neck and lacing the ties at her throat. "Curious."

"I left the white one in the barn," Garman said, pretending he had not caught the feline's name.

"Quite right, Grizelda is no mouser," Lenora murmured, repinning a small square of muslin over the coiled golden braid which adorned her head like a coronet. She approached him with her hands outstretched and, realizing she meant for him to fasten the lacings at her wrists, he complied. "Thank you."

"Shall I toast some bread?" Berta asked. "There's a loaf in the pantry that only seems half stale."

Lenora started to say she was not hungry, but then caught Garman's eye and agreed to take a slice.

Garman pulled his tunic over his head and started his own wash. By the time he had finished, the pile of rats had reached three for one apiece. Lenora was now sat on the bench with the small gray cat lay across her lap. His black and ginger brothers were still prowling restlessly about the kitchen. Garman accepted some bread and butter to break his fast and sat beside her on the bench.

"Do you think your grandfather's kitchen will afford Purcel as much sport?" she asked, eyeing the black cat anxiously. "He seems to have found his calling." She lowered her voice. "He caught two of those rats and Fendrel none." Her gaze dropped to the smallest feline dozing on her lap.

"Certainly not," Garman responded. "My grandfather would never keep such a dirty kitchen."

Lenora sighed. "I do so want to be selfish and keep them all," she admitted. "But it does no good. They must follow their own destiny, like the rest of us. These are Grizelda's second litter, you know."

He stretched out his legs before him. "What became of the first?"

"Charmian was charmed away by the most fashionable tailor in all Aphrany. She took up residence in his shop and has her very own silken cushion to sit upon. Quite the fine lady. Dastian left me for the palace kitchens and a very bad-tempered cook who fed him tidbits and he alone. As for little Minnie, she took a shine to an old soldier my father employs on his estate who is something of a rogue and a swindler. Cats choose where they will, you know. And they won't be led where they bestow their affections."

Garman considered this, eyeing the lazy scrap on her lap. "That one won't leave you in haste," he predicted.

"Dear Fendrel, I hope not," she murmured, stroking him until he purred.

"Hold this," Berta said, thrusting a toasting fork into Lenora's hand. "I want to wash this table down before you eat off it."

Lenora inspected the hunk of bread speared on the sharp end with interest.

Garman reached out and lowered the implement toward the fire. "Hold it steady," he recommended. They both looked up when boots scuffled in the doorway. It was Huw Hainfroy, yawning and scratching his belly. He looked about with surprise at the crowded kitchen.

"You're all in here, I see," he said, blinking as the black cat reached up in a stretch and clawed enthusiastically at his chausses. Absently, he reached down and patted Purcel's head. "We—er—seem to be beset with cats this morning."

"Would you rather rats?" Lenora asked, pointing one slippered toe toward the pile of little limp rodent bodies.

Huw rubbed his eyes, then swiveled around as the maidservant, Martha, came up behind him. "Martha fetch a shovel and take these rats out," he ordered irritably. She pouted, glared at Berta, and then disappeared into the pantry.

Berta sniffed. "I doubt there's very much a shovel in there," she said loudly. Huw looked slightly embarrassed.

"We'll be on our way shortly," Garman interrupted, striving to keep the peace.

"So soon?" Huw's tone was disappointed as he collapsed onto the bench next to him. "My head," he groaned, clutching at it. "Someone had to celebrate your homecoming," he said resentfully. "Even though you would not."

Garman clutched Huw's shoulder. "I can ride over and see you often, once I'm at Matchings Farm," he pointed out.

"Aye, but will you?" Huw asked grumpily.

"Of course."

Martha emerged unhurriedly from the pantry, eating a piece of currant cake slathered in butter.

"Are you deaf as well as idle, girl?" Berta demanded. The maidservant tossed her black hair and turned her back rudely on the old woman, before realizing her mistake. Berta, showing a wiry strength belying her years, took a running leap and landed on the younger woman's back with a terrifying howl.

Lenora almost dropped her toasting fork as Berta set about raining blows on the unfortunate Martha's head, pulling her hair and boxing her ears for good measure. Martha hollered and squawked at last, falling to her knees and wrapping her arms about her in attempted defense. "Mercy!" she yelled. "She's twisted my ears clean off!"

Huw Hainfroy gave a short laugh. "I don't suppose you'd leave your servant with us?" he asked Garman wistfully.

"Certainly not!" Lenora retorted. "I couldn't do without Berta, although, I fear two of my cats do wish to remain with you." They both turned to look at Purcel, who was now hunched over Martha's dropped currant bread, licking all the butter off.

"They're welcome," said Huw dispassionately. "Our last cat died of old age." He turned to Garman. "You remember Winstanton?"

"Aye, he seemed ancient even then."

"Well, the ginger one is called Tybalt and apparently he likes it in the stables. But Purcel seems to hanker after being a kitchen cat," Lenora explained, cuddling Fendrel, her remaining baby close to her chest. Fendrel gave a feeble meow of protest but did not struggle to get away.

Huw grunted, then turned back to Garman. "You'll not leave before Ivo gets up?"

Garman shrugged. "I mean to leave in the next half hour."

Berta hopped off the sniveling Martha. "Now go and fetch that shovel and hop to it!" she said fiercely. Martha clambered to her feet and scurried off. This time likely in search of a shovel.

"I believe I shall go down to the barn and observe Tybalt with the horses," said Lenora.

"Eat first," Garman reminded her, plucking the bread off the end of the abandoned toasting fork and passing it to her.

The meal was a chaotic one. Berta sliced up a currant loaf and toasted that also. Ivo emerged midway through and vowed he, too, would have to see evidence of the budding friendship between his horse and the ginger cat. They all went down to the barn where Tybalt once more charmed the temperamental horse with his presence, scaling the walled partition, and when Pollux lowered his long nose, Tybalt rubbed his face enthusiastically against it.

"Well I never," Ivo spluttered. "What'll you take for him?"

"Nay, I'll take no payment," Lenora vowed solemnly. "Only the promise that if circumstances change and he is no longer welcome here, you will return him to me, and Purcel also," she said, turning to Huw.

Both brothers nodded affably enough, although the gravity of her manner seemed to surprise them. Garman found himself tensing in case either should say anything to offend her about the nature of cats and their importance in the world, but luckily it did not seem to occur to them.

Lenora bade a rather tearful farewell to both cats and climbed into the cart beside Berta.

"I know you've a wife." Ivo frowned. "But you've a home here if you want it."

"Maybe she could make herself useful about the place," Huw agreed.

Garman tried and failed to imagine Lenora in such a setting. "You're generous," he said. "But I've other plans."

"Oh aye?" Huw sounded skeptical as he and his brother exchanged glances.

"What?"

"Can't picture you and your grandfather seeing eye to eye for overlong," Ivo said grudgingly.

The Hainfroys had never really understood his relationship with his grandfather Sutton, he reflected. It was not that he and the old man would disagree, far from it. It was the fact his grandfather would yield to him in every respect that caused Garman such displeasure. If he allowed it, his grandfather would assume the role of deferential servant toward him and Garman found that intolerable.

"I don't mean to stay at the farm overlong," he said instead of attempting an explanation they would find unfathomable.

"Oh? So, this isn't a homecoming?" Huw asked with a heavy frown.

"I came across Sir Miles Danton a couple of months ago," Garman admitted grudgingly after a moment's heavy pause. He lowered his voice. "We spoke of Matchings Halt."

"Matchings Halt?" Ivo gave a short laugh. "You've still that ambition then!"

"What has Sir Miles to do with it?" asked Huw curiously. "The place is overrun with Skenfriths."

Garman glanced over at Lenora, who was deep in conversation with Berta. "The rumor is that old Sir Eliot is on his last legs. When he dies, then Miles will be the head of the family."

"And?" demanded Hugh.

Ivo pulled a face. "Sir Miles means to kick out the widowed lady and her in-laws and sell it to you?"

Garman nodded. "At least he indicated as much."

"You dog!" laughed Huw. "So, you'll get your heart's desire after all these years."

"Didn't I vow I would?" Garman swung up onto Bria'ag's saddle.

"Some would have gone a less devious route," Ivo commented, shaking his head.

"Such as?"

"Marrying the widow."

Garman grimaced. "No, I thank you."

"Yet…" Huw broke off, glancing curiously at Lenora. "You marry this one without a dowry."

Garman bit back his retort. "Her father will pay one. Eventually."

"And if not?"

"If not…" Garman shrugged. "I've money enough for the both of us."

Huw's jaw dropped.

Ivo gave a short laugh. "Careful," he said.

"Of what?"

Ivo pursed his lips. "Maybe your heart's desire has changed, and you just haven't realized it yet."

Garman snorted. "I'll watch out for that."

"It may be too late already," muttered Ivo.

Garman gave him a hard look, but his friend avoided his eye.

14

When Garman had said his grandfather's farm was an hour from the Hainfroys, Lenora had added on another half hour due to the cart slowing him down and she was not far out in her estimation. Trundling up the lane toward the neat-looking farmhouse, Lenora thought it could not offer a greater contrast to the dilapidated Cofton Grange they had left that morning.

Matchings Farm was a neat, well-ordered property, immaculately kept. Two workers were industriously employed in the grounds of the thatched building which was of decent proportion. One appeared to be mending a fence and the other tending to crops. Garman paid them no heed though they turned and stared as they passed. Lenora guessed neither were his relations or they would surely have hailed him.

On reaching the house, Garman swiftly dismounted and set about seeing to the horses. No grooms appeared to attend them, so she and Berta unloaded the cart and Lenora murmured soothing replies in answer to Fendrel's piteous mews. Once the cart was stowed away in one of the outhouses, Garman took their packs from her, and Berta picked up the cat basket. Wordlessly, he led them toward the brown and white timbered house. The women exchanged glances. It did not seem to Lenora that her new husband was exactly filled with joy at his homecoming and she wondered at it.

As they approached the doorway, a man came through it with a look of polite enquiry on his face. He was of middling height, with a short gray beard and very tidy appearance. He checked at the sight of Garman and his face flushed. "Garman!" he exclaimed, came forward a few steps, and then seemed to collect himself, pulling up short. "Is all well, my boy?" he asked, a look of pained enquiry on his face.

Lenora heard her husband answer shortly. "Why would it not be? Are we welcome within?"

Again, the older man's color rose. "Of course, this is your home!" he stammered, moving aside with a polite gesture to allow access to the doorway.

Garman paused, as though for a moment unsure of his own cue. Then he turned back to Lenora and gestured for her to enter before him. Lenora hurried to do so, but when she drew even with them, Garman's hand flew out to stop her.

"Grandfather," he said, "this is my wife, Lenora. Lenora, this is my grandfather, Gerard Sutton."

Seeing the expression of mingled confusion and dismay on the older man's face, Lenora dropped into a curtsey to allow him time to recover. "I am pleased to meet you, Mr. Sutton. I hope you will give me leave to call you Grandfather also."

To her surprise, this request seemed to reduce Garman's grandfather to a state of even more abject confusion. He bowed very low and then shot a look of agonized appeal to her husband.

"Of course you will call him Grandfather," Garman said tensely. "What else would you call him?" He shot a look of challenge at his kinsman, and the older man's gaze dropped before it.

"If that is your wish," Gerard Sutton muttered, but his cheeks were slashed with red and he was clearly uncomfortable at the notion.

"Is my wife to stand on the doorstep all morning?" Garman barked.

The older man sprang forward. "Please enter, my lady," he urged politely. "You must be sadly weary and travel-worn."

"Please call me Lenora," she said as the older man escorted her into the house. "But indeed, I am not overtired for we broke our journey and have only traveled an hour or so this morn."

She had been starting to think Garman's grandfather was displeased at their marriage, but he could not have been more solicitous as he led her into a sitting room and saw her settled in a large chair next to fire.

"If you will excuse me," he said, straightening up from setting a cushion at her back. "I will go and tell Hawise to bring us some refreshment."

"You are very kind."

Garman, who had paused in the hallway to set down their bags and have some words with Berta, now entered carrying the cat basket. "Berta will go with you to the kitchen," he told his grandfather, who nodded and swiftly left the room.

Garman untied the basket lid and set it down in front of the fire before retreating to a seat on the opposite side of the room. Lenora watched Fendrel immediately hop out of the basket and stretch as Grizelda, more cautious, peered over the edge. She felt a pang at the thought of Purcel and Tybalt. What would they be doing now? Would Tybalt have retreated to the stable again, or would he be exploring the fields behind the barn? She hoped he would not venture too far and get lost. As for Purcel, she hoped he would have the sense to get on the right side of that sulky maidservant or he would feel the edge of her broom, she was sure. Almost, she wished she had left Berta there to keep the girl in check.

"He does not mean to be unwelcoming." Garman's heavily spoken words drew her out of her reverie.

Quickly, she surmised he was speaking of his grandfather. "No indeed, he has been very thoughtful," she said, not liking to admit she had been thinking of her pets.

"You're frowning," he said abruptly. "So, something ails you."

"I only wondered that you did not exchange more words by way of greeting," she admitted slowly. "'Twas plain he was pleased to see you."

"Was it?" asked Garman harshly.

"Oh yes," Lenora answered, ignoring his dark glower. "His first impulse was to embrace you, but he held back from it at the last. Perhaps he did not think you would like it." Garman seemed taken aback by her words but made no reply. "Mayhap he should have punched you in the ribs as the Hainfroys did," she suggested wryly. "I think you are more comfortable with that manner of greeting." The ghost of a smile touched his lips, but he held his silence.

At this point, Fendrel made a quick dart toward Garman, sprang up on his knee, and sat there regarding him steadily.

"Well!" said Lenora. "Would you look at that?"

Garman eyed the cat. "What do you want?" he asked. Fendrel opened his mouth on a silent meow.

A step in the doorway heralded Gerard Sutton's return. "Here we are," he said, ushering in a homely looking woman bearing a tray. Catching sight of the cat perched on his grandson's knee, he did a double take and seemed to lose all power of speech.

129

"I'm afraid my third and final kitten has chosen its new master," Lenora said with a sigh. "Still, at least this way, I shall not have to part with him."

"Shall I set it down here, sir?" Hawise prompted when her master stood gaping.

"Er—yes, do," Garman's grandfather answered, clearly flustered.

Hawise set the tray of cheese, crackers, and fruit down on a low table, curtseyed, and then withdrew.

"Thank you," said Lenora, and though she wasn't really hungry yet, she helped herself to a few grapes as Garman's grandfather poured out some foaming ale into cups.

Lenora watched with interest as Garman finally plucked the cat from his knee and set him down on the arm of his chair. Fendrel immediately turned about and started prowling up and down the chair in a purposeful fashion, whisking his tail so that it caressed Garman's shoulder. Lenora smiled to herself. The little cat did not like being ignored. After a few moments he sprang up onto the chair back and settled there in an awkward hunch, rather like a gargoyle, staring down at his master.

Grizelda, meanwhile, joined her mistress, leaning against her skirts and purring. Lenora reached down to absently stroke her milk-white fur as she accepted the cup of ale from Garman's grandfather. "Thank you," she murmured. "Do you have dogs here at Matchings Farm?" In her father's house dogs and cats were raised together and perfectly harmonious. She knew that was not always the case, however.

"Only one dog who lives in the house," replied Gerard Sutton with a smile. "Old Kolby." His glance flickered to Garman before it returned to Lenora. "But you need not worry, my lady, he spends most of his time dozing in the kitchen these days."

"Lenora," Garman corrected him tonelessly.

His grandfather flushed. "Your pardon, Lenora," he corrected himself.

"Indeed, he sounds a most well-mannered dog." Lenora smiled, hoping to put the old gentleman at his ease. It didn't work though, as he was still plainly ill on edge.

"You—er—have you—er…" He cleared his throat. "Been married long?" he managed to finish, fidgeting in his chair.

"But two days only," Lenora answered when Garman was not forthcoming.

"Two days?" he echoed, sounding dazed. "Two days," he repeated almost to himself. "You were married from your father's house, Lenora?" he pursued, sounding faintly anxious. Lenora paused. She had no words of comfort here to allay whatever unspoken fears crowded the old man's brow.

"We wed on the road," Garman preempted her. "Without her family's consent."

Lenora winced at his blunt words. The flush faded from his grandfather's face as he turned very pale. The hand that held his cup of ale trembled slightly.

"Are you well, sir?" Lenora asked him in alarm. She could not bring herself to call him Grandfather when 'twas plain how very unwelcome such a form of address would be.

"Y-yes," he hastened to assure her. "Yes, yes. Just a little— uh—"

"Overcome?" suggested Garman when the old man groped in vain for the right word.

Reaching into his tunic, Gerard withdrew a square of cloth and mopped his brow with it. He stared at his grandson distractedly a moment. "I hope you know what you are about, my boy," he muttered, shaking his head. "Such an inauspicious beginning to wedded life—"

"I am not my father," Garman interrupted him abruptly. His light blue eyes were very cold, like ice. His words arrested the older man, who swallowed convulsively before climbing unsteadily to his feet.

"I'm afraid, my dear, you must excuse me," Gerard Sutton said with quiet dignity to Lenora, though he could not meet her surprised gaze. "I have some urgent business which I must attend to." With a polite bow, he turned and almost hurried from the room.

Lenora turned to her new husband. "Now, just what was that all about?" she demanded. When Garman shrugged, she felt a flash of annoyance. "First Isabeau Hainfroy, and now this!" she exclaimed. "Whoever would have thought you'd have so many skeletons in your cupboard!"

He shot her an irritated look. "I haven't been wed before, if that's what you're thinking!"

Lenora's eyes widened. "That was *not* what I was thinking," she replied in a choked voice, setting her ale down. If anything, his words made her feel worse. My gods, she barely knew anything about him, she thought with some dismay. She had been so focused previously on her escape from court that she had not really given any thought to what she would be running *to*.

He plunked his own cup down with a smothered oath. "Come, I'll give you a tour of the place."

Lenora came to her feet. "We shall have to shut the door on the cats for now," she said. "Until they are familiar with the place." He murmured some agreement. "Have your family been here long?"

He shook his head and held out a hand to her. "No. My father had this place built not long after his marriage."

Lenora looked up with surprise. "So, this is your farm?"

"In name only. My grandfather runs the place." He led her from the room out to the passageway, pulling the door shut behind them.

"It's nicely proportioned," Lenora said, looking around. "The ceilings seem somehow higher than I would expect in a farmhouse."

Garman shot her an ironic look. "You consider yourself an expert on the subject?"

Lenora flushed. This was probably the first farmhouse she had ever set foot in, and clearly he suspected as much. "You're right, of course, I spoke without thinking."

He was silent as he led her from the sitting room into a much larger room with a big arched window, a central fireplace, and a large dining table set about with many books and papers. "In truth," he said. "You probably know as much about farmhouses as my father when he had this place built."

It was a surprising admission and immediately Lenora wanted to ask what kind of people his father came from. If his son was sent to train as squire to a neighboring nobleman, then it could not be from farming stock. She seemed to remember he had described his grandfather previously as a steward, however, Garman's reticence on the subject held her tongue. Clearly, he was not one for sharing confidences. They had to be dragged from him, grudgingly, one by one.

"This seems very like a great hall," she commented. "Only on a smaller scale."

He smiled grimly. "There's a reason for that," he answered, and Lenora waited in vain for him to supply it. When he did not, she sighed and turned her attention instead to the neat piles of books and ledgers scattered about, the clean rushes on the floor and the smell of wax on the wooden furniture. The room was lived in, tidy and comfortable, but she could see no sign of any female presence. There were no looms, or spinning wheels, needlework cushions, or tapestries on the walls.

"How old were you when your mother died?" she asked, unable to stop the questions that sprang to her lips.

"Some two years in age."

"So young? Did you never know your grandmother?"

He shook his head. "She died when my mother was born." Already, he was leading her out of the main hall and into another passageway. Lenora peered into the rooms leading off it. She recognized a pantry and a buttery when she saw them, though she had spent precious little time in either. The buttery was well stocked with casks and barrels and the pantry smelt of fresh bread and cured meats. They carried on to a large kitchen where Hawise and Berta were sat at a table shelling peas. They broke off their conversation when she and Garman entered and looked rather furtive. Hawise started up from her seat.

"Is there something I can fetch for you, good sir? My lady?" she asked eagerly.

"No, nothing, I thank you," Lenora assured her. "My husband is merely showing me the lay of the land."

Hawise smiled and sat back down to resume her task. She was a plump, agreeable-looking woman of some sixty years or so in age with a neat headscarf that completely concealed her probably graying hair.

"You are the only staff here at present?" Garman asked, looking about in some surprise.

"Oh no, sir," Hawise replied. "There's Ada and Margary too, but they're out in the fields today."

"I see."

Lenora crossed the room to where pans were laid out with dressed, prepared meats for the evening meal. 'Twas plain that the staff at Matchings Farm were an industrious lot and could not be a greater contrast to the ramshackle household at Cofton Grange.

"You are content to remain here, Berta?" Lenora asked.

"Oh aye," her servant replied. "Hawise assures me there is plenty for me to be going on with."

"We've always work for another pair of hands," Hawise said with a chuckle. "There's enough clothes for washing and mending to last a sennight!"

Garman had crossed the room and opened another door, so Lenora made haste to follow him. Outside, she found him with his arms crossed, staring out past the neat kitchen garden to the neat fields beyond. She came to stand silently next to him, strangely wary of the stormy expression on his face.

"My parents eloped," he said gruffly.

"Oh!" His words took her aback, and for a moment she was silent. "So that's why your grandfather is so upset," she said slowly. He gave a brisk nod. "But that's my fault! I'm the one who persuaded you to elope."

"It's of no matter."

"But if your grandfather…"

"He'll weather the storm," he said dismissively.

Lenora bit the side of her mouth. She wasn't so sure. "This is not the homecoming you probably envisaged—" she started, but he cut her off with a short mirthless laugh.

"It's not far off," he said. "Don't trouble yourself." She turned to look at his stony profile, unsure what to say that wouldn't make things worse. She had never been the most tactful person. "There's a tournament the day after tomorrow," he said abruptly, scattering her wits even further.

Lenora felt a lurch of alarm. "You're not competing?" she asked in some dismay.

"It's only a half-day ride from here. At Kellingford."

She turned to look at him squarely. "You mean to abandon me here, then?" For some reason, she felt hard used, though in truth, a mere three days ago the plan would have sounded fine to her. "Even though your grandfather cannot even look me in the eye!"

"He's never been able to look me in the eye," she thought he muttered under his breath, but she must have misheard him.

"Well, I mean to come too!" she said with determination.

At this, he turned to face her. "Oh, do you?" he said, his look sweeping her up and down. He uttered a short laugh.

"Something amuses you?"

"You've never been to a rural tournament in your life before, have you?"

"I have not," she agreed affably. "But I enjoy the royal ones very much and I am convinced 'twill be a most interesting experience." He snorted. "You'll take me though?" she asked with more confidence than she felt, her hand stealing into the crook of his arm. For some reason it was imperative that she did not part with him yet. She didn't really want to consider why she felt that way. Maybe, she thought suddenly, they should have left the green string binding them at their handfasting for longer. He might have had a point about that. After all, despite his words, he had not bedded her yet. That meant their union was not consummated if anyone should challenge it. "Garman?"

He gave a start when she said his name, as though he'd been absorbed in thought, and looked down at her hand on his arm for a moment before he spoke.

"Aye," he rumbled. "I'll take you." Then after the faintest hesitation, he added, "Wife."

Lenora beamed at him. Really, it was almost as if he had heard her thoughts!

15

They started out early the next morning at daybreak. Berta wrapped them up some bread and cheese and promised faithfully to keep a watch on Fendrel in their absence. As for Garman's grandfather, he did not make an appearance. Garman's expression was rather grim as they set out, but the more distance they put between themselves and the farm, the lighter his mood seemed to grow. He was practically affable by the time they drew near to the village of Kellingford. At least, Lenora thought, as close to affable as he ever approached. His good mood seemed to take a downturn, however, when Lenora, catching sight of the standards and flags, decided it was time to draw her veils down over her face.

He rolled his eyes. "Is that really necessary? I thought you said it was only courtiers you feared."

"But surely there may be some here competing this day?"

"Maybe one or two," he said after a moment's reflection. "But this is a small affair, and you won't find it frequented like the royal tourneys."

"Well," Lenora said cautiously, "if there aren't too many famous names, maybe I'll reconsider."

"I can't hear you behind that curtain," Garman replied coldly. She didn't quite believe him, but even so, she lifted up her veils and repeated it.

"It's nothing like the royal tournaments," he said, sounding rather bored.

"Are they so different, then?"

"Yes." It was all he gave her, just one word. She waited a moment or two for him to elaborate, then realized he wasn't going to bother. *Oh.* She supposed she would have to find out for herself. Holding her veils to one side, she looked around with interest as they approached the main field where the majority of the tents were set up. To her surprise, she found herself recognizing quite a few of the devices. Certainly more than she'd expected to. There was de Crecy's black tree on a white field, and Kentigern's portcullis on a banner of blue. In fact, all the major players seemed to be here, she noticed with sudden misgiving.

"I thought you said these provincial tournaments were not such glittering affairs!" she said accusingly. "Yet I can see all the usual crowd. Look—Lord Kentigern is here," she said, pointing toward his banner. "And de Bussell too, and de Crecy!" He turned in his saddle to look at her, his expression startled. "I recognize their crests," she said by way of explanation. He did not look pleased by her knowledge. "I told you I like to watch the tournaments," she finished lamely.

"Aye, but not to that extent!"

Why did he look so put out that she knew all his competition's shields? "I know what your device is too, if that's any consolation."

He snorted. "It's yours now too," he pointed out.

"I hadn't actually thought of that," she admitted. What a shame it was so plain and unromantic. She would have much preferred to have had a heraldic beast as their crest. "What does the gate signify?" she asked, thinking of the black field with a white gate on it.

"I couldn't tell you. My father chose it," he replied shortly and turned his attention away from her toward the distance.

Lenora's eyes widened when she heard his coat of arms was that recent. She was just pondering to herself that if so, surely, he should know the blazon and reasoning behind it, when out of the corner of her eye, she spotted it. A red fluttering banner with a black panther.

"Oh no!"

He turned back to her with some exasperation. "What now?"

She pointed to the banner. "Vawdreys," she said hollowly and let her veils fall back over her face.

Garman scanned the field with narrowed eyes. "What of it?"

"You may remember I said I was not overly keen to run into my family," she replied testily. "Sir Roland Vawdrey being an extended member of said family."

He brooded on this a moment. "It does look," he conceded grudgingly, "like most of the crowd from the Autumn Royal Tournament came on here. A lot more than usually turn up."

She supposed that was as close to admitting he'd made a miscalculation that Garman would come. "You'll understand, then, why I choose to wear my veils here?" she said in a muffled voice.

He grunted. "If you must."

"Will there be many ladies in attendance?" she persisted.

"There isn't usually. Sometimes the host may have some womenfolk." He shrugged.

"Who are the hosts here at Kellingford?"

He shot an irritated look her way. "The Kellingfords," he said in the manner of one speaking to an idiot.

Lenora had never heard of anyone by that name and had just opened her mouth to say as much when an eager official bounded in their direction.

"Welcome, welcome gentle sir and your lady fair," he bade them, though the last words were spoken a little uncertainly as he caught sight of Lenora's heavy veiling. "May I take your name, sir knight?"

"Sir Garman Orde and his wife," he answered brusquely.

Lenora lifted her head sharply at his words. He had not given her name. Did he mean for her to remain incognito? Her veiling would enable such a stratagem after all.

The official beamed at them as he flourished his quill and scratched their entry across his scroll. "And your shield?"

"Black field, white gate."

"There are several pavilions set up in the south meadow that are not yet taken," he told them.

Lenora followed the direction of his waved hand to see a field set out with several tents. She assumed the ones that weren't draped in colored flags and banners were the unoccupied ones.

"I require the use of a squire when competing," Garman said after glancing in that direction.

"And to set up camp?" the official asked, peering behind them and seeing no attendant retinue of servants.

"We will need water for washing," he replied shortly. "I can see to the rest of it."

The scribe glanced up in surprise, but something about Garman's expression set him hastily scribbling again. "Very good, sir."

141

Lenora wondered about the provision of meals, and somehow, she had not realized she would be expected to sleep under one of the strange linen constructions. When Garman drew rein and set off in the direction of the tents, Lenora smiled at the official, then remembered she was swathed in veils and nodded her head instead. He sketched a bow, and she set off after her husband. He seemed to be heading for the pavilion set furthest back from the others. Somehow, it seemed rather typical of him that he would shun the company at large. By the time she had caught up with him, he had already dismounted, tied his banner to a pole outside, and disappeared under a hessian flap. Lenora made haste to follow.

Inside, she found him stowing his armor into one corner of the shelter. Lenora swept her veils back and peered around the tent with interest. Three low cots were positioned in the center, a small rather rickety-looking table, and one empty trunk. Lifting the lid to peer inside she found this empty, presumably for their use.

"It's a bit bare," she said critically. "Did we bring our own bedding?"

"Aye," he said, tossing a bundled pack onto one of the beds. "You can make them up, if you're in need of a rest."

Lenora eyed the bundle with interest. "Very well," she said gamely. She was still struggling to unravel the knots when he reentered with a second lot of baggage which he flung down on one of the narrow bunks.

"We'll push these two together," he said, pointing at the two bunks he had not strewn with his armor. They were rather small, Lenora reflected, gazing from the woven mattresses to the bulk of her husband. She would easily fit into one though. She unraveled the blankets and separated them into two piles.

Then it occurred to her that it would likely grow rather cold at night, sleeping out of doors under such flimsy shelter.

"Perhaps we should sleep in the same cot," she said, tapping her finger against her chin.

He gave her an odd look. "We won't fit on one," he said shortly. "Unless you mean to sleep atop me."

"I just mean, I'm just not sure there's enough blankets for me to sleep in the third cot," she explained.

He looked at her, frowning. "Who said you were sleeping in the third cot?" he asked, pushing the two together.

"Oh." Lenora gazed back at him blankly. "I just assumed," she said lamely. "I mean, I've never slept outdoors before, so I didn't know the etiquette."

"It's the same as anywhere else," he said. "A man sleeps with his wife."

Lenora found her face growing rather red. "But you said not many knights brought their ladies with them."

He straightened up. "What difference does that make?"

Lenora bit her lip. She was floundering here. "No matter," she said and shook out the first blanket to lay it over the woven mattress. To her surprise, Garman caught up the other end and started wordlessly to make up the bed with her. She was glad he did, for in truth, she had never made a bed before, and though she had a vague idea, she had to watch him carefully to discover how the corners were tucked. "This is a strange mattress," she commented. "It's not stuffed at all. Just woven materials slung between the outer frame."

"You'll grow used to them."

From this, Lenora deduced he expected her to accompany him to further tournaments in the future. She felt a surprising lurch of pleasure at the notion, and had to bite her lip to keep from smiling as they piled five more blankets on top. "Will we be warm enough?" she asked, surveying the result doubtfully.

"You've got me as well," he answered. "I'm as good as another five blankets."

Before she could respond to this boast, he turned toward the opening where a discreet cough heralded the arrival of servants.

Lenora hastily scrabbled for her veils as they entered carrying two bowls of hot water which they set down on the small table.

"Your host, Sir Roger Kellingford, wishes it known that supper will be served in the Great Hall," one of them announced. "At seven."

Lenora widened her eyes at Garman, but not surprisingly, considering her coverings, he did not react.

"Excuse me, husband," she was forced to pipe up. "But I would rather take some repast here. Alone."

Garman frowned at her. "Why?" he asked pointedly.

Lenora clenched her hands. "I find myself much fatigued from our journey."

He gave her a searching look. "You should have told me," he said gruffly and to her surprise added, "We'll take our supper here."

"I did not mean that you should take your meal here," she protested as the servants piled back out, but he just shrugged.

"I'm not overly fond of the social aspect in any case."

Was her husband a misanthropist? Lenora found herself debating as she hitched her veils aside once more to wash her hands and face in the tepid water. Doubtless the water had been hot when it had left the kitchens, but the house would be some distance away. Drying her face off, she turned back to watch Garman unbuckle another pack. Every move was swift and sure, as though he had done this dozens of times. Perhaps he had. She wondered at his disinterest in the other knights. Her cousin had always taken her to task for not being invested in her fellow mankind, but Garman seemed to take it further than she ever had!

"Do you not have any particular acquaintance among the other knights whose society you seek out?" she asked impulsively.

"Gods no!" He sounded horrified at the notion.

"Is that not unusual?" she asked slowly. "I mean, surely there is some kind of comradeship among the knights."

He snorted. "Is that how it appears from the spectators' box?" he mocked. "That we all get along?" He lifted out the contents of the pack and began sorting it into neat piles. "Get on the bed," he said, nodding toward it. "Take your ease."

Lenora opened her mouth to point out she wasn't tired when she remembered her excuse for not eating with the others. Instead, she slipped out of her ankle boots and climbed onto the bed. Lying on her back, she folded her hands across her stomach. "I would not say that precisely," she said guardedly. "But I suppose I did imagine that there would be a good deal of common ground among your number."

He carried some clothes over to the trunk and deposited them therein. Apparently, her surmises did not warrant a response. She lifted her head off a cushion to watch him. Probably she should take the hint and let the subject drop. "So, you don't like

145

anyone?" she found herself persisting instead. He lifted a broad shoulder and let it fall. "What if I were to ask who has earned your respect as a fellow knight?"

He exhaled noisily. "Are you asking me who is the strongest competition?"

"No," Lenora answered tartly. "For I already know that. I watch the jousts, remember?"

He cast a skeptical glance her way. "Oh really," he muttered.

Lenora raised a finger. "Lord Kentigern," she said distinctly, then added a second finger. "Sir Roland Vawdrey." She passed over that one hurriedly and lifted a third finger. "Sir Jeffrey de Crecy." He made no comment. "On a good day Armand de Bussell can put in a good performance, but he is somewhat inconsistent." Garman's eyes had narrowed. He opened his mouth, then shut it again. "What?" asked Lenora hopefully. "Do you disagree?"

He held his silence a moment, then said raspily: "Vawdrey, Kentigern, and myself are generally considered the best."

"Is that not what I just said?"

"You made no mention of me," he flung at her.

"I was listing your strongest competition," she pointed out with dignity.

He snorted. "I haven't lost to de Crecy in a twelvemonth! As for de Bussell…" The contemptuous curl of his lip spoke volumes.

"I meant no insult," Lenora said, lowering her head back onto the pillow.

"Doubtless you admire the figure they cut sat on a horse, more than their prowess in the field," he said scornfully.

146

Lenora considered this. "De Crecy is handsome to be sure," she said thoughtfully, thinking of his short golden beard and his piercing blue eyes. "But to my mind, his looks are somewhat marred by his manner."

Garman stalked over to the chest and started stripping to the waist for his wash. As though the words were dragged from him, he turned and looked back at her over his shoulder. "What of his manner?" he growled.

"He always looks like his own moustache stinks," she said without thinking. When Garman burst out spluttering and coughing, she added quickly, "I only meant that he looks permanently disgusted by everything and everyone."

Garman gave a grudging smile. "He does," he agreed.

Lenora stared and he turned back to the washing bowl. Had that choking sound been Garman smothering laughter? She propped herself up on one elbow. "As for de Bussell, his looks are not the type that I particularly admire," she persisted, more because she wanted to keep the conversation flowing than that she had any strong opinion of Armand de Bussell's appearance.

Garman grunted, having turned uncommunicative once more. Lenora sighed. Sir Roland Vawdrey was extremely good-looking, so she couldn't in all conscience disparage his looks.

"Of course," she said sadly. "I feel a good deal of fellow-feeling for poor Lord Kentigern these days." She reached up and touched the side of her face, thinking of Kentigern's heavy scarring and his one white eye that was quite blind.

"What do you mean?" Garman asked sharply. He lowered his drying cloth. "You surely do not compare yourself to him?"

"I only meant—"

"That's bloody ridiculous, Lenora!" he thundered at her, flinging down his cloth. "Kentigern has grievous battle wounds! You can scarcely compare them to a mere scattering of pockmarks!"

"Well, I—"

"Do I take it you mean to walk about like a shrouded ghoul for the duration of this tournament?" he asked, his tone biting.

"I must say, I actually think that was a very good notion of yours," she said, lifting her chin.

"Notion of mine?" he asked angrily. "What do you mean by that?"

"Well," she answered a trace of uncertainty entering her voice. "Just that when you supplied your name for the herald, you did not give mine and I assumed it was a deliberate omission. "

"You assumed wrongly!" he cut across her words. He narrowed his eyes as if trying to recall his exact words. "I told him you were my wife."

"Yes," she agreed. "And you left it at that, I thought intentionally."

"Well, you thought wrong," he snapped back.

Lenora slumped back against the pillows. "Oh."

Garman did not speak again until servants arrived with covered dishes for them, and then only to request two chairs were brought for their use. Once these were set down next to the table and the washing water taken away, Lenora joined him to eat their meal of roasted venison, cabbage, and a game pie in a rich egg pastry. Napkins were supplied and another small bowl for washing their hands, but looking around, Lenora could find no cutlery, other than a spoon. She was just about to mention this when Garman passed her his own personal eating knife. He did not speak, or even look at her, just held it out to her handle first. Taking it with a murmur of thanks, she cut up her food into bite-sized pieces and then held it back out to him. He took it back in the same wordless fashion.

Clearly, she was in disgrace. To her surprise, this bothered her more than she would have imagined a mere week ago. A flask of wine had been left for them, but only one cup. Lenora frowned over this a moment, then poured it out and slid the cup across to Garman. He took a deep draught and then handed the cup back to her. Peering in, Lenora could see he had only drained half of it. She drank the other and then refilled the cup. They repeated the process. By then, he had emptied his plate and Lenora had tired of hers. The food was rich, and she was sure they had piled the plates equally. She had eaten at least half of her pie and most of her vegetables. After one more mouthful, she slid the plate across to Garman. He frowned at her.

"I ate more than I usually would, I assure you," she said. His eyebrows rose at this, but he shrugged and finished off her roasted meat.

A bowl of figs and almonds had been left also, and though she was not hungry, Lenora helped herself to a fig and leaned back in her chair. The motion made her chair tilt alarmingly, for the floor was not altogether flat. She shot her hand out to seize the table edge until she had righted herself. "I almost forgot our floor is a meadow," she remarked. "Shall I pour you more wine?"

He dragged his chair back, standing up. "Aye, bring it to the bed." He blew out one of the candles and carried the other over to the cots.

Lenora glanced at the tent flap, but it was down so she could not see the hour by the sky. It seemed early to retire though.

"What about the horses?" she asked. "Are they to remain tethered outside?"

"Certainly not," he retorted, dragging his tunic over his head. "They were taken to the stables already."

"Oh, I did not realize." The servants must have taken them, she thought, asking, "How is it that you do not have your own squire?"

He did not reply, simply continued to strip and climb into the bed. After a moment, Lenora poured his wine and carried it over to him. He took it from her and this time looked her full in the face. "I don't care for the company," he said, startling her.

Lenora gazed at him blankly. "Oh! Did you want me to make up the third cot after all?" she asked, glancing round at the vacant cot which was now piled high with all manner of plate armor.

He twitched back the blanket for her. "I was answering your question about my lack of attendant," he said testily. "I may find your chatter irritating, but I'm hardly likely to banish you from my bed because of it."

Lenora flushed. Her chatter? "No one has ever accused me of chattering before!" she retorted as she started undoing her side lacings. Far from it. "If anything," she added painstakingly, "people complain I am sadly standoffish!" She glared at Garman before wriggling out of her outer gown and draping it over a chair back. "Maybe 'tis because *you* are so unduly taciturn," she added when he said nothing at all, "it prompts me to overcompensate."

"Get in the bed, Lenora."

She sat on the edge of the cot, unpinned her headdress, set it aside, and then removed her stockings and garters. "I need to unpack my things," she said obstinately. "I did not do so earlier."

"Do it on the morn."

"I'd rather do it now," she replied. "I need my comb to braid my hair and—"

"In. The. Bed," he intoned direly.

She turned around, took one look at his face, and decided discretion was the better part of valor. Setting her veils and stockings down on the chair, Lenora moved around to climb in beside him. She did so with exaggerated dignity, her nose pointed skyward. He was infuriatingly rude! The last thing she wanted to do right now was cozy up to him under the sheets. Instead she held her body stiffly away from his as she tucked the blankets around her, scrupulously avoiding any points of contact. He made no comment, but when she finally lay back, he swiftly rolled toward her and yanked the blankets up until their bodies were flush against one another. Lenora regarded him with speechless indignation.

"You'll thank me shortly," he said, "when you feel the cold begin to bite."

Lenora pressed her lips together, feeling thwarted. "I beg you will save your combative nature for the morrow when you have more worthy opponents," she said haughtily. To her surprise, she heard him laugh and turned her head sharply to look at him.

"You don't need to worry your head about that," he murmured, tucking a hand behind his pillow.

"No." She curled her lip. "I expect you're always spoiling for a fight."

"Aye," he agreed readily enough. His eyes flickered over her head and shoulders. Not much else was on display. "That or something else."

Lenora's gaze narrowed as her breath quickened. Surely, he could not mean *that*? Not here? With some alarm, she turned back to contemplating the ceiling. Very likely she was imagining things, but she remembered at the inn how he had compared the act with combat. An act he had since shown no real inclination to perform with her. Perhaps he had lied when he had claimed not to find her repulsive?

Suddenly, he spoke. "This business of obsessively covering your face…" She could hear the scowl in his voice. "It irritates me."

Lenora turned angrily onto her side to face him. Very well, if he wanted an argument, she would *give* him an argument! "Well, I should probably tell you now that under certain circumstances," she vowed with brittle resolve, "I will always wear a veil."

"That seems ridiculous," he said scornfully. When she made no reply, he added testily, "I can see no justification for it." She kept her eyes trained on him, but said nothing. "What possible reason could you have for such exaggerated pageantry?" His tone was cutting. "And what circumstances could prompt such a decision? I can think of none."

"I was thinking, for instance, in my parents' presence," she said with sudden frankness.

He was visibly surprised by her reply, and regretting her outburst, she rolled once more onto her back, staring up at the strangely bunched and draped ceiling. *Say nothing*, she warned herself. *Not one more word.* "Probably," she heard herself say flatly, "because they said my face was a mockery of its former self and it would be better if I had just died."

152

This was met with total silence, and Lenora had just convinced herself that she had only thought the words in her head, when her upper arms were seized in a fierce grip and she was hauled off the mattress and found herself sprawled across Garman Orde's body. She blinked down at him in astonishment. His eyes bored into hers, but when he spoke, his words were quiet. "What did you just say?" So softly did he speak the words that Lenora felt alarmed.

"Well—it doesn't bear dwelling on," she answered breathlessly. "But I must admit, occasionally, when I'm at a low ebb, it just drifts into my mind and—"

His eyes were hard as flint. "They said that to you? Your parents?"

"No! I mean, they didn't intend for me to hear it," she babbled. "They thought I was asleep." He held very still, then suddenly thrust her from him and sat up on the edge of the bed, facing away from her. Lenora stared at his back. "Garman?" When he continued silent, she felt rather alarmed. "I shouldn't have told you, but I think it was festering away in me deep inside." He turned his head slightly at that, but still she could not see his face except in profile. His expression looked carved in stone. Lenora took a shaky breath. "Actually, I think I do feel a little better for having told someone, if that makes sense." She plucked at the blankets. Those words had weighed heavy with her since she had heard them. As if they had been etched on her brain. Speaking them aloud almost felt like an exorcism. She stared at Garman Orde's broad muscular back and wondered why that should be so.

After a moment, he swung his legs back into the bed and slowly eased himself back down on the mattress. "Tell me about them," he said on an outward breath.

"My parents?" asked Lenora in startled tones. He gave a short nod. *What an odd request.* She looked at him sidelong before beginning. "Well…apparently I take after my mother in looks, but she grew rather stout in later life. Perhaps I will too. You might like that, if I grow fat, I mean," she added, but he didn't even give a glimmer of a smile, so she continued. "Apparently she was exceedingly beautiful in her youth. My father was simply wild to marry her from their first meeting. It's funny really as they don't seem to relish each other's company now overmuch." She pondered this a moment. "My mother is rather dissatisfied with her lot in life. She says she should have held out for a duke, but she didn't know her own worth at seventeen. She does not come to court much and spends all her time lying abed and being read to. It's my grandmother who runs the household. She's a very determined woman and never relinquished her grip as chatelaine. Maybe that's partly why my mother is the way she is," Lenora pondered. Then shook her head. "But I don't really think so. My mother has never shown any interest in picking up the reins of responsibility. In truth, neither did I. I always knew I would move away from Hallam Hall once I married." She paused at this point, to wait for any comment, but he gave none. "I was always closer to my father," Lenora admitted cautiously. "He is a prominent courtier and divides his time between our estates and the King's court. I suppose he was disappointed not to have a son to succeed him, but I am their only child. My cousin Kit will inherit the house and lands eventually…" Lenora trailed off, not sure how to continue.

Garman turned his head toward her. "Go on," he said.

"There's not much else to tell. I suppose, like everyone else, they thought I had nothing more to offer the world than my face. I daresay if things had continued and I had not caught the pox, I would have ended up very like my mother. She's rather

154

self-absorbed, you know. Now…I hardly know what will become of me. None of the many fortunes I have had told to me over the years have ever predicted this particular turn of fate's wheel."

He was silent and so very still that for a moment Lenora wondered if he had dropped off to sleep. When he finally spoke, she was almost startled.

"Shall I tell you what will become of you?" he asked suddenly.

Lenora turned her head to look at him. "Please do."

"Whatever you will."

She stared at him, then gave a short laugh. "Well, I suppose my will has carried me this far. Funny, until recently I never realized just how strong it was."

"It's often when life strikes a blow that you discover your own mettle." He spoke almost grudgingly, but Lenora eagerly fastened on to his words.

"I suppose that's true. Maybe if I'd been crossed more in early life…"

"What?"

"My personality would be stronger."

He gave a short laugh. "The gods help me if it was." At her confused look, he cleared his throat. "I find you good to look at," he said after a small pause. "Especially when you're naked."

My body, she thought with surprise. *He's talking about my body.* "Even though I still need fattening up?" She glanced down even though she was covered in blankets.

"I'm not so bothered about that anymore," he said with a shrug. "You've meat enough on your bones to please me."

"Then why—?" She broke off, feeling her face grow hot. "Why have we not…?"

"I want to," he admitted, not quite meeting her eye. "But in the middle of a tournament field might not be the best place."

"Because you want me on my hands and knees?" she asked with a frown and watched the red streaks appear along his cheekbones.

"Not the first time," he said in a low voice that was almost a groan.

"Because you said it would be loud and rough, then?"

He looked pained. "I should not have said that either."

Lenora wondered at that. "Oh. Then you definitely should not have told me that you generally sport with two bedfellows," she retorted.

He looked startled. "When did I—?"

"That first night I sought you out."

He frowned. "I don't recall. What did I say?"

"That I might have walked in on you romping with a pair of wenches."

He relaxed. "I just said that to shock you, Lenora. That is not a habit of mine."

"So, in general, one suffices?"

"You'll be plenty for me." His eyes glanced up and down her blanket-covered body.

"Oh." She considered this. She felt both pleased and relieved by his reply. "And on the whole, I would rather you told me things than not."

"Indeed?" He sounded skeptical.

"Even if the truth is uncomfortable, I would rather know it."

He was quiet a moment. "Do you remember what you said at the inn? The first inn? About your suitors?"

Lenora found herself growing flushed. "Yes," she admitted. "I think I may have misled you slightly, as I did not know what you meant precisely by permitting favors." He turned his head sharply toward her but said nothing. "When I said I did not enjoy fondling or wet kisses," she said in a rush, "I meant pressed to my hand. No one has ever..." She bit her lip. "I don't think that is precisely what you meant." She looked up and found him regarding her steadily.

"No," he agreed gruffly. "That wasn't what I meant."

Lenora took a deep breath. "Do you think that might be appropriate in the middle of a field?" she asked hopefully.

Garman drew in a sharp breath. "You want me to kiss and fondle you, Lenora?" She nodded. "It might not be what you're expecting," he warned. "I'm not interested in pinching your chin or tickling your ears."

"My suitors weren't as bad as all that! No one ever tickled my ears!" She hesitated. "Where would you touch me, then?"

"Wherever I want."

Lenora considered this. "That does not sound so very bad. Besides, I wouldn't want you to touch my face at all." Self-consciously, she reached up to trace the roughened skin at her jaw. Noticing him watching her, she dropped her hand.

157

"Is it sore?" he asked.

"No. I think it is totally healed."

"Why can't I touch it, then?"

"Do you want to?" She was startled.

"Wherever I want, remember?"

"Yes, but—"

"What?"

She took a deep breath in and out. "Very well. I agree."

16

He must have been mad, he thought moments later as his hands roamed over her sweet little body. Lenora Montmayne was not cold as court rumor had it. She was warm and responsive and extremely untutored. She had clearly not lied when she said not one of her wimp suitors had dared even to kiss her lips. She nearly jumped out of his arms with shock when he slid his tongue into her pretty little mouth or squeezed her delightfully rounded buttocks. He had to keep drawing back to utter terse instructions, or she'd just lie there like a stunned mullet.

"Suck my tongue," he demanded. "Pull down your shift."

Dimly, he recognized that he was not treating her with the reverence she doubtless expected, but he had to give it to her, she was following his uncouth instructions to the letter. When her fumbling fingers did not free her breasts quick enough, he yanked the flimsy fabric down and heard it tear. Instead of reproaching him, she gave a soft moan that went straight to his groin.

"Open your legs, Lenora."

She was more hesitant over that one, but fall open they did, though her eyes sought his for reassurance in the dim light. He could have cursed the blankets for impeding his view, but he could hardly throw them off on such a bitter night. His own body felt like a furnace as he settled between her legs and lowered his mouth to one perfect breast. She whimpered and jolted against him as he sucked it into his voracious mouth. Now he was groaning as he tongued her nipple, rubbing his hard cock against her soft belly. *Fuck.* He was going to spill his seed at this rate, which was rather messier than the bit of kissing and fondling she'd asked for. He doubted an extremely virginal

Lenora Montmayne was ready for his seed all over her smooth white belly or that luscious round ass of hers. Still, he thought dimly, for a girl who despised wet kisses, she had swallowed his tongue readily enough.

She panted, her hands clutching fretfully at his shoulders. "Ohhh! Oh Garman." She shuddered. He lifted his head. *Was she...?* He slid one hand between her legs and caught his breath.

"It's a good thing I'm not as prejudiced as you against wet lips," he said huskily, slipping a finger inside her drenched folds. Lenora gave a muffled sound somewhere between a shriek and a squeak. Her legs stiffened, and he slid one finger right up inside her, but even as she uttered a sound of discomfort, his thumb sought out her hidden pearl. "How does that feel?"

She panted and twisted beneath him. "What a strange question—*oh!*"

"What's strange about it?" he asked, stroking his finger. "This is where my cock wants to be, but I don't think you're ready for that, more's the pity."

She dragged in a ragged breath. "I am aware of the mechanics," she said in a voice of strangled dignity that would be amusing if he did not feel quite so edgy with need. "But I—" She broke off with a sob. "Have I—?"

"What?"

"*Wet* myself?" she asked in a voice that shook.

"No, sweetheart," he replied raggedly. He guessed her mother really hadn't spoken to her. "This wetness here is your body readying itself to join with mine. This is how you make me fit."

160

He could almost *hear* her listening to this. "Oh," she said again, this time doubtful, but wondering.

"Give me your mouth again," he ordered. Lenora shuddered, then pressed her lips to his. This time when he deepened the kiss, she was anticipating it, and welcomed the invasive thrust of his tongue with a deep moan that made him feel almost frenzied.

He pushed his finger deep into her and found it gripped in such a fluttering tight sheath that his cock pulsed with envy. This time, Lenora tore her mouth from his. "Garman!" she exclaimed, her tone so panicked that he realized her crisis was almost on her and crushed his mouth against hers to muffle her hoarse cries. If anyone else but he overheard the sounds she made in the throes of pleasure, he would have to kill them, he realized dimly. These sounds were just for him.

He lay tense against her body as it clenched and quivered around him, his thumb circling against her little button, wringing every last drop of astonished pleasure from her until all her limbs relaxed and she released her death grip on him and fell back limp against the mattress. He focused on her sobbed breath, the rise and fall of her chest as her rapture faded. Then he did a very odd thing. Ignoring his rock-hard cock, which was on the point of exploding, he very carefully kissed both her eyelids and all the way down the line of her jaw. He had no earthly idea why. He just knew he had to. She gave a gasp, and if she wasn't wrung out like a limp rag, he knew she would have stiffened or objected to this strange gesture. Luckily, such actions were beyond her right now, as for some reason, it was imperative for him to run the tip of his tongue over the imperfect skin and then kiss her soundly on the mouth.

"You won't like this part," he told her tensely. "I apologize in advance."

He felt her questioning gaze but was pleased that she did not protest or try to pull away as he shifted down her body and shoved her shift up out of his way. Then he took himself in hand and with harsh groans he pumped his cock and released his seed all over her belly and her perfect cunt. When he was done, he fell back on his haunches and fought hard against the ignoble impulse to snatch up the remaining candle and take a good look at his glistening handiwork. For some reason, he was suddenly desperate to see the blond hair between her legs mingled with his seed. For now, he merely contented himself with staring his fill in the murky light and catching his breath. Mercifully, she made no move to close her legs or push him away. Finally, he was able to tear his eyes away and found Lenora watching him in perfect silence.

"Don't move," he said thickly, and climbed off the cot to go and fetch what was left of the water and a cloth. "This will be cold, I'm afraid," he added in a gravelly voice. "But if I don't clean you off now, you won't thank me in the morning." He moistened the cloth and set about cleaning the mess he'd made of her. Lenora lay as meek as a lamb, but he felt her eyes on him the whole time.

"Something to say?" he was forced to ask in the end as he placed the bowl and cloth back on the table.

She licked her lips and he felt a twitch of renewed interest that surprised him so soon. "Why did you say I wouldn't like that part?" she asked curiously.

Garman's eyes widened. *Well...fuck.*

17

Garman woke suddenly around five to the sound of rain. He lay a moment in perfect stillness trying to assimilate himself to both his unfamiliar surroundings and a nagging feeling of unease. Then he remembered and turned hot then cold all over. He'd had sexual congress with his wife. Nay, hardly that. A bit of touching and fondling, nothing more. He glanced down at the blond hair spread over his chest.

She had been practically sprawled across him when he drifted off to sleep. Apparently, they had not moved so much as an inch which was a miracle in itself. Usually Garman could not bear to be even touching with a bedmate when he slept. That's why he always sent them on their way before he settled down to sleep.

Then something else struck him. Lenora had not woken him with her nightmares. For some reason, that also unnerved him, he could not say why. Except...if she was coming to rely on him, then he needed to put a stop to that. Right now.

Abruptly, he set about extricating himself from Lenora's sleeping embrace. She shifted over him with an exclamation of annoyance, burying her face in his chest. He persevered, sliding her sideways off his body and had to dodge a blow to the face from a flailing hand. With a sudden gasp, Lenora twisted away from him and sat up. Then she started grappling with the blankets.

"What are you doing?" he asked sharply. Even in the dim light, he could see she was still half-asleep.

"I need to relieve myself," she answered, throwing her legs over the side of the cot. "Where are my slippers?"

"You need to put your boots on," he told her. "The grass will be wet."

"Grass?" Lenora looked around at him in confusion.

He knew she was still half-asleep. With an irritated sigh, Garman climbed out of the bed and started dragging on some undergarments. "We're in a field, remember?"

She rubbed her eyes and yawned. "So, that's what that sound is." She glanced up at the ceiling. "Will it come through?"

"Depends how heavy the downpour is. Come." He held up his cloak above his head.

"I'm not dressed."

"You need to take a—to empty your bladder, not attend a feast," he reminded her.

"I can't go out like this," Lenora protested, looking down at her abused shift. The neckline was torn in one place from his none-so-tender treatment. He had to remind himself not to ogle as she adjusted it to provide as much coverage as possible.

"No one will see us."

She finished pulling on her boots. "Are you sure I shouldn't put more clothes on? What if we run across anyone else?"

"At this hour? They'd only be about the same business." He gave an impatient gesture. "Come. Get under this cloak."

Lenora walked over to him grudgingly. "You don't need to come with me."

"You're not going outside half-dressed without me," he answered firmly.

"Well, I'm not going to…pee in front of you!" she objected in scandalized tones.

"Why not?" he asked, pushing the entrance aside for her. "You've seen me do it."

"What? I did not!"

"When you showed up in my bedchamber back at Caer-Lyoness."

"I didn't see anything! You had just tucked it away," she argued, then caught herself up.

He had to bite back a smile in the dark. "I won't look. I'll just hold the cloak up so you don't get wet. Head straight in front of you to that line of trees."

Lenora walked unsteadily in the direction he'd specified. "Ugh!" she complained and caught at the hem of her shift to hold it above her knees. "The grass is sopping wet!"

He didn't answer, just walked behind her until they approached the cover of the outskirts of the wood. "Here," he said.

"What?" She whipped her head round.

"Squat down here."

"Squat?" Lenora squeaked. "I will not!"

"Lenora, if you will come to a rural tournament, you'll have to take a piss among the trees," he pointed out bluntly. "You were the one who asked to come."

"It's not—taking a piss among the trees!" she whispered in outraged tones. "It's taking a piss at my husband's feet I object to!"

He lifted an eyebrow at her, then realized she would barely make out his features in this light. "It would take more than that to put me off, I assure you." Now why had he said that? he wondered. He had meant to say it would take more than that to shock him.

"I can't do it," she said obstinately. "I won't. You'll have to stand here and let me just wander off a few yards."

For a moment, he considered reminding her where his fingers had been only a few hours previously. Then he decided against it. "You're not wandering off anywhere without me," he said instead curtly. "It's dark and we're surrounded by strangers."

He heard her frustrated huff, and then, quite suddenly, she dropped down, grumbling and bunching her skirts. "Kindly whistle a tune or something."

He held the cloak aloft. "Really? What if that attracts more attention?"

"Is your whistling really that impressive?"

"Lenora, would you just…"

"Oh, very well!" she said hastily. When she sprang back up moments later, he was sure her face was flaming even though he couldn't see clear enough to tell. "Do you need to—um—?"

He snorted. "Why, are you going to hold the cloak over my head?"

"Why not?"

"You could barely reach," he pointed out, handing over the cloak anyway. Then he took a few steps away and turned his back to her. He heard her gasp and spin around to face the opposite way as he unfastened himself. Maidenly modesty was a very strange thing, he reflected. Not four hours ago she had

166

told him she had not disliked his decorating her with his seed. Now a glimpse of his cock seemed something to be avoided at all cost.

"It hardly seems fair," she mused suddenly, surprising him. "That the whole operation is so much simpler for men."

He grunted, tucking himself back in. "Come on." He grabbed the cloak in one hand and her in the other and they made their way back to their tent, jostling and bumping against one another as they tried to ward off the rain.

"I do hope it stops soon," she said anxiously. "What time do they usually bring around the washing water and any refreshment?"

"Not for a while," he admitted. "The banqueting would have lasted long into the night." Near the tent, she tripped on something and almost fell, and he was forced to wrap an arm around her waist to steady her. "You're shivering. Get back into bed," he said as they ducked back inside.

"I intend to." He heard a rustle and realized she had pulled her shift up over her head as he saw the white garment drift down onto one of the chairs. Quickly he turned his head, but she was already disappearing under the covers. "Horrid wet thing was wrapping around my ankles," she mumbled through teeth that chattered. "Aren't you coming back to bed?"

He hadn't intended to. He knew he wouldn't sleep now, yet for some reason, he hesitated. She was cold and needed him to warm her up. He stripped down to his braies and climbed in beside her. Immediately, Lenora huddled against him. He found his arms closing around her. "You're a mass of gooseflesh."

"I know. You didn't have to crouch with cold, wet grass brushing your bare arse!"

He bit back a laugh. How long, he wondered, would she continue to surprise him? Almost without thought, he slid his hands lower to cup her backside. "These buttocks should never suffer such indignities," he said huskily.

She gave a smothered chuckle. "Sometimes you are almost droll, Garman Orde. I've remarked on it before, have I not?" she said. When he did not answer, she pressed her face to his chest.

It couldn't be comfortable sleeping like that, he pondered moments later as he felt her drift off to sleep. Yet this was the second time she had managed it. He felt her limbs go limp and heavy as she slumped against him. For some reason, that filled him with a strange satisfaction. Why was that? he wondered uneasily. The fact she was comfortable enough to sleep against him naked was also oddly pleasing on some level; he had no idea why. Gently, he stroked a thumb against the indentation of her waist.

He liked how warm her voice was when she was pleased or amused. It flowed through him like a fine wine, making him light-headed and relaxed. Her hair was silky soft where it brushed against his skin. Almost, he wanted to run his fingers through it. If he was another man, an affectionate sort of man, he would give in to the temptation. He lifted his hand, then lowered it again. He was not that man, he reminded himself with a frown. No matter how much she might want him to be.

He wanted intimacy with her alright, but not this kind of intimacy. Physical closeness was all very well and good, so long as she did not start confusing it with another kind of closeness. He swore silently and stared into the darkness. Of course she would. She was a woman. He had taken a misstep somewhere along the way with her, he thought, frowning, else she would not be curling into him like this, making jokes, calling him "droll"—whatever the fuck that meant—and *cuddling* with him.

And it was not only her. What the fuck was he *doing*, tickling her waist and holding her in his arms like this? He shifted uneasily, moving his hands behind his head. He was the one confusing the issue, as he was the one taking the lead in their interaction. Lenora was clueless about men and how men and women should interact. What the fuck had he been thinking? He had even for a moment held her hand outside in the dark, like some kind of lovesick swain. What the fuck was that about? He glanced down at the blond head on his chest. She was a pleasing armful, but she needed to know her place. Which was in his bed and on his cock, but even so, that did not mean they were friends or companions or anything other than he determined.

And on the morrow, he would have to steel himself to make as much plain to her.

18

Lenora woke to the low murmur of voices. She sat up and found washing water had arrived from the house and was being set down on the small table. Garman was up and half-dressed already. As soon as the servants left, he began sloshing the water around, washing his neck and face.

"Good morning," Lenora said, stretching and rubbing her eyes. He glanced over his shoulder at her but did not speak. "What time is your first event?" When he did not answer, she shrugged, guessing he could not hear her above his ministrations, the washcloth wrapped around his neck muffling his ears. Instead she fell to braiding her hair so it was tidily out of the way when it was her turn at the basin. Once this was done, she drew back the blankets, intending to climb out of the bed when he forestalled her.

"Don't bother rising yet," he told her abruptly. "I've told them to bring you food and drink out here to break your fast."

"Oh." Lenora looked up at him. "That was thoughtful, thank you."

His eyelids flickered. "It will be easier for me to get ready if you remain where you are. There's not much room."

"I see," Lenora replied carefully, finally noticing that something about his tone was decidedly off this morning. He sounded somehow surly and confrontational, and she wondered at it, drawing her feet back into the bed.

Although he did not turn his head to look at her as he moved about the tent retrieving his armor and weaponry, she could tell he was avoiding her. The truth was that his gaze would have fallen on her a dozen times quite naturally if he had not been so studiously ignoring her. Lenora considered this as she watched him retrieve his shield from under the spare bunk.

"Will you break your fast here with me?" she asked politely.

"I would have thought the answer obvious. I will not."

Bad tempered was one thing, but now he just sounded bored, she realized with dismay. With her? Already?

"You're off to the main house, then," she observed. He did not answer, but instead shrugged an irritable shoulder. "Am I to come and watch you compete later on?"

"Lenora," he said, turning to look her full in the face for the first time that morning. "Just because I had my fingers between your legs last night does not mean we are now joined at the hip."

Lenora felt her face fall and a ridiculous sensation of disappointment flood her—and something more. It felt rather like hurt feelings, which made no earthly sense. Clearly, he was being as offensive as possible to try to mortify her. But why would he want to do that? Unless, a voice whispered in her ear, this was just his usual practice. After all, likely he turned out all the wenches he'd bedded the next morning and she was just getting a taste of that. He couldn't very well turn out his own wife, so she was getting the next best thing.

"I see," she heard herself say aloud in a funny, detached voice. "Well, I hope you enjoy the company there." She lay back flat on the bed and stared up at the ceiling of the pavilion as she listened to him buckle on his sword. After a moment, she heard his footfalls and the swing of the tent entrance and he was gone. Lenora lay perfectly still, swallowing down a sudden lump in her throat. She felt a ridiculous impulse to cry. *Idiot*, she reproached herself. *Did you think he was your friend? The very*

171

reason you picked him was because you knew him to be a merciless swine. Why are you now hurt to find he runs true to form?

The truth was, she had woken feeling happy and strangely carefree. She could not remember the last time she had awakened feeling that way. If there had been bad dreams, she did not remember them. And now it had all come crashing down around her ears. She hugged her own arms and turned into the pillow to muffle a shameful sob. *Foolish Lenora*, she upbraided herself. *Had you forgotten your ruined face and your ruined future?* Servants would arrive shortly with bread and fish. Was she really going to lie abed, weeping over the fact her husband was an ill-mannered brute? That thought had her bounding up from the bed and dragging her dress from the previous day on.

She was not such a fool, she hoped, as all that. Why should she care where Garman Orde took his meals? Or that he did not care to have her cheer him on in the crowds? She had married him with her eyes open. She was reaping what she had sown. 'Twas just that for a moment, the veriest instant, she had forgotten what kind of marriage she had bartered.

She would not do that again.

Lenora spent the morning alone in the tent. She ate the food brought out to her and had a good wash. Then she unpacked the three gowns and underdresses she had brought with her and set her combs and hairpins on the top of the trunk. It did not take her long to dress her hair for in truth, she was capable of only the simplest of styles. Her maid, Hannah, had always been responsible for the elaborate arrangements she used to wear at court. Still it was a good deal shorter now, only hanging to her middle back, so it was easier to handle.

172

After she had coiled and pinned her blond locks at her nape, she set about dressing herself in a favorite gown of deep rose decorated with gold embroidery at the hem and the cuffs. Very likely it was far too frivolous for a field, but she felt in need of cheering. Then she set about securing her veils onto a gold toque which she perched atop her head and pinned firmly into place. She had only a small hand mirror to check her progress, but she thought she had made rather a good job of it in all. She was just angling it over the top of her head and craning to see it from a different viewpoint when she recognized a voice raised in conversation walking past her tent.

"If he wants his saddle polished again, he can damn well polish it himself, the lazy braggart!" said an indignant voice that sounded strangely familiar. Lenora turned her head sharply.

"I tell you, it's a perfectly reasonable request!" replied an exasperated voice. "You'll get a cuff round the ear if you don't shape up soon, Montmayne. Tell him, Ames."

Montmayne! thought Lenora, her ears pricking up. She had thought it sounded very like her young cousin Kit. Another youth murmured some reply, but it was muffled and she could not catch it for they were definitely moving away now. Lenora set down her hand mirror and crossed quickly to the tent opening to peer out. Walking away from her were three youths, one thickset and stout, one fair and well proportioned, and the other rather gangly with auburn curling hair. Lenora drew in a breath. The latter, if she was not mistaken, was none other than her first cousin.

"We'll see you down the stables in five minutes? Come, Hal," the blond said, peeling away to the left. The heavyset lad followed him.

"I tell you, I'm never playing the dice cup with you again, Ames," Kit called after them ill-naturedly. "You barely left me with the shirt on my back last time."

The blond youth laughed. He really was very good-looking, thought Lenora, and he also seemed strangely familiar. "I wouldn't want your shirt," he said, flexing his arms. "It would confine my muscles too much." His friend Hal guffawed loudly, but Kit scowled.

"I tell you I won't be gulled twice."

"Faintheart!"

Kit flung out his arm in a dismissive gesture, and Lenora watched him disappear into a yellow-striped tent. The other two made off in the direction of the manor house. Lenora hesitated. She had not seen her cousin in months, but in that intervening time he must have become a squire to some knight.

She and Kit had never been close due to the seven-year age gap between them. Still, she had the overwhelming impulse to go and seek him out. After all, what else could she do now that she had tidied her things away, washed, and dressed? Garman had made it perfectly plain to her that he did not care for her company this day and she could hardly set off to the competition field without an escort. Perhaps, she thought, her spirits rising, Kit would accompany her to watch the joust?

After all, why should she not? Her veils would conceal her face. She knew which tent he was staying in. She could walk directly there and visit with him and no one else be any the wiser. Overcoming her indecision, she strode from the tent and hurried with swift steps toward the tent which looked the twin of the one she was currently staying in except for its color. When she reached it, she stooped a moment and stood listening outside the entrance. She didn't want to go blundering in if his new master

174

was already in there. She fancied she could hear someone moving around within, but there was no conversation. Deliberately, she cleared her throat.

"Kit?" she called softly. Something thudded softly, as though dropped.

"Gods rot you!" she heard an adolescent male say. "Who's there?" the same voice added querulously. "If it's you pair of jackanapes, you can sod off after all the trouble you've caused me! And you won't fleece me out of any more coin either! I'm onto you—!" The tent flap was wrenched back, and Kit's wrathful expression was swiftly extinguished. "Who the devil are you?" he asked in astonishment, falling back at the sight of a heavily veiled woman.

"It's your cousin Lenora," she replied matter-of-factly. "Let me in."

Stubbornly, instead of moving away from the entrance, Kit moved instead to firmly block her way. "Nay," he said, shaking his head of copper curls. "You're not her, madam. For she's grievously ill and lies on her deathbed even now." He eyed her swathed head nervously. "They say," he added hoarsely, "her face has clear rotted away."

"Nonsense! I am perfectly recovered now," she told him bracingly and, seeing his reticence, could not resist lowering her voice and stepping up close to him. "'Tis only my pretty face," she added in hollow sepulchral tones, "that is left a ruined shell of what it once was..."

She saw Kit blanch and laughed merrily. "You always were a perfect goose, Kit Montmayne!" she told him, and then felt an arm close around her waist from behind, lifting her into the air and her bottom pinched with great familiarity.

"What have we here? An assignation—?" Sir Lionel's teasing words abruptly cut off as Lenora uttered a startled scream and whirled around on him.

"Leave go of her!" Kit yelled, bounding forward out of the tent and grabbing Lenora's arm to haul her away from the surprised knight. "How dare you touch my cousin! I'll have your hide for this, Emworth, you dog!" He clapped a hand to his hip, and finding no dagger, gazed around wildly.

"Your cousin?" repeated Sir Lionel, looking dumbfounded. He looked from Lenora to Kit in horrified disbelief. "What cousin?"

"Just because her face rotted off," Kit thundered, "does not mean you can take liberties with her body, you blackguard!"

Lenora rubbed her backside distractedly. She could not believe such behavior of her most reverent and respectful suitor. Sir Lionel, who had once kissed her empty glove and blushed over it, had *pinched* her backside, and pinched it hard. He had also been grossly familiar in the way he had manhandled her into his arms. She was shocked to her core. Her scattered thoughts were brought back to earth with a bump when she saw her cousin lower his head and charge at Sir Lionel in the manner of a human battering ram. Sir Lionel, who was still staring at her open-mouthed, did not recover from his shock in time and ended up doubled over groaning as his squire enthusiastically fell on him and started pummeling him with great vigor.

"Kit!" Lenora protested, but was not heard. To her consternation, people seemed to be hurrying toward their altercation. "Kit, stop that!" she hissed, struggling with her veils. Perhaps they could not hear her above the uproar. Finally, she got all four of the veils disentangled and yanked them back. "Stop it right now, you pair of fools!"

Sir Lionel sat up looking pained as Kit dropped his fists. "Lenora!" her cousin exclaimed. "By all the saints, it is you!"

She plunked her hands on her hips. "Is that not what I told you from the outset?" she demanded, then noticed the stares from the crowd around them.

"Well!" grumbled Kit, looking aggrieved. "I'd like to know why my father told me that pack of lies!"

A pair of fellow squires darted out of the crowd and pulled Kit to his feet. Lenora recognized them from earlier. "You're for it now, Kit, my boy!" the chubbier of the two said, nudging Kit in the ribs. "You can't go fighting 'em when the fancy takes you!" The other, the handsome blond boy, regarded Lenora thoughtfully.

"Lady Lenora," a nearby voice said contritely, and she looked round to find Sir Lionel sinking to his knees in the grass. "I can only earnestly beg your forgiveness," he said wretchedly. "I did not realize—that is I scarcely thought—"

"You thought me a disreputable female, trysting with your squire," Lenora supplied with some acerbity, "who was fair game for your wandering hands."

Sir Lionel's face turned scarlet with embarrassment. "I—I—" Words failed him, and he hung his handsome head dejectedly. "I have no defense," he said miserably.

Lenora marveled that this man who had professed himself her devoted servant had seen fit to opportune wenches while she was supposedly on her death bed. He had even had a poem commissioned some months ago, bragging of his steadfast heart that would never waver!

"Why don't you give him a penance, Lady Lenora?" asked the blond squire in a clear carrying voice.

177

"A penance?" Lenora looked around at the murmur of approval from the crowd. She glanced back down at Sir Lionel to find his eyes fixed on her face. Too late, she realized it was on full view of all and sundry. For a moment she was tempted to drag the coverings back over her face, but that would likely look rather cowardly. Besides, everyone had got a good look by now. Instead, she tilted her chin and held Sir Lionel's gaze. To her surprise, he did not flinch away or look at her with sudden dawning horror.

"Will you not commission me, as your humble servant?" he beseeched, as flushed and pleading as he had always been in her presence.

Lenora's mind went blank. Despite being such a beacon to courtly love, she had never been particularly good at its conventions. She darted a look of appeal toward the blond squire and he sauntered forward to her side.

"It would seem appropriate, would it not, for Sir Lionel to make some reparation toward the fairer sex for his rude treatment of them?" he mused loudly, looking like he was enjoying himself. Again, the crowd was in the palm of his hand, nodding and murmuring in agreement.

"What is your name, youth?" Lenora asked suddenly. "For I feel sure I know you."

"Aye, Lady Lenora, for you do know me. I am Cuthbert Ames, squire to Sir Roland Vawdrey."

Lenora gave a quick nod. "Of course! I have seen you many times with my kinswoman the Lady Eden. That is a very good notion, Cuthbert." She looked at him critically. "How would such a penance work?"

He tapped his chin, his blue eyes dreamy. For a moment he was lost in thought and then he spoke. "For the next three months," he said in a ringing voice, "Sir Lionel should take up the mantle of a protector and champion of wronged women everywhere. He should ride hither and thither in search of these wrongs and set himself the righteous task of righting them."

This seemed rather vague to Lenora, but clearly it found favor with the crowd, who broke out into a spontaneous round of applause.

"I will do it," said Sir Lionel hoarsely. "In your name." To her surprise, the gaze he directed on her was just as slavish as ever. She blinked as he rose to his feet in front of her. "Will you give me some token, my lady?" he asked. "I have no right to expect such a thing, base wretch that I am, but it would give me purpose should my resolve fail."

What strange creatures men were, Lenora thought, startled. Only moments ago, he had acted with gross impropriety, and now he was back to being all chivalrous and courtly again! What manner of token could she give him? she wondered. Then suddenly it came to her. Reaching up, she removed the smallest of the head veils, the one only long enough to cover her face, and handed that to Sir Lionel. He swallowed and took it from her as if it were some precious jewel. For an instant, he pressed his own face to it, and then turned rather red.

"Hold hard!" piped up Kit, who was frowning now, his expression turning wrathful once more. "For now I think of it, I seem to remember my uncle wrote that you had run away from court with some knave! Which one of these miscreants was it?" He scanned the crowd keenly, passing a pointed finger over their number. "Speak up! Which one of you induced my cousin to bring disgrace on our family name?"

Beside her, Cuthbert sighed. "He's damnably hotheaded, you know," he said, clicking his tongue.

"Oh, I know," Lenora murmured. "Always has been."

"My fellow squires will stand with me, I'm sure!" Kit continued, clapping a hand to his stout friend's shoulder. "Hal? You'll stand my man in this matter?"

Hal looked rather dubious at the notion. He scratched his head. "Oh, er, yes," he said without enthusiasm and sent a pleading look in Cuthbert's direction.

"Ames?" Kit barked. "You're my second!"

"Yes, yes," Cuthbert murmured. "Simmer down! It's all in hand."

"Lenora!" Kit said imperiously, turning to her. "You will reveal to me now, cousin, the name of the villain who besmirched our family name by fleeing with you without permission."

Lenora had no sooner opened her mouth to try to staunch this new flow of disaster than the crowd parted, and a tall figure pushed through.

"What's going on here?" Garman demanded angrily. Kit took a hasty step back. Garman swung round in Lenora's direction and narrowed his eyes. "Wife?"

Someone audibly gasped. Lenora shut her eyes briefly.

"Wife?" yelped Kit. "You never married *him*?"

"No," uttered Sir Lionel in anguished tones. "Lenora, you cannot have!"

"Well, I have," Lenora said, nimbly sidestepped Sir Lionel, and walked over to Garman.

"Cousin," she said gravely, addressing Kit as though he were a full-grown man and not some fifteen-year-old upstart. "This is my husband, Sir Garman Orde." She placed a warning hand on her husband's forearm. "Husband," she said, addressing Garman. "May I present my first cousin and my father's heir, Christopher Montmayne, the younger."

Garman was perfectly still. Kit looked uncertain for a moment, then his eyes sized up Garman's bulk and guarded expression. He gave a stiff bow.

"There now," her cousin's friend Hal said heartily. He slapped Kit on the back. "Can't say any fairer than that old fellow! All very civilized and proper!" His relief was palpable.

Cuthbert Ames drifted back over to their side. "All seems in order," he agreed, clapping a restraining hand to Kit's shoulder. "Wouldn't you say?"

Lenora noticed uneasily that the crowd did not seem to be dispersing one whit. Did they really imagine that her husband was going to draw swords with a mere youth?

"What's Emworth doing here?" Garman asked in a quiet voice that immediately put Lenora on her guard.

"Oh! He has just begged me for a commission," she said breezily. "He will be leaving on a quest for the next three months and will be setting forth immediately." She shot a significant look at Sir Lionel, who was still looking at her in a forlorn fashion. "Is that not so, Sir Lionel?" At her words he gave a visible start.

"Oh, er, yes, Lady Lenora," he mumbled, bowing. "Immediately." Still his gaze lingered on her sadly until he noticed the ugly expression on Garman's face. He bowed very low, then beat a speedy retreat in the direction of his tent. At least he could take a hint, thought Lenora. Perhaps she had misjudged Sir Lionel altogether.

"Well," said Kit, taking up his cudgels again. "You needn't think I shall remain in his service after this outrage! Why I've never—hie! Leave go I say! I have not finished speaking with my cousin!" He struggled in vain as his two friends grabbed him roughly about his neck and dragged him unceremoniously off in the direction of the competition field.

Garman let his hostile gaze wander over the crowd until people began to melt away. "What was that about?" he growled as Lenora fell in step with him and they made their way in the direction of their tent.

"Oh, just my cousin Kit, you know," she said airily. "I thought I would have some speech with him, but things got rather…heated. It seems my father had sent some word to him about our elopement. His father is my least favorite relation." She grimaced, thinking of her uncle, Sir Christopher Montmayne. "But Kit is rather a dear, although somewhat prone to overreaction. He was determined to find out who had run away with me and causing rather a scene, I'm afraid." Instinctively, Lenora felt it would be better all around if Garman did not hear about the bottom-pinching until after Sir Lionel had made his escape, if at all. "Did you win?" she asked brightly, not giving him time to question her further.

He opened his mouth, then seemed to change his mind about what he was going to say. "Why was Emworth there?" he persisted.

"It turns out my cousin is Sir Lionel's squire," she said after only the tiniest hesitation, as if that explained everything. She hoped devoutly he had not seen Kit attacking the knight he was supposed to be serving. That could take some explaining.

182

Garman came to an abrupt halt. Lenora did likewise. She looked up and found his gaze trained on her. "Did you uncover your face for him or your cousin?" he ground out.

Lenora gasped. "Neither! That is to say, I was forced to uncover it in order to make myself heard above the clamor." She took a few calming breaths. "My cousin had the oddest notions about my fate. By all accounts, my uncle is under the impression the pox left me devoid of every facial feature. Mind you," she reflected sagely, "my father and he are not close, so likely he has not been kept fully apprised of my recovery."

"Well, according to your father, you never will recover," he pointed out brutally.

Lenora blinked. "True," she murmured. "For my looks will never be restored to what they once were."

"Emworth did not seem to mind overmuch!" Garman scowled.

"No," Lenora agreed absently. "He didn't really, did he? Which is funny because I always thought…" Belatedly she noticed the angry gleam in Garman's eye. "Likely he was distracted by everything going on around us and barely had the chance to notice," she finished lamely.

"Is that so?" His tone was singularly unpleasant. He started forward again, catching her wrist in his hand, practically dragging her in his wake.

Lenora bit her lip. "By any chance, did you—?"

"Did I what?" he snapped.

"Lose your event today?" she asked loudly. "You seem to be in a most ill humor!"

"Maybe that's because I just happened upon my wife entertaining a former suitor! My wife," he reiterated coldly, "who assured me she did not intend to uncover her face during this tournament!"

"I was not *entertaining* Sir Lionel," Lenora objected hotly. "And you did not *happen* upon us as though it were some sort of…clandestine meeting! My cousin was there also, and by the time you arrived, some dozen other people were milling around!"

Garman flung back the entrance to the pavilion and ducked inside. Pausing a moment to roll her eyes in exasperation, Lenora followed him. Inside, he started stripping off various pieces of armor and flinging them down in a pile. Lenora hovered uncertainly. She had never been good at placating people, and quite frankly, she was not sure she even wanted to appease Garman, who had been most rude and offhand with her only a few hours ago. Why she should have to soothe his frayed temper, she had no notion! She watched him a moment until he threw himself into a chair and sat there glowering at her.

"I did not mean to incur your displeasure by this," she said at last. "I just wanted to see a friendly face. After all, you made it plain to me that you had no desire for my company this day."

"Excuse me, my lady, good sir knight!" sang out a voice, making them both jump. Servants had arrived with more washing water. Lenora gestured toward the small table and stood out of the way as they bustled around, replacing the drying cloths and soap flakes with new ones.

"We may as well go to the feast this evening," Garman said heavily. "Now everyone knows you're here."

Lenora opened her mouth to argue, then shut it again. After all, he did have a point. And if she had not found it rather dull being confined to their pavilion then she would not have gone in search of company in the first place. She shot a sideways glance at him and found him watching her warily in return. "You could be right," she conceded. "Sir Roland's squire was there, so no doubt he will report back that I am here."

"If Vawdrey comes sniffing around, then I can soon send him away with a flea in his ear," Garman responded coldly.

"I'm sure he won't," Lenora soothed. "But doubtless he will want some response to the letter I received from Eden," she reflected. "Maybe I should write it now, for I will not need to change again." She looked down at her dress and then back at Garman, but he was already turning his back to her, stripping to the waist to wash. The servants withdrew. "I don't suppose you have any writing materials?" she asked, suddenly realizing she had none with her. He shot a derisive look over his shoulder at her. "I'll take that as a no." She had just sat herself down in his vacated seat when they heard a voice ring out loudly outside.

"Is the Lady Lenora within? I have a message for her."

Lenora started to her feet, but Garman interrupted her.

"Who is it?" he roared.

"Cuthbert Ames, squire to Sir Roland."

Garman swore under his breath and placed his razor down. "Come in."

Lenora sat back down again as Cuthbert Ames ducked into the tent.

"Good day to you, Sir Garman," he said with unruffled calm. Garman grunted and picked his razor back up, dragging it down his jaw. "My lady bade me come with a message," Cuthbert said, turning to Lenora.

"Eden is here?" Lenora cried. "I had no notion! She did not come to the summer palace."

185

Cuthbert grinned. "Aye. For the master permitted her to come to Kellingford where there is no risk of pox."

"I'm so glad!" said Lenora warmly and clasped her hands.

"What's the message?" Garman asked, half turning toward them and frowning.

"She asked if Lady Lenora could come to her tent to take a private supper with her this evening."

"No," Garman answered swiftly.

"Oh, but I want to!" Lenora protested.

"The Lady Lenora is attending tonight's banquet in the main house," Garman addressed Cuthbert, ignoring her objection.

"Oh, but that was a last-minute decision!" Lenora pointed out. "Could I not see my cousin? I'd much rather."

Garman's jaw tightened. "I would have thought you'd have had your fill of cousins today."

Lenora paused. "Not at all."

"I had no notion you were so fond of your family members." His tone was cutting, no doubt alluding to the fact she had proposed marriage to him as an escape from family obligations.

"Well, why should you?" she asked aloud. "I do not think we've ever discussed such matters."

He threw down his razor and turned around. "You're accompanying me tonight," he said shortly. "And there's an end to it."

Lenora pressed her lips together as she bit back a stinging retort. Cuthbert, she noticed, was watching them both with open curiosity. "I'm afraid I cannot join her this evening, Cuthbert,"

186

she said after a moment and was pleased at how calm her voice sounded. "Please convey my apologies to Eden and assure her that I will look to see her on the morrow. Perhaps I could join her in watching one of the events?"

Cuthbert grinned. "My master competes tomorrow in the melee. My lady will not miss that."

"Excellent, then I hope I may join her." She shot a look at Garman, who had his arms folded across his bared chest and was watching her narrowly. "Perhaps you could collect me beforehand?"

Cuthbert nodded obligingly. "Of course. Would ten suit you?"

"Most admirably, I thank you."

Looking amused, Cuthbert sketched her a bow, nodded at Garman, and backed out of the tent agile as a cat. She had not a doubt he had been fully aware of the tension between her and Garman and had been highly entertained.

"If you've quite finished making a show of us," Garman said harshly, "perhaps I can finish dressing?"

"I wish you would," Lenora replied sweetly, sweeping her hair pins from the top of the trunk into her hand. She would need to tidy up her remaining veils if she was to accompany him this evening and being confronted by her husband's half-naked body was distracting. She snatched up her hand mirror. One of the consequences of giving Sir Lionel her face veil was that she would not achieve full coverage now. With a sigh, she set about making the best of it she could.

*

Kellingford Manor was a large mishmash of a place that had been added to and built on until the original part of the house,

187

which had once been handsome and well proportioned, was now a sprawling, incoherent maze. Much like their home, the Kellingfords seemed a bewildering hodgepodge of a family that consisted of a rabble of stepsiblings and various cousins who rotated around the central patriarch, old Sir Roger Kellingford, without any direct line.

Lenora had not had more than three introductions than she gave up trying to understand who exactly her hosts were. Instead she curtseyed and smiled, even though her face was mostly hidden by her veils, and was seated next to Garman at a large table with her back to the fireplace in an extremely draughty hall. Garman stretched out his legs before him and gave a startled exclamation when he found his hand licked by a hound lurking under their bench.

Lenora laughed as he wiped his fingers on his tunic with a grimace. "Would you rather he'd bit you?" she asked, reaching down to stroke the friendly dog. "I never did get to meet your grandfather's dog. Kolby, wasn't it?"

"Aye, Kolby," he agreed. "He's old, but he doesn't drool like this one at least."

"I hope Fendrel is not missing you too much."

"Me?" He sounded startled.

"Yes, you," Lenora said absently, having caught sight of a profile she recognized in the dimly lit hall. "Oh!" Eden caught sight of her too, and Lenora saw her eyes widen. Her cousin's eyes were fixed on her in pained uncertainty. Then Lenora remembered she wore a veil. *Curses.* Hesitantly, she raised a hand in greeting. Eden, frowning, returned the gesture, then leaned into her husband Roland's side to speak to him.

"My cousin is here," she pointed out lamely. Garman frowned and leaned forward as the servers placed bread and roasted meat before them and cups of foaming ale. "I wish they had been sat at the same table as us." He made no comment and Lenora fidgeted with her veil, wondering if she should pin it discreetly aside to eat.

"You are lately married, I think?" asked a strident voice opposite them, and Lenora looked up to find an older lady they had been introduced to earlier regarding them eagerly. Her name and relationship to their host she could not recall, but she had the vague idea she was some sort of connection.

"Indeed," Lenora replied demurely when Garman gave no response. For politeness' sake, she was forced to draw her veil to one side and secure it. After all, light in the hall was not exactly bright and beyond their table she doubted many could make out her features.

The woman nodded sagely. "I can always tell," she observed indulgently. Lenora glanced sideways at Garman, who merely looked bored. "Brides have always had a special place here at Kellingford," the older woman declared. "Indeed, my stepbrother has brought at least four home in his time." She laughed heartily at this, displaying her rather prominent teeth.

Lenora smiled politely, though under the table she reached for Garman's leg and clasped him above the knee in a death grip. If he imagined for one minute he was leaving her to the tender mercies of this alarming woman, he was much mistaken!

Garman's hand closed over her own, anchoring it to him securely. "We have been wed almost a week now," he said dismissively.

"A week!" the woman crowed as if at some grand jest and shook slightly with laughter. "Newlyweds," she pronounced, shaking her head. Turning her head, she loudly shouted, "Roger!"

Lenora stiffened as she repeated her call to their host. "You'll pronounce a toast," she boomed. "To the bride and groom?"

"Do not trouble yourself," Garman said curtly, and Lenora winced again. He sounded the most reluctant and surly of grooms.

"You must be the lady who was causing such a stir this morning with two knights fighting over her," the woman said, looking diverted. "Everyone's been talking of it."

Lenora felt a little short of breath. "It was just a misunderstanding, I assure you."

"Fight? What fight?" Garman's tone was suddenly sharp.

"There was no fight," Lenora said, outwardly calm, inwardly cursing the events that had brought her into the dining hall.

"Oh-ho, madam! Is that the tale you'll give him? Then I shall back you up!" The matron gave her an exaggerated wink. "We females must stick together."

"There were *no* two knights," Lenora persisted doggedly. "It was a misunderstanding only. My young cousin—"

"Who fought?" Garman cut in angrily, his hand tightening on hers.

"Why 'twas that handsome young devil Sir Lionel," the older woman said, forgetting her vow of only moments ago. "Only now your wife has sent him away on a quest to repent of his hasty temper."

"Why it wasn't to repent of his hasty temper, Bridgette, lord bless you," boomed Sir Roger from the high table. "But to

190

repent him of his lusty nature!" A gale of laughter went up, which ceased abruptly when Garman suddenly stood up from his bench, almost overturning it. Lenora gasped and righted herself as the dog bolted under the table.

Lenora stared ahead of her in frozen dismay as a deathly hush fell over the Great Hall. Garman was scanning the hall, until his gaze fell on his quarry. "You there!" he shouted, then pointed. "Come here. Now!"

For one horrible moment Lenora thought it was Sir Lionel and he had not shown a clean pair of heels after all. Then she saw to her relief that it was only Kit, looking rather pale. His two friends exchanged glances and then stood up beside him. Lenora's mind raced. What on earth was she going to do? "You're making an utter spectacle of me!" she said in a low, furious voice that she hoped would carry no further than her husband. He ignored her as the three approached. They stood before the table like guilty penitents as Garman looked them over.

"You boy," he said, nodding toward stout Hal Payne, his gaze cold. "Tell me what happened."

Hal swallowed audibly. "I—I wasn't actually there when it blew up," he admitted. "By the time I came upon them, Kit was atop of Emworth and raining blows upon him."

Garman turned to Kit and was silent a moment surveying him. When he did speak it was with a sort of menacing quietness that made Lenora's stomach clench. "Why?"

Kit drew himself up, flinging back his head. "Nothing," he declared dramatically, "will induce me to tell you what transpired—"

191

"Emworth wanted the Lady Lenora to run away with him," cut in Cuthbert smoothly, then took a large bite out of an apple. Lenora closed her eyes as Garman stiffened and the whole room started a hushed whispering that grew to a swelling roar. Cuthbert unhurriedly swallowed his mouthful. "When she refused," he continued, raising his voice to make himself heard above the babble, "Emworth lost his head and tried to carry her off with him. Naturally, when Kit heard his cousin calling for help, he ran to her aid and that is when the fight broke out."

Lenora opened one eye to find the whole hall listening to the tale with bated breath and wide eyes.

"Is that what happened?" Garman rapped out. Lenora gasped, thinking he was asking her, but when her eyes flew to him, she found he was looking again at Kit.

"I—er—" Kit stammered. "That is—"

"Most noble youth!" Sir Roger shouted from the high table. "The honor is yours! We salute you! Kellingford salutes you! What is your name?"

"It's Kit, sir. That is—Kit Montmayne." He bowed, scarlet-cheeked, to the thunderous applause that greeted Sir Roger's words.

"Kit Montmayne! The hero of the day!" Sir Roger yelled above the clamor. "I vow I'll give you today's medal of valor, for all you did not compete in the field! I saw no deed more deserving!" He reached into the pile of the medals and held a badge aloft to loud cheers. "Approach me, lad, and receive your prize!"

Lenora gave a faint moan and gazed out glassily as toasts were raised to her young cousin. Kit received the slaps on the back and hearty congratulations with a sort of dazed bashfulness. She

192

looked pointedly at Cuthbert, who was still eating his apple, but the youth met her eye with an untroubled gaze. *What a cool little liar*, she thought indignantly. Then with some trepidation she glanced toward Eden, who was staring astonished as the rest and applauding Kit's heroics, her husband's arm slung around her shoulders.

Garman lowered himself back onto his seat, reaching for his cup and tossing it back.

"That is not quite how I remember it," Lenora admitted unevenly.

"You had your chance to tell me what occurred, and you did not take it," he gritted out, slamming his cup back down.

"Now, now, it's not the little bride's fault Emworth quite lost his head over her," Lady Bridgette said boisterously.

Garman ignored her, signaling for a server to bring him more ale. Lenora drew in a shaky breath and took a sip of wine. How people could even believe such a tale now her looks were gone was beyond her. She snuck another look at her husband, who looked to be silently fuming. *Oh dear*, she thought with some trepidation. *This does not bode well.*

19

The rest of the night passed between them in stony silence. They barely spoke a word as they made their way back to their tent, and both of them washed and undressed without comment and barely any light. Lenora groped her way into the bed and lay there wondering if she should broach the subject of Garman's ugly mood.

In the end, she did not feel the equal to it and lay there staring blindly into the darkness as she listened to him move about. It felt like she would never relax enough for sleep, but she must have, for the next thing she knew she was being held in a tight grip and terse words were being murmured into her ear.

"—all is well. You're at the tourney at Kellingford. With me."

Lenora lay stunned, her heart pounding as she realized that in her mind, at least, she had been back in the crypt with the afflicted. Garman was hunched over her, his strong arms clasping her to him. "I'm awake," she gasped. "I'm awake."

He grunted, but did not release her, though his hold slackened. "Roll onto your side," he growled. Lenora did so and at once found herself dragged back against his front. "Go back to sleep."

Lenora lay a moment, wondering if she should try to put herself to rights. Her shift felt all tangled up around her legs and down one shoulder. She wasn't sure she was decently covered. Then she dismissed the fact and closed her eyes. Garman's big body was warm against her back and she felt herself relaxing in spite of herself.

"Sir Lionel didn't want to run away with me," she heard herself confess. "He mistook me for a..." Words failed her. "Female of loose morals," she said with dignity.

"What?"

She felt him stiffen behind her. "He pinched me on the backside," Lenora admitted in a small voice. "And caught me about the waist." Garman said nothing, but she heard him breathe out heavily. "You know how much I always disliked being pawed about and no one *ever* dreamed of treating me with such familiarity as that. I was so shocked I screamed. Then Kit attacked him and all was pandemonium." She heard his ragged breathing and fancied he was silent from astonishment. "I think Cuthbert Ames lied out of some mistaken instinct to protect my dignity."

To her astonishment, she heard Garman give a short laugh. "I'd give anything to have seen Emworth's face when he discovered it was you."

Lenora turned her head to try to peer at him, but it was too dark. "I was never so shocked in all my life," she confessed in a rush. "I mean Sir Lionel Emworth! He was always so... proper. Once, he picked up one of my gloves I dropped coming out of the cathedral and he acted so reverently over it you'd have thought it was a holy relic!"

Again Garman uttered a short laugh. "Some men act differently with different kinds of women," he said dismissively, but Lenora's attention was caught.

"Do you?" she asked and for some reason the answer was important to her. She tried to turn toward him, but his hand closed over her hip, holding her in place.

"I don't think so," he said after consideration. "Not as a rule."

195

"No, I don't think you would," she said with relief. "I mean, I can't imagine you would start acting all prim and proper just because a female was of the nobility, then set about pinching tavern wenches' cheeks just because you can."

Garman shifted behind her uncomfortably. "Well, obviously there are some differences," he said.

"Yes," Lenora conceded. "I can see there would be, but I don't imagine you would be such a hypocrite as Sir Lionel."

He was silent a moment. "You almost make me feel sorry for the poor bastard," he said grudgingly.

"Sorry?" Lenora echoed indignantly. "I've very likely got a bruise!"

"You'd better not have," he growled, and she caught her breath as one hand slid around from her hip to her buttocks. "Where?" he asked roughly as his hand circled over her thin shift. "Here?"

She reached back and guided his hand over her left cheek. "Here," she said and was glad the dark hid her blushes. His thumb lightly skimmed the spot.

"Does it hurt?"

Lenora hesitated. "A little."

He swore under breath. "If the skin *is* marked, I'll track him down and beat the living daylights out of him."

She drew in a steadying breath. "You may find it hard to find him," she admitted. "The quest we set him was ridiculously obscure. I daresay he'll just ensconce himself in some remote tavern for the duration." Her voice was scathing.

Garman gave a soft laugh again. "Tavern wenches' chins?"

"More likely buttocks," Lenora corrected him sourly. Garman gave another startled laugh.

"I'm so relieved I didn't marry him," Lenora rambled on. "Imagine having the kind of husband who you can't turn your back on for fear he'll be pursuing serving wenches into dark corners!"

Garman's hand closed possessively over her soft flesh. "If you had married him, you'd have soon been a widow," he vowed.

"How do you mean?"

"I'd have tracked him down and murdered him. You're mine, Lenora."

She let out a hitched sigh. "Yes," she agreed, even though this was pure nonsense. If she'd married Sir Lionel, they both knew Garman would have carried on utterly indifferent to her fate. He had barely been aware of Lady Lenora Montmayne.

"I'm in deadly earnest," he insisted as though aware of her thoughts. His hand continued to shift lazily over her rounded backside.

"Hmm." Lenora gave up, her eyes fluttering shut. "I daresay you would. I wouldn't put anything past you."

He crowded in closer to her, and Lenora felt something hard prodding insistently at her lower back. "Go to sleep," he said needlessly, for she already had.

20

By tacit agreement, they went along to break their fast at the manor house the next morn. Garman watched her pin on the head veils without comment, but before they left the tent, he made her raise her skirts so he could inspect her bare bottom in daylight for any sign of bruising.

"Hmm," he said, dropping to his knees and brushing his knuckles over the swell of flesh.

"Is it bruised?" Lenora asked in a strangled voice, her face aflame.

"You have two purplish spots here and here," he said, pressing finger and thumb to the site.

"Ouch!" She winced.

"He must have pinched hard, curse him."

"He did!" Lenora agreed hotly, then sighed. "But they do say that fleshy areas bruise more easily, and that is without doubt my most fleshy area. It is most vexing for—" At the feeling of his warm breath on her skin, her thoughts scattered. "Garman?" She felt him brush his lips over the tender spot. "Did you just—?" She turned her head.

"A kiss makes it better," he said gravely and winked before rising to his feet. Lenora dropped her skirts and stared at him flabbergasted. He'd just kissed her backside!

"Come along," he said, holding out a hand. Lenora placed hers in it and they made their way toward the ancestral home of the Kellingfords.

On the way, they passed several knights and squires, most of whom had a passing greeting to throw their way. Lenora answered them all, though Garman mostly gave curt nods only. She supposed he had spoken the truth about having no particular friends among their number and marveled at it.

"Do you suppose the Hainfroys ever will compete?" she asked curiously.

He shrugged. "Who knows? I hoped so at one time, but I doubt it now."

"It might be nice for you to have some friends along when you take part."

He shot a look at her. "They're competitive like me," he said dryly. "I doubt they'd enjoy suffering a defeat at my hands."

"Or you at theirs?"

"Even less."

"So having friends at tournaments might be fraught with difficulties," she pondered. "Perhaps it's just as well that you have none."

He smiled grimly and she remembered how much she had enjoyed his laughter the previous night. She would like to see his laugh by daylight, she thought rather wistfully.

"What is it?" His words jolted her out of her ruminations.

"'Tis naught," she said hurriedly. "I only hope we are not seated with the Lady Bridgette this morn. She's so boisterous and has such a teasing nature." He frowned at this, but otherwise made no comment on her sudden aversion to their host's stepsister.

As they ate round white loaves and roasted fish at the long table, Lenora reminded him that Cuthbert was collecting her at ten o'clock to join her cousin at watching an event. It was on the tip of her tongue to ask him in what field he was competing today, but remembering his snub last time, she shied away from enquiring. Suddenly, it was imperative to her that he did not rebuff her as he had done the previous day.

By some miracle, they had managed to get things between them back on an even keel and she did not wish for a repeat of the hostilities that left her feeling surprisingly hurt. Instead she changed the subject and had him explain the strange crest of the Kellingfords which sprawled over the fireplace, a beast which was part eagle and part horse.

"Does Sir Roger have no heir to compete under their colors?"

"He has a couple of bastards," Garman admitted grudgingly. "But their shields do not bear the hippogriff, only the bar sinister to show the circumstance of their birth."

"What a shame," Lenora replied. "The Kellingford family seems very convoluted."

Garman nodded, buttering her another piece of bread. "His heir is a nephew through a half sister and does not bear the Kellingford name. By all accounts, Sir Roger prizes his bastards above his heir, and petitions the King to legitimize his offspring."

"Maybe he will," Lenora murmured, taking the bread. "For his chief advisor, Earl Vawdrey, prizes his own brother for all he is bastard-born."

"True enough," Garman agreed without much interest.

Lenora glanced toward the high table, leaning in closer to Garman. "Which ones are his sons?" she asked in a low voice.

200

Garman placed another piece of fish on her plate. "The two lads sat at the far end of the table in blue tunics," he said. "The one acts as squire to the other."

Lenora looked at two tanned males with good-natured faces who were wolfing down their breakfasts with hearty appetites and untidy brown hair. One was still a boy of about thirteen, while the other was approaching manhood though not yet filled out. "Which one is the heir?" she asked.

"The one sat to Sir Roger's left."

Lenora turned her head and observed a colorless-looking young man with an expression of distaste on his face as he prodded fretfully at his food. Lenora watched him snap his fingers for a servant and open his mouth to complain before catching his uncle's eye and thinking better of it. Lenora pulled a face. "I don't blame him for preferring his sons," she said.

Garman nodded. "Chatton lacks spirit," he agreed, "and does not even compete."

Lenora let her eyes wander over the rest of the company in search of her relations as she waited for Garman to finish his second plateful. She soon spotted Eden sat with her husband, though not Kit, who she suspected must have stayed out late enjoying his celebrated status after receiving his award the night before.

"I suggest you stop watching Vawdrey like that unless you want me to gut him in the next event." Garman's words were spoken low, but with such a sinister undertone that Lenora jumped.

Lenora turned her head, startled. "What??" She stared at him. For a moment, she had thought she had misheard him, but his grim expression put paid to that. "Why do you say that? I was just observing him with Eden, that's all," she explained. "I find the two of them together very entertaining."

He looked at her narrowly, then glanced across to observe Roland whispering in Eden's ear. Eden swatted him away with a reproachful word or two, for she was trying to politely listen to what the lady opposite was saying to her. Roland grinned and wound an arm around his wife's waist. When Eden leaned subtly against him, Roland looked smug.

"What's entertaining about it?" Garman demanded. "She's a shrewish scold and he's a damn fool to put up with it."

Lenora bristled. "That's my cousin you're speaking of," she reminded him with spirit. "And my favorite person in the world!"

His eyebrows shot up to the sky. "Eden Vawdrey?" he repeated skeptically.

Lenora nodded. "She's the best person I know!"

He was clearly surprised by this. "I wouldn't have thought you had any common ground."

"We were brought up together as girls and shared our childhood like sisters."

"Aye, but…" He let his words trail off.

"What?"

"You moved in vastly different circles at court," he pointed out.

Lenora considered this. "You mean because she attended all the intellectual gatherings while I merely paraded my beauty?" Again, Garman looked taken aback, though it was plain that was what he had meant. "That doesn't mean we haven't always cared for each other deeply," she told him sternly. "Eden was always trying to encourage me to improve myself with books and learning."

He snorted. "I can well believe that."

"While I did my best to ensure she made an advantageous marriage," she carried on, ignoring his interruption. He made a noise of rude disbelief at this. "What?"

"By standing idly by while she ran off with your betrothed?" he asked scathingly.

"Oh, is that what I did?" asked Lenora sotto voce. She smiled to herself. Only she knew that she had been instrumental in securing her cousin's match with the youngest Vawdrey, a powerful family at court.

"Are you saying it isn't?" Garman asked in a hard voice, his eyes on her face.

Lenora shrugged. "Oh, I'm saying nothing." It wasn't her secret to tell. Besides, all had turned out as it should. Eden and Roland were madly in love. "Roland Vawdrey was never my betrothed. I told that much to the Queen in front of a large audience. I wonder that you have never heard the tale."

"I've better things to do than listen to a lot of damned court intrigue," he said, pushing away his plate, his lip curling with contempt.

"Well then," she said lightly. "I will not bore you with it now." She could tell her words had not pleased him, but she could not let falsehoods pass about any rift between her and her cousin over Roland Vawdrey.

He escorted her back to the tent after the meal and again, it was on the tip of her tongue to ask him about his event, but she bit back her curiosity. When Cuthbert arrived to collect her, she bade Garman her cheeriest farewell and followed the youth across the field.

Cuthbert showed no embarrassment whatsoever over his conduct on the previous day. When Lenora informed him she had told Garman the truth of what had happened, he gave her a long speculative look. "The lie wasn't for his sake, but for the company in general," he said at last.

"You painted Sir Lionel in the role of would-be abductor!" she pointed out sternly.

Cuthbert looked unconcerned. "He'd likely prefer that to unprincipled philanderer," he said with a shrug. "Unrequited love will fit well with the reputation he has cultivated of romantic swain."

Lenora was privately struck by his shrewd reading of Sir Lionel's character, but held her tongue while she considered how to reply. His next words shocked her rather.

"Have you considered yet how you will convince your husband to take on Kit as his squire?"

"Pardon?" Lenora faltered, almost coming to a stop.

"This way," Cuthbert prompted her, "Roland competes in the melee."

"Oh." Lenora made a grab for one of her veils which was working its way loose. "What makes you think I was going to do any such thing?"

Cuthbert tapped two fingertips to his eyelids. "Second sight," he said matter-of-factly. "It's usually pretty reliable so long as it does not concern my own fate."

"Why does it not work about yourself?" Lenora asked. "That seems rather unfair."

Cuthbert shrugged. "That's how gifts work oftentimes," he said. "It's never troubled me overmuch. I always know my own mind and have little need for guidance."

Lenora thought that was probably true. "You can see the fortunes of others?" she asked and marveled that she was no longer eager to hear her own predicted.

"Sometimes."

"And you see Kit working out as Garman's squire?"

"He never got on well with Emworth," Cuthbert continued, ignoring her question. "It's hard to serve someone you little respect."

"You think he would respect my husband?"

"Oh yes. And if he did not, he'd get a cuff round the ear, I'll be bound," Cuthbert said, absently rubbing his own ear. Lenora found she could believe he'd received many a clout in his time.

By this point they had reached a wooden stand which had been erected with many steps leading up to elevated positions to look down on the field below. It looked a crude imitation of the ones you found at court to watch the royal tournament although it did not bear the attendant trappings of the royal boxes with their banners and pennants and matching page boys.

"My lady sits in the right-hand box," Cuthbert said, gesturing for Lenora to precede him in mounting the steps.

Lenora glanced up and saw Eden waving to her. She hastened up the steps and when she'd reached the top, turned right and hurried to embrace her cousin.

"Lenora!" Eden stood up from her bench and made a sound between a laugh and a cry. "At last! I've been so worried."

They clung to one another a moment, and then stood back to survey the other. Lenora noticed with interest that Eden was wearing a very pretty dress of royal blue with matching sapphires adorning her fingers and the bodice of her dress.

"You look very well, Eden," she said with satisfaction.

Eden put her hands to her thickening waist a little self-consciously. "You notice the differences?"

Lenora nodded. "But only because you are usually so slender. Your brooch is beautiful."

"Is it not?" Eden gestured for her to sit beside her. "Roland spoils me to a ridiculous degree. My jewelry box is overflowing these days."

"It is nothing less than you deserve," Lenora said warmly, taking her seat.

"Now tell me," Eden said, turning toward her impulsively and grasping both her hands. "Is all well with you, cousin? I was never so shocked in all my life then when I heard you were here in the company of a new husband! And when I heard his identity…" Eden's lips pressed together. "I could not imagine how it could have come about!"

"Could you not?" asked Lenora lightly. "Yet you must surely remember how much I enjoy the royal tournaments!" When Eden gave her no answering smile, she pressed on. "All is well, cousin, I assure you." Noticing Eden looking at the veils she wore, she steeled herself for a request to see her face. However, she should have known her cousin better.

"If you say you are happy in your marriage then I must be glad of it," Eden continued with forced cheerfulness. "I must admit, I did not realize Sir Garman ranked among your admirers but—"

"Nay," Lenora corrected her swiftly, "for he did not. Indeed, he has confessed himself wholly unadmiring of my former beauty."

Eden visibly checked her words. "He did?" she said, frowning. "Then—?"

"Our alliance is of recent creation. Since my illness."

Eden pursed her lips as if to speak and then apparently changed her mind. When she did speak, she seemed to be measuring every word. "You will have a good deal of disappointed suitors. No doubt, Sir Lionel's reaction, though very shocking, is an indication of how your former admirers will take the news of your marriage."

Lenora glanced sideways to see if Cuthbert still loitered, but the lad had made himself scarce. "I doubt that very much," she said briskly. "Only consider, the vast majority of them admired my face and nothing more. To give Sir Lionel his due, his regard seemed undimmed by my loss of looks. I must admit, I was somewhat surprised by that fact."

Trumpeting horns alerted them to the fact the combatants were now entering the field, and they both turned to watch as about twenty knights in red armbands lined up, followed by another twenty in navy armbands. Roland Vawdrey, wearing a red armband, raised a hand in greeting which his wife returned with a cheery wave of her scarf. Then Eden leaned forward, lips parted as he took up his place in the formation.

Lenora felt the box lurch and reached out to steady herself. "This structure does not seem terribly sturdy," she commented in alarm, but Eden was not listening. Her eyes were on the field before them as she rested her elbows on the edge of the box. It was amusing to think that only a year ago, Eden had felt nothing but scornful indifference for the lists. Lenora had just

settled herself comfortably after the first charge when Eden
uttered a sharp exclamation and half started out of her chair,
nearly upsetting a platter of grapes between them.

"That villain!" she said hotly and turned to demand of Lenora,
"Did you see that? That ill-judged blow?" Lenora looked at
Eden's flushed face with interest. "De Crecy thinks himself
wholly beyond reproach, but he shall find out differently at this
evening's meal when I tell him just what I think of him!" her
cousin vowed, clenching her fists.

It was not the easiest thing to watch the tournament through her
double veiling. In the privacy of their enclosure, surely she
could afford to dispense with them. Lenora set about sweeping
them to one side and securing them there with a pin. In truth, it
seemed a little rude to expect her cousin to talk to her swathed
in veils. Eden was discreet as the grave. She had evinced no
shock or horror at Lenora's appearance and did not seem to
sneak any side glances that Lenora could tell. "Will Sir Roland
not mind you tackling Sir Jeffrey like that in public?" she asked
with curiosity.

"Mind? Why should he?" replied Eden with surprise. Then she
gave a slightly self-conscious laugh. "He likes it when I get
riled up on his behalf."

"Indeed?" Lenora found herself enjoying this glimpse into her
cousin's wedded life.

Eden nodded. "Oh yes, he loves it when I take up cudgels for
him."

"It's fortunate you've discovered an interest in the tourney
now," Lenora reflected. "As you did not used to care for them
at all."

"Oh well," Eden answered conscientiously. "I really only care about the events Roland takes part in. I would not choose to watch any event on its own merit. I do not truly appreciate the sport as you do." Lenora nodded absently. "Will your husband not mind that you choose to watch the melee with me when he competes in the Challenge to Arms?"

Lenora hastily rearranged her face so Eden did not guess this was news to her. "I'm sure he won't care two pins," Lenora answered lightly. "Why should he? We are not a love match like yourself and Sir Roland." Something about her tone must not have sounded as casual as she had intended, for she found Eden keenly regarding her. To her annoyance, Lenora felt herself coloring up. Shedding her veils had the unfortunate effect of exposing her blushes. "You must not judge our pairing in the same light as your own," she added firmly.

"Must I not?" Eden answered with a curious expression, but then let the subject drop. "Have you heard from Uncle Leofric since your marriage?"

"Not yet," Lenora admitted. "Word will likely not have reached Father yet." She waved a hand about vaguely. "This is our first public appearance as a married couple after all."

"True," her cousin replied. "But word will soon filter back. There are several knights who attend court here, for all it is a backwater tournament."

Lenora murmured in agreement, "I know." She winced. "Garman says it is not usually so well attended." She fiddled with the arrangement of her veils, wondering if she should bring one forward again.

"Do you cover your face constantly now?" Eden asked suddenly. Her cousin's tone was carefully neutral, and she was considerate enough to keep her gaze at the field and not on

Lenora's face when she asked. Still, Lenora felt an implied criticism of her cowardice.

She was silent a moment before replying. "I thought I would initially, but no. You see, no one knows me at Cofton Warren, so it's much easier there. To them I am just a plain woman with a poor complexion." Eden shot a startled look at her at this and made a noise of disagreement, but Lenora ignored it. "It is when confronted with people who knew me before that I wish my features to be obscured."

"I suppose that makes sense," Eden said after a moment or two. "But indeed, you exaggerate, Lenora. Indeed," she insisted at the quick shake of Lenora's head. "You do, cousin. You must strive for some sense of perspective. It is only because you were so very lovely that you feel the contrast so cruelly now." She paused, waiting for her words to sink in. "You are an attractive woman still."

"Eden—"

"I do not just say that as someone who loves you," Eden interrupted her swiftly. "I speak as someone who has eyes in her head and a tongue that speaks true."

Her cousin's words were so emphatically spoken that Lenora paused. "My parents did not think so," she found herself confessing. Again, she had not meant to speak of it to Eden, but she felt the relief of unburdening to her cousin almost instantly. She would not repeat the words for they would only wound Eden almost as much as they had hurt her. She would only live the best life she could, and do her best to prove them wrong.

An angry flush crept up her cousin's neck. "They surely did not say so in your presence?" Eden asked in a voice that quivered with emotion.

"They thought me asleep. They did not mean for me to overhear their conversation."

Eden rallied. "That must have been in the early days of your recovery," she said uncertainly. "Your face was likely still swollen at that point and—"

"No," Lenora cut her off. "For they did not visit me in the early days, Eden." There was a heavy pause after her simply spoken words and then Eden's hand sought out Lenora's. "I wish I had been there," her cousin said, her eyes bright with unshed tears. "I cannot think what my uncle and aunt were about!"

"It was better you were not," Lenora said, returning the pressure of her fingers. "You would not have stayed away while I was infectious."

"Who looked after you?" Eden demanded. "Hannah?"

Lenora shook her head. "Let us not speak of it. It does not bear dwelling on." Something about her expression made the usually relentless Eden give way on this point. "I still have the servant who attended me, and I shall keep her till the end of her days or mine. Her name is Berta."

"Very well," Eden said. "I must meet this Berta someday, for undoubtedly I owe her a great debt." She paused. "If you do not wish to discuss your illness, then I shall respect that. But should you ever change your mind—"

"I won't," Lenora said. "But thank you."

"Then let us speak of other things," Eden said bracingly. The knights were now regrouping on the field with over half of them unhorsed. Vawdrey still retained his seat, so Eden's equanimity was unruffled. "How are you finding married life?" While Lenora scrambled to accommodate this abrupt change of direction, Eden continued, "I felt sorely in need of a confidante

211

in the early days of my own marriage. Alas, I was far from anyone I knew or considered a friend. You have ended up in similar circumstances, I think."

"Yes," Lenora agreed cautiously. "Though you are my only friend and also the only family I am close to."

"Soon, there will be another," Eden said, touching a hand to the slight swell of her stomach. "A niece or a nephew for you to love."

Lenora smiled. "I look forward to it."

"You are finding your way?" Eden asked discreetly. "Sir Garman is considerate?"

Considerate? Lenora's eyebrows rose. Not a word she would ever use about her husband, but she hesitated to say as such, seeing the sudden rush of pink to Eden's cheeks. Was her prim cousin attempting to raise matters pertaining to the marriage bed? "Oh," she said airily. "We are both groping our way about. We shall get there in the end I have no doubt."

Eden frowned. "I know what you mean," she said slowly. "I felt rather at sea myself in those early days," she confessed. "It's hard to remember now that everything has fallen into place, but—" She broke off, biting her lip. "All I can advise is that you try and be as trusting and open with your husband as possible and try not to let other considerations encroach."

"Other considerations?" Lenora asked, feeling mystified.

Eden made a quick gesture with her hands. "Modesty, dignity— that sort of thing. They all go out the window when it comes to—*that*." Eden's face was scarlet now. "I'm sure you have the measure of it by now." She darted a look at Lenora's face.

212

"Um." Lenora tried to school her face into an attitude of wifely wisdom. She really didn't.

Lenora watched her cousin's gaze turn doubtful. "Or haven't you?" Eden looked faintly anxious.

"Not really," Lenora confessed. "Do you think it's very important?"

"Important?" Eden's eyes widened. "Oh, dear me, yes! It most certainly is very important." She leaned forward and lowered her voice. "I think it is one of the ways that you bond as husband and wife. Initially, perhaps more importance attaches itself to the act for your husband, but then given time, your bodies become attuned..." Eden cleared her throat. "Am I making any sense?" She faltered.

Lenora thought about it. "I do not think Garman and I have reached that point yet," she admitted. "You see, ours is more of an *arrangement*," she stressed. When Eden looked alarmed, she added quickly, "As most marriages are for our rank. I am sure that given time we will get there."

Eden sat back in her chair looking troubled. "What do you think is impeding your trust?" she asked practically. "Is there some barrier to be surmounted?"

Lenora suppressed a sigh. Eden was always so practical. Always looking for a solution. "Well," she said, casting about for something that would satisfy her cousin. "There are so many mysteries unexpectedly surrounding him."

"Mysteries?" Eden repeated, looking surprised. "I would have thought Sir Garman singularly lacking in such things!"

For some reason, Lenora found herself bristling at this. "What do you mean?" she asked, and even she heard the unexpected edge to her words. She felt the strangest impulse to point out that some people might think Roland Vawdrey singularly lacking in subtlety or even brains!

Eden bit her lip. "Sorry, I did not mean to be judgmental," she said contritely. "I apologize."

Immediately, Lenora's fingers unclenched. "No, of course you did not," she murmured, wondering at her own swift annoyance. It wasn't like her at all! Usually she was even-tempered, even her sternest critics could not fault her on that score.

"Pray continue," Eden said encouragingly.

"There is something about his family circumstances that I do not quite understand," Lenora admitted, for the first time even to herself. "He owns a farm that his father built, but I do not think his father was from an agricultural background. Indeed, if he was, Garman could scarcely have been knighted after all."

"You have not met any of his father's family?"

"No indeed." Lenora shook her head. "For both his parents died when Garman was very young. I have met only his grandfather on his mother's side—one Gerard Sutton. He runs the farm on Garman's behalf. His manner is a little odd around me. There is some constraint that I do not altogether understand. It is not just with me, but with his own grandson also. He was very unhappy about our unsanctioned elopement."

Eden gave a start and Lenora realized that Sir Roland had been unhorsed and was now under attack from two knights who were rounding on him. They both sat silent until he had beat them off and fallen back among what was left of the red armbands. Eden relaxed again and turned back to her cousin.

"What is his grandfather like?" she asked with interest.

"Scrupulously polite, very proper, and extremely reserved. Nothing," Lenora added frankly, "like my husband." Before Eden could make any reply, she continued, "Then, there are the Hainfroys. They are like family to Garman, yet there is no actual blood between them. Garman was a squire to the late Sir Bernhard and considers his sons to be like brothers to him. It seems they fought side by side in the war."

"I see. Sometimes, when family ties are not strong, people form substitute bonds," Eden reflected.

"There is something else," admitted Lenora hesitantly. "For some reason the Hainfroys disowned their sister, and that reason is something to do with Garman."

Eden frowned. "Did you think of asking your husband about this?"

"Of course I did," Lenora responded with some exasperation. "I'm not some shrinking maiden, Eden!"

Her cousin looked abashed. "No, of course not," she hurried to assure her. "'Tis only that sometimes the most direct line is the best one to take with men, and yet some women seem to shrink from it entirely."

"Not me," Lenora said firmly. "I asked him outright and he declined to talk about the subject."

Eden looked up sharply. "He refused to tell you what lay between them?"

"He did," Lenora agreed without rancor. "He said he didn't have to explain anything, and then he distracted me by telling me what a virile male he was."

Eden nearly choked on her grape. "Lenora!" she protested with watering eyes.

"What?" Lenora realized that some of the hot red color on Eden's face was not due to her choking fit. "Oh, I didn't mean *that*," she said hastily. "He wasn't trying to seduce me or anything. He meant it quite as a matter of fact. He got quite annoyed when I laughed about it."

Eden's expression turned curious. She looked like she wanted to ask something but couldn't quite bring herself to. "I hate to be indelicate," she said at last, "but is there no one else you could ask about his past association with this Hainfroy woman?"

"I thought of that," Lenora admitted, "but have not yet hit on the right opportunity. I did ask him outright if she had broken his heart and he flatly denied it."

A grape slipped through Eden's fingers. It fell down the gaps between the benches. "You asked him that outright?" she echoed, giving up on her snack.

"Oh yes." Lenora nodded. "With a man like Garman, it is pointless trying to be delicate about things. He does not trouble to soften anything he says, and would not appreciate it from others."

Eden blinked. "Lenora," she said with a spurt of laughter. "It seems to me you are being *extremely* open and frank with Sir Garman!"

"Perhaps," Lenora agreed. "But *he* is not returning the favor! Not in every respect."

Eden frowned. "He ought to take some effort to promote understanding between you. After all, you are his wife. Roland did everything he could to make me feel secure about him in the early days of our marriage."

"Ah, but Roland Vawdrey was already in love with you when he married you," Lenora pointed out. Eden flushed slightly and Lenora marveled at it, when her cousin was expecting her husband's child. "You know he was," she added quietly.

"Yes," Eden murmured, glancing back down at where Roland was trouncing his good friend Sir James Attley. "But are you so sure that Sir Garman does not harbor such feelings for you, cousin?"

"Quite sure!" Lenora spluttered. "Our situation is not at all similar."

Eden looked unsure. "Perhaps," she demurred. "Perhaps not."

"It is absolutely nothing alike!"

"I'm not so sure. There was something about his attitude last night at the banquet. I can't quite put my finger on it, but he seemed…"

"Belligerent?" scoffed Lenora. "Bad-tempered? Put out? He is frequently all three of those things. Ever since I have known him in fact."

"Possessive," said Eden decisively. She nodded. "Yes, decidedly possessive. And extremely jealous over that incident with Sir Lionel, who I must say acted with the greatest impropriety. I am shocked to hear he so far forgot himself." Eden frowned. "I had thought him a superior sort of man. He is a patron of the arts, you know, and sponsored at least two of the poets I espouse."

Lenora grimaced. "Some men act very differently with different groups of people," she said darkly.

"I should think they all do," her cousin said forthrightly, surprising her. "But still, that was an infamous thing for him to

217

have done. I was very disappointed. I must say, your husband had every right to be angry about it, Lenora."

"Er, yes, quite," Lenora agreed, shifting uneasily in her seat. "But we had a heart-to-heart talk about it last night before we fell asleep and that is all resolved between us now."

"Oh good! Well, I am extremely pleased to hear that," Eden said with approval. "That certainly sounds most sensible."

Conversation was broken off for a while as Eden's attention solely focused on Roland, who was going toe-to-toe with the final navy armband, Sir Armand de Bussell. As they watched, de Bussell slipped to one knee and the point of Roland's sword was at his neck.

"Yes!" cried Eden, raising her scarf to her mouth. De Bussell flung down his blade in disgust, yielding to the victor. Roland Vawdrey dragged off his helmet and looked toward the box where Eden blew him a kiss. "He won!" Eden crowed. "I knew he would, of course," she added quickly. "Only sometimes the oddest upsets occur."

"I like it when that happens," Lenora mused. "It gets rather dull when the same person always wins."

Eden looked as if she would argue for a moment, but then let it pass. "What shall we do now?" she asked. "It will take the better part of an hour for Roland to see to his horse and change out of his armor."

"Oh, let us go and watch the jousting," Lenora begged, "for it is my favorite event."

Eden conceded and directed Cuthbert to let her husband know where they had gone. Arm in arm, the two cousins climbed down from their rickety perch and strolled toward the next field which had been set up for the jousting.

Again, Lenora was surprised to see the wooden structures lined up for observing the competitors. Her heart sank a little for they seemed somewhat knocked together and crudely constructed. Still, Eden scaled the steps of a vacant one, so Lenora followed her up. This one seemed a good deal sturdier than the last one, so Lenora took her seat on a bench with a relieved sigh.

Her eyes scanned the field as Eden craned forward to make out the banners.

"'Tis Lord Kentigern," Eden said with a little shiver. "I always find him rather terrifying. He is so powerfully built and that blind staring eye…"

"He is a mighty fighter," Lenora said absently. She could see no sign of a white gate on a black shield. Not that she was looking for Garman Orde. Not at all.

"Oh no!" Eden said with the deepest dismay. "How unfortunate for the very first round." She clicked her tongue.

"What is it?"

"Sir Renlow d'Avenant," Eden said in tragic accents. "What cruel twist of fate would choose to pitch him against the likes of Lord Kentigern?"

Lenora peered down at the two figures. Lord Kentigern was a giant of muscle and sinew with a monstrous horned helmet. His opponent looked to be a much less bulky figure, slim and tall in old-fashioned armor that had seen far better days. His family crest was so worn and faded that Lenora could not even make it out on the threadbare pennant, try as she might.

He had no squire, though someone darted forward to hand up his lance. Lenora blinked. It looked rather like Cuthbert. She darted a glance at Eden. "Is that—?"

"Oh yes," Eden said. "Roland is rather a sponsor of Sir Renlow's, you know. He may not look very imposing," she said defensively, "but Sir Renlow is utterly, utterly fearless. If there is any challenge, he will throw himself into it quite without any regard for his own fate. I believe he either broke a limb or ended up unconscious at every tournament last year, and yet night after night, he turns up to the feasting without fail, good-natured to the last."

"So, he will not regard his first round draw of Lord Kentigern in the light of a misfortune then?" Lenora ventured.

"Oh no! It wouldn't even enter his head," Eden admitted. "He sees every challenge as an opportunity to cover himself in glory."

Lenora blinked. "A very estimable young man."

"Yes," agreed Eden doubtfully. "But I wish he had more care for his person. No one else seems to look out for him," she fretted in what Lenora could only regard as a maternal manner. She eyed Eden with surprise. She could not be much older than this Sir Renlow. As if aware of Lenora's scrutiny, Eden fidgeted in her seat. "There is something rather unworldly about him," she said, looking a bit embarrassed. "I can't help but worry about him sometimes."

"Like a monk, do you mean?" Lenora asked in a puzzled tone, but the thunder of hooves told them the joust had begun, so they both faced forward and braced themselves for the impact.

To her embarrassment, Lenora found herself shutting her eyes at the terrific crash of splintering wood on plate armor. When she peeped back again, broken lances lay on the ground next to the mighty fallen figure of Lord Kentigern, and to her astonishment, Sir Renlow remained sat in his saddle. A deathly hush fell over the stadium as everyone took in this strange turn of events.

Sir Renlow struggled to lift his visor, which was either rusted shut or dented out of shape. In the end, he pulled it off completely, exposing his head of light brown curls. He was just dismounting to utter silence when Cuthbert ran forward and threw a bucket of water over the insensible Lord Kentigern. This broke the spell and the crowd started murmuring and nudging each other.

"He won!" whispered Eden, clutching at Lenora's arm. "He won!"

Lenora could not celebrate the win, however, as her eyes were riveted to the stirring bulk of Lord Kentigern, who was lurching unsteadily to his feet, looking like some kind of grotesque minotaur with his fearsome helmet. "Oh dear," she said under her breath. "Look out!"

But Sir Renlow was oblivious to her warning. He approached Lord Kentigern quite unabashed, wearing a shy smile on his face. *Is he quite mad?* thought Lenora with alarm. The crowd seemingly agreed with her, for a horrified hush had once more fallen over them all like a blanket.

Lord Kentigern reached up and fumbled with his helmet, until his horribly scarred face and beard were revealed. "Boy!" he roared. Then suddenly, they were grasping each other's forearms in a companionable gesture. A ripple of surprised appreciation ran through the crowd.

"Three cheers for Sir Renlow!" shouted someone who sounded rather like her cousin Kit. A clamor of cheers rose up and Lord Kentigern was exchanging words now with the jubilant Sir Renlow, who was beaming from ear to ear.

221

"Well, that is certainly a turnup for the books!" Eden commented, sitting back in her seat. "Who'd have thought Lord Kentigern would be so sportsmanlike. He is usually so taciturn at the celebratory feasts."

"It was certainly not the outcome I was expecting," Lenora admitted.

"Roland will be so sorry to miss Sir Renlow's triumph." Eden frowned, looking around. "Oh dear."

"What is it?"

"Your husband approaches," Eden said with misgiving. "And he does not look happy."

Lenora looked quickly around and saw Garman bearing down on them. Eden was right. He looked angry, dirty, and... Lenora flailed about for the word she was looking for. *Virile,* she thought, as the word flashed into her mind insistently. It was the right word after all. She had no idea why she had found it funny when he said it before.

Distractedly she picked up her alms purse and fanned herself with it. "Have you taken a tumble in the dirt?" she asked as he approached. Perhaps it wasn't the most auspicious greeting. His glower seemed to grow even more pronounced.

"What are you doing over here?" he ground out, flicking a brief glance at her cousin and nodding brusquely. Lenora did not dare look at the proper and correct Eden's face. No doubt she would be stiff with outrage at such an informal greeting. Whatever he had been about to say next died on his lips as he noticed Sir Renlow's arm being raised in victory by none other than Lord Kentigern.

"Well, I'll be damned!"

Lenora heard Eden inhale noisily at the curse.

"My husband has long held that Sir Renlow showed potential for greatness," Eden said loftily. "Despite his frequent losses."

"It's Kentigern's magnanimity that shocked me, not d'Avenant's win," he replied, casting a thoughtful look at the brutish giant who was limping from the arena. "If d'Avenant wasn't so dedicated to fair play then he'd have many more wins under his belt, not just this one." His lip curled. "The boy's an idealist." His scorn for idealism seemed plain.

"How old is he?" Lenora asked, scrutinizing Sir Renlow's boyish good looks again. He looked both youthful and slender compared to Kentigern, but then she thought, most people would. She had an idea that Sir Renlow d'Avenant's appearance was deceptive. He moved with the grace of an athlete and the shoulders under his chain mail shirt were clearly muscled. She suspected if she stood next to him, he would be tall and have muscles enough. In truth, he must have, to have knocked Kentigern from his seat.

"He is some three and twenty years, I believe," Eden answered. "'Tis just his open, friendly manners that make him appear still a lad. That and the fact he is always surrounded by a goodly number of squires, rather than fellow knights."

"And why is that?" Lenora asked curiously.

"Oh," said Eden airily. "He is very patient and kind to them by all accounts. Cuthbert often takes himself off for a lesson from him when Roland is too curt or irritable to go over something again. He's never too busy to help them master some skill they lack."

"So he has no squire of his own?" Lenora asked with interest, watching as Cuthbert, Hal, and her own cousin surged forward to help Sir Renlow gather his lances and battered shield and lead his horse around the competing area to receive his victor's accolades.

"No," said Eden, "for he's as poor as a church mouse. Do you not see how battered and rusty his armor is? All castoffs. The d'Avenants are not wealthy, and he is but a third son. When he is captured in the melee, Roland often pays his ransom out of good will."

"That is good of him," Lenora commented, avoiding Garman's eye.

"Indeed, Roland will be sorry to have missed his triumph," Eden said, raising her hands to clap for Sir Renlow when he drew near to their box. Lenora joined her and out of the corner of her eye, she saw Garman nod to him. Sir Renlow grinned back, flushed and happy. Really, if his nose had not been broken at some point, he would almost be too pretty with those features, she thought, and that curling nut-brown hair.

"It seems the other knights accord him respect," Lenora mused and heard Garman snort derisively.

"He's a fool," her husband said curtly, "who believes in knightly virtues culled from storybooks."

Lenora remembered Berta's sour words about quarrelsome knights and the trouble they brought to the streets of Aphrany. "He must know," she said with a frown, "that none of you embody those virtues."

"Oh yes," Eden broke in. "I asked him about that once. He said he does not model himself on what a knight *is*, but what a knight *should* be. He is a most remarkable young man."

Garman looked skeptical. "And what did Vawdrey say to that?" he asked mockingly, looking her cousin straight in the eye.

Eden colored slightly. "He admits it a rather unrealistic endeavor," she admitted stiffly. "But he does not jeer at Sir Renlow's lofty ambitions."

"In your presence, he doesn't," Garman added dryly.

"I have often observed with my own eyes," Eden responded, lifting her chin, "that my husband does not profit by the hostage taking during the melee, or foul play. Unlike *some* of your fellow knights."

There could be no doubt from her pointed tone that she included Garman in this number, Lenora reflected, as he laughed.

"Vawdrey's one of the dirtiest fighters on the circuit!"

"He is not!" Eden gasped. "How dare you try to besmirch my husband's name!"

Lenora opened her mouth to intercede, but a deep voice interrupted them as Roland Vawdrey strode into the box.

"What's this?" he asked, making straight for Eden and pulling her into his arms. Lenora noticed with interest that her prickly cousin made no protest, but even tipped her face up to accept his kiss and cling obligingly to his tunic. "If you mean to tear down my reputation, you'll never manage it in my wife's presence," he added with a lingering smile, his eyes still on her. "She won't hear a word against me."

"Your wife was just informing us you're a staunch supporter of d'Avenant's pure vision of knighthood," Garman said derisively.

Roland's eyebrows snapped together, and he darted a startled glance at his longtime foe before returning his gaze to his wife, where it softened. "Oh well," he said lightly. "He's a good fellow, Renlow. Heart of a lion."

"Head in the clouds," Garman snapped.

Roland's lips screwed up in what Lenora strongly suspected was an effort not to agree. "His notions are sound at heart," he said, sounding hard-pressed.

"He's deluded."

"He has just won the joust," Lenora pointed out.

"He's merely ascended to the next round," Garman replied dampeningly. "Where he'll very likely go crashing out to de Crecy."

"He'll likely win the medal for most valiant at tonight's feast," Eden asserted with spirit.

"Oh aye, very likely," Garman agreed. "A piece of tin you can't even melt down and no accompanying purse. A hollow victory."

"Not to one whose head is in the clouds," Lenora found herself arguing. "One such as he will be trailing clouds of glory for a sennight."

Garman's head turned sharply to look at her and he scowled.

Roland laughed at this. "Very likely," he agreed. "That does sound rather like Renlow."

Lenora rose from her seat. "Should we head back to the tent?" she asked her husband, conscious he had come looking for her. "You will likely want to wash and change," she added for Eden's benefit, as her cousin had seemed startled by her words.

"You do not wish to remain here with us and watch the rest of the day's jousting?" Eden asked her with a frown. Lenora shook her head. "But it's your favorite event," her cousin persisted. Roland slid onto the bench next to his wife and murmured

226

something in her ear. Eden looked from Lenora to Garman and then back again. "Oh," she said. "Well, but won't you both return here after your ablutions? Sir Garman," she said with a regal inclination of her head. "'Twould be pleasant to become acquainted now we are to be family."

Lenora could see Garman was surprised by the invitation. "Should you like that?" he asked Lenora, not quite meeting her gaze.

"It would be nice, but we could always meet up at supper," Lenora assured him. "You could take your ease if you are tired, or we could go and watch the Challenge to Arms if you'd prefer."

"At supper, then," Roland interrupted. "That seems a good notion, what say you, Orde?"

Garman agreed, looking rather guarded. Lenora smiled at her cousin, who was still a little put out that they were to be parted already.

"I won't get up and bow," Roland said. "As we are all family here."

Lenora rose and crossed to Garman's side. He preceded her down the steps and held out a hand to steady her when she followed. As they crossed the field, he drew her hand firmly through his arm. "What a shame you have no squire to help ready your bathing water and lay out your apparel." He shot her a quizzical look, but made no reply. "You must admit one would be useful. Have you never had your own?"

"No," he replied shortly. "I do not have the patience. I leave that sort of thing to good-natured dolts like d'Avenant."

"Is he a good-natured dolt?" Lenora asked doubtfully.

227

"You seem strangely fascinated by him," he said, tension running through his words.

"Do I?" Lenora pondered this. "Mayhap because I have never before seen one such as he."

"Maybe you should have approached him with your offer," Garman said, his words completely devoid of expression.

"Approached him?" Lenora repeated. "Oh, I see. You mean for marriage." She felt her cheeks redden. "How very ungallant of you to say so."

"I'm not gallant. But then, that is why you picked me, is it not?"

Lenora bit her lip. "Are you saying that you wish I had picked another?" she asked with a definite edge to her voice.

"It seems odd you were forced to settle for me, when you still had the likes of Emworth panting after you."

Why did he sound so bitter about it? Lenora wondered. Maybe he wished she had approached Emworth. For some reason, that thought made her feel suddenly rather cold. "I explained that whole incident," Lenora reminded him. "He was not trying to run away with me."

"No, he was just trying to get his filthy hands on my property."

Lenora flushed. *Property?* "Actually, my grandmother's solution to me losing my looks was for me to wed Sir Lionel," she admitted. "But I dismissed that out of hand."

"Why?" He bit the word out as they approached the field of pavilions now, Garman practically towing her in his wake.

"We've already had this discussion," Lenora reminded him breathlessly in her effort to keep up.

"Pity does not inspire lust in a man, Lenora."

"Pardon?" *Lust?*

"Pity was far from what he was feeling for you."

She took a deep breath. "I don't care what his feelings were," Lenora said frankly. "And I never did."

He gave a short laugh at that. "Frank to a fault, aren't you?"

Was she? He practically thrust her into their tent before him. "I don't want there to be any misunderstandings between us," she said as he followed her inside, whipping his chain mail shirt over his head. Lenora's gaze skittered over his heavily muscled torso.

"Don't look at me like that," he said thickly. "Unless you want to be flat on your back."

She caught her breath. "Maybe I do want that," she shocked even herself by saying aloud.

He paused a moment in the act of unbuckling his belt. Lenora could see he was breathing hard. When he spoke it was in a low, steady voice. "I'm covered in dirt."

"Yes, I know. It seems seeing you like that inspires lust in me."

The belt slid between his fingers, and his sword clattered to the floor.

Both turned their heads sharply as they heard footsteps scuffling at the entrance to their tent. "I've brought washing water for you, sir."

To Lenora's mortification she recognized her cousin's voice and quickly retreated to the far side of the pavilion, hoping profoundly he had not heard her.

Garman cleared his throat. "Enter."

Kit ducked in the tent carrying a large jug of steaming water. Lenora wondered if Cuthbert had put the idea into his head. Considering he was hardly known for his humility, he carried the hot water over to the table as meek as a lamb.

"Good of you," Garman grunted.

Kit nodded, picked up the sword belt from the floor, and sat down on the spare bed. He looked over at Lenora. "Had a good morning?" he asked, seemingly oblivious to the underlying tension.

"Er, yes," she said feebly, and made her way over to a chair to collapse in.

"You'll never guess at the upset in the jousting this morning," he carried on with relish.

"She doesn't need to guess," Garman interrupted harshly as he poured water into the bowl.

"I watched the first joust with Eden," Lenora explained.

Kit winced. "Did she ring a peal over your head for eloping?"

"You forget we are the same age." Lenora frowned. "And raised as sisters."

"She could lecture a bishop, that one," Kit snorted.

Lenora opened her mouth to remonstrate with him as she heard Garman's muffled laugh. A quick glance showed her his head was covered in a washcloth. "Eden is—"

"Yes, yes," cut in Kit hurriedly. "Don't you start. I know you are both thick as thieves."

"Then don't say something to provoke my wrath," Lenora replied smartly. "I won't have Eden bad-mouthed in my presence."

"Lord," muttered Kit under his breath.

"And anyway, she did not even attempt to reproach me. She only wanted to assure herself that all is well with me." She felt Garman's eyes on her but did not look his way again. "How have you spent your morning, cousin?" she asked. "Presumably you have only yourself to please now you are master-less."

Kit's eyes traveled over to where Garman was now rubbing a drying cloth over his head. "I tagged along with Payne to the joust," he murmured.

"Which knight does your friend serve?" she asked with interest.

"Sir James Attley. He had a second round draw."

Lenora nodded. She knew Sir James to be a crony of Roland Vawdrey. "I see."

"My father will probably approach some other second-rate knight now Emworth's out of the picture," he said, gloomily plucking at a blanket. "He doesn't have any decent acquaintance to ask. Emworth only took me because of my kinship to you."

"How about my husband?" Lenora asked.

Kit's head whipped around to look at her. "Do you suppose—?"

"Why don't we ask him?" Lenora looked toward Garman, who was lowering his cloth with a sardonic gleam in his eye.

"You wouldn't enjoy serving me," he said shortly.

Kit shrugged. "I know a lot of squires," he said. "And none of them talk of enjoyment when it comes to serving."

Garman seemed to consider this. "How long did you serve Emworth? I'd have to waste my time unteaching everything he saw fit to impart before we even began your training."

"As to that, you needn't worry," Kit assured him blithely. "For I never listened to a thing he said." Lenora shut her eyes a moment. "Man was a damned fool."

"True enough," Garman agreed. "But if you fall afoul of me, you'll know it."

"Aye," Kit said, nodding. "I'd guessed as much."

Garman cast the damp cloth over a chair back and picked up a clean tunic. "What of your father?" he asked.

"Oh, Father said he would wash his hands of me if Emworth cast me off," said Kit cheerfully. "He said I would have to speak to Uncle Leofric to get a new sponsor, as informally I'm his heir, or will be eventually. My father is only thirteen months younger than my uncle and their younger brother died years ago."

"Then it is perfectly natural that my husband should take you on now," Lenora said with composure. "I don't imagine Father knows any knight more appropriate."

Garman grunted and Kit sprang up from the bunk. "Then it's settled!" he enthused. "I'm most awfully grateful to you Sir Garman, cousin," he said, nodding to Lenora and taking a step toward the opening.

"Where do you think you're going?" asked Garman, eyebrows raised. "I did not dismiss you."

Kit paused. "I was going to join my friends at the tilting field," he said slowly.

"You will go down to the stables and become acquainted with my horse, Bria'ag," said Garman coolly. "If after an hour in his company you still want to be my squire, then so be it."

Kit looked a little taken aback. "Am I to groom him, then?"

"If he'll allow it," Garman said, sounding as though he thought it highly unlikely.

Kit nodded again, drew himself up straight, a look of steely determination on his face as he exited the tent, rolling up his sleeves.

"Is Bria'ag so very fierce?" Lenora asked as Garman crossed to the tent flap and secured the ties.

"Get on the bed," he said, ignoring her question. Lenora blinked as he turned and drew his tunic back up over his head so he was bare-chested again. When he took two steps toward her, Lenora started out of her seat and found herself spun around and her lacings yanked this way and that.

"Why are we undressing?" she asked.

"Take off your headdress and those damned veils," he told her precipitately.

They hadn't been covering her face since the joust, but she drew the pins out and removed her toque as Garman was easing her bodice open. At his promptings, she held her arms up and he drew it over her head so she stood in just her shift and stockings.

"That's better. Now up on the bed."

Lenora cast a doubtful look at the fastened entrance. "Won't everyone be expecting us?" she asked, biting her lip.

"You think I'm the only knight seeking pleasure between a woman's thighs right now?" he asked coolly. "Besides, you told me this was what you wanted, remember?"

Lenora swallowed. "Yes, but—"

"We won't go all the way. Trust me." At that, she relaxed and walked over to the bed with a readiness that clearly surprised him as well as her. It seemed she did trust him, she realized. *Well, wasn't that a turnup for the books.*

He followed close behind her as she climbed onto the bed, and no sooner had she stretched out on the mattress than he was on top of her, covering her with his much larger body.

"Aren't you cold?" she asked wonderingly as she ran her hands over the bunched, hard muscle of his shoulders. "Should we get under the covers?"

"No." He paused. "I want to see what I'm doing this time." He stopped and frowned down at her.

"What is it?"

"Nothing," he answered, but still stared.

When she saw his eyes fixed on her face, she braced a hand to his chest and turned stiff as a board. "What is it?" she asked again with dread, catching her breath. Now was not the time for him to notice her ruined face.

"I'm thinking about kissing you," he said gruffly.

"Oh!" Lenora had no sooner wondered why he looked so sheepish about the fact than he was lowering his mouth to hers. She had almost forgotten the hot, wet slide of his rapacious kiss.

Perhaps he should look embarrassed about the fact he wished to mate his mouth to hers like that in broad daylight!

He tore his mouth from hers. "Am I to instruct you every step this time, or do you remember anything?" he asked, his hand yanking her shift down to expose her breasts.

"I'm not your squire!" Lenora retorted hotly. "Really, you have no manners!"

"No, I don't," he agreed. "Now answer my question."

"I remember what you did to me last time."

"Good, now tell me which parts you liked."

Lenora's head spun. "I—I liked your kiss," she admitted.

"Why?" *Why?* Seemingly, her bewilderment was plain. "Why do you like my kiss, when you hated all others?" he demanded, eyes glinting behind lowered lids.

"I have no idea," she said truthfully. "Save that no one ever dared kiss me as you do."

"Show me how they kissed you."

Odd how that embarrassed her when his hand was kneading her naked bosom like it was his perfect right. Huffing out a breath, Lenora reached for his other hand which was tangled in her hair. She brought it to her lips. When she pressed a chaste kiss to his fingers, he went still.

"That's it?"

"Yes," she whispered, unable to meet his eyes. "No wait." She turned his hand over and pressed a lingering kiss to his palm.

"Who the fuck kissed you like that?" he snapped out.

"Sir Symond de Chevenix," she admitted. "But after he did it, I told my father not to admit him again."

"You didn't like it?"

She shook her head and felt him relax. "Though maybe I would, if it was you."

"I never kissed anyone like that," he admitted. "Never wanted to."

"Oh."

"Now kiss me as I kiss you," he said arrogantly and lifted off her, rolling onto his back.

Lenora shivered, finding herself suddenly lying atop the covers in her thin shift. She rolled onto her side so she was pressed against him. How was she supposed to cage him in like he did to her? she wondered. She was not half his size! Reaching around him, she flung her leg over and scrambled atop him in a most unladylike fashion. "I can't really do it the same way," she said unevenly. "For you do not precisely lie atop me like this…"

He made no answer, and when she forced herself to look him full in the face, his expression was shuttered. Inching forward, she found the best way was to brace her knees on either side of his waist and to clap her hands to his face and hold it still as she lowered her lips to his. He went very still when she opened her mouth on his, and for a moment, she thought he wasn't going to participate at all.

Then suddenly, he yielded and she surged forward, sliding her tongue against his. He gave a muffled oath, and Lenora found herself caught up against him by arms as yielding as steel bands. One hand slid under her shift and gripped her backside hard. She winced faintly, feeling the bruise beneath the crush of

236

his fingers. Then she was distracted by the feel of his short hair beneath her fingers as she realized hers were now running through his hair. Had he done that to her? She rather thought this was her own idea.

She rubbed herself against his bare chest and panted against his mouth. "Garman."

"What?" His voice was husky.

"We have to stop kissing now."

"What? Why?" He did not sound pleased.

"You didn't kiss me any longer than this."

"Then I'm a fool," he groaned.

She inched down and he grunted, shifting against her. Lenora hesitated. This was definitely different. She could feel his swollen hardness beneath his muscular belly. "I need to kiss your chest," she pointed out.

"What?"

"You kissed mine next."

He breathed out. "I'm not bothered about that. Just pull down your shift."

She adjusted the neckline of her shift until her breasts were bared and then pressed forward until they brushed against his chest. His chest hair was sparse—though what there was dark gold and patterned in swirls. She ran a hand over his small flat nipples and heard him give a breathless laugh. "Does it not feel good to be touched here?" she asked curiously.

"Not particularly. I'd rather suck yours."

She drew in a breath. "Oh."

"Why don't you feed them to me?" Lenora's wide eyes made him smirk. "I'd enjoy that far more."

She felt her face flame. "Are you in earnest?"

"Deadly, I assure you."

Hesitantly, she eased up his body again, his hands at her waist, urging her up. Cupping one breast, she brought her nipple to his mouth and gasped when his lips fastened there. If his hands were not supporting her, she thought her shaky arms and legs would have given out as she'd hovered over him, biting her lip to stave off her moans.

"Other breast," he prompted her. She hurried to comply. Only one hand was at her waist now, she realized when the other slid between her legs, rubbing her slickness there. "So wet," he whispered. "I want to put my mouth here, Lenora. Will you let me?"

"There?" She stared. "Your mouth?"

He nodded. "Oh yes."

"Why?"

"I want to taste it."

Lenora shuddered. "I don't know."

"Trust me." Again, his words made her feel calmer. She *did* trust him, but his request was so strange. Again, his hands at her waist compelled her. "I need you to turn around."

"Turn around?" Lenora's voice was little more than a squeak.

"You face the foot of the bed," he said.

"I don't know about this."

"I do," he said firmly and rose up on his elbows. "Get on your hands and knees."

Lenora found herself scooting around, her face scarlet when she thought about the view he must be getting. "Garman?"

"Shhh, sweetheart," he soothed her, lifting her shift up to her middle back, his hands squeezing her plump buttocks. "Gods, Lenora," he said thickly. "You have the most beautiful ass in all Karadok."

Lenora's eyes opened wide. Well, that was a compliment she had never received before! She clutched at the blankets as she felt his breath warm on her thighs. "I need you to move back, just a bit."

With a moan of mortification, she closed her eyes and shuffled back. He was asking her to open her legs right over his face, she thought with vague horror. How was she even able to comply with such wishes? She could not believe this was a reasonable request for a husband to make of a wife.

Then the first lap of his tongue through her folds made her thoughts scatter. The second made her catch her breath. The third had her biting on her lip. Then he started alternating between long leisurely swipes of his tongue and short stabbing darts which found that concealed spot again that made her whole body jolt with pleasure. "Oh!"

"Lenora," he said sternly. "If you can't keep quiet, I'll have to stop. And I don't want to stop."

"I don't know if I can," she admitted shakily.

"Let's try. I have every faith in you."

She fell forward onto her elbows, covering her mouth with her hands. Garman gave a growl of approval at the change of angle and set his mouth on her again, his hands, which had been lightly caressing her buttocks, now grabbed a firm hold of them.

What if someone walked into their tent and were to see her hovering over his face like this? she thought with a sort of horror. Spreading herself out for him like this and upside down? Her face flamed even hotter at the thought.

This must be some form of obscure torture, she thought distractedly as she concentrated very, very hard not to yell out, moan, or even worse, plead with him as he lapped and groaned against her most secretly feminine place. She felt herself wet, not just from his tongue, but like before, when he had said her body was making itself ready for his, and his tongue was seeking out every last drop of it.

"Wh-why are you allowed to make noise and I'm not?" she demanded in a strangled voice. "It hardly seems fair—oh!" She was forced to bite into her one hand to muffle a cry. One of his hands had released her long enough to deliver a stinging slap to her rounded backside. Her eyes smarted, but for some reason, the pleasure did not even falter. It twisted higher inside her still, a tighter spiral coiling like a spring, and she realized she was now shamelessly rocking herself against his mouth like a wild creature and clawing at the bedsheets. When she tried to stop, his large hands spread out across the backs of her thighs and dragged her back onto his mouth as he drove his tongue right into her, making her twist and writhe against him in pleasure. "Ohhh!"

Instead of pulling back to caution her to silence, he groaned deeply against her, the noise vibrating all the way through where she ached and fluttered. She trembled, her thighs shook, then one of his hands delved between her legs, spreading her folds and a big finger slid right into her aching depths while the roughed pad of his thumb found that magic spot and rubbed

240

against her. The whole world shuddered, and with a muffled scream, Lenora collapsed face-first on top of him.

*

When Lenora's eyes next flickered open, she fancied it was some couple of hours later. To her surprise, Garman was still stretched out on the bed beside her, his hands folded behind his head. "Have you been asleep?" she asked slightly self-consciously. She couldn't believe she had rolled over and slumbered so easily after all that had passed between them. Yet it had been easier than falling off a log.

"No," he answered.

"Tired after your event?" she asked with a yawn. He had certainly tired her out!

"No."

She turned her head to look at him. For a moment, her heart plummeted to her stockinged feet. Was she about to get the stony treatment she had received last time they had become intimate? But his expression wasn't irritable or closed off this time. He turned his face to meet her gaze squarely and seemed quite content to lie there beside her, their bodies touching, the atmosphere companionable.

"Waiting for me to wake?" she ventured, realizing he must have righted her clothes and set her the correct way up in the bed. She must have been out cold! He had washed and changed his tunic, she realized, and she had slept through all of it! She should probably feel more embarrassed about that, but she felt so very relaxed and well rested that she could not quite bring herself to.

"I thought you might like to go and watch something." He colored slightly and turned away.

Lenora found her breath coming rather fast. "Indeed, I would," she said with a faint smile. "Thank you for waiting." He shrugged again. She guessed he had not much practice being friendly. For some reason, that thought both warmed and encouraged her. "What shall we watch?"

"As you've seen the melee and the joust, I thought we'd watch the bohort."

She wondered if a reluctance to join Eden and Sir Roland for the afternoon prompted his choice. "I don't think I've ever...?"

"They don't have them at royal tournaments. They're usually hashed together by participants rather than the host."

"Well, then that sounds a very good notion." Neither of them made a move. After a moment, she asked: "Did Kit return?"

"No."

"Do you think Bria'ag will have made a minced meat out of him?"

A smile tugged at his lips. "We shall see how strong his resolve is to serve as my squire."

"He may surprise you."

"He already has," Garman admitted.

"How so?"

He turned his head to look at her. "Attacking Emworth," he said after a moment. "That took guts."

"Personally, I think he was only waiting for an excuse."

Again, Garman gave that glimmer of a half smile. She had the strangest impulse to put a finger to the corner of his upturned lips, but knew well that any physical contact between them was limited to a very precise set of circumstances. With a pang, she remembered the way Roland Vawdrey could not seem to keep his hands from Eden whatever their location.

"What?" he asked with a frown.

"Are we growing closer?" she asked on impulse. "I think we are, but I don't want to make a fool of myself."

His frown grew deeper. "What do you mean?"

Lenora tried to marshal her thoughts. "It's hard to explain. If I were to reach for your arm in public for instance. Would you push me away?"

He looked vaguely insulted. "Of course not."

"What if the Hainfroys were there?"

"The Hainfroys? They wouldn't bat an eyelid."

Remembering how the Hainfroys had stared at their every interaction, she found she did not entirely believe him. "Perhaps not to find a wench sat on your lap, but to find a wife…" She trailed off.

"You seem to have some strange notion about the Hainfroys," he said dismissively, but she still did not think he would ever show much affection in public. Some people weren't built that way. With surprise she remembered she had always thought as much about herself.

"I think the Hainfroys are the closest thing you have to a family," she said aloud.

His eyes darted to hers again. He did not speak for a full minute, but when he did, Lenora sat up and paid notice. "My old master, Sir Bernhard, wanted me to marry his daughter, Isabeau Hainfroy," he said tonelessly. "He had us promise him

243

on his deathbed that we would honor his wish." Lenora's eyes grew wide. "Then, she did not wait until he was cold in his grave before running off with a traveling musician called Justin Lind."

Lenora's lips parted into a soundless *oh*. "So that's why her brothers disowned her?" He nodded his head once. "Yet, you say she did not break your heart?" she asked.

He pursed his lips and shook his head. "Nor her father's either, for he was dead and buried."

"You must have felt the snub at the time though?" she said with some sympathy.

He cocked his head as if considering this. "Lind had a bare chin and curling golden hair," he said derisively. "Of course I felt the snub. It was a damned insult to be thrown over for the likes of him."

Lenora gave a gurgle of laughter. "I expect he was the very antithesis of you and the Hainfroy males. Poor Isabeau was very likely sick to death of great rollicking brutes of men."

That did make him smile faintly. Was it just Lenora's imagination or was he doing that more lately? "Very likely," he agreed.

"I daresay he had a pure singing voice," Lenora pondered. "And very likely played the lute like an angel." Garman looked disgusted, so she carried on swiftly. "If you'd lived at the Grange from the age of twelve, Isabeau probably saw you as a third brother, as Huw and Ivo do." His gaze flickered to her at that and he shrugged. "You disagree?"

"I've never really given it much thought."

244

"Did your grandfather Sutton wish you and Isabeau Hainfroy to make a match of it?" she asked, the thought suddenly occurring to her.

He snorted. "I have no idea. I doubt he even knew that was in the wind." He hesitated. "I am not close to my grandfather. To either of my grandfathers," he added, then quickly said, "I never speak of the other one."

"I did not know you had more than one."

"There's a reason for that, Lenora," he said grimly.

"I see. Well, on the subject of relations, if you do end up taking Kit for a squire," Lenora said, "I feel beholden to tell you that his father, my uncle Christopher, is frankly quite dreadful. He is easily the worst of us Montmaynes. It would be extremely difficult if we should have to put up with him darkening our doorstep to rant at us about Kit."

"I wouldn't find it awkward."

Lenora looked at him. "How so? You mean you would slam the door in his face?" she said shrewdly.

He nodded with a grim smile. "Would that bother you?"

Lenora thought about it. "Actually, no. And I don't believe Kit would mind it either."

"Then it's not a problem, is it?"

"Your grandfather Sutton would likely find it excessively awkward," she admitted with a grimace. "He seems to me a very proper and polite man."

"I don't plan on us always living with him at Matchings Farm," Garman said, and Lenora's ears pricked up.

"You do not say *on his always living with us at Matchings Farm*," she said slowly. "Yet your grandfather seems at great pains to point out that the place is yours."

"I'm no farmer," said Garman. "I have no interest."

"Even though your father had the place built?"

"Even so."

"Where do you see us living, then?" asked Lenora, turning back toward him. She felt a prickle of unease. "Is it dependent on receiving my dowry?"

"No," he said shortly. "For in a twelvemonth or so I shall have coin enough to buy it. Anyway, at present it is occupied."

"Where is it?"

"Not far from the farm," he said cautiously. "It's a small estate nearby called Matchings Halt."

"Who lives there currently?"

"A widow and her in-laws. I have reason to believe the head of their family changes soon and the new head will sell."

"He will sell it from under the widow?" Lenora asked in alarm.

"That is no business of ours," he said, rising from the bed and putting a hand out toward her.

Lenora put her hand in his and allowed him to pull her up from the bed. His words troubled her, and not just the part about the widow. What if her father could not be persuaded to part with her dowry? Despite his assurance, he would doubtless need it if he was looking to buy his own estate. They walked across the field arm in arm, and Lenora was only pulled out of her worrisome thoughts when Kit waylaid them.

"I saw to the horse," he said belligerently.

"Did you?" Garman came to a halt.

"Aye," said Kit. "Though you might have warned me it was some kind of test."

"Forewarned is forearmed. Wouldn't have been much of a test, then, would it?"

Kit huffed. Lenora noticed his hose was muddied up to the knee and guessed Bria'ag must have given him some trouble. Still, his expression brightened now. "So it's a done deal?" he asked.

"Depending on your father's permission."

"Oh, that," said Kit airily. "I can get that alright. I'll just have to spend a few days with him to remind him how very ill we get along. He'll be champing at the bit to get rid of me within a sennight. You'll see."

"You will have to return to Caer-Lyoness then?" Lenora asked.

"Nay, I'll be bound for Hallam," he said, naming the ancestral home of the Montmaynes. "Father hasn't been to court in two months. Reckons his old trouble is playing him up."

Lenora nodded, remembering how her uncle suffered from a painful swelling of his feet. "I will write to you at Hallam, then," she said brightly. "Giving you our direction."

Kit nodded. "I shan't leave until after the final day tomorrow," he pointed out. "There's no hurry that I know of." He glanced furtively at Garman, who made no response. "Perhaps I could attend to you on the morrow when you joust?"

Lenora glanced up at her husband, who gave a brief nod. So...he jousted on the morrow.

"Aye," he agreed. "We'll see how you go."

Kit caught sight of someone over Lenora's shoulder and gave a start. "There's Ames," he said quickly. "I've something I need to give him. I'll look for you later."

He started off and Lenora turned to watch him run over and smote Cuthbert on the shoulder. For some reason it crossed her mind that the blond youth might have aided Kit with handling Bria'ag though she could not have said precisely why the suspicion crossed her mind. The two boys fell in step with each other and made their way over to a brightly painted stall where their stout friend Hal Payne could be seen in animated conversation with the younger of Sir Roger's two illegitimate sons. The four of them hailed one another enthusiastically, Kit grabbing Hal Payne in a headlock and forcing him to drop his pastry and yell till his face turned puce.

"Boys are so rough," Lenora tutted. "I must say, these squires seem to have rather more free time than I would have anticipated."

His mouth twisted into a grim smile, but he said nothing. Garman was definitely a man of fewer words than she was used to, but she wouldn't say he hoarded them like a miser. If he had something to say, he said it. If he did not, then he did not mouth empty platitudes. She fancied she was getting rather used to it.

Lenora spent a pleasant afternoon. The bohort was quite easily the least formal event she had ever watched at a tourney. The first part seemed to be an exercise on which knight could throw a lance the furthest. The second round was the same again, but this time with the squires. The most impressive advanced to the next round by turn until their numbers were whittled down to a final few.

"I've never seen the squires compete before," she exclaimed with surprise.

Garman was largely silent, and she found his eyes on her as much as the competition, a fact which he did not seem embarrassed by. It was only halfway through proceedings that she realized she had completely forgotten to don her head veils before leaving the tent.

Garman was leaning back against a wooden railing and watched her distractedly pat her head and glance about. "You didn't put them on again after we climbed out of bed," he said, deducing the source of her agitation. She gave an exclamation of annoyance. "It little signifies, Lenora."

"Only unmarried women wear their heads bare," she pointed out a little tartly.

"No one is likely to forget you're married when I'm right here at your side." Lenora looked up at him. *Well, that was true enough. You could hardly miss him.* "I'll remind you next time," he said and turned back to the action on the field.

Sir Ned Bevan, another close friend of Roland's, emerged the eventual victor of the knights. Lenora clapped enthusiastically with the crowd as Sir Ned bowed, holding his shield aloft. "A worthy winner," she murmured and saw Garman's glower. "You do not care for Sir Edward?"

"I know no ill of him, save that he's a strong competitor and not to be taken lightly."

"Some would call that high praise," Lenora remarked as she rose from the bench. He frowned but did not argue the point.

"You must have had friends among your fellow squires when you were Kit's age," she remarked as the squires once more took to the field with the final five. Cuthbert Ames was one of

249

their number and easily took the prize with his rather unorthodox technique of a run up comprising of five steps of varying length.

"I did. The Hainfroys."

Oh. Of course. Except, they would not have been traveling to and from tournaments with Sir Bernhard, but rather battlefields.

"What manner of master was Sir Bernhard?" she asked impulsively.

"The best. Hard but fair."

"I see." She felt a sudden conviction Garman would take his old master's tone with her cousin and fell silent as she noticed some nudging and murmuring had broken out among the squires' ranks. It quickly progressed to flying fists and Lenora was dismayed to see Kit and Hal Payne in the thick of it as fighting broke out. "Whatever is going on?" she blurted. "Why does someone not stop it?"

"Likely someone said something about their friend's win," Garman said mildly. "I do not think your cousin will accept a slight about anyone he deems of his circle."

"He's too hotheaded by far!" Lenora fretted. "Why do the knights not stop it?" she asked, getting to her feet. To her consternation it seemed to her a good number of the knights were cheering the boys on.

Garman's hand at her shoulder prevented her from moving forward. "Stay here!" he said, striding forward into the fray. Lenora watched him roughly shove Hal and a large curly-headed lad apart, then grab Kit firmly by the scruff of his neck and drag him from a scuffle with what looked like a pair of ferocious-looking twins.

Lenora glared at the knights who were booing to see the sport broken up too soon.

"For shame, Orde!" bellowed one such knight who Lenora vaguely recognized as of impeccable reputation. Garman ignored him, dragging both boys over to the side. "Spoilsport!"

"Kit!" Lenora hurried down the steps. "Why are you marring Cuthbert's win with such behavior?"

"You don't understand," her cousin muttered angrily, though his gaze dropped from hers.

"They call Ames 'witch's brat,'" Hal Payne explained in a hoarse voice, his face scarlet with fury. "And say he uses sorcery to win when he beats them."

"What nonsense!" Lenora said bracingly and ignored the rude gesture Kit gave to someone over her shoulder. "You should rise above such things. Is that not so?" she addressed Garman.

He gave her a level look. "I would not let such a thing pass," he admitted before looking away.

"Oh." She covered her confusion by reaching for a handkerchief for Hal's bloodied nose. At this point, Cuthbert came sauntering over. He looked none too concerned to find Kit with a swollen eye and Hal's nose spurting, which made Lenora wonder if this might not be a regular occurrence.

"My best win by a long shot," he said with a grin. Kit ruffled his hair and Hal slung an arm around his shoulders. "I'll treat you with my winnings," Cuthbert said, holding up a bulging leather purse with a triumphant flourish.

The five of them made their way back through the field of stalls, and Lenora found she and Garman were included when Cuthbert bade them pick out some treats. Lenora selected a marzipan cake and a jelly, flavored with violets. She thought Garman would refuse the offer, but in the end he chose gingerbread, and Hal and Kit picked so many things Lenora wondered if they would spend all of Cuthbert's winnings. He seemed cheerful enough as he handed over his coins.

"What are you boys doing now?" Lenora asked and all three of them immediately looked evasive. "Not fighting?" she asked with misgiving.

"Oh no," Cuthbert assured her. "Though I mean to relieve Harlow of his purse before the evening's over."

"Dice cup," Hal explained when Lenora looked alarmed.

"Which one was Harlow?" asked Garman with grudging interest.

"Colin Harlow, the large braggart with the loud voice," Kit answered darkly.

"Small piggy eyes," put in Hal. When Lenora still looked unsure, he added cheerfully, "The one I was fighting while Kit took on the Carleton twins."

The boys took their leave of them at the edge of the field, giving Lenora many assurances that they would not get into any brawls.

"I'm not sure I wholly believe them," Lenora said as they crossed into the next field.

"You're learning," Garman replied with the ghost of a smile. "There will be mischief, but I doubt they'll come to much harm."

"What about young Harlow?"

"Penniless by morn. Young Ames seems to have a far more practical idea of revenge than mere fisticuffs."

"How wicked of those boys to raise his parentage against Cuthbert."

"Is he a witch's brat, then?" Garman asked without much interest.

"So I believe. He has the second sight."

Garman grunted. "He has connections to a powerful family at court. I doubt anyone would seriously challenge him."

"He seems a most resourceful boy, and not at all cowed," Lenora agreed. "I will have to ask Eden about his precise connection to the Vawdreys." Garman shot a keen look at her. "What did I say?"

"Have you always been so interested in the lives of others?" he asked with a frown.

Lenora's step faltered. "Not really," she admitted. "In fact, one time, someone counselled me I should take more of an interest in my fellow mankind."

He gave a snort. "You could hardly be more invested!"

"In truth, it seems to come quite naturally to me now. Perhaps since my illness passed," she mused. "If you're jousting on the morrow, are you thinking to take supper up at the manor house this evening?" she asked as they approached their pavilion.

"Did you want to?" he asked as he held the tent open for her.

"Not particularly," she admitted.

"Then let's turn in early."

She felt relieved to be avoiding another evening up at Kellingford Manor, for all Sir Roger was so genial.

They spent a quiet evening in the tent. Garman set about polishing his armor and Lenora finished off both his gingerbread and her violet jelly. It seemed he was not a fan of sweet-tasting things, and Lenora felt touched that he had not wanted to rebuff Cuthbert's friendly gesture. She had just washed and changed for bed when a page from the manor delivered a purse and a silver bowl for Garman which was apparently his prize from the Challenge to Arms.

"You won!" she said accusingly. "Why did you not say?"

He shrugged and set the cup down next to the remains of their supper. "You seemed determined to believe I had lost."

"I would not have suggested we skipped the evening feast up at the house if I had known you were to receive a prize," she lamented.

"It little matters."

She frowned slightly, remembering Eden's words. "Do you really care so little for your audience?"

He set down his gleaming breastplate. "I've never cared for the opinion of the crowd."

"What about me?"

He looked startled and uncertain how to answer her for a moment. Then he spat on his breastplate and gave it a vigorous polish. "It makes no difference to me either way."

Lenora eyed him uncertainly, but found she didn't wholly believe him. Eden had thought him angry that morning and he had definitely seemed put out that she had sat watching Roland

Vawdrey's event rather than his own. "I shall watch you on the morrow," she said suddenly.

"I told you it makes no odds to me."

"I'm watching you because I want to," she insisted, "not because I think you want it."

He shrugged and Lenora wondered why he had a mind to make things so difficult. Were all husbands like this? She sighed and lay back on the pillows.

"Go to sleep," he recommended. He now seemed to be oiling the blade of his sword.

Lenora turned onto her side and closed her eyes. When she woke again hours later it was to the patter of rain falling on the tent and to find herself lying cozy in Garman Orde's arms. She lay a moment quiet, before she felt him stir behind her.

"I'm here," he said, lifting his head off the pillow, his voice husky with sleep. "You're here with me."

"I know," she said, turning her head to look at him over her shoulder. It was too dark to make out much. "I wasn't having a nightmare," she assured him. "I think the rain woke me this time."

"Oh." His head hit the pillow again and she felt him relax his hold on her, though he did not move away.

Did he remain half-alert to listen out for her broken sleep? she wondered. And if so…if so, what exactly did that mean?

21

Garman woke at first light. Lenora had turned and curled into him in the night and his arm was serving as her pillow. He lay a moment contemplating her peaceful expression and the way her blond hair felt against his skin.

Gods, if he was not careful, he would soon find himself tickling her ears, he thought with contempt. Then again, no one would ever know. Gingerly, he reached out and gently stroked the silky blond head. Lenora sighed in her slumber. He froze, but she did not stir. Very carefully, he lifted her head and slid out his arm from under her, lowering her back onto the pillows.

Rising from the bed, he made his way over to the tent entrance and peered outside. The grass was still wet after last night's downpour. Hoping it would not affect the joust overmuch, he turned back and pulled on his boots and a tunic to go and relieve himself.

He was just on his way back when he spotted Kit Montmayne carrying two pitchers of water toward their tent. Hailing him in hushed tones, he explained Lenora was still asleep, took the washing water, and sent Kit along to the stables to feed Bria'ag. The longer his horse had between feeding and exercise the better.

When he reached the pavilion, he poured one jug of water into the basin, stripped off his tunic, and began to vigorously wash. By the time he was drying himself, he heard movement in the bed behind him, but did not turn to look.

It was when he began dressing that he could definitely feel eyes on him. Only then did he allow himself to turn and fling a glance over his shoulder. Lenora was lolling against the pillows, watching him with interest. He cleared his throat. "You're awake." A pointless remark, but for some reason he felt the need for speech.

"I am," she agreed after a moment's hesitation.

At the hint of caution in her reply, he turned again to look at her. She definitely had a wary look on her face. Why was that? Then he remembered. His surliness of the other morning. Ah, that would account for it. Frowning, he reached for his razor. "You still want to watch me in the joust this morn?"

"I do," she said.

"Good," he answered and guessed it was a stunned silence that greeted his response. "I intend to win," he added, soaping up his face.

"I'm sure."

He fancied he almost heard her hesitate. "What?"

"I rather thought you preferred me to hold my tongue of a morn."

He considered this. "Tell me what you were going to say."

"I was just wondering if you knew the name of your opponent," she admitted.

"I do," he said curtly. "It's Vawdrey."

"Oh."

He turned again to regard her as he dragged the straight razor down his face. "Will you be conflicted?" he asked tensely.

"Of course not! Though I do not think I shall sit with Eden." At his raised eyebrows, she explained. "She gets very heated. No, really," she added at his skeptical expression. "Apparently she has even been known to harangue Sir Roland's opponents at the celebratory banquet afterward." He snorted and turned back to the basin to rinse his blade. "Has she never tackled you?"

"Never." He frowned. Though he did think she might have spent a few meals glaring at him, now he came to think about it. "I often skip the feasting."

"Even when you win?"

"Especially when I win." He looked at her and could almost see the question trembling on her lips. "I don't care for being congratulated and toasted. I'm not like Vawdrey. I don't court popularity."

She fidgeted a moment, drawing the blanket around herself and tucking herself in. "It's your manner," she said firmly. "You're miserly with your smiles. I'm sure you would have many admirers if only you did not scowl and glower so."

"I don't want admirers."

She sighed and crossed her feet under the blanket. "You're almost as bad as Lord Kentigern and he glories in being disagreeable."

"I don't glory in it. I'm indifferent. The crowd don't mean anything to me."

She was silent at this and looked a little sad, though Garman had no notion why she should. He finished washing and dressing, and when attendants arrived with more washing water, he sent them for bread and fish to break his fast.

Lenora rose and started to get herself ready for the day ahead. When she drew a green dress from the trunk, he found himself interjecting. "Wear the dress you wore the other day."

She looked up startled. "The rose one?" He nodded and she looked pleased. "That's my favorite."

He glanced away, unsure why he'd even made such a request. Then he heard a footfall outside and crossed quickly to the opening. He didn't want servants getting a glimpse even of her shoulder if he could help it.

Taking the food from them, he carried it to the table and set it down. "Come and eat when you're ready." Seeing she was only just drawing on a pale blue stocking under her shift, he frowned. "It'll be cold."

"Well, I didn't want to be in your way by rising earlier."

Again he remembered his prior churlishness. "You're not in my way," he muttered and made his way over to where she was hopping on one foot. "Sit on the bed."

"But I—"

"Give it to me." He held out his hand out for the other stocking and the garters that she held.

"I can do it," she protested, even as she sat herself on the edge of the mattress.

Ignoring her words, he sank down and slipped a bright blue garter over her stockinged foot, sliding it up her shapely calf until it rested above her knee. Then he slid his finger under the band and snapped it, looking up at her startled face. "Do you know why I leave these on during bed sport?" he asked.

She hesitated. "I thought...so my feet wouldn't get cold?"

He shook his head. "Entirely for my benefit." He shook out the other stocking.

"You like the way they look?" she asked in surprise.

"Yes."

"Oh." She appeared to turn this over in her mind as he drew the other stocking over her toes and up her leg, then slipped the other garter into place.

She had already managed to get into a clean shift by herself, so he looked around. "Where's your gown?"

She pointed, and he fetched it, noting the laces were at the sides of the bodice and at the wrists.

"Hold up your arms."

Lenora obliged, and he helped her into the deep pink overdress, swiftly tying her laces.

"You could fasten that a little tighter," she commented critically.

He paused. "You're sure?" She'd gained some flesh in the last week or so, he was pleased to observe. She nodded, so he did as she suggested. "How's that?"

"Sufficient."

He caught her chin between finger and thumb, tilting it up, then dropped a swift kiss on her surprised lips. "Leave your hair loose for now. Dress it after you've eaten."

"Very well."

They moved to the table and Garman piled their plates as Lenora buttered the bread, and for some minutes there was no conversation between them as they ate. "Your cousin Kit will be back presently from the stables," he said. "I'll get him to take you along to the tilting field and see you seated."

She nodded, wiping her mouth with a napkin. "I hope I can get a good seat."

Privately, he thought she might have to settle for what she could get. It was the final day of the competition after all, and the joust was always the most anticipated event. Aloud, he said nothing and wondered if, against all odds, he was growing tactful. "Will you wear a veil today?" he asked abruptly, dispelling all question of tact.

"I shall," she responded carefully. "As all married women do. But not specifically to cover my face, if that is what you mean."

"You know it was."

She paused in the act of raising a morsel of bread to her mouth. "Well, yes," she conceded. "I trust that pleases you."

"Your frankness or the lack of veiling?"

She gave him a level gaze. "Both, I imagine."

"It's good you look to please me these days," he said and wondered if he was deliberately baiting her. She checked, then clearly deciding to rise above any provocation, finished off her food. "In future, I prefer you to have your hair loose when it is just the two of us."

"So you like to look upon my hair, as well as my nakedness and my legs in stockings," she answered lightly. "Never fear, I make sure to note your every preference."

"Yet you do not mention my very favorite feature of yours, I find," he answered and saw the color rise to her cheeks.

"I included that in my nakedness," she said primly, and he was forced to bite back a grin. "I see you smiling," she said. "Though you take great pains to hide it from me."

"I am in deadly earnest, wife."

"Oh, I don't doubt it, husband."

For just a moment, he regretted the fact he had to go and joust with that bastard Vawdrey, when he could be here instead, sparring with Lenora. She must have seen a flash of something in his eyes for her breathing increased and her cheeks glowed. For a moment, it was touch and go if he would drag her into his lap. Then they both heard approaching footsteps and he cleared his throat.

"That will be your cousin now," he said needlessly, for Kit's head was peering around the opening.

"Oh, you're awake, Lenora. That's good for almost all the seats are filled."

Lenora pushed back her chair. "Already?" Her voice was dismayed.

"There was just one box that was still free, so I had Hal save you a seat. Sir James is now out of the running, so he hasn't any duties this morning."

"Oh, excellent." Lenora beamed. "Let me just tidy my hair and you can take me along."

Garman watched her out of the corner of his eye as she swiftly pinned her hair up and added a veil which, true to her word, did nothing to hide her face. "You'd better take a cloak," he said gruffly. "It may get cold or rain later."

"Oh, of course." She caught up a green cloak and looked at him expectantly. "Well, good luck," she said brightly.

For some reason, her polite good wishes annoyed him. "It's not luck that wins me trophies," he growled. "Come here." He wasn't going to kiss her, he told himself, even though he felt the oddest inclination to. She walked over to him, and he reached out, stroking the backs of his fingers down her jawline in a strange sort of caress. He couldn't feel her pockmarks as he wasn't using his fingertips, but it was the place where she was worst marked and they both knew it.

She stood very still, and he flicked a finger against her cheek. "I like it when you're brave, wife." He saw her swallow and nod and then with one last glance, she walked over to Kit, who was watching them both with very round eyes. Then they were gone. Garman turned back to his preparations feeling strangely calm.

22

It seemed to Garman that he was quite unruffled by the hustle and bustle down at the tilting field that morn, which usually irritated the hell out of him. He went about his business, showing Kit how he kept Bria'ag calm and getting him to fix on the last pieces of his charger's regalia. Lenora's cousin showed himself good with horses and competent with armor, so all went as well as could be expected.

He swung up into his saddle and Kit passed up his jousting spear. "Which box?" he asked, lifting his lower visor so the box could see his mouth. Already the crowd was restive and noisy.

"Fourth from the left," Kit answered smartly, showing himself quick on the uptake. "The Kellingford colors hang there."

Garman nodded, slamming his helmet shut. Then he made his way to his start position. He allowed himself only a moment to scan the excited crowd for Lenora. He fastened on her box at once with its large yellow banner bearing the hippogriff. He soon found her in her rose-colored gown talking animatedly to Kit's friend, the young puppy.

Only then did he turn and fasten a cold hard stare on Roland Vawdrey, who was similarly positioned at the other end of the field, decked out in red and black. The marshals were running up and down the field, checking everything was in its correct position, and Garman could not say exactly when he became aware of a disturbance in the crowd, only that he sensed something amiss even as he saw the flags being raised to stand ready.

Bria'ag snorted and tossed his head, trying to see the audience to the left of them, despite the heavy chamfron hampering his vision. "Easy, boy. Easy." But the charger was having none of it. Despite the fact he was generally as indifferent to the crowd as Garman himself, something was definitely disquieting the beast. Garman took his eye off the marshal and instead scanned the crowd. Initially, he could see nothing, but his hearing told him something was very amiss.

Something gave a shuddering groan and then the screams started. He heard the ominous splintering of wood and then one of the boxes began to list drunkenly forward. Lenora's box. Garman's stomach lurched; he threw down his spear and urged Bria'ag toward the tumult. Even as the horse closed the distance between them, he knew he was going to be too late. Before his eyes, the roof caved in and the whole structure collapsed.

23

"Don't move," Lenora heard a voice murmur and felt the cool, damp cloth at her brow. To her surprise, she recognized the voice as her husband's low rumble.

"She's awake," she heard another voice say, and then approaching footsteps. Lenora opened her eyes and squinted up at the concerned faces. Garman, Kit, and some man she could only suppose was a physician.

"What happened?"

"Don't worry about that now," Garman told her swiftly. "How does your head feel?"

"It aches," she admitted, and raised a hand to touch it, feeling carefully around.

His hand closed over hers and lifted her fingers to rest above her left brow where she felt a painful swelling. "Ouch!"

"That's where the roof collapsed on you," he said grimly.

"Roof?"

"Of your box."

"Of course," she said with dawning comprehension. "The whole structure fell."

"It did," he agreed. "With you in it."

"What happened to Hal Payne?" she asked with growing concern. "He tried to shield me from the falling timber and prevented me being hurtled down—"

"Hal's fine," Kit said hurriedly. "Broke his arm, poor fellow, but nothing more."

A small cough sounded. "If I might interrupt?" the physician asked mildly. "Can you feel your legs, my lady?"

Lenora wriggled her feet and winced. "Y-yes."

"It hurts?" Garman asked quickly.

"I just feel bruised."

"You were mostly thrown clear," Kit told her. "Damnably lucky you were at the front."

"I don't feel terribly lucky," Lenora admitted, closing her eyes. "I feel like the most unlucky woman in all Karadok!" Then her conscience pricked her. "I hope no one was seriously hurt?" she asked anxiously.

"Nothing more than a broken bone or two," Kit hastened to assure her.

"Aren't you going to check her over?" Garman barked, turning toward the physician.

The smaller man coughed again. "I think the lady might appreciate some privacy…"

"I'm her husband!" Garman thundered. "Do you think I haven't already seen it all before?"

"Quite, quite," the doctor said hurriedly. "But this young man—?"

"I'll duck out," Kit said, "and go and pacify Eden. She's still fuming she wasn't allowed to tend her."

"Tell her all is well with me," Lenora called after him. Her voice had a wobble in it that embarrassed her. Raising a hand, she tried to cover her face, but Garman was already dragging her up by her armpits. "I'm really quite well," she croaked in a voice that wouldn't convince anyone. Then she burst into tears.

"Shhhh now, Lenora," Garman said gruffly, lifting her into his lap. "You're fine. You're absolutely fine." His large hand was at the back of her head, pressing her face to his chest. "I'm here with you, and all is well."

She stifled a sob and peered up at him.

Seeing her expression, he asked, "What?" in a low voice.

She shook her head. "It's just...that's what you always say. When I have a nightmare, I mean."

He looked at her uncertainly a moment, then glanced at the physician. "Well?" he barked. "What do you want her to do?"

"If the good lady could extend her arms out in front of her," the doctor quavered.

Lenora tried to rouse herself to comply with the doctor's orders, but she felt stiff and sore and winced her way through the exercises until she realized that just induced Garman to snap and snarl at the poor man. Things went quicker after she suppressed her groans and the only one of her bumps and scrapes the gentleman seemed concerned about was the one on her head.

"The swelling must be kept to a minimum with the application of poultices of crushed linseed and ground horseradish root," he finished briskly.

Garman nodded and escorted him out. When he entered again, she heard him fiddling with the tent flap a moment before he turned.

"Let me take a good look at you, Lenora. I need to reassure myself."

She cracked an eye open and gazed up at him. "What do you mean?"

"Come on, arms up." He had her shift whipped over her head before she even realized his intent.

"Garman!"

"Let me see. There's no point for maidenly modesty with me now, is there," he lightly scolded.

"The physician already—" she started to protest.

"That doddering old fool barely saw a thing. You scarcely lifted your skirts above your calves!" he said with exasperation. "Now get up on your feet. I want to see you turn in a circle."

Tottering to her feet, she felt too dazed and miserable to be embarrassed by her nudity. Docilely, she turned a full circle before him. Garman clicked his tongue and suddenly she was filled with misgivings. "What is it?" she asked, trying to peer over her back. "Am I black and blue?"

"You likely will be soon," he admitted and sat down on the bed. "Come here." He helped her back into her shift and she crawled into the bed. He settled the covers over her and lay on top of them next to her. "I've said you're not up to seeing anyone." This was flung at her almost like a challenge.

"Good," said Lenora, raising a hand to the lump at her brow. She gave a faint moan. "I don't want to see anyone." She looked even *less* presentable now, she thought dolefully, a thing she had scarcely thought possible. "I feel terrible." He ran a hand up and down her hip in a comforting motion. Lenora closed her eyes and sighed.

269

"Go to sleep."

She glanced down at his large hand at her waist. To her surprise, it was bound up. "What happened to your hand?" she murmured drowsily.

"It's nothing," she thought she heard him answer as her stinging eyelids lowered.

She did drift into some semblance of sleep but was awakened sometime later by raised voices just outside the tent.

"Did you not see what occurred to my wife?" she heard Garman say in a voice of suppressed fury.

"We did indeed, Sir Garman," she heard another man say soothingly. "Sir Roger and myself were a good deal shocked and upset, but the audience, my good sir. You must consider the audience! Some have traveled a good distance to see—"

"I have no interest in them," Garman cut in ruthlessly.

"The Lady Bridgette begs you will allow the lady to accompany us back to the manor where she may rest in a proper bedchamber and be assured of every comfort," the voice continued in appeal.

"I will see to my wife's comfort and none other," Garman said tersely. "She does not leave my side."

"I'm sure Kellingford Manor would happily extend its hospitality—"

"We have no need of it and will be leaving first thing on the morrow," he interrupted in clipped tones. "I would ask you leave us now, for my wife needs rest."

"Sir Garman—"

"No!" His voice rose on that word but was then lowered to a menacing rumble. Whatever was said, Lenora could not catch, but the tone was ominous in the extreme. Hasty farewells were uttered by the Kellingford deputation and footfalls were heard moving away before the tent flap swished open and Lenora sat up.

"They woke you, I see," Garman said grimly.

"What's happening? Did they want you to complete the joust?"

He gave a short mirthless laugh. "They did." He moved to the table and poured a cup from a jug which he brought toward her. Lenora was startled to see both his hands in fact were bound up.

"What happened to your hands?"

He glanced at them. "It's nothing. Drink this."

Lenora sat up and felt a poultice slide down from her head. She made a grab for it and placed it gingerly back over the lump on her head. Then she took the cup from him and sipped the fruity beverage, her eyes fixed on him the whole time. "How many hours have passed?"

He glanced at the tent opening. "It's about four o'clock."

"Four o'clock?" She was startled. "A good deal of the day has passed."

"It has."

"If the crowd has been waiting all this time…"

"They can wait until Doomsday for all I care."

She watched as he poured himself a cup and then tossed it back. "You said you were going to win," she reminded him, clutching the goblet stem. He said nothing but set his cup down. "I should like to have seen it," she added rather wistfully.

That made him pause. "I would have thought this would have put you off tournaments for life!"

"Hardly! I am not quite so fragile as all that!" She plucked at her bedsheets. "I am aware I was a bit maudlin and indulging in self-pity this morning, but—"

"Self-pity?" he repeated, then shook his head.

"But really, I just have a bump on my head, that is all." She gazed up at him appealingly. "It would seem a shame to let Sir Roland win purely by your failure to present."

He stared at her. "What are you saying?"

Lenora took a deep breath. "I want to watch you compete in the joust," she said, sitting up.

"You've got a lump on your head the size of an egg!"

"What of it?" She shrugged. "My appearance little signifies these days."

"Lenora—"

"Garman," she said, calmly countering his belligerence.

"If you think I'm leaving you here—"

"Certainly not!" she interrupted firmly. "You shall carry me down to the arena. Sir Roger can let me sit in his box after what befell me. I would hardly trust to another. And I shall want Hal Payne sat to my right with his broken arm, and when you have won, you can place the winner's garland on my broken head. That is what I want."

He gazed at her. "You're serious?"

272

"Oh yes."

"You must admit," a voice piped up admiringly from the entrance, "that's plucky of her. Damned plucky. Never knew she had it in her."

Lenora and Garman looked to find Kit, Cuthbert, and a rather pale Hal stood peering in. Kit was looking highly gratified that his cousin was displaying such backbone.

"Hal!" said Lenora, holding out a hand. Hal Payne came swiftly into the tent and clasped her fingers in the hand that was not lashed up along a splint. Garman gave an exclamation of annoyance that Lenora ignored. "I wanted to thank you for your prompt action this morning. I'm sure my injuries would have been far more grievous if not for you."

Hal's round face colored hotly. "It was nothing, Lady Lenora. Nothing at all."

"You can release her hand now," Garman said waspishly.

Hal hesitated a moment, then bowed over her hand and pressed an ardent kiss to her fingers.

"It was a great honor, my lady," he said hoarsely. Lenora deduced that once the boy shed his puppy fat, he was going to be great success at wooing. Even she did not find his kiss distasteful in the slightest. She smiled kindly at him, and Garman clapped a hand to his shoulder, propelling him to the tent entrance where his friends were watching with great interest.

"One of you had better run along to speak to the marshal," Garman said briefly. "And another to Sir Roger, and you, Ames, to your master. Tell them to all make ready."

"Aye."

The boys took to their heels. Lenora slid from the bed to make her way stiffly to the trunk. Her rose gown was thrown over the back of a chair and looked both muddy and torn. She suppressed a sigh and reached for the green and gold one, only to find it taken from her hands.

"I'll help you get dressed, then you help me by fastening my armor buckles," Garman said.

"Very well, first you play lady's maid, then I play squire," she said humorously.

He did not even crack a smile.

24

By the time they reached the arena, it was rather darker than customary, and torches had been lit all the way along the length of the field. Somehow, it lent a more somber air to the proceedings, and Lenora found the field strangely quieted when she arrived on her palfrey which Kit had fetched from the stables.

The audience fell into even more of a hush as Garman led her to Sir Roger's family box and, after lifting her down from the horse's back, carried her right up the steps himself and set her down on the front bench, between Sir Roger and Hal Payne, as she had specified.

Sir Roger, his heir, and his two illegitimate sons, all stood up to bow very respectfully to her, and Lady Bridgette welcomed her with a booming voice and praised her fortitude. In truth, Lenora was feeling a little light-headed by this point, but whether that was due to the incident she had suffered that morning, or the fact she was feeling extremely exposed as the center of all attention, it was hard to say. Despite the decided chill in the air, she felt hot-cheeked and strangely detached from proceedings.

Garman had straightened before her and was looking down at her now, so she forced a smile to her lips and looked up at him. Her mind went blank, for she remembered he had taken exception before when she had wished him good luck. Her brain scrambled for more appropriate words.

"I shall look to see you win, sir knight," she said loudly.

He ignored these words, reaching instead for her hand which he took thoughtfully in his own. Just as she began to wonder once more about those bandages, he robbed her of all thought by carrying her hand to his lips and kissing it rather in the manner of someone who does something unaccustomed that slightly baffled him. He frowned slightly, then turned her hand over and kissed the center of her palm. Lenora swallowed and felt her cheeks go even redder. Sir Roger cleared his throat. Garman released her hand and made his way swiftly back down the steps.

"Well!" said Lady Bridgette. "That's a sight you never thought to see, Roger! Sir Garman Orde acting the chivalrous knight!"

"Don't care what they do, so long as I see 'em joust!" her stepbrother responded roundly. "Begging your pardon, Lady Lenora."

Lenora waved a hand absently. She had leaned forward and placed one arm along the front of the box. Garman and Sir Roland were taking up their positions at either end of the field.

"You've certainly given us plenty of entertainment this week, Lady Lenora," Bridgette continued with relish. "First with Sir Lionel trying to run off with you and now your thrilling brush with death."

"Hardly death!" Sir Roger huffed. "Really, Bridgette!"

"Well, that's clearly how Sir Garman views it. Quite beside himself he was when he pulled her lifeless body from the wreckage this morning."

"What?" Lenora turned from contemplating the field. "What did you say, Lady Bridgette?"

"I said, he looked like a man possessed when he ripped that collapsed box apart to find you this morning, with his bare hands—"

"Shhhh, Bridgette, for Lord's sake!" Sir Roger complained. "They're about to start!"

Lenora turned hurriedly back in time to see the wave of the flag. Garman's charger in black and white thundered toward Roland Vawdrey's in black and red. There was a loud crash as both hit their target of the other's shield and a great splintering of broken lances. The crowd erupted into cheers. Both knights looked jarred, but remained seated and carried on until they reached the other end. Their squires, Kit and Cuthbert, ran to the opposing ends with new jousting spears and officials ran forward to clear away any debris.

"They look to be very evenly matched," Lady Bridgette commented sotto voce.

"Yes," Lenora murmured in agreement. "There is not really much between the top three, I would say."

Sir Roger looked rather taken aback by her words. "Hah! You are objective, Lady Lenora, in any event. Your cousin Eden will have it that none is her husband's equal and any triumph over him is a mere fluke."

Lenora nodded. "I am devoted to my cousin, but she does not have a true appreciation of the joust," she said. "Her only real appreciation is for Sir Roland. Whereas I enjoy the sport for its own sake, and can see that Lord Kentigern, Sir Roland, and my husband are truly experts in the field. Any one of them can win on a good day or lose on a bad. That is part of what makes the joust so very exciting."

"Yet Lord Kentigern went crashing out to a mere novice the other day!" Lady Bridgette observed, looking puzzled.

"Oh no," Lenora said, shaking her head. "Sir Renlow is far from a novice. He just has not yet hit his stride. I believe he will be a very formidable competitor once he does find his feet."

"And loses some of his damned principles!" growled Sir Roger. "Young fool!"

"So, Lord Kentigern was having a bad day," Lady Bridgette mused. "And Sir Renlow, a good one?"

"Undoubtedly," Lenora agreed, gripping the edge of the box as the horses once more charged toward each other.

"It is very informative to be lectured by an expert as one observes," Bridgette said, nodding her head. "Roger usually just yells and stamps his feet, so I have no clue what is happening."

Lenora clasped her hands together as again, both lances broke with a terrific smash, and both combatants were forced to straighten themselves in their saddles.

Sir Roger and his two sons had sprung from the bench with a smothered yell, but now settled down again for the third pass. In the stands, people were starting to drum their heels and stamp their feet.

"This will be the decider," Sir Roger said, rubbing his hands together with glee. The crowd seemed to be teeming with anticipation, a low murmur filling the arena. Lenora wondered briefly where Eden was sitting, then dismissed it. No doubt wherever it was, her attention would be solely focused on her own husband.

Lenora breathed in deeply and stared at Garman as he adjusted his breastplate and thumped at a couple of pieces of armor that looked likely dented. Kit passed him up another lance. Garman felt the weight of it and then wheeled Bria'ag around for the final pass. Lenora gripped the ledge, feeling a little giddy.

Suddenly, she realized she had not yet breathed out. Exhaling heavily, she jumped a little when the crowd started noisily yelling and whistling their support. To her surprise, she realized that some of them were even cheering for her husband.

"It seems we are not the only ones to appreciate the high drama of your situation," Lady Bridgette said dryly. "I've never heard them chant *his* name before."

"He is not a crowd favorite," Lenora agreed faintly. Though you would not have known it at this precise moment.

She scanned the excited crowd before tearing her eyes away and fixing them again on Garman. He cut an imposing figure. She focused on him with her total concentration, tuning out the background noise. For a moment, he almost seemed to move by infinitesimal degrees, his charge forward appearing at no more than a snail's pace to her.

Then all of a sudden, he seemed to blur and hurtle forward at a breakneck pace. She did not hear the clash of spear against shield, she heard nothing, as though suddenly struck deaf to all sound around her. Lenora stood frozen, as though suspended in time, waiting for her senses to return to her. It was the oddest feeling.

Then next, breaking over her was thunderous applause, shouting, yelling, and hooting. She saw in a flash, Roland Vawdrey's black and scarlet colors rolling around on the ground. Garman had reached the end of the run and turned Bria'ag around to hold his lance aloft in victory. Lenora shot to her feet. She saw Cuthbert's blond head as he ran forward to catch Sir Roland's horse, but Lenora had eyes only for Garman. Was it only her imagination, or did he look to her? She clapped her hands together until her palms felt numb. Hands reached out to pat her shoulder, voices hailed her husband's victory, but she didn't really hear them.

"Are you well, my dear?" It was Lady Bridgette, speaking calmly for once in her ear.

"I am well," Lenora assured her, realizing her face was wet with tears. Lady Bridgette nodded, then passed her a handkerchief to dab her face. "I have no idea why I feel so emotional," she blurted. "After all, this is what he does. I've seen it many times before."

Lady Bridgette gave a knowing smile and Lenora stopped talking. Garman was steering Bria'ag in her direction and she saw that he had the victor's garland on the end of his spear. As he approached, the crowd noise swelled louder. Lenora squared her shoulders. She had been given the winner's wreath many, many times, but all those other times faded from her memory. She scarcely remembered them. In truth, they had been only an acknowledgment of her beauty, nothing more. And she had never been awarded it by Garman Orde.

He waited a moment before the Kellingford box, until the crowd noise dipped, and only then did he raise the lance until it hovered before her. Lenora paused. She had never given much thought before to the pageantry of the occasion, but for the first time, she appreciated her role in the story being told before their audience. As any onlooker could see only too plainly, she was no longer the prettiest woman in attendance. However, they would see that in Sir Garman's eyes, she was still deemed worthy.

She looked around smilingly at the expectant crowd. They hushed further and then, bestowing the biggest smile of all on her husband, she reached out and took the flower ring and placed it squarely on top of her head. The crowd burst once more into rapturous applause. Lenora laughed and clapped again. The high spirits were infectious. She felt almost giddy.

Sir Roger was at her elbow, congratulating her on her husband's win. He was asking about escorting her to the feast, but his sister, Lady Bridgette, stepped in and murmured something in his ear. They were both looking over Lenora's shoulder now, and she swayed a moment, feeling almost drunk. Then a hand was at her waist, steadying her. She glanced around and found Garman there, still partly dressed in his armor, his hair plastered in sweat. The next thing she knew she was in his arms and being swept down the steps toward Bria'ag. She tipped her head back to look at him.

"You won," she said simply.

He shifted her in his arms and slung her up onto the horse's back. She had to reach up to adjust her garland of flowers which had slipped down over her eyes. Then he was up behind her and the crowd was cheering again as he rode slowly around the edge of the field. "Enjoy the applause now," he told her in a low voice. "We're not going to the celebratory banquet."

Lenora raised a hand to wave and smile. She noticed Garman's brusque nod of acknowledgment and laughed again. "I feel drunk," she mused. "But I haven't had a drop of wine."

His hand tightened at her waist. "You don't feel faint?"

"Not at all."

He seemed to relax at that. "Shall we go around again?"

Lenora looked at the jubilant faces. "Yes, once more." She sat up straighter, determined to commit this moment to memory. "You're popular, you realize, in this instant."

"Fancy that," he drawled. "And all it took was my wife's brains almost being dashed out in front of them all."

Lenora nodded thoughtfully. "Isn't it funny, what makes people like you?"

She had caught sight of Eden now, with her arms around Sir Roland's waist. Roland grinned ruefully, catching sight of them, and raised a hand in greeting. Garman nodded. Eden laid her head on her husband's shoulder and seemed to be taking his loss far worse than he did.

"I like Roland Vawdrey," Lenora said decidedly. "Don't you?"

"No," Garman growled.

"Oh. That seems a shame to me. He has a good heart."

He did not answer, but that might have been due to the din the crowd were making. This time, when they reached the end of the field, Garman steered Bria'ag through the gap between the stands and they made their escape.

25

They had a simple supper of bread, cheese, and grapes, and Garman was in and out of the tent as she washed and undressed, seeing to his armor and getting his horse stabled.

Lenora smiled to herself as she finally sat in a chair to brush out and braid her golden hair.

"Don't talk to me about liking other men," Garman said tersely as he walked back in again and dumped a pile of armor in the corner of the tent.

"What?" His words startled her. "You mean Sir Roland?" She hesitated. "You misunderstand me. I have only ever considered him as Eden's. It is important to me that her husband has a good heart."

"Well, I don't have a good heart. I have a black heart."

"That's not at all the same," she said dismissively. "I don't concern myself about that."

He straightened up, pinning her with his gaze. "You should concern yourself about it," he said sharply. "Now you find yourself married to me."

She stared at him. "It's fine though," she said, her cheeks turning pink. "It's important Eden has a decent husband as she's a fine, upstanding woman."

His brows snapped together. "And what of you?"

"Me?" She gave a short laugh. "I'm nothing."

"What?"

"I'm nothing," she repeated slowly. "And I knew that even when I was beautiful. So, it doesn't matter if you're an utter swine. We've had this conversation already."

Garman stared at her a moment, then he gave a hollow laugh.

"But as a matter of fact," she said confidingly, "you are not as bad as all that. You have your good points." She set down her hair comb. "I think, as a husband, you suit me very well."

"Because I win when you tell me to?" he asked sarcastically.

"Yes, that was very impressive," she said and saw him struggle not to smile at that. Why did he fight it every time? she wondered. "I think our marriage will be a very great success."

"Are you sure you haven't had any wine?"

She smiled and shook her head. "You don't agree?"

"I haven't dwelt on the matter." His reply was rather crushing, but she wouldn't let that get to her when she was feeling so happy. Reaching across, she carefully straightened the garland where she had set it on the table after removing it to place a fresh poultice on her head.

The garland was not half as impressive as the ones she had received at the royal tournaments, but those had never filled her heart with pride as this one did. She ran her finger over the petals reverently. "Thank you for my flowers," she said dreamily.

He gave her a sharp look and approached her chair. "Lift your head, Lenora." She obliged, and he placed a hand at her forehead, careful to avoid the bruised area. "You're not feverish?"

"No, I don't think so."

His eyes bored into hers. "I gave you those flowers because you told me to, no other reason."

She pulled away his hand. "Oh dear," she said with a grimace. "Is this where you start being rude and insulting to me, terrified I'll misinterpret your actions?"

He gazed at her blankly a moment. "What?"

"Like the other morning? Because if so, I'd rather you didn't speak at all." She stood swiftly and went to move away, but he grabbed her arm, preventing her. "I don't *find* myself married to you, Garman," she spelled out in a brittle voice. "I'm the one who picked you out, or don't you remember?"

He released her arm. "Aye, I remember," he said harshly. "I'm not the one in danger of forgetting."

"Neither am I!" she answered tartly, feeling stung. The clouds she had been drifting among were definitely starting to disperse now and she was coming back to earth with a bump. Lenora sighed; it had been nice while it lasted. The lump on her head was starting to throb and Garman's manner was beginning to irritate her. "I'm going to bed," she said flatly. He did not answer, and she crossed swiftly to the bed and climbed into it.

The next few minutes were spent in silence between them, the only sounds being Garman removing his clothes and washing. When things went silent, she raised her head and found him unwinding a deal of linen wrappings from his hands and inspecting what was underneath. She wondered about those again briefly before he turned around, blew out the candles, and crossed to the bed in pitch darkness.

Lenora held herself stiffly as the bed dipped when he climbed into it. He rolled onto his back and Lenora lay on her stomach with her face turned away from his. Reaching up, she checked the poultice had not slipped from the spot that throbbed at her brow.

Outside she could hear voices in the distance laughing and talking to each other, likely on their way home after the jousting, or perhaps making their way up to the manor house.

"What do you mean by saying you're nothing?" Garman asked out of the darkness in the voice of one severely goaded.

Lenora lifted her head a moment, surprised by both his question and his tone.

"Not much," she said cautiously. "Just that."

"What *exactly*?"

Lenora sighed wearily. "What is the point in going into it?"

"Because I want to know," he persisted.

"Just in the same manner that you know you have a black heart; I know very well that I am an empty husk. I have always known."

"Empty?" His words were sharp. "Explain."

"I have no substance," she said drearily. "I have no personality. You said so yourself."

He gave an exclamation. "That was days ago! Before I even knew you."

Lenora shrugged. "I don't want to talk about it."

"Well, unfortunately for you, it's a woman's lot in life to do things she doesn't want to," he snorted.

Lenora rolled onto her back. "Why are you being so disagreeable?"

"I *am* disagreeable. Everyone says so."

"Is this you panicking because the crowd actually liked you tonight?" she asked, huffing out a breath. Garman was silent. "Because you needn't worry. Fame is a fickle beast and very soon they'll all forget how you won their hearts and cast you aside for tomorrow's favorite."

"Is that what you think they did with you?" he asked shrewdly, and Lenora caught her breath. She was glad the tent was in darkness for she felt her face grow suddenly very hot.

When she could manage to keep her voice steady, she said quietly: "I suppose they did, yes."

"Then you suppose wrong!" he replied angrily, and she thought she heard him grit his teeth. "Emworth still wants you and likely more besides!"

Snatching up a pillow, Lenora hurled it toward where she imagined his face was. "You—beast!" she panted, and her voice shook. "That's not the first time you've suggested I should have asked another! That I was a fool to ask you!" She made a grab for another pillow and found her waist suddenly encircled by two strong arms, as she was borne back down to the mattress.

"Be still!" he ordered. "You've a lump on your head the size of an egg. I'm not about to start wrestling with you!"

Lenora struggled for all she was worth, and found he just bore down on her all the harder, catching her wrists in his large hands and pinning them above her head. For some reason she could not fathom, she was suddenly breathless for an altogether different reason. She remembered how he had previously compared lovemaking to fighting and then wished devoutly she had not.

287

"And for the record, I was not saying that," he said in a low voice. His breath tickled her neck. Finding her efforts to wriggle free futile, and only served to make her hot and bothered, Lenora subsided. As soon as she stopped struggling, all the bruises from the accident that morning suddenly made themselves known to her. "Ouch." She winced.

He relaxed his hold at once. "Where does it hurt?"

"All over!"

He levered his top half off her and settled beside her, one hand still resting on her hip. "Turn onto your side," he recommended. "Most of your bruises are on your backside." When she went to turn toward him, he tightened his hold, preventing her. "The other way. Give me your back." Lenora complied, and he lay very still until she found the position most comfortable. She felt him lift his arm and feel her head to check the poultice was still placed over her brow. Then, very carefully, he shifted into her, pressing his front against her back. That was when she realized she had not been the only one affected by their tussle.

He breathed out gustily. "There's nothing weak about your personality, Lenora," he told her. "I don't know where you got that from. You may not have spent your childhood studying books and music, but you don't lack spirit."

"That's not what you said before," she flung at him over her shoulder.

"When?"

"At the inn, that second night."

He hesitated, running a hand up from her hip to her waist and back down again. Lenora shivered. "That was based on what I'd seen of you at court," he said dismissively. "Even that second night, I knew I had you wrong. Ever since I have known you—" He broke off as though considering his words.

"What?"

"You've been like a force of nature."

She caught her breath. "Me?"

"Crawled out of a pile of pox victims, didn't you? Marched me off to get handfasted?"

She stared into the darkness. "Well…"

"Tricked a guard, cajoled a priest… Need I go on?"

She gave a shaky laugh. "I almost wish you would."

He breathed out noisily. "We're both battered and bruised. And likely exhausted. It's been a long day."

"Yes," she murmured. His hand at her waist felt heavy and comforting. As if guessing the direction of her thoughts, he eased it around her hip in a small circle.

"I shouldn't have picked a fight," he said hoarsely. "You're right. Acting the champion doesn't sit well with me."

She was so astonished by this admission that she lay silent a moment, digesting this. "Well, I shouldn't have struck you with a pillow," she conceded. "Only…"

"Only what?" She heard the faint thread of amusement running through his words.

"If I wasn't a mass of bruises, would you have wrestled with me?"

He lay very still a moment. "In the sheets? Aye." He gave a short laugh. "Don't tempt me when I need to be gentle with you." *Wrestled in the sheets?* From the husky tone of his voice she could tell he was definitely referring to bed sport and shivered a little. "Cold?" he asked.

She shook her head. "No." They were both quiet awhile and Lenora listened to his steady breathing evening out. Very softly she asked, "What time will we set off in the morning?"

"Early," he rasped. "Now go to sleep."

She wanted to ask if they would have time for her to say goodbye to her cousins, but did not want to shatter their momentary truce.

26

When Lenora awoke the next morning, it was late and she felt
groggy. All around her were tidy bundles and rolls of things
that had been packed neatly away. Garman had been busy, she
realized, while she slept on.

Tentatively she reached for the tender spot at her brow and
found the swelling much reduced. A quick scan of the tent saw
she had been left out only one outfit, presumably to travel home
in. She quickly rose, washed in lukewarm water, and dressed.
She was just securing her hair at her nape when she heard a
footfall outside and looked up eagerly. It was Garman and he
was carrying the spoils of his win. When he entered, he set
down a large silver salver and a chinking purse which bulged.

"Good morning," she greeted him affably. "Sir Roger has
awarded you your winnings, I see."

Instead of answering this, he crossed the tent and cupped her
cheek. "How's your head?"

"A lot better, thank you," she said, feeling exasperated with
herself when her cheeks grew warm. He ran a thumb absently
over her jaw as he was wont to do before releasing her and
picking up a couple of the rolled packs. Did he always
deliberately touch that patch of roughened, pitted skin? Lenora
wondered and had to take a couple of steadying breaths before
she spoke again. "Are we now ready for the off?" she asked
croakily.

"I'm just loading up the horses now," he said over his shoulder
as he ducked out of the tent.

Lenora busied herself pinning a veil over her coiled hair and then donning her cloak. "Have you made our farewells?" she asked when he appeared again to grab the last few things.

"Aye," he said shortly. "And gave our direction at Cofton Warren to young Montmayne."

"That's good," Lenora said. "I don't suppose—"

"I also gave it to Ames, for the Lady Eden," Garman interrupted her.

"You think of everything."

He smirked, but made no rejoinder to that, and with a quick glance around to check for hair pins or any small feminine possession he might have overlooked, Lenora took her leave of their pavilion. She felt somewhat mixed emotions about that. On one hand, the materials were starting to look sadly wet and sagging. She was not sure how much longer their shelter would have remained dry. On the other hand, she was not overly anxious to return to Matchings Farm where Garman's grandfather was so polite and disapproving. Still, she would see Berta, Grizelda, and Fendrel, so that was something.

Garman was just packing away his standard banner which had been flying outside their tent. He tucked it into a saddlebag and pinched her chin before lifting her up onto her mare. "What is it?" he asked, so she told him. "You'll miss the tournament life?" he asked with raised eyebrows.

"Yes, I believe I will." She lifted her chin at his skeptical gaze. "And I can mount a horse unaided, you know," Lenora felt bound to point out as she took the reins.

"You've suffered a mishap," he reminded her sternly as he swung into his own saddle. "And if you start to feel giddy or sick, you're to tell me. I can have you up on Bria'ag before me."

"I feel perfectly well this morning, I assure you."

"Well, you've a good color at least," he agreed as he led the way. "Stay close to me."

The majority of the other competitors had not yet risen, so they picked their way among the brightly colored tents with ease and soon left the field and all of Kellingford behind them.

Lenora wondered if Sir Roger would prevail in his quest to get his two sons legitimized. She wondered if Lady Bridgette would spread much gossip about the faded court beauty, whose knight had won the jousting in spite of her fall from grace. Catching the direction of her thoughts with a guilty start, she tried in vain to tamp down the mingled triumph and glee that bubbled through her at Garman's victory.

Her husband was not a chivalrous parfait knight, despite his win, she reminded herself. He most certainly had *not* been fueled by any desire to please her or crown her the worthiest lady in the land. He had won simply because he wanted the purse of silver, not the glory. He despised the adulation of the crowd. Still, she could not quite quash the gratitude she felt at the idea he had won partly because she had told him she wanted it. It gave her a warm feeling deep in the pit of her stomach.

"When do you suppose you will return to Kellingford?" she asked impulsively.

"Same time next year."

"So, it's an annual tournament?"

"Most of them are."

"Will you take me with you?"

He shot her a measuring look. "If you still desire it," he said with a shrug of his shoulders.

"Why would I not?" asked Lenora, startled.

"You'll likely be installed at Matchings Halt by then," he said dismissively.

Matchings Halt, Lenora remembered with a frown, was the fine estate Garman meant to buy from under some poor widow. Though where he would get the funds for that she did not know. Not unless her father handed over her dowry sooner rather than later. She shifted in her saddle uneasily. "I suppose I ought to write to my parents directly on our return," she said without much enthusiasm.

"Likely they'll hear soon enough from your cousins, or someone else at court," Garman answered without much interest.

"Yes, but that would very likely get their backs up."

"Why should we care?"

She shot a searching glance over at him. Did he really not care about her dowry? Or was this mere bravado?

"Don't write to them on my account," he said gruffly. "I won't care if you never speak with them again."

"What about my dowry?" she blurted, astonished by his words.

"I don't need it." The curl of his lip spoke of utter disdain for her father's money. Lenora's jaw dropped. "You think I would take money from a man who had rather you had died than recovered?" he demanded with an angry glint in his eye.

"Well, but…" Lenora's words trailed off. "I did promise you would receive a handsome dowry if you wed me," she struggled on.

"You did," he agreed. "But I went into this weighing the odds of that actually occurring. They seemed slight, even at the beginning. And now…I find I no longer care."

Lenora gaped at him. Did he just say that he'd take her with nothing? That he had taken her with nothing from the beginning? She spluttered a moment, unable to find words. Garman glanced at her dismissively and seemed to consider the subject a closed one. They rode the next hour or so in silence as Lenora furiously turned things over in her mind until her head started to positively ache.

Was it possible that Garman Orde did in fact have some honor to him? He had been furious when she had told him of her parents' hurtful words. She remembered how he had bodily put her from him and seemed shaken by the account. Then he had encouraged her to tell him about her relationship with her family, she remembered. He did have moments where he seemed to behave with decency and proper feeling.

She stole another glance at him. If only he was a little more forthcoming about himself, she thought with frustration. Sometimes it seemed like he drew her closer to him and then took two steps back, pushing her away. "Are you looking forward to seeing your grandfather again?" she asked boldly.

His expression grew distant. "I only saw him three days ago," he pointed out.

She hesitated. "Does he know about your plan to buy the Matchings Halt estate?"

He shook his head, then shot her another guarded look. "I only ever spoke of it to the Hainfroys. Several years ago. When we spoke of…things we wanted to achieve."

He spoke of his dreams to his closest friends, she thought, feeling wildly encouraged by this volunteered information. A boyish Garman having plans to buy his own estate made him seem a lot more approachable. "And did you speak to them of it again the other day when we stayed with them?"

"I believe I did make some mention of it." He cleared his throat, looking a little uncomfortable at the admission.

"What did they say?" asked Lenora curiously.

He frowned. "They were surprised, I think, that I still thought of the place."

"What's it like? Shall I like it?"

His brows rose again. "I think so," he said slowly. "It's a handsome house. Mellowed stone and well-balanced, not ill proportioned like Kellingford or neglected like Cofton Grange." He hesitated again. "It's a fine estate and prosperous, but not a grand one like you're likely used to."

"Small is fine," Lenora hastened to assure him. "I am not well-versed in the running of a household. It will be easier for me to pick up such things in a smaller house, rather than a large one like Hallam Hall."

A smile tugged at his lips before he suppressed it ruthlessly. "Maybe my grandfather could give you some lessons in household management," he added, surprising her.

"Your grandfather Sutton?"

"Aye."

For a moment she wondered why he recommended asking a man who ran a modest-sized farm, but then remembered he had before described his grandfather as a steward. At some point, then, he must have had the running of a sizeable property. "Very well, I shall ask him, if you think he would be amenable to the idea."

He nodded briefly and turned back to scanning the road ahead.

I wonder, thought Lenora, *if I will ever make him out.*

27

Something felt different. Garman had been aware of it as soon
as he woke that morn. For starters, Lenora was using his biceps
for a pillow again and his first impulse was not to shake her off.
Not by a long shot. Of course, he hadn't really objected to her
place in his bed from the outset, but he didn't want to examine
that too closely. So, for now, he simply eyed her profile with
both appreciation and vague unease as they once more
approached Cofton Warren.

It seemed strange to him that courtiers thought her looks now
ruined, simply because she had some roughened texture along
her jawline and her eyelids were crinkly. For that was the sum
total of the damage, in Garman's eyes at least. True, he seemed
to recall there had been a time when he had thought her beauty
gone. But that occasion, when he'd first surveyed her changed
face, seemed a lifetime ago, far longer than a mere couple of
weeks. And he had never thought her life was over due to it, far
from it. If anything, from all he had heard, it seemed to have
been the making of her.

She was still pretty. Anyone who couldn't see that was a fool.
His gut tightened when he thought of the fact others were not
likely put off by a bit of pitted skin either. Like that bastard
Emworth for instance. Lenora was adamant he hadn't been
trying to run off with her, but Garman had seen the look of
longing on his face when he had eyed her. Emworth coveted
her, but he wasn't going to get her, for she was Garman's. His
had been the bedchamber she had crept to that night, and his
was the wrist she had been bound to by the priest. That made
her his, and no man could put their bond asunder. Such
remembrances soothed the jealous tumult of his thoughts until

he could breathe calmly again, which was just as well for they had practically reached the farm now.

"When we get in, you're going straight to bed," he said firmly. She looked washed-out and pale after their four-hour ride.

She looked up quickly, and for a moment, he thought she would protest, but then she seemed to think better of it. "I am a little worn out," she admitted with a wan smile.

"You need a new poultice."

"Berta can probably make me one."

He thought it doubtful of someone who made their living laundering or laying out the dead but said nothing. He'd noticed Lenora didn't like anyone to criticize her stiff-necked cousin or her old crone of a servant. Or her cats. And for some reason he didn't want to earn her displeasure. Maybe because of her bandaged head. Maybe not. Anyway, likely one of his grandfather's staff could oblige with the poultice if her old gallows hag could not.

Some half hour later, they reached the approach to the farm and Garman made haste to dismount his own mount and lift her down from hers. She didn't even protest this time, and he saw her lips were pressed together as if she was in some discomfort.

"Your head?" he asked quietly as a groom came forward to lead the horses into the stable.

"A little sore," she admitted.

"I'll be back out shortly to gather our things," he said over his shoulder to the stable hand. "See the horses are rubbed down."

"Aye, sir."

299

Swiftly he carried her up to the house. "Which way is our bedchamber?" he asked a servant at the bottom of the stairs.

"Master Sutton, he's put your lady wife in the best back bedchamber, sir," she gasped with a small curtsey.

Garman paused. "And myself?"

"The master had your old room aired, sir."

Garman scowled. His grandfather was such a slave to propriety, always. But expecting them to sleep in separate rooms because the marriage was unsanctioned was ridiculous. Recalling to mind the tiny bed in the best back chamber, he headed for his old room instead.

"You don't have to carry me the entire way," Lenora murmured against his shoulder before spoiling the effect by yawning.

"You're exhausted." He threw open the door to his bedchamber and walked her straight over to the large bed. Despite the fact he was an infrequent visitor, his grandfather had allotted him one of the largest front bedchambers as befitted the owner. The big dark wooden bed was dressed in sheets ready for him. He set her down in the middle of the bed.

"Don't move. I'll send up someone to lay the fire and bring you water to wash." She nodded, raising a hand to her brow. Seeing the gesture, he carefully removed her hand to take a look under the poultice. "It needs to be redressed," he said with a frown. "But it doesn't look inflamed."

"Good," she said and closed her eyes.

He retreated and made good on his promises, sending servants up to her and then making his way down to the stables to collect his tournament gear. The next hour was spent seeing things stowed away, and after that, he went along to check on Berta and the cats. He found all three in the kitchen. Berta was sat at the large table humming tunelessly as she pounded away at a bowl of pungent-smelling mush.

"What's that smell?" he said, wrinkling his nose.

"'Tis yarrow root," she cackled. "I've steeped it in vinegar for my lady to put on her wound."

He glanced at it doubtfully. "I suppose you know what you're about."

"I do," she said, nodding her head. "Raised three rascally boys in my time, and what I don't know about cuts and bruises isn't worth knowing!"

He opened his mouth but was distracted from answering by something furry winding its way around his ankles and purring loudly. Recognizing the blue-gray pelt of Lenora's youngest cat, he reached down and lifted the gangly youngster into his arms. "I'll take this one up to her," he said, though why he felt he had to explain his actions he had no notion.

Berta nodded. "His mother has already ensconced herself on the bedcovers."

Garman glanced over to where his grandfather's old hound was dozing at the kitchen fire. "You've had no strife from Kolby with the cats?"

Berta snorted. "Him?" she said, gesturing over her shoulder with her thumb. "He's at the time of life where he cares for nothing except a fire to lie beside and a full stomach. And why shouldn't he?" She looked belligerent. "That time comes to us all."

Garman frowned at her. "I'm sure my grandfather does not begrudge him such comforts in his old age." He glanced over at Kolby, who rolled onto his back and yawned widely.

"Pah!" said Berta, screwing her pestle almost violently. "It's a cruel world for those that can't shift as fast as once they could," she said, pursing her lips together.

Garman looked down to find he was absently stroking the cat's gray fur. "Do you want me to take that up with me?" he asked, nodding toward the paste.

Berta stopped abruptly and stepped back to take a good look at him. "And when did you start acting so handsome?" she demanded but snatched up the bowl and shoved it in his hand all the same. "See she slathers it all over the sore parts, mind." Then she turned her back to him and stomped across the kitchen before wrenching open the door and disappearing.

Garman watched her slam the door shut behind her and met Kolby's eye when the startled hound looked up with a look of enquiry on his face.

"I've no idea," Garman told the dog, then carried Fendrel up to her bedchamber.

"Berta's in some towering dudgeon about something or other," he announced, setting Fendrel down on the bed next to Lenora and the pretty white cat Grizelda.

"There you are, Fendrel!" Lenora greeted the kitten. "Took your sweet time coming up to welcome me back." She glanced at Garman. "I daresay he was waiting for you." He made no reply to that, just watched her pet and kiss the kitten, murmuring to him in a sweet, low voice. "Did you miss us? Did you? Oh, my dear little boy."

He set the bowl of paste down on the table next to the bed. "This is for you."

Lenora glanced at it. "I'm not eating that," she warned.

He smiled sourly. "It's not for consumption."

"What is it for, then?"

"Berta made it for your bruises."

"Oh, I see." Lenora peered into the bowl with interest, then wrinkled her nose. "Why is she in a high dudgeon?" she asked, his words sinking in.

Garman poured a jug of clean water into the bowl and started his wash.

"I don't know," he admitted. "She wasn't so obliging as to tell me." He felt Lenora's eyes on his back and glanced back over his shoulder at her in enquiry.

"Are you being sarcastic?" she asked with sudden suspicion.

"Not especially."

"Well, in my experience, Berta usually does not hold back, but is most forthcoming. Then again…"

He plunged the cloth into the basin, then lathered it with soap leaves. "What?" he asked, almost in spite of himself.

She hesitated. "You are not exactly encouraging when it comes to the sharing of confidences."

He grunted. "Is that your experience of me?"

She fell silent a moment as he dried his face and neck. "No," she admitted. "I was not being fair. In truth, I have confided

303

more in you these last couple of weeks than I have in anyone these last six months."

He turned around and regarded her. She was lying against the pillows in the middle of his bed, wrapped in a black and gold robe which she had donned over her shift after undressing. Her golden hair was coming out of the twist at her nape, falling about her face in loose ringlets. The effect was pleasing and marred only by the dressing at her brow.

"Let's take that off," he said, nodding to it, "and try Berta's cure."

Lenora pressed her lips together in resolve and reached up for the poultice.

"I'll do it," he said, crossing the room and batting away her hands. She submitted to his ministrations meekly and though she tensed when he started applying Berta's paste, did not object. "Tell me if it starts to sting," he ordered.

"It doesn't sting," she answered him cautiously. "Though it does tingle a little."

For the next couple of minutes, he concentrated solely on his task. The flesh was bruised and still swollen, though no longer the size of an egg. He cursed under his breath at the mottled color that was starting to come out. A little lower and she would have blacked an eye.

"I said, was this your bedchamber when you were a boy?" she asked patiently as he wrapped a clean strip of cloth over the treated area. From her expression, he guessed she had repeated the question more than once.

"Yes."

"Rather a large room for a small child." This he ignored. "It must be the biggest bedchamber in the house," she persisted. "I'm surprised your grandfather did not take it for his own."

Garman grimaced. "My grandfather has always been very conscious of my due."

"You mean because as your maternal grandfather he has no claim on the place?"

He pulled a face. "Precisely."

"Well," she said, "it is surely in his favor that he is so scrupulous. No one wants an encroaching guardian."

"In my view, he's always been a good deal too scrupulous," he said, turning away and heading back to the basin to wash his hands.

The bed rustled as Lenora settled once more against the pillows. She looked thoughtful, as though she had every intention of continuing the conversation. For some reason, that did not irritate him as much as he would have expected. Still, he did not mean to encourage her in poking and prying into his family setup, so he would need to nip that in the bud.

He steeled himself up to snub her as he picked up the basin of dirty water to carry out. "I'll send more logs up for the fire," he said, walking to the door.

Lenora nodded, distracted as Grizelda sauntered up the bed to touch noses with her. "Thank you," she said with a smile that somehow warmed him. "Not just for the logs but for this," she said, pointing to her dressing.

He nodded briefly and left the room. He was halfway down the stairs when his grandfather hailed him from the hallway, asking after Lenora. Gerard Sutton exclaimed and tutted over his

305

account of her injuries awhile, bemoaning what a nasty, rough life the tournament one was.

"She loves it," Garman answered coolly, which seemed to halt the older man's flow of conversation abruptly. "By the by, did you say anything to Lenora's servant? About her being past a useful age?" he asked.

His grandfather looked startled. "I?"

"Someone has," Garman said darkly. "So, I want you to make it known that she is a fixed part of our household. Lenora trusts her as none other and holds that she owes her her life. We won't be casting her off when she outlives her usefulness."

"The servant Berta, you mean?" His grandfather looked uncertain. "I don't think anyone would dare to cross her," he said. "And she seems to be keeping herself very busy about the place. But I will ask Hopkirk if anyone has fallen afoul of her. It seemed to me she and Hawise were going along very well together in the kitchen."

"Hawise?" Garman repeated slowly. "Is she not the one whose grandsons run your stables?"

"*Your* stables, my boy," his grandfather corrected him gently.

Garman ignored him. "Maybe that's why," he muttered.

"What's that?" The older man looked bewildered.

"It seems Berta is estranged from her own children," Garman said absently, scratching his neck. "Maybe spending time with Hawise has touched her on the raw."

His grandfather peered at him. "You mean…because Hawise has two generations of her offspring about her here helping run the place?"

Garman nodded. "Quite." Then he noticed his grandfather regarding him oddly. "What?"

"Oh, nothing my boy. Nothing at all," Gerard Sutton assured him with a cautious smile. "Only that I can see a new influence at work on you. One that seems highly beneficial."

Garman scowled. "Well, you needn't expect us to sleep in separate bedchambers in that case, need you?"

Gerard Sutton colored. "That is your own affair," he said primly. "I merely wished to give you options should you not be on such terms."

"Sharing a bed, you mean?"

The older man visibly bridled. "I did not intend to put you out of temper about it, my boy. I just wanted to be sensitive to any issues that may remain unresolved."

Garman cast him a withering look. "In fact, we came across two of her cousins at Kellingford. They are quite reconciled to our union. Her father's heir is shortly to become my squire."

"Indeed?" Again, his grandfather looked a good deal taken aback. "I will say, that sounds very promising." He hesitated. "Has her father attempted to make peace with you at all?" he asked, a look of pained enquiry on his face.

"No, and even if he did, I'm not interested in making peace with him," Garman retorted bluntly.

His grandfather tutted. "My boy," he said, shaking his head. "Extremely imprudent, if you will allow me to say so. Very ill-advised indeed to be at odds with your own kin."

"We've had this conversation before," Garman said dryly. "Albeit, another version of it."

His grandfather sighed. "Very well, I have made my feelings clear on this score," he admitted. "And will say no more about it."

"I'd appreciate that."

"I was wondering only yesterday if word might not have reached Twyford Castle of your marriage," his grandfather said, casting a furtive glance about.

His words brought Garman up abruptly and he gave him a furious look. "I believe I've asked you before not to speak of that place in my hearing," he said angrily.

His grandfather quailed. "I only thought—"

"Well, don't!" Garman growled. "I haven't undergone some miraculous change of opinion on that subject, I assure you!"

Seething, he carried the basin into the kitchen and set it down with a thud. Trust the old man to shatter his good mood, he thought caustically. They had always rubbed each other the wrong way and that wasn't likely to change anytime soon.

28

Lenora slept soundly all afternoon, with the cats at the foot of the bed. She awoke suddenly to the conviction that rain was coming into their tent. Blinking up at the beamed ceiling, she foggily recalled she was at Matchings Farm, Garman's boyhood home, and wondered where her husband was right now. No sooner had the thought entered her head than she heard the door quietly open and close. Lifting her head from the pillow, she saw him enter the room soft-footed as a feline.

"There you are," she murmured. "I just had a dream our tent was leaking."

"Better a tent than a boat," he said with a wry twist of his lips.

"I've never been on a boat," she admitted with a yawn.

"Do you want to join my grandfather downstairs, or take your supper here in our room?"

"Where will you be?"

He paused as though he had not considered it. "Where do you want me to be?"

"By my side," she answered truthfully, then knew a moment's panic he might not appreciate this.

"Then I will be." He shrugged, and she relaxed.

"My head feels fine," she said as he approached and peered under the dressing. He grunted at this, and Lenora perceived it must be coming out as an ugly bruise. "Does it look very unsightly?"

"It's turning purple."

"Don't people say the worst of the pain is passed once the bruise comes out?"

"That or something like it."

Was it her imagination or did his replies seem a little more clipped than usual? Lenora gazed up at him. "I believe I will take my supper downstairs," she said decisively.

"Very well." Absently, he trailed the backs of his fingers down her cheek and reached out and stroked Fendrel's head. The little cat had stalked up the bed with a reproachful meow when he approached. "I'll let them know," he said, straightening up.

"I'll get dressed."

"Don't bother." He cast a look over her. "Just put that robe on you wore earlier. It looked presentable enough."

"I can't come downstairs in a robe," she protested.

"Why not? You're decently covered. Besides, it's only my grandfather and me at table. You'll be back up to bed directly after."

Bossy, thought Lenora, but did not protest. As soon as the door closed behind him, she rose, donned her robe, and made for the looking glass. She could do nothing about the dressing stuck to her brow with the strange mixture Berta had prepared. Still, she tidied her hair around it, washed her face, and then pulled on some soft pointed slippers.

She hardly missed her lady's maid at all these days, she reflected as she left the room and wondered if Hannah had left her father's employment or remained on. She ought to have asked Eden. No doubt her cousin would know. As she approached the bottom step, she heard voices in a room off the hallway, one of which was clearly her husband's.

"I've told you before," he said with chilly detachment. "I don't give a damn what the old man wants. I'd see him hanged before being reconciled with him."

Lenora froze a moment on the stair. She had not realized things were quite *that* bad between Garman and his grandfather. Then, to her considerable relief, she heard the other speak and realized he was talking *to* and not *about* Gerard Sutton.

"I wish you would not talk in such a wild fashion—" the older man started querulously, but Garman's upraised voice suddenly cut through his words.

"Is that you on the stair, Lenora?" he called.

"It is," she answered guiltily, and took the last step.

"Come in here and join us."

Following his directions, she walked quickly into the large chamber where a long table was laid with their supper. Both men rose, and Garman rounded the table to catch her hand and draw her down to sit at his left.

"It's a cold collation," Garman's grandfather said apologetically. "We eat simple fare on a Friday as a rule."

"I am perfectly content to eat such foods," Lenora answered truthfully enough, though she wondered what the hardboiled eggs were seasoned with. They appeared to be steeped in vinegar and strewn with parsley which unfortunately brought Berta's bruise treatment to her mind. Avoiding the eggs, she settled instead for roasted onion salad and helped herself to a dish of fried root vegetables with bacon.

To her interest she noticed that Garman's grandfather ate only sparingly and eschewed wine altogether. She wondered if he had ever been in holy orders and wished her husband was not so close-lipped at all times.

"What are you thinking of?" Garman asked her with disarming shrewdness as he poured her a goblet of wine.

Lenora almost dropped her spoon. "Nothing much." Her mind raced. "I was just remembering Father Udolphus," she prevaricated and to her annoyance colored hotly.

He frowned. "Who?"

"You remember, the hermit who married us?"

"Father Udolphus, did you say?" asked Gerard Sutton with interest. "I think I've heard of him. Is he not the famous Head Abbot at Pryors Norton?"

"Can't have been," Garman answered with a frown, though in truth, he had looked the part. "This one was a hermit dwelling on a roadside."

His grandfather coughed. "I believe this abbot spends six months of every year living as a poor friar serving the community. He believes it keeps his soul untainted by the trappings of his worldly station."

Garman remembered the hermit's manner and pondered the likelihood they were one and the same. Accepting the probability of this with a shrug, he turned to Lenora. "Thanks to your character assassination, the good abbot heartily despised me."

Lenora choked on the mouthful of wine she had just taken. "I had forgotten I blackened your name to him," she admitted ruefully.

"Blackened it?" he mocked. "You stripped me of all human decency."

"Hardly that," Lenora objected, setting down her goblet. "I merely invested you with the qualities of my wicked seducer."

A knife clattered against the table, and they both turned to find Garman's grandfather listening, his eyes round, his face pale.

Lenora started. She had forgotten they were not alone. "Did you know," she said hurriedly, "that my own father thought the life of a holy nun might suit me at one time?"

"Did he?" Garman asked coolly. "I fancy I can guess precisely when that thought occurred to him."

Lenora's startled eyes met his own glittering ones. Was he angry? She took another hasty sip of wine.

Gerard Sutton cleared his throat. "Is that why your father did not wish for your marriage, my dear?" he asked, sounding as though he was making an effort. "He wished you to devote your life to the gods?"

"Not exactly." Lenora winced.

"He wanted her to marry Sir Lionel Emworth," Garman interposed heavily.

"And I refused," Lenora added.

"You had some material objection to your father's choice?" the older man asked, clearly striving to conceal his disapproval of such filial impiety.

"Oh yes," Lenora agreed. "You see—"

"Sir Lionel could not keep his hands to himself," Garman interrupted cuttingly.

Lenora's eyes flew to his. "Well, yes," she agreed. "He is the sort of man who corners maids when no one is looking." She could see Garman's grandfather was a good deal taken aback by such frank speech. "I find I do not trust a man who acts differently when he thinks himself unobserved. Your grandson, for instance, would not moderate his behavior one whit, regardless of audience."

Gerard Sutton blinked. "That is probably true," he agreed in a faint voice, and Garman grinned wolfishly. Lenora hastily covered her own mouth with a napkin.

"And then," she said, lowering the napkin, striving for a calm, even tone, "there was the fact that I wished to marry your grandson." She did not dare to look at Garman at this point, just smiled brightly at his grandfather. "You see, I have always been a great follower of the jousts."

"I see," said Gerard Sutton faintly, though his expression was disbelieving. "You are of an—um—romantic disposition, Lenora," he said with a sad smile. "Like so many young women."

An uncomfortable silence hung over the table a moment as all three of them registered that Gerard Sutton thought she was heading for a big disillusionment. "I do not think so," Lenora rallied after a heartbeat. *Was that true though?* She thought of her previous preoccupation with fortunes and true loves, and colored hotly. Mayhap she had been rather foolish and ill-informed in the past. Gerard Sutton shook his head, plainly not believing a word she said, and Lenora found herself growing stilted and awkward at the idea he believed her head over heels for his grandson.

When Garman firmly escorted her up to bed at the close of the meal, she was almost tongue-tied in bidding his grandfather goodnight. They were halfway up the stairs when she glanced back down and found the old man watching her sorrowfully.

314

"What's wrong?" Garman asked as he opened the bedroom door for her.

She bit her lip. "Your grandfather thinks me the biggest fool in the county," she said, slipping past him.

He gave a short laugh but stayed by the door. "He thinks I seduced you and stole you away, more like."

Lenora gazed back at him, feeling troubled. She sank back to sit on the bed. "Does his opinion really not bother you?" she asked curiously. He shrugged his large shoulders. "You will not trouble, then, to tell him the truth?" she persisted.

"And undo all your hard work? When you took the trouble to tell him such a pretty tale?"

Lenora's face flamed and she looked away. She deserved that, she supposed, but right now all of her playfulness seemed to have trickled away.

"You look tired," he said abruptly. "Get into bed."

"Where are you going?" she asked quickly.

"I thought I would ride over and visit with the Hainfroys."

"Oh." She had no idea why she felt so put out. She plucked at the embroidered bedcovers. "I see."

"You're dog-tired," he said again. "And need your rest."

Lenora nodded. It was nothing but the truth, but for some reason she felt ill-used. When he went to shut the door after him, she said, forestalling him, "I wish you will enquire how Tybalt and Purcel are faring. If they are not suited to life at Cofton Grange, you could bring them back with you." Even she could hear the wistful note in her voice.

315

For goodness' sake, Lenora! she told herself crossly. *He'll think you're pining for him and he hasn't even left yet!* He gave a nod and quietly shut the door behind him. Falling back onto the pillows, Lenora stared at the ceiling. It was the strangest thing. She felt…she didn't know *what* she felt precisely. Out of nowhere, it occurred to her that this prickling resentment she felt at Garman leaving her side now could be…jealousy.

She propped herself up on one elbow and stroked Fendrel, who had jumped up on the bed beside her. The more she thought about it, the stronger her conviction grew. She was jealous of the Hainfroys, for her husband sought out their company in favor of her own. The realization winded her. Until now, her favorite person in all the world had been her cousin Eden. But Eden had a wide circle of friends and acquaintances and Lenora had never begrudged her them or any time they spent apart.

Before now, she'd had admirers drop her, citing her indifference, and paying court to other beauties who actually bothered to flirt and flatter back. Lenora had never felt even the faintest flicker of resentment or sorrow at their abandonment. Her mother had said she would one day pay for her coldness to her suitors, but she never had. Why, then, did she feel these stirrings now?

It wasn't even as if he left her side to visit with another woman! In vain she told herself that he had not seen the Hainfroys in a long time, and indeed, they were like brothers to him. The gnawing feeling did not subside. Doubtless, she told herself sternly, it was because she had spent too much time in his company. Closeted in that small tent with him, she had started to imagine there was only the two of them against the whole world. But their marriage was not to be of that sort, she reproached herself. It was an arrangement, not a partnership. Why had she forgotten that? Nay, not forgotten precisely. She pressed a hand against her chest. It was not her memory that was at fault, but something else.

Fendrel meowed, startling her. "He's gone to visit your brothers," she said, striving for brisk, and sounding only forlorn. This wouldn't do! Hauling herself off the bed, she moved around the room, undressing and washing and preparing for bed. She needed to put a stop to this. No doubt it was a product of her illness, this inclination toward neediness and melancholy. They were not true facets of her nature and never had been.

She needed to collect herself. As she loosely braided her hair, she strove to remember her original intent in pushing for this marriage. Ah, that was it! It had not been a husband she craved, but a home of her own. A safe haven away from prying eyes and the world that now had no place for her.

Disquieting thoughts pushed into her mind, giving her no peace as she blew out the candle and climbed under the covers. Was it even true, her conscience whispered, that the world had no place for her? She remembered the cheering crowd at Kellingford, her cousin Kit, Cuthbert, Hal, Lady Bridgette, and even Sir Lionel. None of them, she thought, moving restlessly, acted like she was no longer a principal player in life's game. They acted as though... As though she still had a role to play. Could it be that it was only her parents who considered her life to be over?

She stared into the darkness, wondering what her father would think when he heard she had been crowned at a tournament, despite her ruined face. That Sir Lionel had still desired her, or at least her back view in any case. Would her father regret his hasty judgment that she belonged on a heap now? Almost, she was tempted to write him a breezy letter, listing her triumphs in a casual offhand manner.

317

Nay, she thought, turning over and dragging the blanket with her. Maybe she should write to Queen Armenal herself! Her eyes gleamed and she had to smother a chuckle. How the dark-eyed Queen would revel in such gossip. It would whip around the court like wildfire. Armenal would insist on regaling everyone with it until they all grew quite sick of the story.

But then, Lenora thought regretfully, the Queen would write summoning her to court. Or even worse, show up here with her retinue on a state visit. She imagined Garman's grandfather's horrified reaction to visiting royalty. She had better not, she thought with a sigh. Fendrel, irritated by her restlessness, jumped off the bed and sauntered over to lie before the fire. Lenora flipped onto her back again. What she really needed was some new purpose to distract her from feeling empty or lonely when Garman inevitably abandoned her in these strange surroundings.

She had Berta, she reminded herself. And a new kinsman in Gerard Sutton. True, she still had to win him over, but what if she enlisted his help, she thought, remembering Garman's saying she could do worse than to learn household management from his grandfather. After all, had it not been her hastily formed resolve to learn how to run her own home? She remembered Garman's plan to buy a pretty estate nearby and wished it had not involved the throwing out of its current inhabitant. Why was nothing straightforward these days? She closed her eyes. And now she would probably lie awake for hours and hours, she thought, and promptly fell fast asleep.

The next morning, she woke to find herself alone in the bed and a maid pouring water for her into a basin. Blinking at the sunlight streaming through the window, she wondered if Garman had stayed at Cofton Grange for the night or returned home to a different room. Unbidden images of the Hainfroys' comely servant, Martha, crept into her memory. After all, the girl had watched him avidly on the occasion of their former visit. Recognizing him as a virile male, she seemed to remember had been Garman's opinion. Ignoring the flash of irritation this caused her, she climbed resolutely from the bed.

"Did my husband return last night?" she asked in what she hoped was a light, airy fashion, petting first Grizelda and then Fendrel's sleepy heads.

"Nay, milady," the servant replied with a look of severe disapproval on her face. Sensing there was more to come, Lenora gave her a look of bright enquiry. "Those Hainfroy brothers be awful wild, milady. When they gets together with the young master, one night's carousing can quickly turn into seven."

"A whole week?" Lenora exclaimed.

The maid nodded. "Mind, they was a few years younger then," she conceded grudgingly. "But Master Garman, he were never good at keeping Master Sutton informed of his whereabouts and that's the sad truth of it. Powerful worried Master Sutton's been over the years on his account." She shook her head and gave a gusty sigh.

"Your name is Ada, isn't it?" Lenora asked, lifting a soft red wool dress out of the trunk.

"That's right, milady." A flicker of gratification flashed over the woman's face that her name had been remembered.

Lenora gave her an encouraging smile. "Do you think Master Sutton would be willing to give me a tour of the place today and show me the lay of the land?"

Ada gave her a surprised look. "Sure to, miss. He's a very kind and obliging master *he* is and would deny his family nothing." She pressed her lips together grimly again and Lenora guessed she was thinking hard thoughts about Garman's attitude toward the older man.

She was tempted for a moment to press for more information, but decided she had better go slowly. Old servants could be tricky to handle without giving offence, and she didn't want to cause them to close ranks against a newcomer who trod clumsily and set their backs up. Thinking that Eden would be proud of her strategic thinking, she thanked Ada for the hot water and made haste to wash and dress. Ada stuck around to help her fasten her laces, but as soon as she was clothed, Lenora dismissed her to her other duties and dressed her hair herself.

Her own appearance in the looking glass startled her. She was flushed and bright-eyed and even her wild hair didn't detract from the fact she looked surprisingly well. Maybe she was feverish, and that was what had given her such a good color? She turned this way and that before the large oval mirror. Had she regained some of her lost figure? She was definitely filling out her robe better than she had before.

Reaching for a hair comb, she started trying to bring her disordered locks under control. Peering under the plaster, she found the bump on her head so vastly reduced that it barely even seemed a lump anymore. Gingerly, she pulled the plaster away and dabbed at the area with a damp cloth to remove the last of the paste. She would go without the dressing for today. Perhaps now she looked less scrawny and didn't have a large poultice stuck to her head then her husband would deign to sleep in the same bed as her?

Gerard Sutton had already broken his fast when she made her way down to the parlor, but another servant hurried through and fetched her toasted bread and a bowl of spiced wine which she plunked down before Lenora and then hurried off with a distracted curtsey. Clearly the servants had many duties to fulfill around the farm and would not stand around waiting on her as they did at court.

On finishing her meal, she made her way thoughtfully to the kitchens where she found Grizelda and Fendrel already partaking of a fish dish and purring around Berta's ankles. "Good morning," she greeted her servant. "How are you, Berta?"

Her maid grunted, eyeing Lenora's forehead. "Took off your poultice, I see," she said sourly.

"Yes, it's a good deal better today, and I found the paste smeared all through my hair and made things vastly uncomfortable. Although," she added hastily, "'twas vastly efficacious and I am sure quite reduced the swelling. Thank you."

"Humph."

"How are you finding Matchings Farm?" Lenora asked, lowering her voice confidentially. She glanced down the length of the kitchen and found only Hawise at the far end, busily employed hanging fresh herbs up to dry.

Berta shrugged irritably. "It's a roof over my head. No good asking for more in this life. Not in my experience."

Lenora's brows rose. Garman had been right. Something was bothering Berta. "Your quarters are comfortable?" she asked softly.

"Aye."

"The tasks assigned you not too arduous?"

"Hah! I've done a lot worse in my time." Still her tone was bitter. The kitchen door opened and shut, and Lenora and Berta turned to look as a tall youth stepped inside and took the strands

321

of rosemary from Hawise that she was stretching to hang on the hook.

"Let me, Granny," he said cheerfully and then stooped to kiss Hawise's craggy cheek.

Lenora was surprised to see a starkly bitter expression creep over Berta's face. "So Hawise has family here," Lenora murmured.

Berta's expression went blank. She slammed a bowl down on the table. "If that's all, miss, I've got work to do," she said rudely.

Lenora's startled gaze flew to Berta's resentful expression and then back to Hawise, who was beaming up at her grandson. "Can you direct me toward Master Sutton's whereabouts?" she asked carefully. "I would have a word with him this morn."

"Johnny?" Berta shouted, making Lenora jump. "Where's the master?"

The amiable youth grinned. "He be up the long pasture, Miss Berta," he said in a soft countrified drawl.

"Would you escort me there?" Lenora asked and saw a panicked look cross the young man's face.

"Now, Johnny," Hawise scolded fondly. "Don't 'ee stand there lookin' foolish when the mistress asks ye a request. Look lively, do."

"O' course, miss," he stammered, dragging off his hood and shifting from one foot to the other. "Wasn't my intention to be disobligin'." He stole a look at Lenora from under his blond lashes and blushed.

"That's very good of you, Johnny," Lenora responded and ran to fetch her cloak, for it looked cold and crisp outside though the sky was very blue.

Soon they were walking briskly in the direction of the Long Meadow. Lenora decided to drag some conversation from the tongue-tied young man. "So Hawise is your grandmother. Did she find you the position here at Matchings Farm?"

"My granny, father, and uncle before me, they all work for Master Sutton," Johnny told her bashfully.

"He's been here a good while, then. Did you work for Master Garman's father before that?"

"Nay, missus," Johnny said, shaking his head. "Master Garman's father barely saw out the building of the place before he was taken by the plague."

"I see," Lenora echoed slowly. "And Garman's mother, was she also a plague victim?"

"That she were," Johnny concurred. "A sad day for the master when his only child was taken."

Lenora looked up quickly. "At least she left him her son to raise, so he was not left without kith or kin."

"Aye," he conceded, scratching the back of his head. "But—" Johnny hesitated. "'Tweren't the same, miss, begging your pardon. On account of Master Garman's status. 'Tis true he's his blood and all, but still…'tain't the same."

"His status?" Lenora puzzled. "I don't think I quite—?"

"Lenora!" Gerard Sutton's voice rang out close by in slightly alarmed tones. "Is all well, my dear?" His small, neat figure hurried over to her, rolling up the piece of parchment he had been holding. "Should you be out here in the light of your recent injuries?"

Lenora waved this aside. "I am quite healed up, as you see, Grandfather," she said, doggedly determined to pursue their acquaintance, in spite of his seeming reluctance. She fancied he started slightly at the familiarity but ignored his reaction. After all, had not Garman himself said she should address him thus? "I am come to see you, on my husband's advice."

Again, Gerard Sutton looked discomforted. "Indeed?" he wavered. "He is back, then? I had not expected to see him before midday at the earliest."

Lenora plastered a brave smile to her face. "No, he is not back," she admitted. "But we discussed this matter days ago, whilst we were at Kellingford, in fact."

"I see," he answered, though plainly from his expression he did not.

"I have a great hankering to learn household management, you see," Lenora plunged on determinedly. "He suggested that you would be an excellent mentor."

"Garman suggested this?"

"He did." She hesitated. "I believe my husband mentioned at one time you used to be a steward, so I thought—"

Gerard Sutton's head whipped around to face her. "He told you that?"

"Well—yes." Lenora stared at his shocked tone. "Have I said something amiss?"

"What did he tell you?" he asked eagerly. "Tell me exactly."

324

"Why, that if I wished to learn household management, you would make me a good teacher. As I said, he had told me previously you had been a steward, so it seemed quite a natural recommendation for him to make."

He huffed out a breath. "And nothing else?" He sounded disappointed. "Would you walk this way with me a little?" He gestured politely.

Lenora fell in step beside him, cudgeling her brains. "He explained about his parents," she said slowly. Again, Gerard Sutton seemed to hold his breath. "That they eloped without their parents' consent. That seemed to explain your own attitude toward our marriage," she wound up frankly.

Some color stole back into the older man's cheeks at this. He went to speak but seemed to check himself. "I apologize if you find me unwelcoming, Lenora," he said stiffly.

"I don't," she contradicted him. "Not unwelcoming precisely."

He clicked his tongue. "No doubt I seem sadly standoffish to you."

She considered this. "Not that, but I do not think a state of perfect accord exists between you and Garman. So, as his wife, I can hardly expect to be welcomed by you with open arms."

He turned a little pale. "This is very difficult," he muttered almost to himself. "Very difficult indeed. If only one knew how to proceed for the best."

He was so different in every respect from Garman that it was small wonder they were not close. "Was it difficult, even when he was two years old?" she asked.

"Yes, even then." His mouth twisted, and he rubbed his brow distractedly, swinging around to regard her searchingly. "I'm afraid I cannot elaborate, but if you are truly in earnest about learning household management—"

"I am," Lenora cut in coolly.

"Then I will most happily take up your instruction."

"Immediately?" she enquired.

He blinked a little at this. "If that is your wish."

"It is." She inclined her head. "For I have nothing else to occupy myself with at present."

"Very well, then, my dear. We will begin at once."

Lenora spent an informative afternoon with Grandfather Sutton. First, he showed her the outhouses, the two barns, and the stables, introducing her to his core staff of five men. During the harvest, he explained they would be obliged to hire more hands, but for the most part, these sufficed.

Then the pair of them rode out to take in the five-acre spread of ripening wheat and rye for the autumn harvest along with vegetable patches of onions, peas, and beans. Returning that evening tired but keen to share her exploits, Lenora was disappointed to find her husband had still not returned from Cofton Grange. Swiftly masking her chagrin, she washed and changed and joined his grandfather for a filling supper of minced mutton in a piecrust served with spiced roasted parsnips. Over the final course of lightly fried crackers and cheese, Lenora found she could not disguise her yawns.

"Doubtless it's all that fresh air," Gerard Sutton commented with a smile.

"Very likely," Lenora agreed. "I had not expected to spend so much time out of doors today, but I found it most instructive."

"It's best to start with a thorough grounding of the household resources," he replied, dabbing the corners of his mouth with a napkin. "I'm pleased you found it interesting." He hesitated. "You were very pleasant company today, my dear," he added, both surprising and gratifying her.

After supper, Lenora made for her bedchamber and ordered a bath which she lingered over. Suppose Garman should come home while she was bathing? The memory of that first night in the inn sprang to mind, when he had climbed in her bath with her. Lenora bit her lip, a blush rising up her neck. She did not think she would mind if he wanted to share it with her now, she thought, slightly surprised by the direction of her own thoughts.

It seemed she was ready to move forward with their marriage, but sadly, Garman was now dragging his feet. He did not return before she turned to gooseflesh and was forced to climb out of her bath. Nor had he returned when she blew out her candle and drew up the covers. Even the cats shunned her bed, curling up together in front of the fire.

When next Lenora woke, it was to hear someone moving around clumsily in the dark. A smothered oath let her know it was Garman. He had clearly forgotten the proportions of the room, she thought, listening to him fling off his clothes and then stumble and stub his toe. He swore again, then groped his way toward the bed. Why had he not lit a candle? she wondered and felt glad he had not trod on Fendrel's tail.

When the mattress dipped, she realized he was climbing into her side of the bed. She had just roused herself to slide away to make room for him when his arm slid around her and drew her back roughly against his big, hard body. He let out a half sigh, half groan the moment they made contact and pressed a sloppy kiss into the side of her neck before settling his head on the pillow beside her own.

Smelling strong spirits on his breath, she wondered if he was sotted. "Have you been drinking solidly for the past two days?"

"Aye," he agreed drowsily. "Why? Are you about to act the scolding wife?"

"I'm not sure," Lenora mused. "Why did you not stay away another night?"

"Didn't want to," he growled.

Lenora's ears pricked up at this. "You didn't? I expect your friends were eager for you to stay on," she speculated.

"Why should I if I don't want to?" His tone was aggrieved. "You're as bad as Huw. Going on at me."

Lenora mulled this over. "I was only thinking of you riding home in the dark. You're lucky you didn't end up in a ditch."

He snorted. "Know that road like the back of my hand."

"Well, I expect you know this room, but you've nearly tripped a half dozen times."

He made no reply to this, and she thought he had fallen into a doze when he suddenly asked in a gravelly voice, "How's your head?"

"My head is quite healed, thank you. Yours, however, will be sadly aching on the morrow."

"Nay, wife, for I'll dunk my head in a basin of cold water and be right as rain."

He had addressed her as "wife" at least a half dozen times now, she told herself sternly. There was no reason for it to make her feel so fluttery and out of breath. "Why not simply have a bath?

I had a bath this evening," she carried on recklessly. "I had hoped you might return for it."

She felt him lift his head off the pillow. "Why?" he asked blearily.

"I think I've gained some flesh and wanted you to corroborate," she answered lightly.

He was silent a moment. "Remind me to check in the morning," he said thickly and shifted against her back. "Tease."

Lenora held her breath as his hand slid between her thighs to cup her there in a shockingly proprietary fashion. Her pulse raced in some unexpected places. Then very softly, he began to snore.

Oh.

29

Garman woke suddenly to find himself alone in his bed. At least, he had thought he was alone until he felt a furry creature tucked into his armpit. A smothered exclamation later, he realized it was the little gray cat Fendrel and relaxed back onto the pillow with a groan. His mouth was dry and something was niggling at his memory.

A quick glance about the room showed Lenora was nowhere to be found. Squinting at the window, he guessed it was around midday. Fendrel began to vibrate, emitting a low buzzing sound which Garman was dimly aware indicated feline satisfaction. At least someone was satisfied, he thought darkly. He wasn't sure how much longer he could hold out with this considerate husband shit.

His decision where to spend the last two days had less to do with catching up with the Hainfroys than avoiding Lenora while she was recovering from a head injury. When he had insisted she share his bed, he had not anticipated how bloody difficult he would find restraining himself. He rubbed his brow and huffed out a frustrated breath.

If anyone had told him this time two weeks ago that his marriage would still be unconsummated at this point, he would have laughed them to scorn. But the fact remained, he'd barely touched her. And that needed to change. Soon. He was not a considerate man, and the strain was starting to tell on him. She barely seemed to leave his thoughts these days and other women didn't even register with him anymore.

What the hells was it about Lenora Montmayne that had him champing at the bit? He couldn't remember a partiality for one particular woman since the days of callow youth. The one that sprang to mind had been a black-haired barmaid with a lusty laugh and ample charms. Absolutely nothing like Lenora.

Not to say that Lenora did not have a nice laugh, he conceded, rolling out of bed, for she did. In fact, for a spoiled court beauty, she was easily entertained. He doubted many highborn wenches would have been content in that tent at Kellingford, with the mud and having to piss in a field, but she had seemed almost sorry to leave it.

Most of the time, she seemed to make up her own amusement, he reflected as he upended the half jug of cold leftover washing water into the empty basin. Quite often, at his expense, he thought with a wry twist of his lips as he leaned down to plunge his face straight into the water. That damned guard at the palace and the priest who'd wed them sprang to mind. He stood upright, cold water trickling down his neck.

She'd had a lively disregard for his wrath from the first, he thought as he scrubbed a cloth over his wet hair and shoulders. Despite his ugly reputation, she hadn't flinched. His throat went dry as he remembered her standing up in that damn bathtub at the inn, letting him look his fill at her naked, dripping body.

Then suddenly, her words from the previous evening came back to him. *I had a bath this evening. I had hoped you might return for it.* His eyelids flickered. She couldn't have meant that the way it sounded…could she?

Pulling his tunic over his head, he tried to remember what his own response had been. What had he said to that? He couldn't even remember. Cursing himself for a fool, he dragged on his braies and fastened his chausses. Below stairs seemed strangely deserted. It was only when he entered the kitchens that he found Hawise humming tunelessly as she prepared vegetables for a stew.

"Where is everyone?" he asked, glancing around.

"Berta accompanied the master and Lady Lenora into town," she answered smartly.

"Town?"

"Wednesday is market day," she reminded him. Garman frowned. Why the hells did Lenora want to go to a provincial market? he wondered with irritation. "Would you be needing something, sir?" she asked, setting down her knife and wiping her hands on a cloth.

He shook his head distractedly. "What time did they set off?"

"Straight after breaking their fast." She glanced at the window. "And should be back before ere long."

He grunted and waved a hand, indicating she should carry on with her stew. She beamed at him and took her knife back up to commence chopping onions. "How is Berta getting along?" he found himself asking, propping his hip against the table.

Hawise frowned slightly. "She's a hard worker," she said lightly. "And never needs to be shown any task more than once." He nodded at this, guessing there was more to come. In the silence, he reached for a round loaf and cut himself a thick slice. Hawise cleared her throat. "No doubt, leaving behind her old life and her family hasn't been easy."

Garman paused in the act of slathering on some butter. "No doubt," he repeated.

The old woman directed a shrewd glance his way. "Relations ain't always the easiest to get along with. I know when my Jem married his Annie, there were a few ruffled feathers at first. Soon blew over though," she remarked sagely. "All water under the bridge now. Folks just need to learn how to get along."

Garman raised his piece of bread to his lips, then lowered it again. For a moment he had a sharp suspicion she was speaking directly to him. He narrowed his eyes.

"Look over there," Hawise recommended, nodding in the direction of the kitchen fire. He glanced over to the hearth where Lenora's white cat was curled up next to his grandfather's old hound. "Kolby's reconciled at any rate," she said with satisfaction.

As if disturbed by this mention of his name, Kolby stretched out by the fire and yawned, rolling onto his stomach. Grizelda fussily rose and resettled herself against him. Almost apologetically, the dog smacked his lips together and lowered his head onto his front paws. "We'll all learn to rub along together in the end," Hawise said with satisfaction. "You'll see. Mind, I have no clue where the little gray is this morn."

Garman cleared his throat. "He's still abed," he admitted.

Hawise's eyebrows shot up her head, but she said nothing on that score. "I daresay he'll find his way down here when his belly starts rumbling," she said comfortably.

"Very likely," he agreed and wandered back out of the kitchen toward the front of the house, still eating his bread and butter. If the party had left at first light, they should be returning any minute. Cofton Warren was a small town, and if Lenora was hoping the marketplace would rival those of Aphrany or Caer-Lyoness, she would be sadly disappointed.

On impulse he made his way down to the stables to check on Bria'ag, who seemed none the worse for their midnight ride home. "End up in a ditch indeed," Garman muttered as he stroked the horse's gleaming flanks. He felt a flicker of annoyance that Tybalt had felt no impulse to bond with his own destrier yet was now inseparable from Huw's stallion. "Pollux is nothing compared to you," he assured his horse.

"Was you wanting something, Master Garman?" a voice asked doubtfully from the next stall. Garman exclaimed and Bria'ag stamped a mighty hoof. Glancing over the partition, he saw a wide-eyed groom peering up at him, clutching a broom.

"No," he responded shortly. "What time are you expecting your master home?"

"Oh, anytime now like as not," answered the groom. Garman nodded briskly and exited the stable.

His head was not sore for he rarely suffered, and the bread had settled any slight queasiness. Still, he felt irritable and out of sorts. Where the hells was his wife anyway? Should she not ask his leave before sauntering forth here, there, and everywhere? He kicked a pebble and scowled.

He should have stayed longer at Cofton Grange, instead of haring back here to her side. Huw had been most put out by his insistence on leaving, though Ivo had merely laughed as though he were in on some grand jest. "She won't vanish into thin air if you stay another night!" Huw had snapped. "What's so special about her anyway?" he'd jeered. "Certainly not her looks. And by your own account she's no heiress either."

Garman frowned; he hadn't fought with either of the Hainfroy brothers in earnest since they were lads, but Ivo had been forced to step in at that point, for Garman had Huw by the throat.

Brawling, his old master would have called it, and either knocked their heads together or emptied a bucket of water over them. But old Sir Bernhard had been dead now for over four years and their boyhood fights were long behind them. Doubtless the vast quantity of drink was partly to blame for his loss of control, but not all. *No*, he thought, clenching his fist, *not all*.

The sound of hooves and voices had him wheeling around to see the approaching cart. Lenora's laugh drifted over, and he started forward to meet them.

"Ah, you're back, then, my boy," his grandfather hailed him, pulling on the reins. He looked to be in high spirits for once with a flush on his cheeks and a sparkle in his eye.

"Aye," Garman said grudgingly and reached up for Lenora to climb down. She gazed down at him somewhat quizzically. "What?" he asked, sounding surlier than he'd intended.

"How's your head?" she asked archly as he swung her down.

"Fine, how's yours?"

"You needn't snap," she reproached him as she turned to reach back up to take some parcels from Berta. Garman grasped her upper arms and moved her bodily to one side as he took the boxes in her place.

"I can get down meself!" Berta said sharply when he held out a hand to her. He rolled his eyes and reached into the back of the cart for the bulging sacks.

"Allow me to take some of those," his grandfather protested as Garman slung them over his shoulder. He sent a withering look in his grandfather's direction. The old man was only half his size and he was more than equal to the task.

"Here comes Johnny now," said Lenora brightly. "He can carry some of them."

Johnny came hurrying over, hands held out. Then he caught Garman's eye and visibly quailed.

335

"I've got these," Garman glowered, and the crestfallen lad hastily retreated.

"Um, very obliging of you, my boy," his grandfather murmured. "You needn't worry that I've let her overtax herself. We've kept a careful eye on her the whole time, isn't that right, Berta?"

Berta hitched an irritable shoulder, which everyone seemed to take as an affirmative.

"I feel absolutely fine," Lenora assured him, taking the older man's arm. They smiled at one another in perfect accord, and Garman fell in step behind them with Berta, his mood a good deal more akin to the sour old woman's.

"Soused, were you?" Berta asked with a sidelong look. "I know that hangdog look."

"I feel perfectly fine," he retorted.

"They do say," Berta mused. "That a good cure for morning fog is to wash your pizzle in salt and vinegar water."

Garman glared at her. "I haven't got morning fog," he said coldly. "And even if I did, I wouldn't be putting *my pizzle* anywhere near such a concoction."

"Actually I might have got that wrong," Berta admitted, tapping her chin. "It might have been to dip your ballocks in it, not the pizzle."

Mercifully, Hawise flung open the door for them at this point, and they were divested of cloaks and purchases.

"We managed to buy cloves," Lenora told her sadly. "But the Spicer had only limited stock today and no nutmeg whatsoever. He did say that by this time next month he should have received a shipment."

336

Garman snagged Lenora's arm when she would have followed both Berta and Hawise to the kitchens. "It's time for you to rest now," he growled.

"He's quite right, my child," his grandfather interrupted when she would have argued. "You've been on your feet all morning."

"But I feel quite recovered now," she protested as Garman maneuvered her toward the stairs.

"An hour or two's rest before supper would doubtless be most beneficial," Gerard called up after them. "I'll have Ada bring up water for you to wash."

Lenora twisted around to look back at Garman over her shoulder. "Your grandfather has not yet finished today's instruction."

Garman propelled her firmly up the steps with his hands on her shoulders. "Instruction?"

"Household management," said Lenora smugly. "I'm proving a most apt pupil."

"Oh?" He gazed down at the top of her head. "You've started on that, have you?"

"We started yesterday, actually," Lenora sniffed. "While you were dallying with your friends."

Dallying? "I see." He closed the door firmly behind them and steered her toward the bed. "Sit, and I'll take off your boots."

Lenora sat on the edge of the bed while he unfastened her ankle boots. A knock on the door heralded Ada's arrival with a steaming pitcher of hot water. Lenora thanked her and rose to set about her ablutions. "Why are you taking off your boots?"

she asked in surprise, catching sight of him as she dried her face on a cloth.

He didn't answer, simply crossed the room to stand beside her, washing his own hands. Lenora shrugged, but when she went to walk to the bed, he caught her elbow. "Let me see," he said, putting his hands carefully to her brow and parting the hair there. She waited patiently, head bowed as he inspected the small cut and the slight remaining redness. "It's healed well."

"I told you," she said. "I'm a good healer. It's my secret talent."

He grunted, releasing her. "You are surprisingly resilient," he admitted, watching her climb onto the bed.

"I'm not really tired," she said, flipping onto her back.

"No?" He walked to the edge of the bed. "Then maybe it's time I continued *my* instruction."

"Your instruction?" She gazed up at him. "And what are you teaching me, pray?"

"How to please me," he answered shortly.

She turned rather pink at this. "I'm already learning how to be a good housewife. There are limits to how much I can learn at any one time."

"Then I give you permission to drop the household duties for now," he said arrogantly.

"Oh, you do, do you?" she spluttered as he lowered onto the bed beside her. "How good of you!" He wasn't fooled though. Under the bluster, she was nervous. He frowned absently; didn't she know by now that she had no need to be nervous around him? Reaching for her, he drew her close. "Tell me if I do anything you don't like," he said, almost surprising himself.

Her eyes met his. "I thought I was supposed to be learning what you like?"

"We'll both be learning each other's likes," he corrected, his gaze dropping to her lips. "Now, if I remember correctly, you like my kiss."

She caught her breath, and he lowered his mouth to hers. The burst of pleasure he felt at the simple touch of her lips against his shocked him. He had got that wrong, he realized dazedly. *He* was the one who liked her kiss. More than liked. He loved it. Especially when she made that sound deep in her throat.

Why had he not been doing more of this? He drew back his head, breaking the kiss. "Wrap your arms around me," he demanded. *And what else? Oh yes.* "Run your fingers through my hair, like last time." He had only just a chance to see her eyes widen in surprise before he crushed his lips to hers again. He felt her hands press against his back, clasping him to her. Then one slid up to his neck and into his hair and he lost it, deepening the kiss, turning it into a carnal mating of mouths.

Was he being too rough? He eased up his bruising grip, the hard press of his lips and rolled onto his back, taking her with him, so she was now in the superior position. He couldn't trust himself to be considerate, he realized too late. He'd let her dictate the pace.

Immediately, Lenora scooted in closer, pursuing his kiss. Her fingers tugged at his roots; she opened her mouth over his and moaned. *Ah gods.* She liked it. His head reeled. Perhaps she knew she could trust him after all? When her tongue lapped at his, he growled deep in his chest, his hands sliding around to grab her ass. Her legs were on either side of him now and she was practically astride him. He wanted her naked and grinding on top of him. The feel of her skirts reminded him he'd left her clothes on for a reason. *Right.* She was a virgin. He shuddered.

339

Gods, he needed to be gentler. He lifted up his hands to ease her head back from his.

"What is it?" she panted, eyes glazed, her hair coming loose from its arrangement and tumbling loose about her face. His cock pulsed hard seeing her like this for him. Fuck, she might not be beautiful, but she was desirable as hell, and *his*.

"Lift up your skirts." There was only a moment of hesitation before she released him and began bunching up the fabric. "Show me," he said shakily.

Her head jerked up. "What?"

"Bring it up here." He licked his lips and Lenora's face flamed.

"Um."

"We did this before too," he reminded her unevenly. "Remember? In the tent."

"Yes," she squeaked. "But…but I was…" She made a helpless gesture.

"Facing the other way, I know. It makes no difference. Come and sit on my face, Lenora."

"Garman!" She was shocked, but he was past caring.

"Now!" he rumbled, and with a muffled sob, she fell forward, edging up his body inch by inch, the tangle of skirts preventing her from moving faster.

He reached down and started unlacing his crotch. The dull, almost painful throb of his cock needed relief. He took himself in hand and groaned as she hitched up her skirts, parted her knees, and showed him her pretty slit.

"Fuck," he whispered. "Perfect." And it was. So perfect he had to close his eyes an instant or he would have released at the sight of her. He slid his hand up his throbbing shaft and squeezed the tip hard. He didn't want to spend himself on the sheets. He wanted to release deep inside his wife.

"Garman?"

"I can't wait," he groaned earthily. "Have mercy and give me a taste."

She whimpered as one of his hands grabbed her hip to urge her up and over his chest. "What if you can't breathe—oh!"

Then I'll die happy, he thought, moaning against her slippery pink cunt. So good. He could have been sampling this divine honeypot between her legs for the last two weeks. *What the fuck had he been thinking?* He dragged his tongue between her slick folds and over her pretty pearl again and again, delving into her tight sheathe in a tease that had his cock twitching in anticipation. Her wetness maddened him. His cock jerked in his own tight grip, but still he couldn't drag his mouth away. He strained his ears to catch her hitched breathing, his hand clasping and unclasping on her trembling thigh. He still hadn't had his fill when he heard her wail and felt her convulsing around his swirling tongue.

Only the overwhelming impulse to spill his seed made him disentangle her limbs and roll her under him. "Open wider," he grunted, sliding his hips into the cradle of her thighs. Her blue eyes blinked up at him. "Wrap your legs around my back."

Her eyelids drifted closed, and he bit back a short laugh. "Lenora, I'm about to take you," he warned.

"I don't care," she murmured. "I'm feeling too blissful."

341

"Well, I'm about to wake you up," he said. "With my cock." He rubbed it against her wet heat.

Her eyes flickered open at that, and a look of faint alarm washed over her face. "That's not going to fit!" she gasped, glancing down at his angry-looking manhood. "Why does it look so different now?"

"Because of you," he said, opening her nether lips with his fingers and easing his length against her slick folds. He flexed his hips and stroked it against her with agonizing slowness, deliberately grazing her sensitive bud and making her gasp. "You'll make it fit, Lenora, you're so nice and wet. You're going to open right up and take me deep," he promised huskily. "And next time you'll want it there. You'll ache for me as bad as I do for you."

Her eyes were big and round now, as she listened to his every word. "Very well then," she said in a choked voice. "But first—" She broke off.

His head jerked up. "What?"

Her chest heaved. "Can you do that thing? That thing you did before?"

"Anything," he promised raspily. "Tell me."

"When you—" She released her stranglehold on the back of his shirt and covered her face with her forearm. "Touched me where I'm ugliest," she said on a sob.

His eyebrows snapped together. He stared down at her uncomprehendingly. "You're not ugly anywhere," he said tersely.

"You know what I mean," she said in a muffled voice.

"No, I don't." He grabbed the arm blocking his view of her face and shoved it up above her head. Her eyes were squeezed shut. "Look at me." She shook her head. "Look at me, Lenora." A tear trickled down her cheek. It felt like a splash of cold water to his back. *Shit.* "What are you talking about?"

"M-my jaw," she stammered. "My eyelids."

What the fuck? Had he touched them? He gave his head a slight shake. "What did I do?" Another tear. He was fucking this up. Reaching down, he adjusted his cock so it lay harmlessly against her belly, and carefully lowered his chest to hers. "Sweetheart, why are you crying?"

"I don't know," she confessed shakily. "Sorry."

"Don't," he said and ducked his head to press a swift kiss to her jaw. "Here?" She nodded. "You think you're ugly here?" he asked softly and trailed small kisses down the pitted skin. "This little rough patch of skin?" he asked incredulously.

"Yes," she whispered.

"You're wrong. It's not ugly. Not even a bit." No response. He frowned and hovered over her. "These eyelids are the reason I started liking you in the first place." Her eyes sprang open at that and she stared at him. "Close them," he ordered. "I want to kiss them."

Her eyes shut obediently, and he pressed the most careful, lightest kisses of his life against her crinkled pink lids. She was holding her breath, he realized and waited. Then he saw the moisture seeping out from under her lashes.

"Why are you crying, Lenora?" he groaned. "Should I stop?"

"You like me?" she asked in a small voice.

What the hell? "Of course I fucking like you." He stared down at her thunderstruck. But really, how could she know? He was pretty taken aback by his declaration himself. "I like you," he said firmly.

"But…" She hesitated. "You don't like anyone."

"Bullshit," he said flatly. "I like you. A lot."

She swallowed. "I like you too."

Fuck. What was happening? And why did his chest feel so tight? Then he remembered he'd been sporting a raging hard-on for the gods alone knew how long. All his blood must have rushed to his dick. Of course, if he had even a spark of decency, her distress would have made him go limp by now. He cursed and went to roll off her. Her knees tightened around his hips and she wrapped her arms around his neck, preventing him.

"Where are you going?"

"Nowhere," he said gruffly. "I just don't think I should be forcing myself on you when you're upset."

"Forcing? You're not," she said calmly. "Don't go." Then she unwound one arm and placed her warm palm against his chest where it had felt most constricted. Did she know how it ached then? His eyes shot to meet hers as the warmth spread out over him. But her hand was already sliding down now, down over the jumping muscles in his stomach until she wrapped her fingers around his neglected shaft. He made a strangled noise in the back of his throat.

"I don't really know how to touch you back," she admitted, puffing out a breath.

"You're doing fine."

"Really?"

344

He nodded. "Though if you keep doing that…" He winced, his fingers closing over hers. "I'm already way too primed." Still, he could not resist moving her hand in a slow stroke that made the sweat bead at his brow and his hips jerk.

She settled back against the mattress and let her knees fall apart on either side of him.

He inhaled sharply. "Lenora."

"Yes, Garman."

"I shouldn't—" he said, even as his hand slid up one milk-white thigh. The blondness of her hair there was only one shade darker than that on her head. He stroked his thumb through the damp curls and watched her sigh. "Are you sure?"

She nodded and he settled over her, bracing his weight on his forearms, still gazing down at her face.

"The first time for women is not supposed to be good," he said regretfully. "But I'll try to make this as easy as I can."

Her arms slid around his back as he reached down and adjusted himself to her before pressing forward. He saw the wariness creep into her open gaze, a wince, a smothered yell, and then he pressed his mouth to hers as he breached her virginity and slid home. *Finally, thank the gods.*

She wasn't with him for this part, but he was acutely aware of her every shaky breath. Somehow, despite his pleasure, he found himself moderating his thrusts without too much effort. True, he had to squeeze his eyes shut to concentrate. The feel of her around him was like nothing else. It was strange how aware he felt of the clench of her fingers at his back as he luxuriated in the tight, silky clasp of her. How often he felt compelled to press his lips to hers. These were new impulses, entirely foreign to him. He would worry about that later.

345

For now, he would have to concentrate on pulling out before he reached crisis point. She had not been insulted when he had spent on her smooth belly before, so she would allow the liberty this second time. Spending inside a woman was not an indulgence Garman Orde had ever allowed himself since he came of age to seek a woman's company. Old Sir Bernhard had explained the consequences of such actions.

When he felt his brow begin to bead with sweat, he groaned and told himself his exertions had gone on long enough. He needed to withdraw. *You don't need to*, a voice whispered in his head that sounded very like his own. *This is your wife. Any brat you got on her would not be left behind, for she would raise it.*

For a moment he struggled to remember why he wanted no legitimate issue either. *My revenge*, he thought desperately, but for once, the notion did not hold him in the icy grip it usually wielded. How could it, when the hot clasp of Lenora's body had him in its thrall? A tingling in the base of his spine warned him too late that his control was quite gone. He had left it too late and overwhelming pleasure had snuck up on him. His eyes flew open, fastened on Lenora's answering startled look, and he lost himself in her with a series of deeply satisfied moans.

*

Afterward, he lay behind her, eyes closed as his chin rested on the top of her head. It was easy to drown out the alarming thoughts jostling to the front of his mind when he still held her in his arms. He would worry about what he'd done later. For now, his body felt too happy about it to pay any heed to the clamoring concerns.

"We'll have to go down to supper soon," Lenora pointed out. Garman frowned. For some reason he had the notion she should be content to lie like this with him for as long as he saw fit.

"Only, I've had a busy day and I'm quite hungry," she continued.

"Go to sleep," he murmured.

"I'm not remotely tired." She turned her head to look back at him, and he gave a sound of disapproval. "You probably need to catch up on your sleep," she pointed out, "after your late night, but I'm going to get up now." He tightened his hold about her waist, and she smothered a laugh. "I'll send Fendrel up to cuddle with you." He opened an eye at that. *Cuddle?* "Your grandfather will be expecting me at table, and I don't want to disappoint him."

She didn't seem to mind so much about disappointing *him*, he thought with a twinge of annoyance. Still, he released her, as against all odds, it turned out he was a considerate sort of husband.

To his surprise, he did not drift off to sleep as she moved about the room despite the fact he was both sated and tired. He watched as she emptied the dirty water out of the window and then poured the rest of the clean water out of the jug into the bowl. It would be cold now, he thought, watching her lift her shift to wash discreetly between her legs.

Suddenly, he wished he had waited until nightfall and they had been fully undressed for bed when he took her virginity. Lifting her skirts like that in the middle of the afternoon had possibly not been the most thoughtful consummation of their marriage. And now she proposed to go downstairs and eat a meal without him. It was…strangely dissatisfying.

"It's good we waited until we had each other's measure," he said gruffly, raising himself up on one elbow.

She lowered her skirts and regarded him with surprise. "I thought you were waiting until I had fattened up a little," she said with a teasing smile. "And my hipbones didn't stick out too much."

He was silent a moment. In truth, his initial reluctance had made little to no sense to him now. She had been both pale and wan, but it had been something else that had held him back and he was damned if he knew what it had been. "It wasn't because you were too skinny," he said shortly, dropping back onto the pillow. "It was something else, though I hardly even knew it at the time."

"You mean other than the fact you weren't particularly attracted to me?" she asked lightly.

"What?" He was almost startled by her words.

"You were most frank and upfront about it, I thought. I respected you for it."

"I seem to remember I showed you my cock was hard enough to get the job done," he pointed out.

"You most certainly did not show it me!" Lenora spluttered, tidying her hair at the small glass. "You put my hand on it. Over the covers."

He shrugged. "Either way, I was capable, but the timing seemed wrong."

"I suppose you were being considerate of my maidenly feeling," she said thoughtfully as she added a hairpin. "As we were two strangers staying in a procession of inns."

He snorted. "Doesn't sound like me."

"Well, if not that, then what was it?"

He shifted uneasily on the mattress, trying to find the right words. "If I'd had you then, it wouldn't have been like this. It's better this way."

"You mean, because we know each other now?" she asked, her expression softening.

He gave a murmur of agreement, but it wasn't that precisely. That had never stopped him before. No, it was more the idea that he could ruin something if he'd taken a misstep with her.

Maybe it was the way she had been so fearless around him from the outset. He'd liked that, he realized. Liked it a lot. He'd recognized her bravery from the very first, though at the time he wasn't sure if it was partly due to her being foolhardy. He had never really understood why he'd accepted her proposal.

Then she'd been so damn impudent, the opposite of what he'd always thought her. Putting that guard to blush, telling that priest he'd already been enjoying his conjugal rights. The memory tugged his lips into a reluctant smile. He had told nothing but the truth after all. He liked Lenora Montmayne. He'd liked her from their first interaction when she'd lifted that damned veil, letting him see her damaged eyelids.

She had guts and the idea of putting a shadow in those clear blue eyes when she beheld him, of giving her a reason to fear him, had left him cold from the outset. And he suspected that rutting her in a damp inn, while other patrons could likely overhear, would have given her a very real disgust of him. That was why he had not done it. Not because of any lack of attraction or consideration of maidenly modesty.

He had held back, because if not, he had known on some level that he could ruin some potential future between them. Like this moment right now, he thought with dawning realization. She pulled on her boots while he debated the wisdom of imparting any of this to her.

"Does that mean you won't be taking me on all fours?" she asked conversationally, startling him out of his reverie.

He met her eyes squarely. "Oh, I'll be doing that alright," he said. "Just as soon as you're ready for it."

Lenora laughed, jumped out of her chair, and hurried out of the room.

30

"Thank you, Margery." Lenora smiled at the girl after accepting her plate of beef stew and reached for the dish of fried beans which she helped herself to sparingly. She had lied when she told Garman that she was hungry, for she had eaten two pastries in town and a small bun as she walked through the market. It had just felt *essential* for her own defenses that she immediately put some space between the two of them.

The sight of him, all content and wanting to *talk* to her, instead of turning immediately cool, had frankly terrified her. If at that moment, he had said something, *anything* that might hurt her, she might never recover from it. Her drawbridge was down, and he had stormed her castle. The last time that happened…had not ended well. If her cousin Kit had not come along to distract her, she was not sure what she would have done.

She was still a coward, she thought despondently, even now. Remembering her recent tears under him, her fist tightened around her spoon in mortification. Why had she turned so…so *emotional*? He didn't want emotion from her. It wasn't that sort of marriage, she told herself crossly. Acting in that foolish fashion had just forced words from him that he didn't want to say and probably, she thought with a pang, did not actually mean.

She was an idiot.

"Is everything alright, my dear?" Gerard Sutton peered at her anxiously from the other end of the table.

Quickly, Lenora schooled her features. "Oh yes, Grandfather," she assured him. "Just a little tired."

"Garman does not join us for supper, it seems," he said, tutting. "No doubt last night's proclivities…"

His words were cut short as they heard a firm tread on the stair and then the door swung open.

"Good evening," Garman said evenly and crossed the room to sit on the bench next to Lenora.

To her annoyance, Lenora felt her face color hotly as she felt his eyes on her face. "I thought you would sleep," she said aloud.

"Did you?"

She looked up sharply, for there was no intonation to his words, but he met her eyes calmly enough.

She made to stand. "Let me call for Margery to fetch you some stew," she muttered, but he caught her wrist to prevent her from rising.

"Margery!" he roared. Then turned to her. "No need." Hurried footsteps were heard in the passage. "More stew," he said succinctly. Margery rushed away to oblige.

To Lenora's embarrassment, Gerard Sutton seemed to be watching their exchange with a certain keenness. "No doubt Lenora has told you, my boy," he said, beaming, "that she is taking to her wifely duties with great keenness and aptitude."

Lenora closed her eyes briefly against Garman's answering smirk.

"Oh, I agree," he rumbled gravely. "Though she could scarcely be enthusiastic enough for my tastes."

"That is good to hear," his pure-minded grandfather uttered, holding up his goblet for the returning Margery to replenish.

The maid set down a large bowl of stew for Garman and moved around the table, pouring out three cups of wine.

"This is a flavorsome stew," Garman said, surprising everyone, for his table conversation was usually sparse. "Hawise is a good cook," he added. "I had some conversation with her earlier in the kitchens whilst she was preparing it."

Lenora's and Gerard's startled eyes met across the table. "You did?" His grandfather faltered.

"Aye." Garman paused. "We had some speech about Kolby and the cats."

Lenora's head turned sharply. "Is everything alright betwixt them?" she asked anxiously. She had heard of no altercations, but then she had been out for a good deal of the day.

"Very harmonious," he said. "He and Grizelda doze quite happily before the fire together."

Gerard gave a small dry cough. "That is good to hear in all events."

"Begging your pardon, sirs, but the little gray is curled up there now," Margery put in, setting the stopper back in the jug of wine. "Curled up in between Kolby's front paws, he is, as if he'd knowed him all his life!"

"Fendrel," Garman supplied, surprising the company at large once again. "Is the gray's name," he elaborated when his grandfather looked quite bewildered.

"Ah yes," Gerard said hurriedly. "I believe Lenora considers that Fendrel has chosen you for his master, is that not so?" he asked, bestowing a smile on his new granddaughter.

Lenora's answering smile was a little forced. She had not really expected Garman to embrace his role as Fendrel's protector with such aplomb.

"Cats apparently exercise their own will when it comes to such things," Garman said without any obvious amusement. He turned to Lenora. "I can report that Tybalt and Purcel are flourishing at Cofton Grange."

Lenora colored hotly. How could she have forgotten to ask after Fendrel's brothers? "Oh, I'm so glad!" she blurted, almost dropping her spoon. "For I have often worried that Tybalt might be quite crushed beneath a horse's hoof in their stable."

"Or Purcel treated cruelly by that slovenly servant of theirs?" he suggested. "You need not worry, for she's run away after some harsh words from Ivo. They are currently having to shift for themselves."

Lenora's eyes widened. "So, they have no servant at all?"

"The place must be quite at sixes and sevens with two bachelors running it," Gerard hazarded. "It is quite a large property from what I recall."

"It's in a state of complete and utter chaos," Garman agreed. "Except for the stables, of course. That's all Huw and Ivo care about at any rate." He paused. "They were fools to disown their sister. Isabeau would have kept the house in some order at least."

Lenora digested this in silence, but Gerard fidgeted in his seat. "It is most regrettable when such matters tear families apart," he said unhappily and shook his head.

Garman's expression tightened a moment, but then he glanced at Lenora and seemed to relax. She wondered if Gerard Sutton

354

had disliked his own son-in-law so very much that he always felt the need to lament his daughter's match.

"You're not eating much stew," Garman commented as he scraped his own bowl clean.

Lenora looked down at her own helping which she had been pushing around with her spoon. "I'm afraid my eyes were bigger than my stomach." She pulled a face. "I ate too many treats in the marketplace this day."

Gerard chuckled. "I was surprised myself when you managed that second custard."

"Oh, but they had so many delicious flavors on that stall." Feeling Garman's gaze on her, Lenora lowered her own to her plate, feeling suddenly self-conscious. Her bold words from the night before came back to haunt her. *I think I've gained some flesh and wanted you to corroborate.* She would not have been so daring if he had not been intoxicated. She hoped most heartily he had forgotten that episode altogether.

"Margery, will you have a bath sent up to our room after supper?" Garman said casually, dashing her hopes. She did not dare to raise her eyes, but instead steeled herself to nibble on a green bean. She also wished to goodness she could take back that comment about him taking her on all fours! At the time she had been feigning an insouciance she did not feel.

In truth she felt sore between her legs and far from keen to repeat the marital relations for a while at least. True, he had warned her it was not particularly pleasant for a first time, and he had spoken true. Well, at least the actual culmination of the act had hurt, she corrected herself. The first part had been…pleasurable in the extreme, though somewhat shocking.

Eden's words stirred in her memory. What was it her cousin had said? Something about the bodies of husbands and wives becoming more attuned as time went on. She must have meant that marital relations get better, Lenora thought, for certainly Eden evinced no apparent revulsion at Roland Vawdrey's touch these days. She remembered fleetingly how they had stood entwined at Kellingford. No, she did not imagine her cousin shrank from the physical aspect of marriage. Eden would have told her quite truthfully if it were some odious duty that must be performed with gritted teeth each time.

"Will you have some fig tart, milady?" Margery asked from behind her, making her jump.

"What? Oh, no thank you, Margery," she said hurriedly.

"You're probably tired," Garman said slyly, "and should retire directly after your bath."

"I had a bath last night," she said quickly. "I had thought the bath for you."

He gave her a level look. "Oh, it is for my benefit," he agreed with a gleam in his eye and Lenora directed an alarmed glance his grandfather's way. Luckily, Gerard was directing Margery how large a slice of pie he wanted and was oblivious to their exchange.

She shot Garman a reproving look, but he only winked at her.

*

Lenora busied herself around the room as her bath was filled with buckets of hot water. She felt sure the servants must think her a most unreasonable mistress, demanding a bath two nights in a row. She was halfway through tidying her jewelry box when Garman came into the room and picked up the last pail of

356

hot water, dismissing the servant and shutting the door behind them.

"Your bath awaits," he said, emptying the last bucket into the tub and setting it down. He moved over to the bed, sat down, and pulled off his boots. She watched covertly as he lowered himself onto his back until he was fully outstretched and placed his hands behind his head. "Don't let it get cold," he recommended.

Lenora lifted her chin and finished placing her brooches and rings back into the box before she made any move to remove her gown. This wouldn't do, she thought, fumbling with her laces. She was no shrinking maiden. She glanced over at Garman's still form. "Won't you join me?" she asked coolly. "As you did that first night?" She saw his eyelids flicker and was pleased to think she could still take him aback.

He cleared his throat. "This tub is not so big as the one at the inn," he said regretfully. "Besides, I thought you might be sore."

Oh! Lenora's startled gaze met his. He was being solicitous, not lecherous! Immediately a good deal of tension left her body and she almost breathed a sigh of relief. "I am a bit," she admitted, loosening her bodice enough to wriggle out of it. "Thank you. That is most considerate."

"I'm trying," he said and turned his head as Fendrel jumped up onto the bed next to him and started to loudly purr. Lenora's gown dropped to the floor and she whipped her shift over her head. She watched Garman pet Fendrel's small head as the cat extended his claws to dig into his chest.

"I like the way he maintains eye contact with me as he shreds my tunic," he remarked wryly as he carefully detached the cat's claws.

357

Lenora laughed as she stepped over the edge of the tub and sank into the water. "When they're young like Fendrel, they have not yet learned to temper their strength. As they get older, they grow gentler with us."

Garman grunted as Fendrel circled about, kneading the bed covers and whisking his tail. "Not the most restful animals, are they?"

"Kittens aren't," she conceded. "Their natures are playful and adventurous. But mature cats can be very restful. You have observed, I am sure, how calm and loving my Grizelda is."

"She certainly looked affectionate when I saw her ten minutes ago," he agreed. Lenora looked up from lathering soap leaves in her hands. "Sat on Hawise's lap," he explained. "By the kitchen fire."

Lenora smiled. "It's a great relief to me that they are all fitting in. Purcel and Tybalt included."

"They seem to have the run of the Hainfroy place," Garman said, watching Fendrel curl up in the center of his chest. "Purcel knocked two candlesticks and a fruit bowl off the shelf and no one batted an eyelid."

"Oh dear," Lenora murmured. "He must be running riot. Do you think there is any likelihood the brothers may invite their sister home to impose some order about the place?"

He shook his head. "They'd never stomach Lind about the place. Fellow plays a harp."

"Maybe they should marry?" Lenora said boldly. That might stop their carrying on. "Why don't you suggest it?"

He snorted. "Who'd have them?"

Lenora tipped her head to one side considering this. "I suppose," she said, grimacing, "they would need wives with money."

Garman shrugged. "The estate could certainly use it."

This remark had the unhappy result of reminding Lenora of the property Garman aspired to buy. The one her dowry would doubtless afford him. "What was the name of that estate again?" she asked. "The one you mean to purchase when you have enough saved."

"Matchings Halt," he said shortly.

"It must be close by, I think. As this is Matchings Farm." He nodded, stroking Fendrel's short, sleek back. "Could we ride out and see it one morning?" she suggested tentatively.

He frowned. "It's currently occupied," he reminded her.

"The present occupants are unaware that it will soon be up for sale?" she asked and he nodded again. Lenora hesitated. "I think you said it was a widow?"

"A widow and her in-laws," he agreed.

"Where will they go?"

"That is hardly our concern, Lenora."

She pursed her lips and wrung out her washing cloth. "Is she wealthy?" she asked slowly. "Does she have other properties?"

"I neither know nor care."

"Do you dislike her for some reason?" she asked, hoping there might be an explanation for his callousness. Maybe the old woman was unpleasant or hard and grasping?

He merely looked surprised by her words. "I can barely remember her," he said. "I think her reputation locally is good."

Lenora sat up and looked at him hard, her arms crossed over her breasts. He returned her gaze unflinchingly. *Well.* "Yet you would dispossess her of her home without a thought," she persisted.

He shrugged his massive shoulders. "Life is hard. She is no concern of mine."

Feeling unaccountably disappointed, Lenora groped around the bottom of the bath for the washcloth. She had washed her hair the night before, so this time she simply concentrated on cleansing her body. Garman's attitude toward the widow displeased her, reminding her of his own reputation as a stone-hearted brute.

She did not speak for several minutes simply concentrating on her ablutions. Then she covered her front with the cloth, rested her head on the edge, and lay back to soak in the water. She had no reason to feel this way. She had married him *because*, rather than in spite, of his reputation. Why then, did she feel so deeply dispirited when he spoke with frankness about his own lack of compassion toward some female about to have her future thrown into jeopardy?

Then it hit her. It was because *she* identified with this female. Her own security had been snatched from her overnight in a similar fashion. She had retired to her chamber one day, secure in her future, and emerged weeks later as a figure only fit to inspire pity in the hearts of men.

Then again, she had married Garman Orde precisely because she knew he was pitiless. She swallowed. Had she so easily forgotten this same fact? Glancing over at the bed, she watched his large hand caress the small gray cat. It *was* hard to remember sometimes, she thought wistfully. For had he not shown her true consideration in the past few weeks? She remembered his anger when she had told him of her parents' words. It had seemed genuine enough at the time.

"The water must be growing cold," he said, pulling her out of her thoughts. "Don't linger and catch a chill."

The water had indeed grown cool. Wordlessly, she clambered from the bath and reached for a large sheet to wrap around her shivering body. She made for the fireplace and crouched there on the hearthrug. A footfall behind her told her Garman was approaching, so she did not start when she found herself enveloped from behind with another blanket.

"You're cold," he said gruffly, moving his hands up and down her arms.

"Yes," she agreed quietly and sat passive as he rubbed her body dry.

"You're my concern, Lenora," he said in a low voice as he swung her up into his arms and carried her over to the bed. He paused. "Where do you keep your clean shifts?"

She pointed to a trunk on the far side of the room and he went to retrieve one for her. She held up her arms as he pulled the white linen garment down over her head and then tucked her in. Then he stripped down and joined her under the covers, tucking his big body behind hers, one arm wrapped firmly about her waist.

Fendrel meowed, feeling neglected, before making his way to the foot of the bed and settling against their feet. Perfect silence reigned for a few moments, and Lenora closed her eyes, listening to the crackle of the fire.

"Tell me something," Garman said out of the blue, quite startling her.

Lenora waited, but nothing more seemed to be forthcoming. "Tell you what?"

"Anything." He almost sounded grumpy. "Something not many people know about you."

Lenora stared at the wall. Well, this was awkward. Was this where she confessed that she had only grown a personality in the last three months? She bit her lip. She had no personal revelations to impart. "I—I told you once before that I used to be obsessed with fortunes and fortune-telling," she said, blushing even into the darkness. He made no answer, and she felt sure he thought this was poor fare as secrets went.

"One time," she rambled on, "a wise woman told me I was a high branch on a venerable old tree. She said the lower branches flourished but I was stunted and bore no leaves." Her voice broke. "Then she said there was a curse on my pretty face, but later I thought she must have meant that my pretty face *was* a curse and that was why I had not grown right as I should."

"What do you mean?" he prompted when she lapsed into silence. "Not grown right?"

"Because all I did was rest on my laurels of beauty, instead of becoming a well-rounded person," she explained. Then quite suddenly, a thought occurred to her that had her reeling. "Garman, it's only just occurred to me! Maybe she did mean my face was cursed and she was foretelling I would fall victim to the red pox." She gasped. "I never thought of it that way before!"

Garman snorted beside her. "Horseshit," he said heavily. "You're not stunted."

"Well, maybe not now," she concurred. "Maybe I am finally putting forth shoots." He huffed out a breath of air at this and was in all likelihood rolling his eyes. "Have you never had your fortune told?"

"Never."

"Not even when you were a child?"

She felt his head rustle on the pillow beside hers and guessed he was shaking it. Suddenly she felt his fingertips come up to rest gently against her jaw in that familiar gesture of his. He ran them lightly over her uneven skin there.

"I like your face better now," he said, his voice raspy. "This texture here adds character."

Character? In spite of herself, Lenora felt a warm glow start in the pit of her stomach. "Yes," she murmured, her eyes drifting shut as he drew her in closer to his body. His words were strangely comforting to her soul, and when she drifted off to sleep, she felt soothed and surprisingly calm.

31

The next morn, Lenora woke first. She lay quiet and still, surprised their positions had not altered during the night. Garman's arm was still about her, his head shared her pillow. Remembering their conversation the previous evening, she found she did not, nay, *could* not believe him wholly callous.

If 'twere so, he would not treat her so tenderly or want to know more about her, surely? When she had wed him, it was true she had thought he would prove an uncaring, neglectful husband. She had believed they would lead practically separate lives with few points of contact. However, that had not proved to be the case. As such, she needed to rethink the working terms of their relationship.

The problem was, she pondered, that currently she brought nothing to the table. When she had approached him, she had done so in the firm conviction that she had a sizeable dowry that would end up in his lap. So far, that had not materialized. Pressing her lips together, she grimly resolved to write that very day to her father. In truth, she could put it off no longer. Mayhap if she presented Garman with her dowry, he would take on board her objections to dispossessing some poor widow of her own home.

Thus resolved, Lenora reached for Garman's hand to prize it from her waist.

"It's early," he objected, his grip tightening. "Go back to sleep."

"Listen to the birdsong," Lenora remonstrated. "It's growing lighter by the minute."

He lifted his head and glanced at the window. "Nay, it's still dark and I doubt very much you rose this early at court."

"No, for I was a spoiled beauty who kept town hours then. Now I am a country housewife and must rise at the crack of dawn," she told him firmly. The next thing she knew she was under him, flat on her back and breathless.

"Is that so?" he rumbled above her. "Well, I think you'll find, my fine lady, that country wives have other duties to fulfill before they go about their day."

"Other duties?" she squeaked. His fingers were bunching her shift up to her waist.

"I don't suppose I could persuade you to take this damned thing off, could I?"

"It depends."

"On what?" He paused; his eyes glinted down at her.

"Well." Lenora turned red. "If I'm to be flat on my back, then I'll take it off," she blurted. "But if you mean for me to be on all fours then I want to keep it on."

She thought his breathing turned rougher a moment. "Why, Lenora Orde," he said thickly. "I do believe you mean to deprive me of the sight of your luscious ass. Which is very contrary of you when you know how much I enjoy it."

She took a deep breath. "I'm self-conscious about it," she admitted. "It's always been far too big for my frame!"

He gave a short laugh. "Keep it on, then, be my guest. It won't impede my enjoyment, I assure you."

Lenora gasped as with no apparent effort he flipped her onto her front, lifted up her shift, and ran his hands over her exposed buttocks.

"Garman!" She squirmed against the mattress.

"Ah, Lenora," he groaned. "If only you could see my view. I'm one lucky bastard."

She gave a breathless laugh. "I've seen it in the mirror, and I don't like it."

"You should see it through my eyes," he said richly and ran another slow hand over her left buttock, cupping it gently. "Though the bruising is a little distracting. Does it hurt?"

"No. Bruising from the collapsing stand?" she asked, not wanting to ask outright about Sir Lionel's pinch mark.

"Mmmm," he agreed. "Do you remember what I did last time? In that field in Kellingford, to make it better?"

Lenora's eyes widened. "Umm…" He moved down and she felt the brush of his lips there against her skin again and again. "You kissed it," she breathed out.

"I did," he said huskily. "If you weren't bruised, I'd bite it too."

"You would bite my bottom?" she asked as if unsure what she was hearing.

He gave a muffled laugh. "Yes, but only very gently." Then he was turning her over again, onto her back. "Hold up your arms. We're getting rid of this." He tugged at her shift, and she held her arms aloft as he stripped it off her. Obviously, she was not getting the all-fours treatment today, she thought with some relief. "Open your legs, Lenora."

After a heartbeat, she did so, and he moved down the bed. "What are you doing?" she quavered. Was he looking at her there?

"Shh," he said, trailing gentle fingers over the curls between her legs. "Let me familiarize myself with you. Did you know your hair down here is nearly as blond as that on your head?"

366

"I have seen myself naked for many years," she pointed out. "Besides, that's no different to you."

"No different to me?" She could hear the amusement in his voice.

"The hair on your body," she clarified. "I—I noticed when I came to your room that first night."

"What did you notice, Lenora?" His voice was rich and warm. "Tell me."

Greatly daring, she reached down to his belly button and lightly touched the tip of her finger to the dark blond trail of hair that started below it. "Here," she whispered.

He sucked in a breath. "You're telling me the Flower of all Karadok had her eyes fixed on me down there?"

"I doubt anyone would call me that these days," she said ruefully. "But yes, I had never seen such body hair before," she admitted. "I thought about it the next day."

His lips twitched at that confession. "Touch it," he invited, pressing her hand to that patch of hard, flat stomach. She felt the muscles tense and flex as she tentatively ran her fingers over his warm skin and tickled the scattering of short hairs. She had to be careful, for Garman's engorged manhood was standing straight up and practically knocking against the back of her hand at this point.

"Where does it…?"

"It runs all the way down."

"I wonder why." She frowned. "For 'tis not enough to keep your tummy warm."

His breathing hitched. "Maybe it's to draw our female's attention to what's below," he suggested.

"This wasn't standing to attention like this before," she said, deciding to take the bull by its horns and boldly reaching for him. His breath hissed between his teeth despite her gentle touch. "I could hardly fail to have noticed it."

"No," he said shortly. "I was too surprised to get hard."

"And I did not tickle your fancy," she said softly. "Not then."

"You can tickle it now, any time you want, Lenora," he rasped.

She laughed. "Why thank you, kind sir." She ran her hand up and down his length in gentle exploration.

"Harder," he gritted out. "Take me more firmly in your grip."

Eyes wide, Lenora gently squeezed him. "You're sure it does not hurt when I do this?"

"No," he answered.

"It feels good?" The expression on his face was a strange mix of pleasure and something else.

"I've got as much hard cock as you can handle," he promised.

"I'm struggling to handle it now," Lenora admitted frankly, bringing both hands to circle his girth.

"Open your legs, I want to touch you too."

Her face aflame, Lenora bent her leg so one knee was raised in the air. Garman reached across and cupped her mound, running his thumb through her hair before sliding his thumb down and dipping inside her there. His eyes flew to meet hers when he found her wet and he groaned. "Just from touching me?"

She nodded then drew a ragged breath as he touched that sensitive spot concealed there and circled it. "Oh!" she cried out softly.

Garman muffled an oath. "Your hand feels good, really good." He shuddered. "But this." He slid his fingers inside her and Lenora whined. "This feels fucking incredible. Tell me now if you're too sore to take me, Lenora, and I'll spend in your hand."

"I— It's not too sore," she said, blushing hard.

He shifted over her, not breaking eye contact even for a moment, then reached down to line up their respective parts. Feeling the broad head of his manhood poised at her entrance, Lenora squeezed her eyes shut and braced herself, her hands clutching at his back.

"Wrap your legs around my waist."

She did so and felt him shudder as her body opened up to him. He entered her, edging slowly forward, biting his lip. Suddenly she realized he was exercising a good deal of will to go carefully with her. Of a surety, this was not the bestial taking he had described to her that first night at the inn.

Perhaps then...perhaps, after all... Her thoughts scattered as he surged forward, and she expelled all the air in her lungs in surprise at finding him seated so deep inside her. She blinked up at him. She had not felt that tearing flash of pain like last time or that jarring burn.

"All is well?" he asked tersely. She nodded and he thrust again with a deep groan, sinking into her by the last few degrees until their nether hair touched. "Gods," he uttered, his eyes rolling back as though indeed he were having a religious experience.

While it did not hurt, Lenora reflected, it definitely felt strange and a little uncomfortable to take him into her body like this. She wondered that men liked it so well. Then his hands were smoothing the hair back from her brow and he was kissing her there very gently, then down her jaw—*oh*.

Without him bidding her this time, she closed her eyes and felt his lips softly touch her eyelids. Then he kissed her mouth, lazily, as if he had all the time in the world and as though his loins weren't quivering below and his hips weren't pressing forward hard against hers, demanding and insistent for all they were still.

In spite of herself, Lenora allowed herself to relax, to be delighted by the stroke of his teasing tongue. She almost jumped when she felt one hand close around her breast, his thumb pressing against her nipple in a toying manner that made her catch her breath. He had not really lavished much attention on her breasts before, though he had once called them a pretty pair, she remembered as he plucked it now between finger and thumb. She bit back a moan at that, feeling an answering squeeze between her legs which startled her.

Garman's hips gave an involuntary jerk and he broke their kiss, staring down at her with wild, tormented eyes. "You liked that?" he panted.

She gazed up at him with parted lips. "What?" she asked confusedly. Still watching her, he squeezed her nipple hard and Lenora gave a strangled cry, digging her heels into his back as she felt herself tighten around his girth, squeezing him tight. Again, he gave a harsh groan and his hips thrust harder this time and she felt him jerk deep inside her. Oh…gods that felt strange.

"So sweetly sensitive," he said hoarsely and nuzzled his face against her other breast. Lenora's breathing grew ragged as he

370

kissed it, first sweetly and then with increasing lasciviousness, touching his tongue to her nipple and finally sucking it wholly into his mouth.

"Oh!" she wept, clawing at his back, and now she was the one pressing her hips hard against his, straining to get closer and closer. "Please!" she implored, tears starting from her eyes. Was she crying? Her mind reeled as her whole body quickened with overwhelming sensation, most of which seemed to emanate from where they were so intimately joined.

The next thing she knew, he was looming over her, his hands at the backs of her knees, holding her pinned open to him as he slammed into her again and again, his face dark, his expression stormy. Lenora sobbed with relief and pleasure. He could not thrust into her hard enough. Her body's clasp on him was so tight she was feared she would cause him an injury.

After his initial lust was spent, he released his grip on her knees and collapsed heavily over her, one hand in her hair guiding her mouth to his. His hips were still moving fitfully, and he released a harsh, continued groan into her mouth as he shuddered above her. She held very still until she felt him stop trembling. Then he began breathing again at a regular pace and pulled his face back from hers. He was flushed and had a strange look in his eye.

Suddenly an awful thought occurred to her. "Did I hurt you?" she blurted in concern. Maybe all that groaning had been in pain? She relaxed her furious grip, resting her hands instead on his shoulders. His lips trembled and then he did the oddest thing. He gave a low, breathless laugh. Lenora stared. She didn't think she'd seen him laugh before, at least not like that, she hadn't. He looked utterly relaxed, his eyes half-shut and his lips still quirked into a smile.

371

"You half killed me," he said hoarsely. "But I'd have died a happy man."

When he untangled himself from her moments later and collapsed on his back at her side, Lenora let her eyes drift shut. She meant to rest them only a minute, for the room was growing light, however when next she opened them, the sun was high, and she was alone in the bed. Lenora gasped, threw back the covers, and made haste to wash and dress. The water was lukewarm at best, so she guessed she had been asleep at least a couple of hours after Garman had his way with her.

The tips of her ears burned as she hurried down the stairs. With a bit of luck, her husband would be in the stables or about some business and she would not have to face him just yet. She almost jumped out of her skin when he hailed her from the foot of the stairs.

"She wakes," he said with lifted brows. "I thought you'd sleep till midday, you slept so soundly."

Hearing the deep satisfaction in his voice, she lifted her chin. "I'm quite refreshed now, thank you," she said primly and tried to slip past him on the bottom step.

He caught her about the waist and clasped her to him. "Is that so? It seems I have an effective remedy for when you wake too early, wife." His finger under her chin prevented her from evading his gaze. "Though now I come to think of it," he said thoughtfully. "I could use it at bedtime too, to ensure you get a good night's rest." Lenora's cheeks burned. "So silent? It seems I have a cure for your pert tongue too."

"I am not pert!"

He merely laughed at this and planted a kiss firmly to her lips. When she neither made protest nor went to move away, his kiss lingered, then turned exploratory. Lenora's head swam and she leaned into him.

A cough nearby had them both turning their heads, and they found Gerard Sutton and Huw Hainfroy regarding them both with round eyes. Lenora gave a faint moan of embarrassment, but Garman's arms tightened around her. After a couple of heartbeats, he swung her down off the step and tucked her into his side. "Huw," he said shortly.

"You have a visitor, my boy," his grandfather said awkwardly. "I will go and ask for some refreshment to be served," he added and hurried away.

Lenora looked from Garman's stony expression to Huw's one of hangdog wretchedness. What was going on here?

Huw swallowed. "Good morning, my lady," he said, scratching the back of his head, and Lenora realized he did not recall her name. Why should he? He had made precious little effort to speak to her on the previous occasion as she seemed to remember.

"Good morning," she said pleasantly. "I trust all is well at Cofton Grange. How is Ivo?" she added politely. Ivo was definitely her favorite out of the two brothers.

"He's well," Huw answered, looking startled. "Very well."

"And your horse? Pollux, I believe was his name?"

Huw colored at this, as though aware she was scoring definite points. "Aye, he's well—the cat too. Tybalt," he added hastily when she opened her mouth, as though to assure her he knew his stable cat's name.

Finally, Lenora graced him with a smile. "Tybalt," she agreed. Huw blinked. Now Garman was looking thunderous, she noticed, glancing up with surprise.

"How can we help you?" Garman asked pointedly with a hard stare.

Had they fallen out? "Let us go into the inner parlor," Lenora suggested. "Unless…" She looked from one to the other again. "You need to have some private speech about some matter…?"

"Nay," both of them objected almost simultaneously.

Lenora frowned, but took a step in the direction of the parlor and found Garman keeping pace with her, one of his arms still wrapped about her shoulder. After a moment's hesitation, Huw Hainfroy followed them, and they were all seated at the table.

"Forgive me, but I have not yet broken my fast," Lenora said smoothly. "Will you not join me in taking some repast?" She gestured toward the fare of bread, butter, and preserves that was laid out on the table. Ada bustled in carrying a plate of salted cod and pickled herrings to add to the spread.

Huw was looking warily at Garman, but seeing nothing in his expression to dissuade him, he gave a nod of thanks and reached to tear himself a hunk of bread. Lenora relaxed as Garman poured ale into three cups.

"How are you finding things at Matchings Farm?" Huw asked with visible effort. "My lady," he added again in the manner of someone rather rusty with the term.

"Please call me Lenora," she told him and again felt Garman bristle at her side. Which was strange, she thought, when he had told her several times that the Hainfroys were the closest thing he had to siblings. Without thinking, she laid a hand on his thigh under the table. Garman stilled, and feeling suddenly awkward, Lenora went to withdraw it, only to feel his own hand come down on top of hers to prevent its removal. She glanced at him quickly, but his expression was impassive.

"I am still finding my feet, I think," she answered Huw's question belatedly. "Garman's grandfather is helping me find my way."

Huw nodded, his mouth full of bread. He swallowed. "It will take a while, no doubt."

Lenora remembered that she had used to leave this kind of small talk to others and wondered what Eden would make of her spinning out polite conversation in this way. She fancied her cousin would be much impressed at her progress in such matters. "You must be looking to engage a new servant at Cofton Grange," she heard herself say aloud as she helped herself to a bread roll. "Now that you have dismissed Martha."

Huw froze with his cup of ale halfway to his lips. "Heard about that, did you?" he said, glancing briefly at Garman. "Didn't exactly dismiss her, if truth be told. She took umbrage and left us to keep house for some fat widower in Upper Lenton."

"I see," Lenora murmured, reaching for the butter dish. "Well, perhaps Hawise might know of someone looking for a situation?" she suggested.

Garman looked doubtful at this, but shrugged a shoulder and Lenora promised to enquire. Huw thanked her for this, and Garman expressed his intention of setting up a quintain in the stable yard and spending the better part of the day in training there with Bria'ag. After a moment, Huw cleared his throat and asked if he might stay and watch. Garman agreed and they set off for the stables.

Lenora was stood at the window, still wondering what the visit had been about, when she spotted Garman striding back from the stables alone. She turned from the window in surprise as he came back into the room. "I've left Huw at the stables," he announced as soon as he crossed the threshold. He stopped before her with a heavy frown. "You won't have any luck finding them a new servant, so I wouldn't even try."

"Why?" she asked with surprise.

He paused a moment before replying. "It's not a respectable position," he said. "In a household with two bachelors."

Lenora considered this. "Servants come in all shapes and sizes," she pointed out. "They could have a manservant or a mature widow. Or even a married couple." He grunted at this. "Of course, the place is sadly run-down," she conceded. "Whoever they took on would have to have plenty about them."

"That's not the half of it," he said forthrightly. "They swear like sailors, practically live in the stables, get drunk every night, and walk muddy boots throughout the whole house."

Lenora snorted. "Berta would soon knock their heads together."

He looked thoughtful at that. "Berta, you say. Would you spare her though?"

Lenora straightened up with alarm. "Certainly not!" She flushed. "I did not mean to suggest her for the world. You misunderstand me. I mean to keep Berta close by me for the past service she has done me. I asked her when we left Caer-Lyoness if she would throw her lot in with mine, and I meant every word of it!"

"No, I do understand that," he said, reaching for her hand. "You may not have noticed, but—" Lenora waited as he absently turned her hand over and then engulfed it between his own two hands. "Berta is not particularly happy here."

Lenora started. "Why, what has happened?" She remembered guiltily that she had observed as much herself over the past week. "Has there been some falling out among the household staff?"

Garman shook his head. "Nothing of that sort. She's too fierce and my grandfather's servants far too mild."

"What, then?"

He shrugged. "I don't think it suits her, fitting into a household that is already established. Then, too, she has no family here and seems to feel the loss."

Lenora bit her lip. She remembered there had been some estrangement. "She has several sons," she said slowly. "But I seem to recall the last of them had recently left her to take a wife Berta did not like. I think they must have all set up their own families and she got left behind to fend for herself."

"Think it over," Garman recommended. "She would be in her element scolding the Hainfroys and bringing order to their mess. She could carry on like a fishwife there and no one would so much as raise an eyebrow." He glanced at her shrewdly. "She could keep an eye on the cats too."

Much struck by his argument, Lenora said nothing. His words made sense, but she hated the thought of releasing Berta from her service. Had she not told Eden that the woman would have a home with her for life? "Let me consider the matter," she said at last, withdrawing her hand from his. "For while 'tis true that she may not fit in particularly well here at the farm, we will have need of her ourselves when we set up our own household."

377

"That may not be for a few years yet," he pointed out dryly, which reminded her she had to write to her father. When Garman said he'd better be getting back to his training, she asked Ada to bring her paper and ink and sat up to the freshly cleared table to compose an overdue letter to her family at Hallam Hall. After staring at the paper fixedly for a moment or two, she dashed off the following:

Dear Father

I hope this letter finds you well and Mother and Grandmother also. I imagine you may have heard the news of my marriage already, but if not then I am happy to inform you that I am now the wife of Sir Garman Orde and currently residing at the address given above.

I must beg your forgiveness, she wrote with a grimace, *for the manner in which I impart this news. Circumstances were such that I did not feel confident after my late illness to divulge my choice of bridegroom to you. I hope you can forgive my hasty flight from court. Regrettably at that time I did not feel that I had any other course open to me.*

It is my wish that with the fullness of time we can be reconciled to one another and you can welcome my husband into the family.

I remain your affectionate daughter.

Lenora

It was rather brief, she thought, gazing down at it. She could well imagine that her father would bristle when he read it. Especially if her uncle Christopher had received news of their marriage before him, but that could not be helped.

She had no doubt that strange rumors of the tournament at Kellingford would have reached court by now and shivered slightly to think what people would make of it. As for her father, she knew his habits well enough to know he would have returned to his country seat by now, so hopefully had been spared the worst of the gossip.

At least she had both her first cousins on her side, she thought as she searched in Grandfather Sutton's writing box for a piece of sealing wax. She had no sooner dripped the hot wax onto the fold than he came bustling into the room, asking her if she wanted to go to accompany him on a stock-take of the cellars.

She gave him her letter, and after glancing at the direction, he said he would see that it was sent off without delay. Lenora went upstairs and changed into her most serviceable headscarf and a cloak, for she had been warned the cellars were both draughty and dusty, and she then spent an instructive afternoon helping Gerard to inspect the stores.

32

Garman returned to the house that afternoon feeling pleased with his progress. Not only had he spent several useful hours in training, but he had finally persuaded Huw to attempt the quintain, which was more than he ever managed previously.

Without a doubt, his friend had only agreed to try to get back in his good books, but by the time Huw left, he genuinely seemed to be enthused about learning to joust. The only downside was that he was now urging Garman to spend a few days with him at the Grange to instruct him and Ivo in the rudiments.

The timing did not seem right to Garman, though he could not say why precisely or give his friend any excuse that would not embarrass them both. It was only his private conviction that he and Lenora were finally settling into a rhythm for their married lives together.

Still, he felt he owed it to them, and his wife would have to realize she was further down his obligation list. In his head this made perfect sense, for the Hainfroys were his oldest friends and he owed them much. He did not quite understand himself why he felt reluctant to leave her for a week or two. It wasn't like she would be going anywhere and besides, he competed on the circuit and would soon be leaving her for weeks at a time as a matter of course.

He was quiet at supper, listening to Lenora and his grandfather chatter over their plans for the week ahead. He ordered a bath for their room after dinner, for he had worked up quite a sweat that day, and pondered how best to break the news of his imminent departure.

"Have you given any more thought to the situation with Berta?" he asked as he lowered himself into the tub before the fire that evening.

Lenora was looking over her trunkful of gowns with a critical eye. "A little," she said grudgingly. "Which of these two dresses would you say was the more serviceable?"

Garman eyed both gowns she held up. Both looked frivolous in the extreme. "The blue," he lied.

"Blue?" She gazed back at the two dresses. "You mean this mauve one?" she said, lifting one up higher. He gave a short nod. "Truly?" She turned the dress about and eyed it with misgiving. "You don't think the cut of the sleeves a little…fussy?"

He thought it was a court dress, but what was the use in pointing that out? Nearly all her gowns were. "And what conclusion did you draw about Berta?" he persisted, rubbing the soap leaves briskly between his palms.

Lenora sighed. "I don't want to lose her," she admitted. "Though I can see what you say makes sense." He grunted and was just soaping under his arms when she added, "I wrote to my father today."

Garman looked up quickly. "Why?"

"I couldn't put it off any longer in good conscience."

He wanted to tell her she should not have bothered, but he had already made his feelings about the matter plain. She must have done this for her own peace of mind, he concluded with a frown.

"It seemed rude not to write when he's bound to hear it from another source," she said lamely. "I would hate for my uncle

Christopher to break it to him for he would be sure to do it with a breathtaking lack of tact."

"Tact?" Garman echoed, lowering his washcloth. "He could scarcely be less tactful than your own sire." He left the unforgiveable words unspoken but, from her flush, he knew they were both thinking of the same thing. *'Twould be better if she'd died, rather than suffer this cruel fate.* The words hung heavy between them.

"What do you want a plain dress for anyway?" he asked gruffly after a moment had lapsed with neither of them uttering a word. "One day in the cellars is surely plenty."

Lenora had set the blue to one side—*or what did she call it, mauve?*—and was now carefully refolding the orange gown and setting it back in the trunk. "Your grandfather is entertaining some visiting neighbors tomorrow evening. I did not want to be too ostentatiously dressed for it." A flicker of uncertainty passed over her face. "I want to look…approachable and friendly," she finished with a nod.

Visitors? Garman rolled his eyes. Maybe his visit to Cofton Grange would not be untimely after all. "I won't be here," he said shortly. "I mean to spend a week or so at the Hainfroy place."

Lenora straightened up from the trunk and stared at him. "A week?" She blinked.

"Maybe two."

"*Two* weeks?" Lenora placed her hands on her hips.

"Aye, wife, two weeks. What of it?"

"I just *told* you that I am to be introduced to your neighbors tomorrow eve—" she began briskly, but he cut her off.

"They're not *my* neighbors, Lenora. They're my grandfather's."

"And what of me?" she demanded.

"What of you?"

"Is this not my home at present?"

He leaned back against the side of the tub and regarded her, brows drawn together. "You are making your home here *for now*," he corrected her.

She drew herself up to all of her unimpressive height. "You said only this afternoon that we might not have our own place for a couple of years at least," she pointed out. When he said nothing, she added accusingly, "It seems to me you spend as much time at the Grange as you do here!"

"That has always been the case," he answered, which was true enough. He had lived more years there as a young squire than he had here as a squalling infant, all told.

Lenora slammed the lid of her trunk and took a step toward the door.

He grabbed the edges of his tub. "Hold, wife!" She froze. "Come and wash my back," he ordered.

Her eyes flashed, and for some reason, that was enough to dispel his bad mood. "I'll call for Hawise," she said, narrowing her gaze at him.

"Hawise hasn't bathed me since I was three years old. You can do it," he said, holding out the cloth. For a moment she considered defying him, and he braced himself to spring from the tub. Then her chin came up and she stalked across the room, snatching the cloth from him with an ill grace that had him biting back a grin.

"Soap!" she bit out, and he handed her the flakes, leaning forward to present his back to her. The cloth slapped his shoulder blades, almost making him jump. She muttered under her breath as she dragged the cloth down the planes of his back.

"Speak up," he recommended. "I can't hear you."

"You should be glad of the fact," she said darkly, and he laughed.

"*Now* you laugh?" she huffed. "I've been wanting to hear an honest laugh from you for weeks and this is what makes you throw back your head in mirth?" For some reason, the admission made him catch his breath. "There!" She threw the cloth into the tub with a splash and took a hasty step away from the tub. Garman's hand shot out and he caught her wrist, preventing her escape. He tugged on it lightly, bringing her back to the edge.

"I did not say I was done with you, wife."

"Oh? What do you want now?" she asked. "Your hair washing?"

He grinned. "Nay, for I've washed it already. It's you that has need of my services."

"I do?" She gave him a skeptical look.

"You don't remember? You asked for my help with something."

"I don't—" She broke off and colored, so he knew the precise moment she realized what he was referring to. Their eyes met and held. "You're the one in the bath this time," she prevaricated.

"Come and join me. We've shared before."

"That tub was bigger," she pointed out.

"So, this time you can sit on my lap. We're better acquainted now."

"Better acquainted?" she echoed with a quirk of her brow, when in his opinion, she should have been querying if he really meant his lap.

"Stop stalling," he said, releasing her hand and leaning back in the tub. "You wanted my opinion and I mean to give it."

Lenora huffed out a breath. "Oh, very well," she said and swiveled around, presenting her back to him, hands on her hips.

He sat up so fast, water sloshed over the sides of the tub as his wet fingers fumbled with her lacings. It did not take long to get her divested of all clothing and draw her into the bath. "Set your other foot here on the other side of me," he said, planting her foot next to his hip and guiding her down onto his lap. She lowered herself gingerly, astride and facing him. She made no mention of his obvious arousal.

"I'm barely submerged to my waist," she complained.

"Which suits my purpose admirably."

She cocked an eyebrow at that, crossing her arms over her breasts and leaning back. "What purpose would that be?"

"Admiring you."

"I shall turn all to goose pimples!"

"You won't get the chance," he promised, his eyes roaming over her.

Catching his expression, she flushed, then uncrossed her arms, resting her hands on the sides of the bath. "Well, what is the verdict?" she asked quietly. "Have I flesh enough to please you yet?"

"Aye," he rumbled deep in his chest, his hands coming to rest on her waist before sliding down. "I see plenty to please me. I would not spare you this night if today was our wedding day."

She gave a short laugh as he ran his thumbs over the swell of her hips. "That's reassuring."

He watched her expression turn thoughtful.

"What?" he asked softly.

"I was just thinking that it's fortunate, is it not? That you prefer comely wenches to beauteous ones."

His thumbs stilled. "Lenora—"

"Don't," she said quickly. "Whatever you're about to say." She placed a finger against his lips. "I prefer your brutal honesty. I think I told you that once, though I'm not sure you believed me."

"I wasn't about to be dishonest," he growled.

"No, but no doubt you felt obligated to say something nice."

Garman placed a hand on either side of Lenora's face. "Lenora," he said firmly. "I *never* feel obligated to say nice things."

"No, but—"

"When I say I like the way you look, it's a simple statement of fact."

"Well—"

"Stop arguing."

"I'm not, I just—"

He yanked her forward roughly against him and slammed his lips into hers. Lenora lay sprawled against him for a moment, but then her arms came up to wind about his neck. He found one hand sliding into her long, silky hair while the other gently stroked her cheek. He felt an almost overwhelming impulse to both soothe and ravish her at the same time, which must be why he felt so conflicted and ached like a hot coal blazed in his chest.

She made a muffled sound and shifted in closer to him. He clapped one hand to her backside while his other slipped between their bodies, seeking out that sensitive spot between her legs. The needy whimper she gave when he found it made his breath catch in his throat. He pulled back from their kiss to watch her face. "Why do you avoid my eye, wife?" he asked huskily.

She huffed out a breath. "It hardly seems decent when your hand's…where it is," she whispered back.

A sudden thought occurred to him. "Tell me if anything's uncomfortable." He frowned slightly. He hadn't exactly been taking it easy on her these last couple of days.

"Not uncomfortable," she mumbled. "But—"

"What?" His fingers stilled. Was she in discomfort?

"Aching," said Lenora on a sob.

He swore, his breathing growing ragged. "Aching?" he repeated softly, adding a finger and thrusting deep.

"Oh!"

"Ah, wife," he said with deep satisfaction. "I can see you're going to keep on pleasing me."

"Garman," she groaned, resting her brow against his.

"Do you want me there, Lenora?" She nodded her head. "Say that then, love."

"I want you here." Her hand slid down his neck, past his chest, right down to his aching cock. He bit back an answering groan and wrapped his hand around hers, stroking his shaft with their intertwined fingers.

"You remember that first time I touched you, in the tent? When I spilled my seed on you?" She looked surprised by the direction of his conversation but nodded. "You did not find it…unpleasant?" She shook her head this time. "That's good, because I'm going to pull out of you before I spend from now on," he said raggedly.

"Why?" she asked with surprise.

"We had this conversation, remember?" he asked tightly as his hips bucked beneath her.

"We did?" She looked uncertain.

"I don't want children," he panted. *At least*, a voice whispered in his head, *you never wanted them before.*

"Pulling out would prevent that?"

"Yes," he bit out.

"You didn't pull out the last two times. What if…"

He felt a lurch in his chest that confused him. It wasn't fear or panic. And it definitely wasn't anger. What was it, then? "If we made a child?" he asked, swallowing.

"Yes. What if we…made a child?"

Something about her tone of voice had him looking at her sharply. "Unlikely," he said. Then closing his eyes an instant, he stilled her hand on him. "I want to be inside you," he said raggedly. "Not for long. I'll withdraw when I get close."

She nodded with complete trust. He wished he had as much faith in himself. "Will we get out of the tub, or—?"

"No, no time," he said, squeezing her waist and hauling her up onto her knees. Hands trembling, he seized her thighs in his big hands and urged her to straddle his inflamed cock.

"But," Lenora objected desperately, "how does this work?"

"Gods, woman, just sit on it," he implored her. "Before I explode!"

Lenora looked up quickly, her eyes seeking his. "But you just said—?"

"I want you to mount me, Lenora," he said, interrupting her rudely. "Now put your wet pussy on my cock like a good girl." His hungry gaze was between them, between her legs as he jostled her into position.

Lenora gave a frustrated sob. "But—" She gave a keening cry as with scant ceremony, he lowered her onto his hard staff.

"Fuck, yes, Lenora," he groaned as he entered her, and she began to slide down his length, swallowing him slowly inch by inch.

"Garman," she breathed, her eyes wide with panic. "I don't think I can like this. You feel so…"

"Say it."

"Big, you feel really big and thick."

He groaned again, his hands squeezing on the fleshy globes of her buttocks. "Take what's yours," he urged. "It's all yours, so take it like a good wife."

He had absolutely no idea where these words were coming from. He couldn't remember ever saying, let alone thinking, such thoughts before. Mind you, he'd never taken a wife before, so maybe that accounted for it.

Lenora closed her eyes and let her head drop back as she sank down a further couple of inches. "I can't," she moaned. "Have mercy."

He gave a mirthless grin. "You'll find no mercy from me in this marriage bed," he said thickly and delivered a ringing slap to her backside. Lenora gave a startled moan and sank down further. "You'll take all or nothing, my girl," he rumbled darkly.

At this threat, Lenora's eyes flew open, and he felt his chest well in the grip of some emotion when he saw the desire in their depths. She was in almost as bad a state as him. "I'll try," she blurted. "Don't pull out."

"You've nearly taken me," he whispered and began massaging her backside again. "Look." His own eyes were riveted to where their bodies were intimately joined. Lenora glanced down and caught her breath at the sight.

She bit her lip. "Spank me again," she said breathlessly. His hot gaze flew to meet hers. "On the other cheek this time."

He gave a short rumble of laughter. "I wasn't sure you'd realized how much wetter you grow when I do that," he mused and delivered one stinging blow and then another. Lenora cried out and sank down the last couple of inches until she had taken him as deep as he could go. "Oh gods," she cried, her head lolling back.

He felt the deep clench of her body and had to close his eyes to withstand it. This was no mere flutter or ripple of delight around his girth. Lenora had shot past the lower levels and was at the peak already. He felt a sweat break out as he realized he would have to work to withstand the pleasure or it would all be over before it had even begun!

"Fuck!" Garman roared, jolting forward, his grip hard on her hips. Lenora's glazed eyes fixed on him in alarm. "I can't—oh, fuck me," he gritted out tersely as he felt himself begin to throb within her. Then his arms were around her, pulling her in closer until she was plastered against him, and his hand was tangling in the hair, yanking her tight against him and his mouth was covering hers. He needed to ease up on her. She would not like having her mouth mashed against his like this. Even if she felt soft and willing in his arms. He could feel the throb and spurt of his cock inside her. It was the strangest sensation in the world even though this must be the third time he had done it. He dragged his mouth from hers, his hand sliding down her back to her clench her hip.

"Garman," she cried, sounding panicked as he felt.

"Yes," he grunted. "Wrap your legs around my back. *Now Lenora!*" He barely recognized his own voice; it was so gravelly. Lenora's eyes were blue like a clear summer sky. She sobbed with relief and struggled to rearrange her limbs to comply with his demands. He heard her ankle knock against the side of the tub as she floundered a moment. Probably she had pins and needles. He reached around her, grabbing, pulling, urging her to wrap her legs tightly around him. She crossed her ankles and held on tight as he shook with the sheer force of his release.

391

Then his hand was in the hair at her nape again, turning her head as he crushed his mouth to hers, seeking something desperately as he gave her his seed. She wrapped her arms around his neck, so she was clinging to him like a limpet, draining him of his life force and curling into him like she never wanted to let go.

He wasn't sure how many minutes later it was that she uncrossed her ankles. The water was definitely cooler now, and if she wasn't plastered so firmly against his body heat, they would surely be shivering. Her face was pressed into his shoulder as if she wasn't ready to look him in the eye yet.

"Did I say to do that?" Garman growled.

"No, but—"

"I'm not pulling out," he said confrontationally, and Lenora paused.

"Oh?"

"Not till I'm ready." *Fuck*, he was a boorish lout. Even as he recognized the fact, he felt powerless to change it. She'd just have to accept him as he was. Exerting a huge effort, he dragged himself up and out of the water, still carrying Lenora in his arms. As he lowered her carefully to the floor, he slid out of her, but it wasn't his choice to break contact.

He should let her wash between her legs, he thought, grudgingly handing her a cloth. She flushed as he glanced down between them and then cleaned herself up with hurried swipes of the cloth. She bent down to rinse the cloth in the bath and then handed it back to him with flaming cheeks. He handed her the nearest drying cloth before he set about cleaning himself. He should probably feel more annoyed about his lack of restraint but found himself unequal to it. How could he when he felt such bone-deep satisfaction?

Lenora wound the cloth about herself and made her way exhaustedly toward their bed. Garman finished drying himself off, his eyes never leaving her. When she started groping about the bed for her shift, he glanced back toward the floor next to the tub where it lay in a puddle of water. He watched her blond head emerge to blow the candle out on her side of the bed.

"Can you fetch me a clean shift?" she asked drowsily.

"No, you don't need it. And don't bother trying to fall asleep before I get in the bed. You know you can't sleep without me there."

"Then I shall have to learn!" she retorted, her voice only slightly muffled. "As you won't even be here."

"Mayhap I'll ride back at midnight one or two nights," he said lazily, rubbing a cloth over his arms. "And sneak up here at dead of night." She made no reply to that, and he flung the cloth down on a chair before making his way to the bed. "Lenora?"

"I'm asleep."

"Should you like that?" he asked, sliding between the covers until he found her curled-up body.

"I should not care at all!" she retorted with spirit.

He dragged her back into his arms. "Liar. You'd like it as much as me."

But in his heart of hearts, he doubted she even could. He sighed as their naked bodies came up flush against each other. He wondered at the strange feeling creeping over him. What was it? His eyes were drifting shut when he came up with the answer. *Contentment.*

393

33

The next morning, he rose at dawn, packed up his jousting gear and armor, and set off for Cofton Grange. Lenora was still soundly sleeping and small wonder, for he had been insatiable the previous night and twice woke her in the night, wearing her out with his ardor. It must have been about two weeks now since she had suffered any bad dreams.

She had attempted to remind him of his resolve to withdraw, but he had stopped her words with his mouth, until she gave up, accepting he was holding nothing back.

On reaching the Grange, his satisfaction soon trickled away and even though he kept himself busy, he found himself strangely plagued throughout the day with recurring thoughts of his wife. Even physical exertion, usually an effective refuge from persistent notions, failed him. Huw fumbled a charge; Garman bawled at him and thought of Lenora. Ivo complained of the vamplate and how unwieldy the lance rest felt on his breastplate; Garman cursed him soundly and thought of Lenora.

Doubtless it was the fact she had him enthralled in the bedchamber, he told himself uneasily as he washed up for supper. She was certainly proving an apt pupil in that respect, and thinking of her warm and willing made both his breath and his loins quicken. It occurred to him he was a damn fool to leave his bed when she lay in it.

But it wasn't only that, he thought with a frown as he sat down to a table thick with dust and bit into slightly stale bread. Looking at the Hainfroys across a table was a far less pleasant prospect than the one he was fast growing used to. But how could he have grown so domesticated in so short a time? He did not care overmuch about the toughness of the meat in the thick stew for he had eaten far worse. Nor for the fact he had to draw and heat his own water for washing or take a bath before the kitchen fire. No, it was her person he missed rather than any attendant comfort or convenience.

If things weren't quite so barbarous here, he could perchance have brought her with him. But the thought of setting her in a damp bed, expecting her to set her fair hands to a dirty house which was not her own did not sit right with him.

He could not help but wonder what she was doing at this precise moment as Huw clapped him on the back and Ivo filled his cup with ale. They were expecting visitors at the farm, he remembered, and she would be wearing her mauve dress. He frowned suddenly, wondering at the identity of his grandfather's neighbors. If it was the Dauntreys, they had at least two sons of marriageable age.

"You frown, brother," Ivo chided him. "Yet you said yourself that last pass I made was credible enough and you've seen many a worse in the field."

Garman grunted and refused the strong red wine Huw was holding out to him. "You'll need clear heads on the morrow," he growled, but knew the Hainfroys would not heed him or train any the less hard tomorrow for drinking tonight. It was simply habit with them. The brothers were in exuberant spirits, flushed with triumph and thoughts of their new endeavor.

They debated now enthusiastically how soon they could enter a country tournament to gain some first-hand experience. Garman wondered how long he would have to wait before they would be snoring their heads off and he could steal away to Matchings Farm. When he had suggested such a thing the previous night to Lenora, it had been in jest, but the idea had since taken root in his mind. Why should he not? It was no more than an hour's ride away, somewhat less. He could be there and back and neither brother none the wiser.

Purcel jumped up onto the table beside Huw's plate and meowed. Garman watched with raised brows as Huw absent-mindedly fed the cat from his own plate. He did not think even Lenora would approve of that. Finding the Hainfroys a servant would be difficult, a wife nigh on *impossible*. He would have to remember to tell Lenora as much.

*

By the time he reached Matchings Farm it was pitch black, though the moon drifted in the sky, giving him some silvery light to show his way. He stabled Bria'ag and made his way stealthily into the house via a side servants' door. He was soft on his feet when he chose to be, and though he had to pause when passing the kitchen for there was movement within, he slipped up the side staircase without much ado. He caught a glimpse of Hawise's grandson banking the kitchen fire and old Kolby flickered a canine eyebrow at him, but otherwise none stirred.

He did not pause to knock at his bedchamber door, but instead passed straight through and found Lenora wide awake and propped up on a mountain of pillows, a ferocious frown at her brow. He checked at the expression on her face and tipped his head to one side.

"Have you been waiting for me, wife?" he asked. The notion was a strangely pleasing one. At his words, Fendrel perked up from the foot of the bed and jumped down, running over to him with a faint cry.

"No, for I did not realize you were in earnest when you said you might return at nightfall," she said with a frankness he found irritating.

His brows snapped together. "Then why are you still awake?" he asked, sitting on a chair and pulling off his boots. He gave the kitten an absent pat on the head which set it purring.

"I have much on my mind," she said crisply and held up a sheet of paper he had not noticed she had on her lap. "Such as this letter from my grandmother, who it seems has been hearing all sorts of rumors about me and what happened at Kellingford."

He shrugged. "Your letter should reach them soon in any case."

"I doubt that will appease her," she said, looking troubled. "It was not exactly newsy."

He gave her a hard look before unfastening his belt. "What *did* you write, then?"

She chewed her lip. "Only that I was well and did not feel I had any other course of action open to me other than elopement." She hesitated. "I wrote in the expectation of them soon being reconciled to our news."

"A bold wish, all considered," he commented, drawing his tunic over his head. He did not want to talk about Lenora's fucking foolish family but could not see how he could in all decency say as much, then tell her what he did want from her. Namely, her sweet little body. And, he added thoughtfully, her mouth.

She sat up, regarding him keenly. "Yes, but why should they not be? My father had no great opinion of Sir Lionel above any of my other suitors." When he made no answer, she added belligerently, "Besides, I want my dowry."

He flung the tunic down next to his boots. "Why?" he asked pointedly and partook of a hasty wash with long-cooled water.

"Because," she spluttered, "I have every right to it. And we need it for our own place as you do not wish to settle here."

397

He paused a moment, then started shucking down his braies and chausses. "I told you," he said, "that I have that in hand. Your dowry is neither wanted nor needed."

She fell silent at that, but it was far from a contented silence. He stepped out of his leggings and kicked them to the side.

"You did not ask," Lenora said in a strange voice, "the name of your grandfather's guests for supper this night."

He paused by the side of the bed, unashamedly naked. "So, tell me, then."

"It was Skenfrith," she said accusingly. "The Lady Beatrix and her two sisters-in-law. Very young for a widow, I thought, and an extremely sweet and agreeable lady. Your grandfather was quite in raptures extolling her virtues and charitable work. She spoke on the subject of her home with much warmth. Apparently," she added, fixing him with a cold eye, "it has been in her family for *generations*."

Garman gave a short laugh. "What of it?" he asked, whisking back the sheets and climbing into the bed beside her, drawing her firmly into his arms. Lenora made some token resistance, but he drew her inexorably against his naked body.

"I am sure you are aware that I am talking about Matchings Halt," she said stiffly. "The estate in which you have your beady eye on."

He smiled against the top of her head. "I am aware," he admitted.

She took a deep breath. "Well, I've decided I don't want it," she said forthrightly.

"What do you mean?"

398

"Just what I said," she replied frostily. "I don't think it's right that we should dispossess Lady Beatrix and turn her out of her own home—"

"*We* wouldn't be," he interrupted her.

Lenora pursed her lips. Clearly, she was holding back, and strange to say, he wanted to hear what it was, almost in spite of himself.

"What?" he bit out. "Let's have it."

She puffed out a breath she was holding. "Only because you are getting some kinsman of hers to do the dirty work," she said, angling her head and glancing up at him.

She had mettle; he'd give her that. She looked a little wary after delivering this piece of wifely defiance, but otherwise remained quite still and recumbent in his arms.

"You think I don't care to get my hands dirty?" he asked, raising his brows in challenge. Likely she would back down now, he thought with a flicker of something like disappointment. But perhaps, just perhaps, she would not.

"I don't think you would particularly care about that," she said reflectively after a moment. "I don't think you care a damn for your reputation."

He gave a short laugh. "Not just a pretty face, are you?"

"Not anymore, no," she said and the slight wobble in her voice annoyed him. He had given her no reason to feel insecure about her looks.

He caught her chin with his fingers and forced her gaze back up to his. The gleam of defiance in the blue depths of her eyes pleased him. He smiled. "You know I like the way you look,

Lenora," he said softly. She swallowed and nodded. "But that doesn't mean I am going to let you run rings around me."

She moistened her lips. "I won't change my mind," she said. "I'm giving you fair warning that I will do anything in my power to find us an alternative. If that means securing my dowry to do it, then so be it."

His eyes narrowed. "I won't have you groveling for it, wife."

"Groveling?" Her angry gasp reassured him.

"You heard me. And if it comes to warnings, then let me give you mine. For I mean to have Matchings Halt. It has been my ambition since I was a mere boy."

"Very well, we've both made our intentions plain," she said gamely. "The battle lines are drawn. Let's have a fair fight and may the best man win."

That did draw a smile from him. "You won't win, Lenora, but I give you leave to try if it amuses you."

"By fair means or foul?"

"By whatever means you like," he drawled. "You still won't win."

"I'm willing to take my chances," she said.

He pinched her chin. "Do your worst," he recommended and lowered his head to press his lips to hers. Lenora leaned into his kiss, and he lay back, pulling her atop him. "Let's get this off you," he rumbled, tearing his lips from hers. She wriggled about as he dragged it up her body, aiding and abetting him in his quest to get her equally naked.

"You'll have to be quiet, Garman," she recommended conspiratorially as he dropped the garment over the edge of the bed. "If anyone hears us, they'll think it most odd as you're not supposed to be here."

"*I'll* have to be quiet?" he said lazily. "You're the noisy one."

"Me?" She swiped at his shoulder and he laughed.

"Very well, we were both quite loud last time, unless I misremember." His hands slid down to cup her rounded backside, and he brought her up firmly against his hard, aching flesh. "Ah Lenora," he groaned. "I've been half-hard since I saw you abed."

"You're a good deal more than half-hard, husband," she said and undulated against him in a way he found wholly distracting.

"Keep moving like that."

Immediately she stilled her hips. "Like what?" she asked, sounding self-conscious.

He gripped her buttocks and urged her closer. "Like you just did," he growled against her ear and delivered a stinging swat to her backside. She hissed and moved her hips tentatively. "Good," he rasped. "Now do it in earnest."

She slid her arms around his neck and lifted her face to his. Unable to refuse the silent invitation, he took her mouth again greedily as she ground her hips against him.

Unable to help himself, he slid one hand over her delicious rear to delve between her legs to seek out the slippery folds betwixt them. They both moaned when he found just how wet she was there, and he took no time to tease and rub her to the point where she had to tear her mouth from his to try to stifle her cries with her hand.

"Shall I make you reach it this way first?" he mused. Lenora sobbed and hid her face in his neck. "Or will that make your legs too weak for what I want?"

She could make him no reply by this point, just shuddered. This seemed to make up his mind.

"Get up, wife. On your knees. It's time for me to show you what I like." He practically had to arrange her limbs himself as he folded her forward onto her hands and knees and settled behind her. He knelt there for a few heartbeats, steadying himself and running his hands over her lush backside. "Do you trust me, Lenora?"

"Yes." She didn't even hesitate.

That sobered him. "If I'm too rough, tell me." She nodded and he took his cock in hand and guided it between her legs, pressing it to the pretty pink petals there but not seeking entrance, not yet. "That's it, get me nice and wet, Lenora, so I can slide right in to the hilt." She moaned softly and moved against him. "Not yet," he said, swatting her backside admonishingly. "I haven't given you my mouth, so we need to make sure you're good and wet."

She rocked against him, and he bit back a grunt. "I'm ready!" she protested as he angled his cock for another teasing slide.

"Stop rushing me, wife," he said, squeezing her hip, but she was hunching her shoulders and grinding against him in earnest now.

"Please!" she gasped and Garman swore. She always got so wet for him it made him light-headed. "You're sure you're ready?"

Her head dropped between her shoulders. "Yes!"

He had only so much self-control. Positioning the thick tip of his cock at the cleft between her legs, he pushed forward, his brow beading with sweat as he felt himself engulfed in the hot, tight grip of her cunt. He needed to go slow and steady, he warned himself as he felt the jolt of pleasure at the base of his spine as she took him deeper still. *Fuck*. He wanted to be so deep inside her that he didn't know where he ended and she began.

Where the fuck was this coming from? He needed to keep himself in check. Even as the words ran through what remained of his mind, his fingers closed tightly on her hips and jolted her back onto his greedy, impaling cock as his hips surged forward hard. Lenora cried out. Garman froze.

"Lenora—?" Then he felt it, the fluttering around his cock turned into a viselike clench and pull against his hard flesh. He groaned with relief and pleasure at the sensation. "Sweetheart, are you—?" Her low wail answered him. *Thank fuck for that.* He stopped fighting it and gave in to his baser nature as he thrust with abandon against the fullness of her soft, ripe ass.

Lenora's arms gave out before he had his fill, but he barely paused in his onslaught as she turned one cheek to the mattress and strove to catch her breath. He was like a man possessed. This might be his favorite position for bed sport, but he had no memory of feeling like his heart might burst in his chest before, or that he might black out from the sheer, overwhelming pleasure. Finally, the sensation of fullness in his ballocks could be ignored no more, and he spilled inside her longer and harder than he could ever remember, until he sank on top of her with a groan. She barely murmured a protest as he crushed her to him and pressed his face into her neck. He wanted to breathe her in, felt as though he could not get enough of her.

After a few moments of ragged breathing, he managed to rouse himself enough to release and roll off her. Even then, he could not resist a quick kiss to her shoulder. Kissing shoulders was not something he had ever felt compelled to do before, he thought, staring at the delicate shoulder blade and the perfection of the turn of her neck. Why was that? Even as his eyes drifted shut, he promised he would allow himself the pleasure of kissing her entire body next time from head to foot. He steadfastly ignored the tremor of alarm that registered somewhere in his thoughts. He could do what he damned well liked to his own wife and she would have to suffer it.

"What are you thinking about?" she suddenly asked, looking over her shoulder at him.

For some reason he answered truthfully. "Why it is that I can't seem to get enough of you," he murmured, too tired and replete for evasion. He saw the small smile that curved her lips. "That pleases you?"

She nodded, looking deliciously flushed and sated.

"Just as well," he grunted. "Though more prudent wives might be alarmed."

"By your monstrous appetites, you mean?" she asked drowsily.

That surprised a grin out of him though he was still too exhausted to laugh. Instead he found himself reaching for her hand. She pressed her palm to his and watched as he intertwined their fingers.

"What are you thinking of?" he asked, surprising even himself.

"Bedchamber doors," she answered with a yawn.

"What?"

"I'm glad I picked yours, Garman Orde," she said, her eyes drifting shut.

For some reason, his heart, which had been slowing to its regular thud, quickened again for an instant. Then he, too, allowed his eyes to close.

34

It had been a week since Garman had left for the Grange. And every night thus far, under cover of darkness, he returned to her side. He climbed out of her bed again before dawn and set off for to run the Hainfroys through their instruction. Lenora had started to sleep in late to recover. She strove to make up for her morning laziness by attacking her new household duties in the afternoon.

Today, she had come to market with Ada in the horse and cart. Smothering a yawn, she stopped at one stall and turned over a few wares before drifting to the next. Ada was with her and bustling about with industrious zeal. The maid had clearly done the market run a hundred times and could do it in her sleep. The only commission Lenora had was from Grandfather Sutton, who had a fancy for an eel pie that had struck him that very morning.

This gave her some leisure to turn over in her mind the problem she was currently working on. Just what it was that Garman found so desirable about Matchings Halt? For if she discovered this, she felt sure she could find an alternative to it that he would like as well. She ticked off on her fingers what she had managed to glean thus far about that estate.

One—it was neat and well maintained with seasoned orchards and well-stocked ponds and fields of choice livestock. Two—the property was compact enough that it only needed a knowledgeable mistress and a conscientious steward to keep it well-run. Three—the house itself was a fine handsome property with a solar, great hall, and kitchen gardens as well became a nobleman's demesne. Four—the grounds were well laid out, fertile, and flourishing. The soil was good, the land regularly rotated for crops to leave areas fallow for recovery.

So far, so good. These practices were all those of good stewardship and Garman's grandfather had already explained several of these techniques to her. The problem was, securing an estate where such care had been employed and embedded over a period of many years, with a household of trustworthy and faithful retainers who cared about the land as much as their overlord. And that would not be so easy a task. In truth, it was starting to feel nigh on impossible.

Lady Beatrix had kindly extended an invitation for Lenora to visit her at any time she so wished, but something held Lenora back from taking this step. For what if, in the end, she could not prevent Garman from negotiating with Beatrix's relative to usurp her from her home? Then it would seem as though Lenora had been complicit in the takeover and had been spying out the land. She could not bear for Lady Beatrix or indeed Garman's grandfather to think such a thing of her.

Lenora wrinkled her nose, realizing she had ill-advisedly chosen to dally next to the fishmonger's stall. Turning from left to right to scan the different traders, she nearly bumped into a tall figure in a shabby purple cloak for the second time that morning. "Your pardon," Lenora apologized politely. The stranger looked at her rather hard and inclined her head in acknowledgment before retreating. Lenora gazed after her, wondering who the tall, rather good-looking girl was, now watching her covertly from a table of woven wares made from rushes, reeds, and canes.

She was a young gentlewoman, if Lenora was not mistaken, and was accompanied by a servant hanging back at a discreet distance. She looked much the same age as Lenora and was dressed in a dark purple brocade gown which must once have been very fine, but now looked rather threadbare and appeared to be patched rather than embellished with stretches of a plainer more hard-wearing fabric.

Clearly the woman was watching her, perhaps for an opportunity to approach her, and Lenora found she was curious enough to give her an opening. "Ada," she said, beckoning to her own companion. "Would you kindly remain here at the fishmonger's stall while I move on? Master Sutton hankers for eel pie for supper. Only I can't bear the smell of it, so I shall await you further along."

The servant nodded obligingly, though she cast a curious look over Lenora as though inspecting her for something. Maybe she thought there might be a particular reason for her oversensitive nose. Lenora blushed. There surely had not been time for her to catch with child already or in any case, Garman did not seem to think so.

They probably should have another discussion about children, Lenora thought, considering the disparity between his intent and his actions. She moved along a couple of stalls deep in thought. In truth, it was probably not the ideal time to start a family when they had no settled home and their marriage was still unaccepted in certain quarters. Then again, with a child in her belly, her father would be less inclined to kick up a fuss about his permission not having been sought.

After a couple of minutes of wandering, she realized the purple-cloaked stranger had decided to take the bull by its horns and was headed in her direction wearing a tight smile. "I must apologize for approaching you in this fashion," she said, running Lenora to earth beside a potter's stall. She sounded rather out of breath, her face turning a dull red. She had a good-looking if somewhat haughty face with dark gold hair worn in two braids that had been woven around her head in a style that had been the height of fashion some ten years ago. "We have not been introduced and I am very conscious of the fact you must think me forward indeed."

"Pray do not worry about that," Lenora told her in what she hoped was an encouraging manner. "I know so few people in this neighborhood that any new acquaintance is a pleasure to me."

The other's face flamed quite scarlet at this, and Lenora wondered at it. "Your name?" she prompted gently when the other appeared tongue-tied. Even this simple request seemed to cause the stranger some difficulty.

She almost reared back. "How awkward this is," she forced out at last, clasping her hands together tightly. Lenora could see the cuffs were fraying although they had been much repaired. "You see, we are by way of being related—by your recent marriage." Clearly, each word was forced out and caused the stranger acute discomfort.

"Oh," said Lenora with exaggerated easiness. "So, you are a relation of my husband, Sir Garman Orde?" She was intrigued, as other than Gerard Sutton, she had not heard of any living relatives.

"Not one that he acknowledges, I'm afraid," the other responded quickly.

"I see," said Lenora calmly, though in truth she felt quite in the dark. "Perhaps you might tell me your name?"

The other gave a start as if only just realizing she had not already given it. "I am Lady Magda Orde," she said and sank into a graceful curtsey. "And your husband's first cousin."

Lenora responded in kind. "And I am Lenora Orde," she said, though her married name still felt rusty on her tongue. She recognized the similar coloring between the cousins, the dark blond hair, the pale blue eyes, and the shared height.

"I know," replied Magda frankly. "You were pointed out to me on a previous occasion. You see, I have a message to pass along to you." She looked around a little furtively at this and reached into a shabby-looking pouch attached to the belt around her hips.

"A message for me?" asked Lenora in some surprise. "From whom?"

"My grandfather, the Earl of Twyford," replied Magda on an outward breath. She had retrieved a folded-up paper, which she held out now to Lenora.

"Your grandfather?" Lenora repeated as she took the missive almost without conscious thought. The strangest feeling of foreboding was stealing over her. Had not Garman once said something about a grandfather he did not acknowledge? "Am I to take it the earl is also Garman's grandfather?" she asked slowly.

"He is," Magda agreed. She darted a curious look at Lenora. "You did not know this?" she asked, clearly taken aback.

"No, I did not," Lenora said heavily, her fingers tightening around the letter. So much for the lowly knight she had meant to marry and follow into obscurity! The grandson of an earl! She felt a tingling feeling of ill foreboding along her spine as another thought occurred to her. "Pray do not tell me Garman is your grandfather's only grandson."

Magda's eyes widened as shook her head slowly. "Nay, I cannot," she said in a low voice. "For he is in truth our grandfather's rightful heir."

Lenora took a deep breath. So, Garman was a future earl of the realm! "He did not tell me *any* of this!"

Magda stepped back, alarmed at Lenora's vehemence. "I apologize," she said rather stiffly, "if the news is unwelcome."

Lenora pulled herself together with an effort. "'Tis only something of a shock," she prevaricated. "I apologize if I was ungracious."

The other woman hesitated but inclined her head. "I'm sure that was only natural." She cast around a harried look as approaching footsteps heralded Ada's return to her mistress and with a hurried curtsey, Magda retreated back to her former position next to the basket weaver's stall.

"Got 'em, milady," Ada said triumphantly. "Enough for two pies, I'll be bound."

*

It was not until Lenora was sat in the cart on the road home that she retrieved the missive from her pocket and broke the wax seal. A sidelong glance at Ada showed her that she was fully occupied with the horse's reins.

Madam, the letter started in a spidery hand.

I suspect you are as curious to meet with me as I with you, and if you wish to exercise a beneficial influence over your husband's life, you will doubtless meet with me for evening supper on Thursday the fourteenth at Twyford Castle.

For reasons you will appreciate, I cannot extend this invitation to you in person. I regret that I will have been most villainously misrepresented to you by one whose loyalty and station in life should have stayed his lips forever. I make no doubt it is he who hath blackened my name to my grandson.

I do you the courtesy of imagining you have enough wit to separate fact from outright slander.

411

And remain

Jarin Orde, Earl of Twyford

Lenora read it through twice with raised brows before refolding
it and slipping it into her purse. Who did he mean? Surely he
did not refer to Gerard Sutton, who had never breathed so much
as a word about another grandfather living, let alone blackened
his name. Today was Tuesday the twelfth which meant the
proposed meeting was in two days' time. Where even was
Twyford Castle? she wondered. She had heard no mention of
the place. Stealing a sideways glance at Ada, she debated
quizzing her about it, before deciding against it. She would wait
for Garman tonight and task him with an explanation.

At supper, Garman's grandfather was in a genial mood,
possibly due to the eel pie. Questions trembled on her lips
several times about the Twyfords, but she restrained herself.
Garman's father must have been Jarin Orde's heir. Yet he had
married the daughter of a steward and built this farm. It didn't
really make sense, however she thought of it.

Retiring early, she brushed her hair and left it loose about her
shoulders, expecting her midnight visitor. She read her letter
again, then slipped it under her pillow, remembering how
stricken Gerard had looked and how his hand had trembled at
the news his grandson had eloped. Lenora wondered if that was
what his own daughter had done. Entered into an unsanctioned
marriage with a young nobleman?

She lay back on her pillows as Fendrel nestled into her side.
Reaching out, she stroked his soft gray fur and the little cat
purred. Grizelda was already lying at her feet in an elegant
stretch. These past few nights the cats had settled into a rhythm
of starting their night on the bed, then jumping down when
Garman appeared to retreat to the fire. When he took his leave
in the early hours and the ashes turned cool, they would spring

412

back up onto the bed to keep her company. They seemed to be taking to their new lives as fishes to water. Certainly, they were growing fat and spoiled by the kitchen staff. Hawise was a definite favorite with both.

Thinking of Hawise brought Berta to mind, and Lenora's brow furrowed. She still had not determined what best to do where she was concerned. Certainly, Berta seemed to be growing sourer and more morose by the day. She even seemed to take some sullen delight in poisoning the atmosphere in the kitchens, which fell silent when her moods grew particularly ferocious, slamming down implements and screwing her face up savagely when anyone spoke to her.

Once or twice, she thought Garman's grandfather had tried tentatively to raise the issue, but he was far too tactful to complain her servant was causing discord among his own. Lenora sighed and rolled onto her side, glancing at the window. Garman was late tonight. Mayhap she would close her eyes a moment, just so she was refreshed when he arrived. The next thing she knew, sunlight was in her eyes and her ears assailed with birdsong.

He had not come.

Neither did he come the next night. At the prospect of waking alone on Thursday morning no clearer of her own decision, Lenora felt almost beside herself. What should she do? On Wednesday during supper, she opened her mouth twice to raise the subject with Grandfather Sutton but could not quite bring herself to do it. After all, did not the Earl of Twyford's letter malign him atrociously? He would no doubt be mortified if he were aware of the contents of the letter and she would not hurt his feelings for the world.

After supper, she retired to her bedchamber, washed, undressed, braided her hair, and reached out a hand to pull back the covers.

Something stayed her hand. Turning from the bed with an exclamation, she donned a robe over her shift, stuffed her feet into some slippers, and snatched up the letter before making her way downstairs.

Gerard Sutton was tidying away some papers in the front parlor.

"Grandfather?"

He looked up in surprise. "My dear, what is it? I thought you were abed. Do you feel unwell?"

Lenora took a deep breath. "I need to speak to you about something that happened. At market."

He looked instantly alarmed. "Is all well? Ada made no mention of any incident—"

"Can we sit?" she asked. "I would ask your opinion, if I may."

"But of course." He gestured to a seat. "Let me just stoke the fire," he fretted. "Dear me, I have let it die down, I had no notion we would need it again." She waited as he fussed with a poker and added a log or two. "You are warm enough?" She nodded and he sat opposite her.

"Grandfather," she started earnestly. "I was approached with an invitation to dine tomorrow evening from the Earl of Twyford."

Gerard Sutton's eyes almost started from his head. "Th-the earl?" he stammered. "Invited you to dine?"

"He did."

"Twyford was surely not in the marketplace?" He sounded shocked and horrified at the idea.

"Oh no. The invite was hand-delivered by one Magda Orde, who I am led to believe is Garman's cousin."

He nodded. "Oh yes. I had heard Rulf had a couple of daughters," he muttered, standing up and then sitting back down again.

"Rulf?" Lenora asked gently, seeing that he was going to need careful handling.

"Garman's uncle," he hesitated. "The earl's younger son."

Lenora clasped her hands together in her lap. "I do not think you will be surprised to hear that Garman has told me none of this."

Gerard Sutton sighed unhappily. "No, my dear, not surprised."

She hesitated. "Would you tell me?"

He stared at her in dismay. "I hardly know what to do for the best," he fretted. "It is unfortunate indeed this happened when Garman is away from home."

"I do not think," Lenora hazarded shrewdly, "that the intention was for me to share the invitation with my husband."

He looked a good deal taken aback by this. "You think it was meant to be a clandestine arrangement?"

"Indeed, I do, from the terms in which it was couched." She paused. "I would show it to you, Grandfather, but—"

He glanced at her shrewdly. "It contains some slur against my character, then?" he said with a rueful smile.

Lenora colored. "I think so, although I did not altogether understand its meaning."

He sat quietly a moment. "May I see it?" he asked.

"Only if you promise not to be offended, for I can assure you that I speak as I find and shall not be swayed in my own formed opinions by that of others."

He gave a quick smile. "I hereby swear I shall not be offended by aught Twyford has written of me." Lenora handed the missive over and watched him scan its contents quickly and then return to the start and read them again at a slower pace. "I see," he pondered. "And I agree, this was meant to be a clandestine supper invitation." He sighed. "He has not changed, the old devil. Though probably his desperation is growing great."

"Why should he be desperate?"

"He has no heir," Gerard said, shaking his white head. "Or rather, he has one that he has no control over. One that holds his own birthright in utter contempt." At those words, a look of such sadness stole over the old man that Lenora reached out to him and they clasped hands.

"Is he a bad man, then? The old earl?" Lenora asked softly.

"Bad?" Gerard looked startled. "No more than many men who head noble families I daresay. He is proud, selfish, and stubborn. But if he was bad, then he has been amply repaid for it." He swallowed before continuing. "I was born and raised at Twyford Castle," he said brightly. "My father was steward before me. There have been Suttons serving Ordes for generations." His gaze softened. "My only child, my daughter, Anne, was raised at Twyford, for I was steward there, too, by the time I was thirty. She had a happy childhood too. She was a good girl, my Anne. Not beautiful, but bonny in her own way like her mother. We were happy together, but then her mother died, and Anne grew into womanhood." A shadow crossed over his face.

"Merek Orde should never have fallen in love with her, but gods help us, fall he did. So much so, that he wanted to marry her. Their family marrying into ours… Can you imagine?" He fell silent and Lenora squeezed his fingers. "You can guess how Twyford felt about his eldest son matched with his lowly steward's daughter. Her catching his eye was not to be wondered at for they had been children together, but making her his wife…?" He shook his head.

"They eloped?" Lenora interjected quietly when Gerard fell silent.

"Aye, that they did. And his lordship raged fit to throw himself into an apoplexy. Vowed to cut him off without a penny, to petition the Crown and have his title passed to his younger son. If such a thing were even possible for the estate is entailed. I'm sure you know better than I how these things work." Lenora nodded. "Anyway, 'twas all for naught. Merek had an inheritance already from his mother's father, old Lord Edland. He built this farm and they settled here and had a son."

"What of Lord Twyford? What did he do?"

"By this point, I'd been banished from Twyford and joined my married daughter here. But I heard he married his younger son to the heiress he'd intended for the elder." He smiled sadly. "I haven't been back to Twyford Castle in twenty-seven years."

To her surprise, Lenora thought she detected a note of yearning in his voice. "You miss the place?"

"It was my home," he said simply. "And all that I knew. I thought I'd die there one day, in service like my father and grandfather before me."

Lenora frowned and plucked at the arm of her chair. "This is a fine farm," she pointed out.

"It is."

"Yet, you are not fond of it?"

"It is not my home. I am merely caretaker here for Garman's sake."

Lenora breathed out. "But Garman does not view it as his home either."

Gerard nodded slowly. "I know," he sighed. "His parents died here. I sent him away as a page to Sir Bernhard while he still a boy. I did my best by him, but I do not deceive myself all has turned out as it should." He looked uneasy. "In truth, I never saw it fitting that he should view this place as his rightful home. He will be Earl of Twyford before ere long."

Lenora frowned. "The only ambition he has confided in me is to buy a small estate," she admitted. "He makes no mention of a castle or title coming his way."

Gerard looked troubled. "He has not spoken of it for many years to me, but when he was a boy, he spoke quite wildly of—" He broke off, moistening his lips. "I fear, through no agency of my own, he resents Lord Twyford. Country folk talk, and I make no doubt he had accounts of his father's treatment that poisoned his mind against his grandfather. Then, too, while he was still young, he was summoned for a visit to Twyford. Against my better judgment, I permitted him to go. When he returned—" He took a deep breath. "He seemed to hate the earl and banned me from ever mentioning his existence again."

"Well," said Lenora. "That is small wonder. Lord Twyford probably spoke ill of you and his mother, so it's not to be wondered at." Her words seemed to startle him. "After all, the earl only wrote me four lines, yet in those scant few lines he managed to scrawl an insult relating to you," she pointed out.

418

"I assure you; I have never bad-mouthed his lordship to Garman over these years, not once. Indeed, I would not deem it fit—"

"I believe you," Lenora interrupted him hastily. "It seems to me that Lord Twyford has only himself to blame for Garman's ill opinion of him."

"So, you will not go?" To Lenora's surprise, Garman's grandfather sounded sad.

"You think I should?"

He did not speak for a long time. Then when he did, he said heavily, "I do not think it is my place to advise you on the best course of action, Lenora. But"—he leaned forward in his seat—"I do not think there will be many more such opportunities for a reconciliation to be made between our families. This is perhaps the last time such an overture could be made." He pressed her hand. "If you do go—"

"I will go," she interrupted him and thought for a moment he looked both startled and glad.

He closed his eyes. "Could I request, my dear, that you are discreet among the servants? 'Tis only that I should not wish it to become common knowledge—"

"I will make my arrangements with Berta alone," she assured him. "You need not worry about that."

*

"Berta?"

Her servant looked up from scrubbing the washing with an irritable twitch of one shoulder. "Well, what is it, miss?" she snapped in exasperation, dropping the tunic into the suds with a splash. "You been worriting about me all mornin', I vow! 'Tis almost as bad as that time you were fixin' to run away!" When

Lenora did not speak, only gazed back at her, Berta's black eyes narrowed with suspicion. "What you a-plottin' of now? I never knew such a girl for tricks!"

Lenora raised a finger to her lips and glanced around the kitchen. Hawise was right up the other end, kneading happily at her dough and humming a tune to herself. "What makes you think I'm plotting anything?" she murmured conspiratorially.

"Cos I knows you!" Berta retorted with a snort. "That great lummox of a husband of yourn ought to keep you on a tighter leash! Askin' for trouble he is, leavin' the likes of you here to your own devices!" Her mouth worked crossly, but Lenora wasn't deceived. Berta was entertained. The brooding look had left her eye and it glinted now sharply as a bird's.

"As a matter of fact," Lenora admitted, leaning forward, "I do have something afoot, and I have need of your help."

"Hah!" Berta wiped her clawlike hands on her apron and rocked back on her heels. "Let's hear it, then."

"I've had an invite to supper at Twyford Castle," she whispered. "Have you ever heard of it?"

Berta's eyebrows rose with surprise. "Twyford Castle?" she repeated slowly. "Why now, I do think I have heard tell of it," she muttered, fingering the hairs on her chin. "Only I never paid it much heed. A soft, gossipy bunch here." She sniffed contemptuously. "Country folk!"

"Think now, Berta!" Lenora implored. "This is important. Do you think you could find out how far it lies from here and the direction by this afternoon? We would need to take a horse and cart and be there by nightfall."

"What you be a-doing of there?" she demanded in a whisper.

"Meeting with an earl," Lenora admitted.

"Pah!" Berta spat. "It's too late to be angling for a title now, girl! I seen the way that Master Garman looks at you. If you think he'd ever let you go, you're much mistaken! He'd beat you soundly if he heard tell of you cavortin', mind," she cautioned.

"I won't be cavorting," Lenora muttered, though what she really wanted to ask after was the manner in which Garman looked at her. "I'll be unearthing dark family secrets," she added mysteriously.

"What's that?"

"I'll tell you all about it," Lenora vowed. "If you promise to accompany me as chaperone."

Berta snorted again. "Chaperone! That be a new role for me."

Lenora gave her a level look. "Speaking of new roles, there's something else I would discuss with you," she admitted, adding hurriedly. "Away from here and in private though. Do you think you could manage the arrangements, Berta?"

The old woman shot her a considering look. "Aye, I could manage 'em, alright," she said grimly. "And I will."

*

And so, it was some few hours later that Lenora found herself sat next to Berta in the horse-drawn cart bowling along the road for Cofton Mallet in a southerly direction. Twyford Castle it turned out was only an hour and a half of decent road away, which boded well for their return journey in the dark. Lenora shivered and drew her cloak closer for her fine red and gold damask gown was cut for glamorous effect and not warmth. She wore a single flashing ruby at her décolletage which might be

421

considered somewhat rash in a female traveling a lonely country road at night, but she had not wished to involve any of Grandfather Sutton's staff lest it left them open to reproach or even punishment.

Neither had she wanted to tax Garman's grandfather further for clearly the Twyford connection was not spoken of at Matchings Farm. She outlined Garman's proposal for Berta's relocation to the Grange at the outset of their journey. When Berta neither railed nor exclaimed at the idea, Lenora calmly went through the various points in favor of the scheme, though she was keen to point out that Berta was under no obligation to go and could return to Lenora's service at any time.

"Indeed, Berta, I hope you know that you will always have a home under my roof," she stressed. Berta appeared to think it over in silence and no more was said. Lenora felt both nervous and excited as they drew closer to the gray stone castle which loomed out of the dark like a great stone monolith in the failing light.

"What a huge place," Lenora gasped. "It will take us another half hour at least to reach its door!"

And indeed, she was right. As they trundled up the tree-lined avenue of the approach, she craned her eyes to make out the monstrous sprawling pile concealed in the shadows. She'd had no idea that it would be such a big estate. Why, it made her own father's place, Hallam Hall, look like a mere lodge house!

Even Berta had turned quiet, staring up open-mouthed at its towers and turrets. "'Tain't much smaller than a royal palace!" she marveled. Quietly, Lenora agreed, but what's more, she thought, it would take a king's ransom to run such a place. She frowned, recalling Magda Orde's frayed cuffs and patched-up dress. A fortune that would soon dwindle away under the demands of a property so vast. If she wasn't mistaken, one of the towers was showing signs of damage even in this failing light.

On reaching the courtyard, they were greeted by an aged servant who held a torch aloft to light their way and a young boy led their horse and cart away into a dilapidated stable. Lenora and Berta followed the stooped old man along a stone passageway which looked rather like a servants' walkway, and she wondered greatly at this approach. Along they went through a somewhat meandering route until they reached a large wooden door which the servant paused at. "The banqueting hall," he said woodenly. "Will you be a-letting me take your cloak, milady?"

Somewhat loath to lose her warm cloak within these chilly stone walls, she nonetheless handed it over and smoothed her long blond tresses over her shoulders, adjusting her small veil to lay neatly down her back.

"I'll be following you along to the kitchens," Berta said stoutly when he turned to her. "And I'll keep mine, thank you kindly!"

He nodded, then fumbled at the door latch. Flinging it wide, he announced in a quavering voice, "My lord, I present the Lady Lenora Orde!"

Lenora blinked at the gloom within. There barely seemed enough candlelight to see by in the huge chamber. A puddle of yellow light shone feebly at the far end of the room, so she made her way in that direction. As she grew closer, she realized several figures were sat around a table on a dais.

"Look out for the floorboard just there, it is rotted through," a voice called in warning, and she realized it was the girl she had met at market.

"I thank you, Magda," she called back as she nimbly sidestepped the hazardous area.

"Come and sit here, girl!" an enfeebled yet autocratic voice demanded. "Beside me." Lenora drew near and made out that a wicked-looking old man sat at the head of the table with sunken cheeks and overbright eyes. Like his home, he had the air of a ruin about him. His frame, which must once have been tall and straight, was now twisted and thin, though dressed in fine robes of deep burgundy. His thin hawklike face was lined with bitterness and disappointment, and unlike Garman's full, sensual mouth, his was hard and cynical.

As Lenora stepped up onto the dais, she counted three women including Magda sat at the other end. An older woman of about fifty years sat opposite Earl Twyford dressed in navy blue satin. She had a haughty, well-bred face and a large steepled headdress with a wide velvet band which entirely concealed her hair. Her forehead was so high that Lenora thought she must have shaved it and plucked out her eyebrows as her own grandmother had once said was the fashion in her own youth.

To the lady's right sat Magda Orde, and to her left, another girl who looked very like Magda only younger and sullener. Lenora noticed the younger daughter had a crutch resting on the back of her seat. Both girls were dressed in finery that looked rather shabby around the edges, though that could have been that the outdated styles looked somehow worse contrasted with their youth.

As Lenora curtseyed and sat in her chair, Magda threw her a look of agonized apology as though she felt bad about what was to come. Lenora smiled reassuringly back at her. Five years at court meant she was not cowed by a fancy title or ill-mannered men. She turned to survey the Earl of Twyford with some interest, looking for a resemblance that was only vaguely present. Though, if she tried to imagine this man in the flush of youth, perhaps…

"Well, madam," he said harshly, interrupting her thoughts. "Have you looked your fill?"

"I have not," she admitted frankly. "For I am looking for a family likeness."

He gave a crack of laughter. "You won't find it here, though perhaps in the long gallery. There is a portrait there of myself at the height of my beauty." His mouth twisted mockingly. "And one of my own father. There you will find it sure enough."

"I would be glad to see them, my lord," Lenora murmured as a servant shuffled in with a platter of roasted mutton. "I believe I can see one between my husband and his cousin," she said, smiling down the table at Magda.

As though reminded of his duty, Earl Twyford waved an irritable hand toward the other end of the table. "My daughter-in-law," he said with distaste. "Jehanne and her two daughters. Magda you have met, and Agnes."

Lenora inclined her head and saw Lady Jehanne's head move infinitesimally. A proud, disagreeable woman she looked too, but then, shut up in this mausoleum, who could blame her? Magda gave a strained smile while her sister's lips moved as though in greeting, but she stared down at the table with a ferocious scowl.

"Do you not envy me my company these past twenty-five years?" Earl Twyford asked contemptuously. "A merry bunch, are they not?" Mercifully, he did not wait for an answer but motioned for his wine cup to be filled by a scared-looking servant who darted out of the shadows. Lenora waited while the meat was carved.

425

Lord Twyford's plate, she noticed, had barely a morsel placed on it, and seeing the way his bony hand clasped and unclasped the arm of his chair, she wondered if some of the lines on his face might not be due to constant pain. He had the look of a sufferer who does not admit to his malady. His color was not good, his breathing shallow and uneven. "Well, madam, what said your husband of this visit?" he asked tightly once the servers had withdrawn again and the food served.

Lenora paused, lowering her spoon. "As to that, my lord, I was not so imprudent as to tell him of it."

Again, he gave that short bark of laughter. "A canny woman," he said, looking down the length of the table. "Did you hear that, Jehanne? This one knows how to handle a man." Lady Jehanne bristled and he turned back to Lenora. "Or do I overestimate you?"

Lenora considered this a moment before replying. "I do not know," she said truthfully. "I have not long been married and before that, I did not care about men at all."

He gazed at her keenly, one of his long fingers tapping against the tabletop. Lenora noticed a large gold signet ring which rolled loosely above the middle knuckle. "Did not care for them, eh? But by all accounts, they cared for you." Lenora's brows rose with surprise. "Yes," he said with a chuckle. "Word still reaches me now and again of the wide world. And when I heard of my grandson's marriage, you may be sure I made enquiries as to the lady. I heard all about the once beautiful Lady Lenora and her squalid fate."

Lenora raised her chin. "Have you looked your fill, my lord?" she asked boldly. "As to my fate, I have been reliably informed it will be whatever I choose to make it."

"Who told you that?" he asked with a sneer, raising his cup to moisten his thin lips.

"My husband," she replied serenely and was pleased to see the cup quiver in his hands with surprise.

"He told you, no doubt," Lord Twyford said, his tone diamond hard, "that I sent for him some years ago. When he numbered some fourteen years."

Lenora shook her head. "He does not speak of any of you," she admitted frankly. The earl's color rose to a violent hue. "Did he come here to Twyford Castle, then?" she asked, hoping to distract him from the inevitable explosion of wrath.

"Aye, he did," the old man admitted, thrusting out his chin. "Wherein he showed himself to be an ungracious, unmannerly churl!"

"And by that, I suppose you mean he did not fawn on any of you or trouble to make himself agreeable," Lenora answered mildly.

Garman's grandfather spluttered. "If you think I enjoy being flattered and fawned over, you are a fool, girl!"

Lenora leaned back in her chair, looking him over. "I don't say that you enjoy it, my lord," she said slowly. "But I daresay you *were* expecting it. And very likely you were looking forward to rebuffing the pretensions of your upstart grandson, and putting him in his place," she added shrewdly. "Unluckily for you, his rightful place is your heir apparent." She steadfastly ignored Lady Jehanne's shocked indrawn breath.

"I do realize that, Mistress Impertinence!" he snapped back at her, and she noticed he did not argue her point. "Perhaps I did take the wrong approach that time," he conceded after a moment, surprising not only her. "But I tried again when he reached twenty-one, and you may be sure his reply was none the prettier. Said he'd throw his cousins out on the street before I was cold in my grave and watch this place rot to its last timber." His eyes glinted. "Now what do you say to that?"

She found she could well imagine a young Garman flinging that in this highhanded old devil's face. "I daresay you took entirely the wrong approach with him," she admonished. "And now you're paying for it dearly."

The old earl snorted. "Oh, so it's you that's got the handling of him, is it?" he asked with heavy sarcasm.

Something about the expression in his eye was oddly hopeful, though Lenora noticed with alarm. It would not do to get his hopes up. "Oh no," she said quickly. "Garman is his own master. I only mean that I know how *not* to get his hackles up from the outset." Lord Twyford merely grunted, eyeing her with a challenging gleam in his eye. "He'll never come to you on bended knee, you know," she said simply. "He wouldn't know how."

"Fine talk!" jeered the old man contemptuously. "He'd sing a different tune given half the chance!"

"Oh no," said Lenora firmly. "Your problem is that Garman is a man of his word and not fine speeches. When you heard him say he would let this place rot to its timbers and throw your dependents out into the street, he would have meant every word."

One of his cousins gasped, Lenora guessed it was Magda, but she did not look across at the womenfolk. She was watching the earl's knobbly fingers tighten on the arms of his chair so hard they turned white. Was that concern about his granddaughter's fate? she wondered. Or that of his sprawling estate? She fancied she knew the answer.

At this, Lady Jehanne could no longer stay silent. She flung her head back and said in a low, angry voice. "If you imagine Sir Garman would escape the judgment of his friends and neighbors by taking such action, you are vastly mistaken!"

Lenora glanced across at the lady. "He has no friends," she answered simply. "And moreover, cultivates none. He cares not the snap of his fingers for neighbors save for the Hainfroys and they would not blink an eye to see him exact his revenge."

Lord Twyford gave a chuckle of amusement at that.

"His reputation," the older woman rallied in a loud, throbbing voice, "would surely suffer beyond repair! He would not dare—"

But here she was forestalled by a sharp crack of laughter from her father-in-law. "We Ordes have never given a damn for the opinion of others," he put in scathingly. "My grandfather dispossessed a whole brace of orphans when he wanted to expand the southern border of his estate. Burned their cottages to a rubble."

Lovely, thought Lenora, noticing how the old man's eyes gleamed with unholy glee. Perhaps Garman's savagery was not learned from old Sir Bernhard after all. Maybe it was bred in the bone.

"You aren't an Orde, Jehanne," the old man continued dismissively. "You only married one!"

Lady Jehanne drew herself up, pursing her lips. "My fortune was squandered on this estate. Both my daughters—"

"Don't speak to me of your pair of mewling females!" he spat contemptuously. "I'll say this for that steward's brat. She gave my son an heir!" His thin lips worked angrily. "Which is more than you ever did, for all your stiff-necked pride!"

This was too much for Lady Jehanne's dignity. She flushed scarlet and rose jerkily from her seat. "I will not sit here and be insulted in my own home," she said in outraged tones.

"Hah!" the old man muttered. "Enjoy it while you can, my dear. My grandson means to throw you out on your ear and reduce these hallowed halls to mere rubble." The last few words were filled with such a wealth of bitterness, and Lenora held her tongue as Lady Jehanne exited grandly from the room, her daughters swept along in her wake.

"Is there no provision made for the girls?" Lenora asked as soon as the door had banged shut.

"None," he answered harshly. "And they are hardly girls." His lip curled. "They ought to have been married off years ago."

"Oh, I agree," she replied calmly. "Why did you not see to it?"

He regarded her beadily through his bright eyes, then gave a lopsided smirk. "You're not afraid of me at all, are you?" he said with grudging respect.

"Certainly not. After all, I am not under your yoke."

He gave a dry chuckle. "I can see now why he married you, even though you lost your looks."

Lenora ignored this. "I shall speak to Garman," she said impulsively. "About his cousins."

He arched a thin eyebrow at her. "You should not waste your breath," he advised her. "I doubt very much he could be induced to stir himself on their behalf."

"Oh, but I've quite made up my mind they should be provided for."

At this, the Earl of Twyford gave a disbelieving huff. "You'd never find a pair who'd take their like, not without a hefty bribe."

"You might be surprised," Lenora told him, lifting her chin. "Connections," she said vaguely.

"Connections!" Lord Twyford repeated disparagingly. "I've not been at court for over fifty years. All my connections are long since dead and buried."

"I didn't mean with you," Lenora responded with some spirit.

"Oh-hoh!" The earl gestured to one of his servants to fetch the wine. "Refill my granddaughter's cup." Lenora set her goblet down while the servant hurried to comply. If she was not mistaken, the old man had taken something of a shine to her in his own, rather acidic way. "A connection to the Montmaynes, you mean?" he asked, giving her a hard look. "Are you not still in disgrace with your own father?"

"Doubtless," she agreed. "But I did not mean a Montmayne connection, but rather one of Garman's own." At his raised brow, she added, "The Hainfroys."

The earl went into a paroxysm of coughing. "The Hainfroys!" he gasped as soon as he was able.

"Indeed, they are an old and venerable family, are they not?"

"Venerable?" he wheezed, still having trouble catching his breath. "Their line was sprung from country squires and has now degenerated to the state of barbarous yokels!"

She was not fooled though; he was not offended at the idea but instead derived some dark amusement from it. She suspected it was his haughty daughter-in-law's reaction he anticipated with such relish.

431

"I have heard it said on good authority that old Sir Bernhard's dearest wish was to marry Garman to his daughter, Isabeau Hainfroy."

"Impudence!" muttered the earl without much heat.

"But when she eloped, that hope was thwarted. Ivo and Huw Hainfroy quite regard Garman as a third brother, but I am sure they would like a binding family link to him. Such as," she finished triumphantly, "marriage to his first cousins."

The earl hunched a shoulder. "Think you could bring that off, do you?" he asked skeptically. "I think you overreach yourself. Especially as you say he is not under your sway."

"He isn't," she swiftly concurred. "But he can recognize when his wife speaks plain sense, I hope."

"Humph!" Lord Twyford took another swig of wine. "You've some opinions of our own at any rate. What my grandson will make of them is another matter."

"And you would not object to the match?" Lenora prodded.

"I?" He shrugged. "I am indifferent. Jehanne would have plenty to say about it though." His eyes gleamed.

"She is still a handsome woman," Lenora said thoughtfully. "And could very likely marry again."

"Cleaning house, are you?" He sat up in his seat. "If you were to take your seat as mistress here," he said slyly, "you would not want the place filled to the rafters with inherited womenfolk."

Lenora regarded him sternly. "Stop plotting, my lord. I am merely trying to avert them being flung out on the street."

"Pah!" he said with a quick gesture of his hands. "That does not concern me. Securing the future of my estate—that is what consumes me! This land has been in our family for generations. It deserves its rightful master."

Lenora remained silent. From what she had seen, Twyford Castle was a monstrously large and ramshackle concern of faded grandeur. The estate was likely neglected and in poor repair, badly in need of investment of both time and money. Garman had no affection for the place, quite the opposite. His intent was to buy Matchings Halt, a comfortable and pretty estate which could be run on a much smaller and tighter scale with less money, servants, and overall effort.

She glanced at the earl who was sat rigid with affront that his grandson had no interest in taking up the helm. Lenora sighed. It was difficult not to pity the old man, despite everything. "You look tired, my lord."

"Nonsense!" he snapped, though the lines about his mouth looked very marked, as though he was in some considerable pain.

"Can I call for an attendant, my lord? Or some medicine?"

"Don't fuss now, I can't abide it!" he rapped out sharply. "You will undo my good opinion of you entirely if you start with that now."

Lenora rolled her eyes. There was clearly nothing to be done with the man. Perhaps it was an Orde trait.

"You will tell me now about my grandson's reputation," he said so casually that she realized it was important to him. "You mentioned it earlier, and I admit to some curiosity."

"Garman's reputation?" repeated Lenora in some alarm. She hesitated.

"Now, none of that!" he admonished, holding up a crooked finger. "I want the unvarnished, plain truth!"

"Do you mean his reputation at court? Or his reputation in the tournaments?" she stalled.

He gave her a sharp glance. "Everything, and no holding back, mind!" He leaned back in his chair, clearly trying to find a way to get comfortable.

"Well then, he is considered to be entirely ruthless, arrogant, cold, brash, and heartless," she admitted on an outward breath. "A merciless opponent in the field and a brutal fighter. He is a man that gives no quarter and cares not for the good opinion of others."

Lord Twyford pursed his lips. "So," he said after a moment's pause, "it is as I have heard reported. There is precious little of the weak Sutton blood flowing through his veins." He sounded inordinately pleased by this.

"I spoke of his reputation, not his character," Lenora said with more force than she'd intended. "Of course, he has some good traits that he keeps from prying eyes." At the older man's unconvinced expression, she added, "There is a side to him that he reveals only to his intimates, who have his confidence."

"Oh, that." The old man shrugged. "So long as he keeps that to its proper place. You will not expose him, I imagine."

Lenora blinked. She wasn't sure they were at all on the same page. Toward the end of the meal, the earl slumped down in his seat as though all energy was expended, and his speech slurred. Lenora gestured for one of the attendants she saw lurking beyond the candlelight to come forward, but when they tried to help the earl out of his seat, he grew quite heated and angry.

"Damn it, I won't be dragged from my own hall in front of my guest!" he spat angrily. "I shall remain here until she takes her leave of me."

"Indeed, I will need to set off very shortly if I am to keep the wool drawn over my husband's eyes," she said quickly and earned a gleam of amusement from his.

"He will beat you soundly before ere long, I daresay," he gloated. "For all you are a cozening piece." He rapped his hand against the tabletop and held his hand out palm up. For a moment she was not sure what he wanted but laid her own hand upon it and felt her fingers gripped with surprising strength. "Tell me quick," he panted. "The boy. You'll bring him up to scratch? He'll be the Earl of Twyford after me and I've had precious little handling of him." His mouth twisted. "It won't be long now."

"He does not require that I should handle him," she answered. "For he's already his own man. And a fine one at that."

His fingers tightened even further, and Lenora bit back a wince. "I've a black heart, my dear," he said in a low voice. "Make no mistake. I enjoyed all my mistakes heartily, save one." He shot her a look. "You understand?"

"You mean…" She hesitated. "Garman?"

He grimaced. "Should have had him here." He winced. "Should never have renounced my Merek! Rulf was nothing to him, nothing at all!" Pain racked him a moment, and Lenora would have called for the servant if he had not leaned so far forward his nose almost touched hers. "Take this now," he said, drawing the large gold ring from his finger. "Take it!" he snapped when she made to protest. "It will be his in any case, soon enough." He pushed her fingers back to close around the heavy ring. "Tell him…" He hesitated. "Tell him his wicked old

435

grandfather died with only one regret in his black heart. Now," he said on a wheezing breath, "Oates will take you to the gallery and you will first look at the portraits and then return home."

She opened her mouth to say farewell, but he waved her irritably away, so she lowered him back into the seat and looked around for Oates, who proved to be the same old man who had shown her in. She straightened up and Oates plunged into the shadows so she was forced to hurry after his retreating footsteps. Shivering, Lenora climbed a winding stone staircase in his wake, until they came out on a draughty platform above the banqueting hall.

Oates held his flaming torch aloft, and Lenora saw he was gesturing for her to behold a large portrait of a flinty-faced man with familiar cold turquoise eyes and dark blond hair. He was not as strongly built as Garman in the shoulders and she could not imagine her husband wearing a jeweled chain about his, but in spite of that, the resemblance was a striking one. *This must be Garman's great-grandfather*, she thought. *The present earl's father*. She looked back at Oates, and he took this as a prompt to move to the next portrait.

The next was unmistakably the present holder of the title. The artist had captured the cold calculation in those eyes almost perfectly, the cruel twist of the lips. He wore his hair longer than his father had, and Lenora could only suppose his raiment to have been the height of fashion in his day. He was tall, but not so athletic as the first earl, for all he held both sword and shield. Lenora drew a shocked breath when she beheld the shield. For though the same colors as the black and white crest Garman displayed, the image was quite a different one. On this shield, the white field displayed a black heart shedding three drops of blood.

Lenora turned light-headed as she remembered those words outside Bonbartle cathedral long, long ago spoken by a man in multicolored rags. *Your true love shall be a mighty lord with the emblem of a bleeding heart.*

The device of the Earls of Twyford.

35

Lenora did not remember much of her journey home. Berta, picking up on her mood, was largely silent, though she reached across to pull Lenora's cloak and hood tighter about her when they threatened to fall open. Lenora's head reeled, though her heart beat steadily in her chest still. Almost as if it had known all along. All those years she had pored over heraldic devices for a bleeding heart, she thought. And the knight who should have borne it scorned it for another.

"You'll catch your death," Berta grumbled. "Then where will we be?"

Lenora only shivered and huddled closer to Berta, leaning her head on her shoulder. *And still, I ended up married to him all the same!*

"They say in the servants' quarters that the old earl is half-dead already," Berta commented. "And lives on thin air and malice alone."

"They probably speak true," Lenora muttered, her hand closing so tightly over the signet ring that it cut into her palm. "I think he must be dying."

"Powerful interested they was in you and Master Garman. What with you being the next Earl and Countess of Twyford, I mean."

"I expect they would be," Lenora commented. "I hope they are not expecting us to sweep in and mend all the leaking rooves and crumbling towers."

Berta snorted. "They're past praying for a good master, I daresay. This one had a vile, evil temper by all accounts. Cast out one son and made the other's life a living hell."

I should never have renounced my Merek! Rulf was nothing to him, nothing at all, Lenora recalled. "He owned quite freely that he was a wicked old man," she murmured.

"Did he now?" Berta sounded diverted by this. "Won't be recanting on his deathbed, then?"

"Highly unlikely, I'd say. His only regret…" She hesitated, remembering Berta's own family circumstances.

"Is what?"

"That his only grandson will not be reconciled to him."

Berta lapsed into silence beside her, and she found herself explaining about the two granddaughters Garman had vowed to throw out into the street and how Lenora had found herself thinking of the Hainfroys as prospective grooms for them. Berta snorted, but for once held back from any derogatory comments, and they completed the rest of the journey in relative silence. Lenora guessed it must be some time after ten o'clock as the cart took the corner for the farm.

"What's all this?" asked Berta in surprise, sitting up in the seat.

Lenora glanced up and noticed with dismay the inordinate number of lights blazing in the windows and some activity out the front of the building. "It's not a fire, is it?" she asked in some alarm. She craned forward. The figures of various people seemed to be milling about outside.

"No," Berta answered ruminatively, casting her a sidelong look. "Though I fancy it might have been discovered you're missing."

Lenora's heart sank. "Oh dear! Even so, that doesn't account for the sheer number of people about the place." Her eyes grew wider still. "But surely I know that carriage?"

She knew, too, that upright figure stood ramrod straight next to Grandfather Sutton in the doorway. It was Lady Dorothea Montmayne stood next to her cousin Kit. "It's my grandmother," she announced in stricken tones as someone else stepped out from behind her. "Oh, and my father too." They were being besieged with Montmaynes.

"That's not the worst of your problems," Berta said dourly.

"What do you mean?" It was hard to see how this could get any worse. Berta raised a hand to point at three figures stood by the stables. There stood her husband, arms folded and wearing a dire expression on his face. Alongside him lolled the Hainfroy brothers, looking frankly intrigued. What on earth were they all doing here?

"You're about to get that hiding," said Berta, "that you been asking for ever since you wed him."

"I most certainly am not!" Lenora retorted, though her heart did quail a bit at the prospect of explaining where she had been tonight. Oh bother! And it's not like she could face him with the insouciance she had been used to feel. Not now she knew for certain he was her true love.

The cart had not even come to a stop before he was reaching up to pluck her out of the seat and swing her roughly down.

"What kind of games have you been playing, Lenora?" he demanded angrily, retaining a firm grip on her upper arm as he marched her toward the house. Indeed, was fortunate he had, or she would surely have tripped and fell. "I gave no leave for you to leave the farm!"

"Why are you back so early?" she gasped in response. "I thought you were staying at the Grange for another week."

"I'm the one asking the questions here!" he bit out, swinging her around to face him. "Good gods, madam! Are you aware of the upset you've caused here?"

"Well, but I've only been gone four hours." She squirmed, feeling her face turn red. As soon as she said it, she realized she'd said the wrong thing. His eyes swept over her and she realized her cloak had swung back and revealed her finery.

Garman's nostrils flared and he grabbed both her upper arms in a bruising grip. For a minute she thought he'd shake her, but then his expression turned icily glacial. "Oh, only four hours?" he said in a voice of cutting coldness before thrusting her away from him so violently that she stumbled backward some steps. "Is that all? You didn't feel it necessary to inform any of my grandfather's household where you were going or when to expect your return?" His voice was rising again now, and Lenora cringed, glancing toward the crowd that was now watching avidly from the doorway.

"Husband," she appealed. "Will you not save your reproaches until we are alone? I am aware that I owe you some explanation, but as you can see—"

"I don't give a fuck who can see us, Lenora!" he roared. "I want to hear from your own lips where you've been! For I can scarce believe what my own grandfather has told me!"

She took a deep breath in and out again. "I had an invitation to dine at Twyford Castle," she answered clearly, and everyone turned suddenly very still.

"Is that so?" he asked with such silky smoothness that Lenora turned suddenly cold all over. "I could hardly credit it could be true."

441

She swallowed. "I made the acquaintance of Lady Magda Orde in the marketplace and she kindly—" She broke off as his face turned dark with anger and he turned on his heel and strode away. "Wait!" She made to run after him, but suddenly Grandfather Sutton stepped forward.

"Child, no," he said quietly but firmly. "Let him go."

Lenora turned toward him blindly. "But—"

"Let him go. Now, come inside and greet your relatives who have traveled some distance to see you."

Lenora's face crumpled. "But, Garman!" she sobbed, glancing in the direction of the stables where he was headed.

Gerard Sutton hurried to her side to prevent her from following on her husband's heels. "Hush now!" he said soothingly. "Leave him to calm down awhile," he urged, when to her utter embarrassment Lenora turned toward him and burst into tears.

36

Grandfather Sutton helped Lenora over the threshold as tears poured down her cheeks, and she clung to his arm for all the world as if she had broken a limb. She could see her own father and grandmother staring at her in astonishment. Now she came to think of it, she could not remember the last time she had cried in earnest. At court she had always been lauded for her perfect composure.

"Come this way to the parlor," she heard Gerard call over his shoulder. "Hawise, take these gentlefolks' cloaks and hoods."

"Lord Lenora," said her cousin Kit, looking discomforted. "Anyone would think he had taken a stick to you, the way you're carrying on!"

Lenora didn't pay him any heed but allowed the old man to lead her into the front parlor and fuss over her, sending for a hot spiced wine and some honey biscuits. She wiped at her eyes until she noticed through bleary eyes that her family were sat awkwardly around her.

"Hello, Father," she sniffed. "Grandmother."

"Here's a pretty mess, daughter," her father said, mopping his brow. "I can scarcely make head nor tail of what goes on here! Save that you are now serving your husband with the same flighty behavior you subjected us to!"

"I'm so sorry, my dear," Gerard tutted, settling her into a chair. "I'm afraid I was forced to admit to Garman your whereabouts and he took it most ill—"

"It's not your fault, Grandfather."

"A most well-proportioned room," Lady Dorothea interrupted loudly as she drew off her gloves. "And a most welcoming fire." She turned to Gerard. "I thank you for your hospitality, Master Sutton. Now perhaps, you might be so good as to explain exactly what my granddaughter has done to provoke her husband's wrath?"

Lenora opened her hand and stared down at the large gold signet ring resting on her palm. She heard a collective gasp as she lifted it with her other fingers and inspected the Orde family crest. "A heart weeping three drops of blood," she said aloud.

Her grandmother blinked. "You're not still harping on about that ridiculous premonition—" The words froze on her tongue. "What is that?" she asked sharply.

"It is the signet ring of the Earl of Twyford."

"Who pray is the Earl of Twyford?" asked her father, sounding bewildered. "And why do you have his ring?"

"The ring is for Garman. *He* will be the Earl of Twyford before much longer."

A heavy silence fell over the room.

"An earl you say?" her father asked faintly. "Orde is to be an earl?"

"Twyford?" echoed her grandmother. "Twyford…a northern title, of course, but still…"

"Countess of Twyford," murmured Sir Leofric Montmayne cautiously. "That has a goodly ring to it. Yes, decidedly a goodly ring."

"Allow me," said Kit, springing up from his seat and helping Ada and Hawise bear their trays of refreshments into the room.

"Thank you, kind sir." Hawise beamed at him as the mulled wine was poured.

"I'm Sir Garman's new squire," he told her confidingly. "It was my trunk taken above stairs."

"Fancy that now! You don't say!"

Lenora listened to them all exclaiming and carrying on in the background. She felt rather numb, and though she could feel the heat of the fire, she shivered remembering Garman's cold anger. She had known he would be displeased, she told herself. Yet, she had plunged ever onward, determined to learn the secrets he concealed. *By fair means or by foul*, she had warned him she meant to pursue her goal.

"…Lenora?"

She jumped. "Your pardon, Grandmother."

"Are you unwell still?"

"No, no. I am quite recovered." Suddenly, it occurred to Lenora that this was the first time Lady Dorothea had seen her since her illness. She gave her a level look. "Do I look unwell to you?"

Her grandmother pursed her thin lips. "You look unhappy, child."

"Oh, well. At this present moment in time, I am."

"I confess, your father's account of things had me anticipating far worse."

Sir Leofric broke off speaking to Gerard Sutton. "Well, I did not know at that time he was a prospective earl," he said plaintively. "No one informed me as such."

"That is not what I meant," Lady Dorothea barked. "Don't be a fool, Leofric!"

Lenora's father puffed out his cheeks and reached for a biscuit. "Well, I confess it all seems to have worked out quite providentially all things considered!"

"Let me see the ring." Lady Dorothea held out a thin hand, and Lenora passed it over to her.

She inspected it at leisure. "Of course, 'tis mere coincidence it fits in with your childhood fancies," she said uneasily as she handed it back.

"You know it is no such thing, Grandmother," Lenora admonished her.

Her grandmother shrugged. "If I had been told that the weeping heart was Sir Garman's device then I would have understood the significance of you running away with him at once! Though I still think it a rash step and most ill-considered of you."

Lenora held her tongue. After all, what was the point in explaining? She saw Gerard Sutton's confused look and sent him a quick reassuring smile.

The sound of horse hooves outside had Kit rushing to the window. "Oh, they've gone," he announced. "That's too bad, I wanted to have a word with Sir Garman about my training." He turned back to Lenora. "Will they return on the morrow?"

She gave him a rather strained smile. "He undertakes his friends the Hainfroys instruction at present and is concentrating his efforts on that."

"My grandson stays presently at Cofton Grange, an estate some few miles hence," Gerard cut in hastily. "Allow me to apologize that he does not tarry to welcome you."

Lenora's cheeks burned when she saw her grandmother's raised eyebrows, but her father seemed to swallow this snub without rancor.

"No doubt, he has much to occupy himself with his impending earldom," he said, nodding with satisfaction. "Is there an estate to accompany the title?"

37

The house had fallen quiet long before Lenora managed to get off to sleep that night. Bedrooms had been allotted to her family members and trunks carried up the stairs. She found herself craning for the noise of a footfall on the stair that she knew would not come. Staring up at the ceiling, she considered the ramifications of the day. Garman had no doubt gone storming off to the Grange, and she had no idea when he might return. Possibly his grandfather Sutton was in his bad books also.

She spent a night tossing and turning and woke heavy-eyed the next morning to be told she had a visitor awaiting her already in the back sitting room. "I didn't want to put her in the front parlor, milady," Ada told her anxiously. "On account of your kinfolks already in there."

"Who is it?" Lenora asked blearily as she flung back the blankets. For a moment, she had hoped it was her husband, but he would hardly await her downstairs.

"Didn't I say?" asked Ada, bustling from the room. "Why it's that Lady Magda Orde from the castle."

It was some half hour later that Lenora made her way to meet with Magda. She devoutly hoped the girl was not expecting good news about Garman suddenly overcoming his aversion to them all. However, when she caught sight of Magda, she looked just as harried as ever.

"I do apologize for that terrible supper last night," she said, rising from her chair as soon as Lenora entered the room. "Alas, I'm sure you thought us all exceeding strange. I can hardly bear to think what you must have made of the conversation at table."

She shuddered slightly. "I'm persuaded things must be very different at court."

"Different, yes," mused Lenora. "But I assure you there are many eccentric personalities to be found there that rival even your grandfather."

Magda relaxed a little. "You are kind," she said abruptly. "For some reason, I did not expect that from the reigning court beauty."

Lenora gave a startled laugh. "Oh, but I am far from reigning." She made a gesture to her face. "Those days are far behind me."

Magda flushed. "Your pardon, I did not mean to—" she began, but Lenora waved her apology aside.

"That was badly done of me," Lenora said. "I did not mean to make things awkward."

"I think," resumed Magda after a slight pause, "that even before—you must have been kind."

"Not especially," Lenora admitted, gesturing to her to be seated again. She took a chair opposite her. "I was mostly disinterested and aloof. I have only recently joined the human race. Since I lost my looks, I mean."

Magda looked at her curiously. "Really?"

"Oh yes. I did not trouble myself to have any interest in my fellow creatures before that. I was very self-absorbed."

Magda frowned. "I find that hard to imagine," she admitted. "You have such a lively interest now in your acquaintance. I think you must be too hard on yourself."

"No, it is quite true," Lenora insisted cheerfully. "But thank you for the compliment."

Magda looked confused for a moment, as if unaware she had paid her one. Then she seemed to give herself a little shake. "I must apologize also, for the manner in which we left your presence the other night also, after supper. You see, Mother was so very angry." She raised her eyes to meet Lenora's, and the expression there wavered a moment. When she spoke again, she sounded rather breathless. "Mother said she had a furious interview with Grandfather about it the next morning."

"Oh?"

"Yes, she was quite beside herself after it." Magda ran a fingertip over the grain of the wood on the table before her. "She—she said that Grandfather confided our cousin has a definite plan for my sister and me." She darted a look at Lenora and blushed again. Lenora's brain raced. *A definite plan?* "But perhaps she misunderstood about that?" Magda twisted her hands anxiously as Lenora wondered what on earth the old earl could have told their mother. "About," prompted Magda, lowering her voice, "the Hainfroy brothers, I mean." She bit her lip.

"Oh!" said Lenora slowly. "He told her that, did he?" But apparently the Earl of Twyford had pretended the scheme was Garman's and not Lenora's suggestion. She caught her breath. That wicked old man! Doubtless he had meant to torment the Lady Jehanne with it. Opening her mouth to reassure Magda on that score, she suddenly noticed the odd expression on the girl's face and closed it again.

"I don't suppose that my cousin had any idea of which brother to betroth me to?" Magda asked with a slight telling hitch in her voice.

Interesting, thought Lenora. If she wasn't mistaken, proud Magda was already invested in one of the rough and ready Hainfroys. She hesitated. Huw was the elder brother and perhaps Ivo's scar would make him more sympathetic to Agnes's plight.

"Huw?" Lenora suggested tentatively and saw the unmistakable flare of disappointment in Magda's eye. "Perhaps I have that wrong," she pondered aloud. "Would Ivo be more palatable to you?"

At that, Magda gave a little start and seemed to remember herself. "I assure you it would make little difference to me," she said woodenly, in what Lenora could plainly see was an outright lie. She was suddenly exceedingly curious to learn what past lay between Ivo and Magda.

"Actually, now I come to think of it," Lenora said thoughtfully. "I think I have it the wrong way around. I believe Garman said he meant Ivo for you." She cast a sharp look in Magda's direction and noticed the shallow breathing and the quiver of her hand as she raised it to her lips. *Aha!* She was not mistaken!

"R-really?" Magda breathed. "Ivo Hainfroy for me?" She swayed slightly in her chair.

Lenora hid her smile behind her handkerchief. The girl was clearly almost giddy at the prospect. Lenora was suddenly wild to know what lay behind her liking for Ivo, but knew Magda was far too reserved to ever tell her. "I wish you'd tell me your history with Ivo," she said on impulse and watched Magda succumb to a coughing fit.

"I—I dare assure you cousin, that—that naught lies between us—" the girl forced out as soon as she could draw air into her lungs.

Lenora made a hasty gesture of dismissal. "Your pardon," she said kindly. "I did not mean to pry. It was most wrong of me. You'd hardly think, would you, that my cousin upbraided me

451

mere months ago for not taking more of an interest in my fellow creatures! Now I am the most prying female alive!"

"No, no." Magda gulped. "I did not mean to imply—"

"Please don't trouble yourself," Lenora said easily with a smile. "I should not have asked."

"He kissed me once," Magda blurted. Then she turned quite puce.

"Ivo?" Lenora's eyes widened. For some reason she had pegged Huw as the one who would be popular with ladies, not Ivo.

"He was just a boy," Magda continued in hushed tones. "It was nothing to signify. He did not," she said sadly, "even know who I was. I daresay he would scarce remember it. But I—never forgot," she finished wistfully.

"It was your first kiss?" Lenora guessed.

Magda was silent a moment. "My only kiss," she said quietly.

"How was it that he did not know your identity?" Lenora puzzled.

"Oh dear," said Magda. "It's not the easiest tale to tell. You see, I should not have been there that day, but it was such a beautiful spring day. And my old nurse's daughter Joan used to play with me. She told me there was a fayre on the village green that day, with dancing. It was May day." She cast a look of appeal Lenora's way. "It was very wicked of me—"

"Nonsense!"

"You see, Joan gave me the loan of her headscarf and we went together. She told everyone I was her cousin who had come to stay from Leigh Green." Magda's eyes glazed over at the memory. "We walked arm in arm through all the crowds and drank apple wine."

"How old were you?" asked Lenora, trying to picture the scene in her mind's eye.

"But fifteen years."

Lenora pictured Magda at fifteen, a little softer, a little less brittle and haughty. And of course, if she was pretending to be a cousin to Joan, her shabby dress would not be such a source of shame to her. Magda probably felt free as a bird under the blue sky that day. Perhaps for the first time and only time in her life.

"Yes," said Lenora softly. "I can imagine."

"Joan had taught me all the dances, of course, when we played together. So, I—I joined the dances with her." Magda's voice faltered. "You are probably not familiar with country dances," she said apologetically. "But there's one where the menfolk join in and whisk you away to the edges and then all the maidens spin back into the center."

Lenora nodded encouragingly.

"Well." She lowered her voice. "Ivo Hainfroy caught *me* up, and after the third time, I did not spin away. We broke away from the dancing and walked around the fayre together, hand in hand." Her gaze skittered away from Lenora's. "I'm sure this all sounds exceedingly foolish to a sophisticated courtier such as yourself."

Lenora shook her head. "Did you tell him who you really were?"

"Of course not!" Magda sounded quite shocked. "I was Joan Inver's cousin from Leigh Green. He would not have cared in any case. I was just a village girl he kissed when he was seventeen." Her voice was practical and forced. "He will not even remember it."

"*You* remember it," Lenora pointed out.

"Of course I do," sighed Magda. "It was the most thrilling day of my life. But I'm sure for Ivo Hainfroy there were many sunny May days and many dances on village greens. I was just one of a long succession of willing girls to kiss." She looked back at Lenora. "I'm sure that story was extremely disappointing and not at all what you were expecting."

Lenora gazed steadily back at her. "I thought it was wonderful," she said staunchly. "And I am vastly grateful to you for telling it to me."

Magda broke out in a startled laugh. "I can quite see why you were so popular at court."

Lenora raised a hand to her pockmarked face and lightly traced the scarring at her jaw. "No, you can't, Magda," she said wryly. "But I thank you for the compliment."

38

Strangely enough, the interview with Magda Orde had the effect of stiffening Lenora's resolve.

She broke her fast with her father, who ate a goodly quantity of herrings and then hummed and hawed awhile before telling Lenora that she had made the best of a bad situation.

"Thank you," she said gravely. "I hope you will tell Mother that all is well with me."

"Your mother will agree with me, I am sure. She will be pleased you are to be a countess."

Privately, Lenora thought her mother would be most put out that her daughter had achieved one of her own ambitions, but she kept this to herself. "I saw Eden at Kellingford, did you know?"

"Kit told me, young scoundrel," her father said mildly. "Everything seems to be going well with that marriage at all events."

"They are a most devoted couple," Lenora agreed.

"Orde, um—he, er—" Her father frowned and stroked his whiskers. "He does not look to be the easiest man to live with."

Lenora lowered her spoon and regarded him thoughtfully. If Eden had seen Garman manhandling her the way he had the night before, she had no doubt her cousin would have had plenty to say. Her father, however, only wanted to skate over the subject. Garman's prospective title made any behavior acceptable it seemed. "In the main we get along much better than last night. He is somewhat displeased with me at present."

"Hmmm." Sir Leofric gave her a fleeting look from beneath his brows. "Well, you would marry him, daughter." He clicked his tongue. "You shall reap what you sow."

"Indeed."

He looked up sharply at that but checked himself before speaking. "I wanted you to marry Sir Lionel," he said fretfully. "Which you refused. Yet by all accounts, he is still devoted to you. At court, they speak most highly of his chivalric heart. The Queen herself has been most touched by his steadfast regard for you."

"Oh, do they? He is back at court, then? Enjoying the attendant fame." *So much for his penance*, thought Lenora cynically.

"Apparently he is having a new poem written to your lost beauty."

Lenora rolled her eyes. "If he is not careful, my husband will hear of his moping and carrying on."

"Do you suppose he will do his duty and attend court when he achieves his earldom?" said her father hopefully.

Lenora could only suppose he looked forward to introducing his son-in-law, the Earl of Twyford, to his acquaintances. "I doubt it somehow."

Her father sighed. "A great pity. Duty to one's sovereign is paramount."

"Garman is a northerner," Lenora pointed out. "His duty lay in serving the Blechmarsh army in the late war."

Her father looked startled, as if this thought had never occurred to him. "Karadok is now united, daughter," he said, rallying himself. "And all late rebels have long since surrendered."

456

"This is true, but you do not see all that many northern courtiers, you will admit."

"The Marquis of Martindale did spend a whole month at Caer-Lyoness last spring, you will remember?"

"To please his southern wife," Lenora agreed.

This her father grudgingly conceded. "Well, well," he said. "Mayhap you could accompany him to the winter palace in Aphrany for the royal tournament later this year?"

Considering the display they had subjected him to of their current marital discord, Lenora could only envy his optimism. "We shall see," she murmured in lieu of any other response.

Her grandmother, Lady Dorothea, ran her to ground later that morning as she sat with the household accounts Gerard had left her to study. They had not held Lenora's attention long, and she was soon pondering how to approach the issue of Garman's cousins. That seemed far pleasanter to dwell on than her own woes.

She had just decided to send for Berta when her grandmother swept in, wearing her cloak and outdoor shoes. "You will accompany me on a walk now, Lenora," she said grandly and, not waiting for an answer, promptly exited the room. Lenora, given little choice, went to fetch her ankle boots and followed her. It was a fine blue sky and she did not require a cloak, only wrapped a mantle about her shoulders.

She caught up with her outside, and they proceeded past the kitchen gardens and through the gate into the orchard. Lady Dorothea walked briskly, though a little stiffly, taking small neat steps, her back ramrod straight as ever. "A well-maintained place, this. Master Sutton seems a conscientious man."

"Oh, he is, very. He is teaching me household management."
Though, if she ever were to end up mistress of monstrous
Twyford Castle, she had no doubt its running would be quite
beyond her. She thought of its neglect and disrepair and almost
winced.

"And how do you enjoy that?" Lady Dorothea asked. "You
certainly showed precious little aptitude for lessons as a girl."

Lenora pulled a face. "I am trying to change, Grandmother. For
the better."

"Oh, I believe you. Indeed, I see some improvement already."

Lenora looked up, feeling her grandmother's eyes on her face.
She lifted her chin. "How do you find my face?" she asked and
heard her grandmother's swiftly indrawn breath. "I'm sure
Father prepared you for the change the pox wrought on me."

"Your father's a fool," her grandmother sniffed. "Prepared me
indeed! He and your mother talked a great deal of nonsense."
She lapsed into silence a moment before speaking again. "All
three of my sons were a sad disappointment to me, Lenora."
When Lenora looked up in surprise, she gave a quick gesture
with her hands.

"I can speak to you this way, now you are a grown woman, and
a child no longer. Leofric at least was not vicious as
Christopher and Godwin were. Unfortunately, his wife was ill
chosen." She pulled a face. "His father would give him his head
in the matter which was a mistake. He chose a pretty face over a
decent character. Your mother encouraged his worse traits until
they eclipsed all his good ones."

Lenora considered this in silence.

"It was the opposite way with your grandfather. I took care to
cultivate his better points, and he flourished under my

458

attentions. Sadly, I gave him too great a sway over our children. At the time, I thought it took a man to raise one. By the time I realized my error, it was too late." She sighed.

"Hey ho, 'tis done now. I was more fortunate by far in my grandchildren, and I took great care to exert as much of my will as possible in their molding." She gave Lenora a level look. "You were the one I worried about the most, as you resisted my efforts the most."

Lenora bowed her head.

"I feared you would go the way of your own mother."

"Perhaps I would have," Lenora admitted, "had I retained my beauty."

"No one retains their beauty, child," her grandmother corrected her sharply. "Your own mother grew sadly fat and her stupidity started to show in her expression." Lenora blinked. "Your father retains only the most spurious of crumbs of affection for her. Their marriage was a disaster." They carried on past the pear trees in silence.

"I had no idea you set so much store on one's chosen helpmate," Lenora admitted.

"Of course you hadn't. Your head was too full of rubbish about true love."

Lenora set her lips. "I should warn you, I still believe in true love, Grandmother," she said firmly.

"Oh, do you now? Why, then, I must ask, did you not marry that mooncalf Emworth? He has spoken many vastly pretty speeches about you."

"Vastly pretty and vastly empty speeches," Lenora corrected her. "Besides, he is not my true love."

459

"And that brute you married is?"

Lenora's steps halted. "Yes, he is rather a brute," she agreed evenly. "But he is also…" Her throat closed over words like *considerate*, *thoughtful*, and *compassionate*, though at times she thought he had demonstrated all three qualities. The memory of poor Beatrix Skenfrith's fate bothered her too much to utter them. She groped for words that were true. "To those he feels a sense of kinship or belonging toward, he demonstrates great care and loyalty," she said earnestly. "He is capable of kindness and decency and a whole host of other qualities. 'Tis only—" She broke off, frowning furiously.

"Yes?"

"His good opinion is rather hard to achieve," she admitted. "He has an outer shell which is hard to crack. But once you have, there is great sweetness to be found within."

Her grandmother gave a short laugh. "I doubt he would thank you for such a description."

"Likely he would not," Lenora admitted. "I would not even attempt to explain except to yourself or Eden."

"Hmm. Still, I do not think he will ever be known for a great philanthropist," Lady Dorothea said, screwing up her face.

Lenora laughed. "Assuredly not. I do not think he will ever care for more than a handful of people in his whole life."

"But you are one of them?"

Lenora paused. "I thought perhaps I was getting there," she said slowly. "Though I do not deny, I have set myself back a few paces on that path."

"How so?"

Lenora clasped her hands together. "My actions last night," she admitted. "He holds no love for his paternal relations and no doubt thinks my visit with them an act of disloyalty."

"That is unfortunate," her grandmother conceded. "Incidentally, why *did* you visit with them?"

"Curiosity," said Lenora simply and did not notice her grandmother's startled look. "And I am trying to solve a problem at present that is rather thorny." She did not really want to explain about Matchings Halt, so she cast a sidelong glance at her grandmother to see if she could get away with skipping over that part. "'Tis about our living arrangements and not worth discussing right now, but I am trying to find my way to a different outcome to that which he desires."

"Curiosity?" her grandmother echoed. "You? My most serene and empty-headed granddaughter?"

Lenora flushed. "I have been taking more of an interest in others of late. Some more so than others," she admitted. "Eden lectured me most roundly on the subject before my illness. While I recovered, I confess I did ponder her words and resolve to improve myself."

"I see, and this outcome that you wish to thwart your husband over," Dorothea began with interest, making Lenora flush guiltily. It seemed she had not gotten away with it after all. "It is a matter on which you feel you must intervene for his own good."

Lenora turned toward her with a gasp. "How did you—?"

Her grandmother smiled. "Did I not just explain that my own marriage was run on very similar lines?" Lenora stared at her grandmother a moment before they moved on. "I am pleased," Lady Dorothea said shortly. "Yes, very pleased on the whole.

461

For I always thought it would take something drastic to shock you out of your complacency. Though I confess, I did not imagine you would undergo quite so rigorous a trial by fire. You have been forged anew by it. I see a better and stronger Lenora before me."

She halted their progress abruptly. "We have come far enough. Come, let us return to the house. I shall speak to your father about returning to Hallam on the morrow. That should give you time enough to concentrate on repairing this tear in the fabric that occupies your mind at present." She gave a short laugh of amusement. "It greatly pleases me to think of you wrestling with thorny problems, child." She shook her head. "I foresee this will be the making of you."

"Thank you, Grandmother," Lenora responded, feeling oddly touched. She slipped her arm through Lady Dorothea's. "Perhaps I should tell you about my servant, Berta, and my husband's cousins on the walk back. For they, too, greatly occupy my mind at present." When Lady Dorothea looked intrigued, Lenora began to outline her half-formulated plans.

*

The rest of the day passed peaceably enough. Lenora's family announced they would be leaving on the morrow, except for Kit, who would remain in his current role. Lenora slipped down to the kitchens before supper for a word with Berta. She found her servant oddly quiet and thoughtful.

"Your father gave me a handsome tip," she admitted. "For 'chaperoning' you, he called it." She sniffed.

"He made no mention of it to me," Lenora said.

"Probably ashamed of his previous shabby treatment!" said Berta with malicious glee. "Mistress Berta, says he, I would be remiss if I wasn't to reward you for your care of my child."

"Have you had any more thoughts about the Grange?" Lenora asked casually. "Only I intend to ride out there tomorrow. After my relations have left. They leave late morning."

"On what pretext?" Berta asked, narrowing her gaze. "Delivering me up like a sacrificial lamb to them savage brothers?"

Lenora gave a short laugh. She could hardly imagine anyone less lamblike. "My excuse is that I am delivering my husband's squire, my cousin Kit."

"Best save me for your next visit's excuse, then," Berta said irritably. "For I still ain't made up my mind to it!"

"Very well, you shall have an extra few days to ponder," Lenora said magnanimously. "Do you have any questions about your proposed employment you would like me to put to them?"

Berta considered this a moment with a tip of her head. "Whether my bed be in the attic," she said at last. "For my old bones can't abide steep steps. And don't bother askin' after where that idle girl slept, for I've no doubt she warmed her masters' beds, and those days is long behind me!"

Lenora spluttered. "Berta!"

"Humph!" She stomped off and Lenora made her way to a farewell supper with her family.

The Montmayne family representatives left the next morning. Her father managed to convey by a few quiet words that he would ensure her dowry was delivered in the next month or so. Her grandmother touched a gloved hand to her cheek and nodded, and they were gone. She and Kit waved them off, and her cousin ran after their carriage to the bottom of the drive.

"Just making sure they had truly gone," he said cheerfully when he reappeared, rubbing his hands together. "We've seen the back of them till winter. Do we set off for the Grange now?" he asked eagerly. "If so, I'll saddle the horses."

"We'll have to take the cart," she pointed out. "If we're taking your trunk with us." Who even knew how long Garman intended to hole up at the Hainfroy place. "You may be there a while."

"The cart?" Kit sounded appalled. "I'll just stuff some things into a sack and sling it behind my saddle. Never fear!"

He was as good as his word and emerged some half hour later with a bag which he hefted toward the stables. Lenora went in to fetch her cloak and don a hood and some gloves for though the sun shone, it was cold when you strayed into the shadows.

They set off before noon and Lenora found she remembered the way pretty well. They had to ask directions only once from a passerby. She glanced at Kit as they approached the somewhat dilapidated outhouses. "The Grange is rather run-down I'm afraid," she said, though she did not know why she felt the need to make excuses.

Kit just nodded. "I daresay it's an aftereffect of the war," he said sagely.

Lenora was startled. "Pardon?"

"Well, when I was at Kellingford, Hadrian told me lots of the estates round these parts got neglected and left derelict while their owners were fighting in the wars. You remember Hadrian? Sir Roger's youngest son."

"Yes, I remember him," Lenora murmured, recalling Sir Roger's two illegitimate sons. She had not even considered the war being a factor. It had all seemed so far removed from a pampered southern courtier such as herself, and she had been little more than a child at the time. "The war has been over some six years or so now though," she added.

"Yes, but after losing, a good deal of northerners were stripped of money and land by the Crown," Kit pointed out. "Men were lost as well as revenue, workers, and masters both. Some estates never recovered their losses and were left to fall derelict. Hadrian said many mighty houses fell with the Blechmarsh cause."

Lenora bit her lip, looking sideways at Kit. "Yes, I suppose that must be true. Garman and both Huw and Ivo served along with Sir Bernhard Hainfroy as his squire."

"And they are now training in the joust?" Kit asked with interest. Lenora nodded. "Hopefully I can join their lessons with them," he said keenly, then caught sight of something. "Someone's coming out to meet us."

Lenora's head whipped around, but to her disappointment she saw at once it was not Garman. It looked to be Huw Hainfroy, she thought with a sinking heart, for she could see no distinctive scar on his cheek. Plastering a smile to her face, she sat up rather straighter in her saddle. "Hello there," she called. "I have brought my husband's squire to stay with him while he is under your roof. This is my cousin Kit Montmayne. Kit, this is Huw Hainfroy."

Huw, she thought, was looking at her rather askance. "You'd better come into the house," he said warily.

"Shall I stable the horses?" Kit asked as they dismounted.

"Aye." Huw pointed in the direction of the barn. "Yonder. There's empty stalls enough. You'll find my brother there," he called after Kit. He turned back to Lenora, she thought, with some reluctance. "Will you step into the kitchen?"

"Happily," Lenora said. "Will we find Purcel within?" she asked, referring to the eldest of Grizelda's kittens.

He grunted. "This time of day he's usually sunning himself at the window."

Such proved to be the case. Purcel regarded them drowsily through heavy-lidded eyes before making a soft chirruping noise of surprise and clambering down to wind his way around Lenora's ankles. "He's grown so big!" she exclaimed. "Look at his shoulders! He's three times as long as poor Fendrel!"

Huw gave a grudging laugh. "Aye, he's grown fat on the rats he catches. There's none left in the house now, so he's forced to roam into the barns for his sport."

"And Tybalt? Does he still haunt the stables?"

"Oh aye, you'll not find him far from the horses. He and this one have their own distinct territory marked out these days. If they find the other encroaching, they'll roll around in the dirt spitting and fighting each other."

"They fight?" Lenora exclaimed with dismay.

"It's often the way with brothers," he said dismissively and crossed the room to pull the door shut. Lenora watched him with interest.

"Garman's above stairs," he said shortly.

"At this hour?" She was frankly surprised.

"He got blind drunk last night, and we had to carry him to bed."

466

Lenora blinked a few times. "Oh. Is that—?"

"Not normal for him, no." Huw was setting down a jug of ale and two cups, so was clearly making the effort of hospitality. "Take a seat on the bench."

Lenora sat down and suffered Purcel reaching up to claw her skirts with enthusiasm. "You savage," she reproached him. "Does he no longer sit on laps as civilized cats do?"

Huw scratched the back of his neck. "Not usually no. Though he'll sit alongside you companionably enough."

Lenora patted the bench invitingly. "Come, Purcel." He cast her a contemptuous look and sprang up on the table. "Purcel!" He whisked his tail in her face and meowed. "Someone's getting rather above himself," she murmured, running a hand over his sleek fur.

"Did you tell Garman that Isabeau likely saw him as a third brother?" Huw asked suddenly.

Lenora looked up in surprise at the abrupt change of subject. "I believe I did say something of that sort. Why?"

"He said it last night," Huw admitted. "Along with a lot of other stuff."

Lenora hardly liked to ask what Garman might have spoken of when in his cups, so wisely said nothing. After a moment, Huw reached for the ale and poured them both a drop.

"Do you remember my servant, Berta?" Lenora asked brightly.

"Berta? Oh aye. She was the one jumped on Martha's back," he said with a grin. "And pulled half the hair out of her head."

"Yes, that is she. Well, I've asked her to consider coming to you here at the Grange for a time. To help you get things running smoothly."

Huw looked rather struck by this piece of news. "Good of you," he said. "We wouldn't refuse her help and that's a fact."

"She's still considering the offer, but I think she will take it. She has a place with me for life, if she ever desires to return, but I don't think Matchings Farm suits her. It's too…" Lenora groped for the right word. "Confining for one of Berta's temperament."

"What does that mean?"

"The order is too well established for her to throw her weight around," Lenora explained.

He grunted at this. "Well, she would have free rein here, though there's precious few people for her to boss here except for us and the cats." As if on cue, Purcel jumped down from the table and sauntered over to his favorite spot at the window where he commenced cleaning himself.

Lenora shot Huw a speculative look as she sipped her ale. "Have you and your brother never considered taking wives?" she asked boldly.

Huw almost spat out the mouthful of ale he'd taken. "Wives?" He coughed. "Nay."

"How old are you both? You must surely be of an age with Garman? Some twenty-seven years?"

"I'm twenty-nine," he corrected her. "Ivo is twenty-eight. Garman is the youngest of we three."

"Oh, well," she told him. "I'd say it was high time, wouldn't you? Especially if you now intend to be off competing on the tourney circuit. Who will keep the home fires burning while you are gone? Who will feed your poor cats?"

Huw wiped his sleeve across his top lip, removing the foam. "Eligible maidens are not exactly beating a path to our door," he said dryly.

"You know, your sister, Isabeau, was not the only means of joining your family with Garman's," she said confidingly.

"What's that?"

"Did you know that Garman has two first cousins of marriageable age?" Huw stared at her. "I should think your father would approve of having his last wish respected, wouldn't you?"

"Two cousins?"

"Magda and Agnes Orde," Lenora told him. "Have you never heard of them? They reside not far from here at Twyford Castle."

His eyes screwed up. "Oh aye," he snorted. "I've heard of them. A pair of ill-tempered, haughty bitches. Is not one of them a cripple?"

Lenora remembered the crutch resting on Agnes's chair and then how she had hobbled out in Lady Jehanne's wake. "Agnes walks with a limp, it's true, but it does not stop her getting around. Speak now if that is an issue, for she would be the one for you."

He flushed at that. "And why is that?"

"Ivo has already made a conquest of Magda."

His eyes practically bulged out of his head. "Ivo?" he said with a short laugh. "Nay, I'll not believe it."

469

"Oh yes. He seduced her many moons ago on the village green."

Huw stared at her. "That does not sound like my brother," he said, shaking his head.

Lenora shrugged. "It was before the war," she said, and from the hard look he gave her and the way his gaze fell away she knew she had spoken shrewdly.

"I see," he murmured.

"Think it over," she recommended and was just lifting her cup to her mouth when the door burst open and Garman stood glowering on the threshold.

"Good morning, husband," Lenora greeted him, only the slightest tremor in her voice, try as she might to repress it. He wore no tunic and was bare to the waist.

Huw wheeled about in alarm. "We were just talking," he said, hastily jumping up from his seat.

Garman came into the room, his eyes never leaving Lenora's face. "What the hells are you doing here, Lenora?" he snarled.

"I'll leave you to it," Huw murmured, making hastily for the door. He paused before opening it, looking back uncertainly at Lenora.

"Good day, Huw," she told him reassuringly. "We will speak further on the matter. Mayhap tomorrow or the day after."

He nodded and let himself out of the kitchen.

"What the fuck do you need to speak to Huw about?" Garman demanded, lifting a pitcher of water and drinking it straight from the jug. Once he had swallowed his mouthful, he lifted it higher and sloshed some over the top of his head before setting it crashing down, and then shaking himself like a dog.

"A heavy night?" Lenora asked sympathetically.

He glowered at her. "You didn't answer my question."

"Oh, I was just telling him about Berta," she replied with a half-truth.

"She's come?" He looked around quickly.

"No, not yet, but I believe the idea grows more palatable to her by the day."

He gave a short, abrasive laugh. "You came all this way to tell him that?" He shot her a scornful look. "A wasted journey. You were so desperate, then, to flee your father's company."

Lenora could not quite conceal the fact she flinched at his harsh words, though she tried. "They have gone back already this morning," she said quietly.

He accepted this without comment, taking another long drink of water. "What are you doing here?" he asked abruptly as he lowered the jug. "I did not send for you, and I will not. You are mistaken if you imagine I want you here."

Lenora took a deep breath. "I have brought my cousin Kit, who you agreed to take on as your squire. I trust your displeasure with me will not mean you going back on your word."

He slammed the pitcher down so hard she jumped. "I'm not a man who goes back on his word," he said softly. "As you will find out to your detriment."

Lenora felt the color drain out of her face. "Did you swear, then, to exact revenge on your father's family?" she asked quietly.

"I did," he answered without even a pause.

It stands to reason, she thought even as her blood ran cold. She imagined him as a thirteen-year-old, standing before the gates of Twyford Castle, hate in his heart. Perhaps that was why he did not want children, she thought suddenly. *So, the line would end with him?*

"I have thought of a more poetic revenge for you," she said desperately. "One that kills two birds with one stone."

He said nothing, merely narrowed his eyes at her.

She licked her lips. "You told me once that Sir Bernhard wished to join your family and his, in wedded bonds. You have observed yourself that your sworn brothers the Hainfroys are badly in need of helpmeets."

"I remember saying no such thing."

"Think of Lord Twyford's horror if you were to barter a match between your Orde cousins and the Hainfroy brothers," she said, leaning forward. "Your aunt Jehanne would be frankly appalled at such a notion. She's a proud and haughty woman—"

"And what of a dowry?" Garman snapped. "Do you really think a sensible man would take a woman without one?"

Lenora's chin came up. "My father has promised to send mine within a month. I can pay their dowry out of my own."

"Yet another matter!" He slammed his palm down on the table. "In which you defy me. I told you I would not have you begging."

Lenora felt the last of her color leech away. "And I told *you* that I would do no such thing," she replied with quiet dignity, rising to her feet. "Tell me now if I need take Kit back with me."

472

"You need not," he ground out.

She nodded to him and hurried toward the kitchen door, her vision suddenly blurry with tears she would never allow to fall while there was still breath in her body. She was halfway down the path toward the stables when she thought she heard something overturn and smash in the house behind her.

Quickening her step, she hurried to the stables and found Kit there sat on an upturned bucket deep in conversation with both Hainfroy brothers. They broke off abruptly when she appeared. "I must leave you now, Kit," she said, making for her horse. "Garman knows you have arrived, but you must tread carefully around him today, for he has a sore head."

"Is that what you did?" asked Ivo sarcastically. "Trod carefully?"

Lenora led her horse out. "I'm afraid not," she admitted. "And now I very much fear he has overturned your kitchen table." She grimaced as both brothers stared at her open-mouthed. "I will see you either tomorrow or the next day," she said. "As soon as Berta has made her decision." Swinging up onto her saddle, she set off on her return journey to Matchings Farm.

She was about halfway home when she had the sensation of eyes on her. Looking back over her shoulder she spotted a figure in the distance that it seemed to her was none other than Garman himself sat astride his horse, Bria'ag. She slowed down to give him the chance of catching up with her, but apparently, he did not want this, for he also slowed down, maintaining the distance between them.

Frowning, Lenora continued on her way and found that though he kept her in his sights, he made no effort to gain on her. As she turned up the driveway for Matchings Farm, he turned abruptly away and rode off. The only conclusion she could draw was that he wanted to see she reached home safely. For some reason, this warmed her heart, and by the time she walked into the farm, a small smile played about her lips, in spite of all her worries.

39

It was late afternoon that Garman strode down the hallway at the farm after ascertaining from a servant that Lenora was sat in the front parlor. He had heard nothing from her since her visit to the Grange some two days earlier. It seemed longer to him than that, for she haunted his thoughts by both day and night. Flinging open the door, he discovered her curled up in the window seat with her white cat, holding a list at arm's length which she seemed to be regarding with frowning absorption.

She lowered the page and sat up as he shut the door behind him. "Garman—?"

"Well?" he said rudely, crossing his arms. His face assumed a look of chilly indifference.

Lenora gazed back at him. "Good morning?" she hazarded.

"Is it?"

She glanced toward the window. "The weather continues fine and bodes well for a good harvest."

He said nothing to this, just gazed at her stonily. How dare she be lolling on cushions while he felt churned up like this? He uncrossed his arms and paced across to the other side of the room, then turned on his heel and stalked back again. "You have news of Berta?" he bit out.

"Oh yes," she said. "She came to me last night and agreed to the move. I feel sadly conflicted about it, but I quite realize it is for the good of all involved. I shall miss her, of course."

She made no mention of missing him, he noticed savagely and glared at her. "Yet you sent no word of this news to the Grange, despite your promise."

"Well, I was going to ride over this afternoon and deliver Berta with her belongings," she explained calmly.

Which reminded him of something else. "There will be no more of this riding around the countryside unaccompanied," he said coldly.

She stole a look at him through her eyelashes. "I was not unaccompanied though," she pointed out. He checked at that and cleared his throat. Lenora lifted the white cat off her lap and placed her carefully on a cushion. "Does she look fatter to you?" she asked with a trace of anxiety. "I'm hoping it is only too many tidbits and not another litter of kittens on the way."

He eyed the cat distractedly. Was she fatter? He had no clue. He angled his head to read the discarded list she had been studying with such care. It looked to be a list of jellies and conserves.

Noticing the direction of his gaze, Lenora sighed. "Your grandfather asked me to study the plans for the autumn fruit crop and give the kitchen any suggestions I might have. The trouble is, I have no ideas on the subject, for I am sadly ignorant."

Garman gave himself a mental shake. He was getting distracted. "I didn't come to talk to you about candied fruits," he said contemptuously. She bit her lip, and he struggled a moment with conflicted feelings himself.

"What did you come for then?" she asked quietly.

"You suggested something the other day," he said with soft menace. "An alternate means of revenge on…my Twyford relations."

"Yes? You have discussed it with the Hainfroys?" she asked, holding her breath.

"I have." He paused. "They're agreeable, strangely enough."
She looked hugely relieved at this piece of news. He steeled
himself. "But if you think this lets you off the hook, wife, you
are sadly mistaken."

She swallowed. "I'm listening."

"I find I cannot forgive you for going behind my back. A wife's
loyalty should be to her husband."

"My loyalty *is* to you," she insisted. At his disgusted gesture
she leaned forward. "Garman, it is, I swear it."

"Your empty words mean nothing to me, Lenora, for I judge
women as I do men, by their actions," he said harshly. "And it's
too late to try and get around me now, for I've seen what lies
beneath your pretty ways and deceitful tongue!"

She winced at his words but, if anything, sat up a little
straighter. "I am sorry you feel that way," she said quietly. "But
I must act as my conscience prompts me."

"Well, you can act as you like in future, for I've had a bellyful
of you. As much of you as I can stand."

He heard her indrawn breath but paid it no heed. His words
were hard and measured and gave no quarter. "If you feel so
much concern for my cousins' fate, then you will not object to
taking their place in the grand scheme of things, will you?" You
could have heard a pin drop at his words.

Her head snapped up at this. "What do you mean?"

"You can take their place," he repeated coldly. "In my grand
revenge."

"I don't understand you."

"Your lack of understanding is not my concern," he said grimly. "Pack your things. I want you out of here within the hour."

"Out?" She stared at him. "Husband—?"

"Out. Pack your things up. Now!" His words were angry and loud. He practically shouted them at her.

Lenora sat perfectly still for a moment, then she rose composedly to her feet. "Very well," she said bracingly. "May I ask where I am to go?" she asked conversationally. "Or is that none of your concern either?" She made her way toward the door, looking back over her shoulder. "I suppose I could return to my father's house..." she mused, reaching for the door latch.

"You will do no such thing," he gritted out. "I told you, you will be taking my cousins' place."

She turned to look at him over her shoulder. "At Twyford Castle?" She looked stunned. "Well, I suppose there is a certain poetic justice to that." She pulled a face. "So, *I* am to be left there now, in a moldering ruin for the rest of my days?" she asked.

He did not answer for a moment. Could not. He imagined her blond head with the ruins falling down around it, and it crossed his mind for the veriest instant that he was cutting off his own nose to spite his face. Angrily, he dismissed the notion. "Aye, that's it," he said curtly. "You're so curious about Twyford Castle, you can become intimately acquainted with it."

"Yes, I see. Quite neat," she murmured, and something else he did not catch for it was under her breath. Almost he asked her to repeat it, but stopped himself. After all, what did it matter? Soon he would be rid of her cursed opinions and irritating words altogether. For some reason, that thought caused him to feel something so akin to pain that it quite took his breath away.

478

"Will you arrange for Berta to be delivered to the Grange as I won't be here to sort that out now?" she asked with such distant politeness that he could not speak. "I would like to keep my word in that respect."

He shrugged. "I will see to that matter. It is no longer your concern," he heard himself respond.

She had her hand on the door now. Why did he feel like this? So empty, with the bitterest taste in his mouth? His throat and chest still burned with anger, but something held him back from unleashing the scalding tirade upon her that would give it relief. Without looking back, she left the room, and he stared at the spot she'd vacated. He realized there could be only one explanation for not bawling and yelling at her as he longed to. He did not want to burn his bridges with her. Which was fucking ridiculous as he was effectively exiling her now. He was walling her up alive in the tomb that was Twyford Castle, the place he hated most in all the world. Why then, was he still holding back his wrath? It made no sense. He was done with her, he swore. Finished.

She had gone against him and now she would have to pay the price. He would have to harden his heart against her, he thought grimly. He was halfway across the room at this point, and almost tripped over his own feet. His heart? Where had that come from? He had no heart. Everyone knew that. Even Lenora. What was it she had said to him on that first night? *I have no doubt you would lead whatever woman you married a dog's life.*

She had gone into this with her eyes open, for all she had looked so still and stricken when he had ordered her out of his life. The memory of her expression caused a pang. Almost he'd regretted his words the moment they had left his mouth. Indeed, when she had started up from her seat, he'd been half inclined to push her back down in it and tell her she was going nowhere. He shook his head. When had he ever been anything other than resolute? Their marriage had been a mistake. An act of impulse which he would come to regret. He did already regret, damn it. And he was putting an end to this debacle now.

He would deliver her to Twyford Castle himself. Cast her down at its gate and issue his instructions for his cousins to be delivered up for the parson's noose within the week. He set his features as he wrenched the door open. There was no going back now.

*

It was dark by the time they reached the castle. Neither he nor Lenora had uttered a word the entire journey. Both were on horseback. She had packed no more than one bag of belongings, for he would not wait and had vowed he would send the rest of her things, including the cats, on after her. She held her head as high as a queen, her profile cold and proud. Why he could not stop his willful gaze from seeking her out was beyond him. He was weak where she was concerned, and it was as well he tore her from his flesh now before she became even more embedded. As it was, he suspected the wound would fester for years. Probably his whole damned life.

To his surprise, the approach to the courtyard was lit with torches and several white faces bobbed before them in the dark.

"Milady!" cried one old man, running forward. "Gods be praised, you done it! You brought the master in time!"

"Oates, what is it?" Lenora asked, reaching down and clasping the old dotard's hand.

Tears streamed down his wobbly jowls. "He's fading fast now, milady, and won't last the night." He sent a fearful look in

Garman's direction. "The physician says he's in a delirium, but every now and then it clears, fit to break your heart."

"Take us to him," Lenora ordered.

Garman's head jerked up, but she was already dismounting. He hesitated a moment, unsure whether to spur Bria'ag on now and leave. What decided him was the fact Lenora did not even look at him. She adjusted her hood, smoothed her cloak, and strode after the scurrying servant up the stone steps.

With a heavy frown, he swung down from his saddle and passed his reins to a waiting attendant.

"My lord," the servant mumbled and turned away before he could correct him.

Taking the steps two at a time, he caught up with them as they ducked into a dimly lit passage. The place was a rabbit warren and appeared almost subterranean in its darkness. There were two more flights of steps before they reached a large bedchamber hung about with faded tapestries and dominated by a large carved wooden bed overhung by a large red canopy. In the midst of it lay a wreck of a man he dimly remembered as Earl Twyford, though the waxen, hollowed-out face was barely recognizable to him.

"The Lady Jehanne does not sit with him?" Lenora asked, approaching the bed.

"Not she," Oates said bitterly.

Garman's expression grew yet more guarded as Lenora sat down on some wooden steps attached to the high platform of the bed. He heard her murmur something, but she kept her voice low and sweet so he could not catch it. Earl Twyford's eyelids fluttered and his eyes fixed on Lenora's face. He did not speak, though at her prompting, his gaze swept over her shoulder to lie with an arrested expression on Garman. On seeing him, the old man seemed to grow increasingly agitated, and Lenora jumped up and hurried over to him.

"Speech is beyond him now," she said urgently. "Come and take his hand." Garman stiffened. "You need say no words." Her hand made a grab for his, and he almost jumped out of his skin, realizing she had not voluntarily touched him in days. It must be that which prompted him to let himself be led meek as a lamb to the bedside. Lenora placed her hands on his shoulders, pushing him down until he sat on the steps, the spot she had just vacated.

Then she lowered her hood and reached for something around her neck. "Put this on," she whispered. "Just while you hold his hand. You can take it off again directly afterward." He frowned as she slipped something onto the little finger of his left hand, which felt like a heavily encrusted ring. Then she took his hand and placed it on the blanket next to the Earl of Twyford's.

"There," she said, and Garman felt the cold and waxy hand twitch and clutch at his. The earl's mouth worked but he uttered no sound. He felt the old man groping around his fingers until he found the ring, and then he gave a sigh that rattled horribly. Garman watched as the sunken chest rose and fell in painfully shallow breaths, thrice more and then halted forever.

Oates gave a sob and grabbed at one of the curtains. Lenora bowed her head. The Earl of Twyford was dead.

40

Lenora found Magda and Agnes huddled around a small fire in the solar. Both looked white-faced and were showing signs of considerable strain. Magda rose to greet her and drew her close to the fire to sit with them.

"It's over," Lenora said in quiet tones as she sank onto the cushioned bench between them. "Your grandfather is dead."

"You were there at the end?" Magda asked. "I'm glad. He would not let me sit with him, not after this morning."

"So, your husband is earl now," said Agnes blankly.

"I suppose so."

"Where is our cousin?" Magda frowned. "We were told you both arrived at the eleventh hour."

"He is gone back," Lenora said flatly.

Magda looked at her. "He surely has many business matters to wind up," she said, clearing her throat.

"Doubtless," Lenora agreed listlessly. "I am to remain here." Not for the world could she elaborate on her meaning, but she saw the sisters exchange startled looks.

"Mother is gone," said Agnes, making her sister exclaim.

"What do you mean?"

"I walked in on her packing her trunk. She *said* she had a widowed cousin she would go to in Ankadine."

Lenora felt a flicker of interest in the way Agnes had stressed her words. "You do not think she has gone to a cousin?" she asked.

Agnes pulled a face. "Not unless the widowed cousin has a bushy black beard and answers to the name Sir Walter Dalton."

"Agnes!" Magda exclaimed, sounding shocked. "I'm sure Mother would never—"

"Oh, what is the point in being so mealy-mouthed about it, sister?" Agnes said crossly, reaching for her crutch. She swung herself up and looked down at them both. "Mother has fled into the night and we are now all left alone to fend for ourselves. The roof leaks, the chimneys smoke, and we have absolutely no means of supporting ourselves—" She broke off with a sob.

"Agnes—" Magda started.

"No, don't!" She flung up her free hand to shield her face. "I'm off to bed. If you leave me for ten minutes, I shall contrive to be asleep by the time you join me." They watched Agnes hobble from the room with great determination, despite her uneven gait.

"You share a room?" Lenora asked.

"Oh yes. So few of them are habitable. Shall I show you to Mother's bedchamber?" Magda asked. "It's actually one of the few decent ones." Lenora could well believe Lady Jehanne had bagged herself one of the better rooms. She followed Magda across the passageway.

"It is this one, cousin," Magda said, opening the door. "I assure you it looks a good deal more cheerful by day." She crossed the room to set a candle on a large studded trunk. "I shall go down and request a fire to be laid, clean bedding, and water for you to wash."

"Thank you, Magda."

Magda hesitated by the door. "Is all quite lost?" she asked softly, leaning against the door. "If so, I'm sure none of us could blame you—"

"Certainly not," Lenora replied with a confidence she did not feel. She sent Magda a brave smile. "In seven days' time. You shall see."

Magda looked uncertain, but gave an answering smile before departing.

The next few days were not pleasantly employed as Lenora felt herself beholden to take her part in the vigil held over the old earl as he was laid out. These proceedings were not hurried as though the servants of the Twyford estate were not large in number, they all wanted their turn to pay their respects.

Two older women washed the body and wrapped it in a winding sheet as Magda, Agnes, and Lenora took turns to sit in attendance as various visitors trooped in and out. Magda told Lenora that the memorial brass had already been engraved for the chapel some months ago at great expense. "For he would have the family crest enameled with black and red," she whispered in some disapproval.

Tenants on the estate were not permitted to sit with the corpse, Magda explained evasively.

"Not that they'd want to," Agnes chimed in darkly, and Lenora could only guess that the earl's tenants were not fond of him.

He was interred on the third day, and their procession to the family chapel was a gloomy one. Lenora and Magda carried funeral wreaths of rosemary for Agnes could not manage a wreath as well as her crutch. If Lenora felt somewhat out of place for having met Lord Twyford only twice before his death,

485

the sisters clearly did not question her right. Both freely addressed her as cousin and seemed to accept her presence as a matter of course.

Oates led the procession, freely weeping as he rang his bell. Monks from the nearby monastery followed with their mumbled prayers, then a gaggle of the strongest servants carrying the shrouded and wrapped body. Magda, Agnes, and Lenora followed the body as expected of womenfolk. Magda's hand slipped into hers as they stood with bowed heads listening to the abbot speak a simple sermon.

"Grandfather told him 'make it brief, man,'" Agnes whispered. "He could not abide being dictated to even in death."

The earl was placed with ceremony into his casket and the monks sang their dirge. Lenora found herself looking over her shoulder more than once in the forlorn hope that Garman might make an appearance though she knew the odds were slim. She told herself he had been there when it counted and had eased the old man's passing.

Lenora's eyes fixed on the memorial brass during the sermon. She found it to be beautiful and privately thought the earl had been right to insist on the enameling. He was depicted in full armor, laid out with his shield over his breast and every detail of the Twyford crest was striking in its coloring from the black heart to the three drops of scarlet blood it shed. Her mind wandered back to that fateful day in Bonbartle, and her throat ached as she remembered the fortune-teller's words.

The heavy mood that had descended on them did not lift for the rest of that day, or the next, for it rained on and off the whole time. After supper, she found Oates hovering at her elbow.

"Yes, Oates," she asked, turning to him.

"Your pardon, milady, but a few of us was wondering if you might bring Master Sutton back to the fold as it were. Now that his lordship…" He cleared his throat. "Now that there is no quarrel to prevent it."

"You knew Master Sutton?"

He looked shocked. "Oh yes, milady. We were boys together here."

Lenora nodded. "I remember he told me he was raised here."

"Most of the servants here have been here for generations," said Oates, his chest puffing out. "'Tis a wicked shame the Suttons were driven out of Twyford. There's been Oateses and Suttons here since dawn o' time."

"In that case, you must have known Anne Sutton, Garman's mother."

"Knowed her well," Oates said promptly. "A more pleasant-spoken girl I never knew. And if some was shocked when her forgot her station, we knew the fault didn't lie at her door, nor her father's. Master Merek were a force o' nature, he were. Few could stand against him when he wanted something and that's a fact. Even the old master could not sway him from a course he'd determined on."

Lenora nodded thoughtfully. "I see."

Oates hesitated. "If anyone can get this place running on an even keel, it's Gerard Sutton. A wonder with the account books and such, he is."

Privately, Lenora thought it would take more than Garman's grandfather to get the place set to rights. It would take a miracle. By her own reckoning of the last three days, only a quarter of the castle was even habitable. She dreaded to think what state its grounds were in.

"I have not yet received word of my husband's plans," Lenora said cautiously.

Oates looked disappointed. "Even if his lordship don't never set foot in here again, he could send Master Sutton in his stead, could he not?"

Lenora's face fell. *Never set foot here again?* Was it so obvious to all that Garman loathed and despised the place?

"Oates," Magda called, "come away now and leave Lady Twyford to digest her meal. I have need of your help."

Lady Twyford. She had still not adjusted to that either, she thought as she sent Magda a grateful look. She would sit with a book for as long as she could stand and only then retire to bed. If not, she knew she would lie awake until the small hours tossing and turning, unable to sleep.

Agnes joined her in the great chamber, and they sat in companionable silence before the fire. Lenora had a book she had found with many illustrations of plants alongside cramped handwriting describing their properties. Agnes was sat whispering to a tiny wire-haired dog which her grandfather had forbidden her from keeping indoors due to his incessant yapping.

For three years, poor Agnes had been forced to keep Gorvenal in the stables, but the last few days had seen him swap this life for one of beds and cushions and his mistress's lap. He cocked a defiant eye at Lenora now, as if daring her to question his place. A bark trembled excitedly on his lips, but his mistress shushed him, so he contented himself with a whine and a darkling look.

Lenora thought of Grizelda and Fendrel and hoped her cats were well at Matchings Farm. She was not overly worried for she knew they were quite spoiled there, but she missed them all the same, and all of a sudden, a great wave of loneliness threatened to overwhelm her. In vain, she told herself this was not to be wondered at. In the last six months her circumstances had changed so often it was a wonder her head did not spin!

Perhaps, a voice whispered in her ear, she had been a fool when her life had been spared those few months ago. Carving out her own future had not gone so well. Maybe after all, she should have been content with something less ambitious, such as becoming Eden's charity cause. She knew full well her cousin would not have grudged her a place under her roof.

The thought was an oddly depressing one. Then her eye fell on the Twyford coat of arms above the fireplace. But…if she had *not* eloped with Sir Garman, then she would not have fulfilled her destiny. Her heart swelled and she was comforted. Her coming here was fated. She had *not* taken a misstep. And if she had not come to supper at the castle when invited, then she would never have known about the bleeding heart. Perhaps more importantly, the old earl's death would have been all the more bitter for the absence of his heir.

A log dropped in the fireplace with a shower of sparks, and Gorvenal leaped up barking in his mistress's arms. Lenora started violently from her thoughts.

"Hush now, Gor!" Agnes scolded, kissing his scruffy face. "I'm sorry, cousin, he is not yet used to life indoors."

"That's quite understandable," Lenora assured her.

"I shall bathe him tonight," Agnes continued, sniffing the curly gray hair. "For he has a certain odor lingering that is not entirely pleasant." She thrust his small, wriggling body in Lenora's direction. "Pray tell, what do you suppose it is?"

Lenora gave an obliging sniff and wrinkled her nose. "Yes... Perhaps he has rolled where foxes have been," she suggested delicately. Gorvenal gave a low, indignant growl.

"Gor!" his mistress implored, and he promptly licked Agnes's face by way of apology.

"I meant no offence," Lenora assured him, though in her opinion, Agnes would find cats much easier to keep. She yawned and, realizing her book was doing the trick, bade her cousin goodnight and rose to climb the stairs to bed.

Her feet felt heavy as she climbed the many stone steps. She felt weary, not so much in body as in heart. It was exhausting keeping up a façade when inside she felt quite desolate. Would Garman soften in his attitude toward her, she wondered, or was she just deluding herself? Sometimes in the middle of the night she feared that just because she could not imagine a future without him in it did not mean he felt the same about her.

Opening her door, she entered the dark bedroom where the glow of the fireplace was the only light and set her candle holder down on the large trunk next to her bed. Straightening up, she pondered a moment. *Should I write him a letter?* she wondered. Surely, she would have to take some kind of action soon if he did not come to her. She could not simply drift on like seaweed without direction. She glanced over to the window where she knew Lady Jehanne had kept a writing case. Then she froze. A tall figure sat there silently regarding her from the shadows. *Garman.*

He didn't utter a sound. Just met her gaze squarely and impassively. For a moment, she wondered if it was a trick of the light and her own mind. Then her eyes adjusted, and she made out his features plainly. He was watchful and tense, despite his stillness, and she realized he was waiting for her reaction.

She cleared her throat. "Husband," she greeted him calmly. He nodded and Lenora moved to the foot of the bed and sat there so they were directly opposite each other. "What happens now?" she asked softly, hoping the candlelight would not show her pallor or tiredness.

"Parlay," he replied abruptly.

"Parlay?" It was not what she had expected or hoped for.

"We agree terms," he elaborated, and Lenora felt a jolt of cold fear.

"For separation?" she croaked, grasping a bedpost.

"What? Fuck no," he replied angrily, then seemed to check himself. "I should probably warn you now, if we can't agree terms, I'll just drag you off with me. I'm *trying* to be civilized." He glared at her.

Lenora felt so relieved she almost sank down on the bed. Then she felt something spark at the base of her spine. "I apologize if I'm being dense," she said carefully. "But terms for what? Last time I saw you, you made it very plain that you wanted me out of your life and were done with me."

"I was angry," he said flatly. "And—hasty," he added with a rasp in his voice. Lenora waited as he seemed to struggle with words. "Just tell me what you need from me, Lenora."

"Need from you?"

"In order for us to get back to where we were. Before everything—"

"Fell apart?"

His eyes fell away from hers. "Before I pulled everything apart," he admitted tersely.

"I don't need anything from you, Garman," she said, lifting her chin. "I have a leaky roof over my head, and I have no doubt I can carve a life for myself here if I must."

"I'm sure you can," he said roughly. "But I can't spare you. You may not need me, but I need you."

Lenora looked up, her breath coming fast. "What of your grand scheme for revenge?" she forced herself to ask. She thought he colored slightly, but it was hard to tell in the shadows.

He held her gaze. "I'm done with it. I'm only hurting myself."

Lenora swallowed, forcing herself to take a deep breath in and out. Her brain raced, trying to remember how parlay was supposed to work. You laid out the terms for negotiating a truce, she thought. So, if she overplayed her hand now by demanding he lived at Twyford Castle, she could then allow herself to be negotiated down to his simply *not* purchasing Matchings Halt.

Do I have the nerve to ask for such a thing though? she wondered. What if he ended up flinging off, enraged again? Negotiations were tricky things, were they not? Then again, she had no experience of diplomacy to draw on. She would simply have to plunge on and hope for the best.

"I want you to take up your rightful place here, at Twyford Castle," she said outrageously and watched his face, waiting for him to explode. "We can use my dowry to instigate much-needed repairs."

His face blank, he answered her coolly, "This place is a bottomless well, Lenora. Your dowry would disappear without a trace."

492

Lenora shrugged as though with supreme unconcern. "You regularly win purses of gold at the tournaments, do you not? Those would supply us with steady income enough."

He snorted. "They would also be swallowed up into dark nothingness!" He took a deep breath, as if striving for calm. "An estate of this size is an unwieldy beast with a monstrous appetite," he pointed out.

Lenora nodded; she could not dispute the fact. "Oh yes, but on my father's death, I have no doubt he will leave me his vast fortune. He has no other children and is not overly fond of either of my cousins."

"You want to throw every coin we have at it? When we could live in comfort and wealth at Matchings Halt?" He was clearly incensed at the notion, but fighting to remain calm.

Lenora nodded, and when he fell silent, decided she had better go all in. "Don't forget," she continued rashly. "We have something the old earl was forced to live without these past twenty-seven years. We have your grandfather Sutton. Oates has been telling me that when he ran this place, it had tenants who were happy and paid their rent and—"

"Half the farms lie empty and are practically derelict," Garman cut across her words angrily.

"I know that, Oates explained. But we could spend my dowry on getting the farms renovated for new tenants," she said as inspiration struck. She was really on a roll now.

"The farms?" he echoed. "Not the roof? Not the—"

Lenora shook her head. "The farms," she repeated insistently. "The family could be moved into the west wing of the castle entirely where conditions are best."

"To camp there until money trickles in to mend the roof?" Garman asked acidly.

"Precisely. You will have to win gold at the winter tournament, of course." He stared at her a moment as if incapable of speech. "Grandfather Sutton will move back to the castle and we would rent out Matchings Farm—"

"I couldn't ask him to do that!" he interrupted in blunt refusal.

"Why? He does not consider the farm to be his home. Do you know where he thinks of as home, Garman? You will never guess." When he did not speak, she said softly, "It is here."

"What?" he burst forth. "You think his dearest wish is to live as a servant again?"

"Oh Garman," she sighed. "He grew up there, it was his *home* and his father's home. And his father's father. He loves Twyford Castle probably as much as the earl did. If he could get his hands on the account books and the running of the place again, he would *love* it! Especially if he could turn things around, don't you see? That would really show everyone that the old earl's downfall was throwing out his right-hand man!"

"He's his own master now," Garman pointed out, looking thunderstruck. "You mean to tell me he'd rather return to some subservient position than be his own man in his own home."

"I know he would," Lenora said simply. "He was raised to be steward here, it's in his blood. And if you gave him someone to train up to take over after him, he would be absolutely in his element. Grandfather Sutton," Lenora concluded, "is one of those people who has to feel useful. Otherwise, he becomes disheartened and loses interest in things."

Garman was looking at her hard now. "And do you know what kind you are?"

Lenora was thrown for a minute. "I think so," she answered slowly.

"I doubt it very much," he said with a short laugh. Was he insulting her? Lenora flushed, then he stood up, confounding her. "Very well," he said shortly. "I agree to your terms."

Her mouth fell open. "What?" she gasped faintly.

"I yield," he said steadily. "Whatever you want."

Lenora stared. "Wait, I—"

"I don't think I can wait," he admitted bluntly. "But if you need this night to come to terms with our reconciliation, then I'll sleep elsewhere. Another chamber, I don't care if it leaks so long as we remain under the same roof." He cleared his throat. "Or we could formalize it now." His gaze slid to the bed then back to her.

"Another chamber?" she echoed. "No, I don't want you to go!"

"Good," he said harshly and reached for her, pulling her up into his arms. At the feel of his strong arms around her, Lenora melted into him with a grateful cry. "If you're tired, we can just sleep," he said, and she felt his lips at her brow. "Just let me hold you." Her head reeling, Lenora felt herself swung up and carried over to the bed. "You look tired." His voice cracked. "And small wonder. I should never have left you in a household of death—"

"No, I'm glad for it," Lenora said as he laid her down. "For I think your cousins were at breaking point. Your aunt, the Lady Jehanne, has abandoned them."

He grunted, slipping her shoes off her feet. She thought he uttered "Small mercies" but she wasn't sure.

"Garman, I don't really—"

"Hush now, we've thrashed out the main terms," he urged. "Let's discuss the details later. For now, I want to concentrate on this. On you and me."

She tried to catch his eye as he loosed the laces to her gown, but he was intent on his task and would not meet her gaze. She lifted her arms obligingly as he drew her gown over her head and then he drew the covers over her.

She rolled onto her side and watched as he speedily undressed and then slid in beside her. In an instant, his arms were around her, his face resting against the swell of her bosom. Lenora raised one hand to run through his short hair, and the other to stroke against his face.

"You came to me," she said, half wonderingly.

"Did you doubt I would?" he asked gruffly in muffled tones. "Eventually?"

"In my lowest moments, yes."

His grip tightened almost painfully. "I can scarce breathe," she said with some amusement. Grudgingly, he relaxed his hold. "Who showed you to this chamber? You could not have guessed it was mine."

"Magda," he said shortly. "And that excitable servant who cries a lot."

"Oates."

"Yes, him."

That must have been where they disappeared to after supper, she thought. "Did you come from the Grange?" He shook his head. Lenora hesitated. "The farm?" she guessed and felt him nod. "You've been staying at the farm?"

With a huff, he lifted his face from her breasts. "Yes, these last three days," he admitted. She noticed that he looked as weary as she felt. Sliding her hands from the back to the front of his head, she cupped his face. "You look tired."

"I feel it," he said. "Why aren't you giving me a harder time?" he asked hoarsely. "You should be angrier with me. Why aren't you?"

Lenora blinked. Did he not think she had demanded enough from him already? "Part of this is my fault," she admitted. "I should have spoken to you before attending the Earl of Twyford here. And also, I said some unforgiveable things on that first night."

"When?" He lifted his head, looking surprised.

Lenora coughed. "I mean, when I approached you and asked you to marry me," she clarified hurriedly. "When I said those things about how you'd treat a wife worse than your dog," she said, not quite meeting his gaze. "It was wrong of me and—"

"Why?" he interrupted her with a shrug. "That is my reputation after all. You said naught amiss." He hesitated. "Some might say I *have* treated you—"

"You most certainly have not!" Lenora argued hotly. "You are the very best of husbands!"

"The very best?" he spluttered. "My gods, I doubt anyone else would say so!"

Lenora turned thoughtful. "I think I need to learn to be more conciliatory," she confessed. "And avoid confrontation more."

"No," he said, turning onto his back. "I like that you don't back down. No one ever dares stand up to me like you do."

Lenora smoothed a hand across his chest. She was silent a moment, savoring his warm, hard body next to hers again at last. "I want to tell you something," she admitted. "But I'm scared to."

"Don't be," he replied on an outward breath. "I don't want you to be scared to tell me anything ever again."

She ran a finger over his collarbone, following its progress with her eyes. "When I was beautiful and foolish and you never spared me a second glance…" she started hesitantly. Garman's hand grasped her hip firmly, but he held his tongue. "I used to be very, very superstitious," she carried on. "It was sort of my only interest in life, other than my cats." She stole a glance at his face, but he showed no visible reaction. "A fortune-teller once told me—"

"If this is about you being stunted—?" he interrupted her.

"No, no," she assured him. "It's a different one."

"Or there being curse on your face—" he started warningly.

"Nor that one either. It's nothing bad," she said hurriedly. He huffed out a breath and gave a short nod for her continue. "This one was a figure in colored rags outside the abbey at Bonbartle. I was twelve years old. He—he told me about my true love." Her face turned scarlet and she did not dare meet Garman's level gaze. "I think it might be why I had no interest in any of my suitors and why I took so much care to learn all the heraldic devices of all the knights I ever came across." Now she'd started, she found it hard to continue.

"Continue," he said gruffly.

"He—he said my true love had the device of a bleeding heart," she said with breathless wonder. When he said nothing, she continued. "You are familiar with the crest of the Earls of Twyford?"

Garman frowned. "'Tis a black heart on a white background and there are three drops of blood—" She broke off as Garman rolled her under him. "Really, Lenora?" he growled. "You needed this to prove I'm your true love?" He raised an eyebrow at her. "Have you not heard a single thing I've said to you?"

Lenora swallowed. "You—you did not speak of love," she pointed out shakily.

"Yes, I did," he insisted. "With every single word I spoke."

"You did?"

"Aye, with every word and every action."

"You did not say so specifically."

"No, I did not," he agreed. "And neither, wife, did you."

Her gaze flew to meet his. "I did not have the nerve."

"You've nerve enough for plenty," he growled.

Lenora caught her breath. "But you—for me, I mean?"

"I'm here, aren't I?" At her frown, he added roughly, "You gave me sleepless nights and restless days. I ached for you, here." He grasped her hand and slid it over his heart. "Right in my black heart."

The smile dropped from Lenora's lips. "You did?" she whispered, feeling its steady beat beneath her fingers.

"Constantly. Even when I was saying harsh words, they pained me to speak them. Inside, I was torn and bleeding."

"Oh." She moistened her lips. "I wanted you to come for me. I trusted you would, but underneath, I was so afraid you would not." Her voice wobbled. "You're proud. Your grandfather said it's an Orde trait."

"I would always have come for you," he said roughly. "I would have come," he repeated. "Though in truth, my pride held me back as long as I could stand it. Even on the ride over here, I was clutching at lame excuses to give you. Such as Fendrel missed you or was wasting away. He's fine," he added quickly at her expression of concern.

She breathed out then. "I'm glad it did not take longer," she murmured and smiled up at him.

He placed his hands on either side of her face. "I love you, Lenora." His words wiped the smile right off her face. She never would have dreamt he would say it first.

"I love you too," she answered in a choked voice. "Garman Orde."

She watched his shoulders relax and a smile tug at his lips. "Not because of some ragged soothsayer," he insisted. "Though, if his words put you off looking at other men, then I suppose I am indebted to him on that score."

She laughed. "Why, then?" she asked curiously.

"For your own sake," he answered readily enough. "For your quick wits, the fact you laugh when least prudent, your determination to forge your own way." He looked at her long and hard. "For the fact you make the least likely people love you."

"Meaning yourself?"

"Most of all myself. But there are plenty of others. Berta, my cousins and yours, both my grandfathers," he said dryly. "I've a feeling you're only getting started."

She nodded at that and smiled. "I'd like to think so," she began shakily and then he was kissing her.

"I'm sorry," he whispered against her jaw. "I missed you. I was a fool."

Lenora felt her heart swell in her chest. "I missed you too."

"Your family must think me the biggest churl in existence."

"I don't think so," she said with a gurgle of laughter. "Your new title has reconciled my father to you almost entirely."

"Almost?" She dropped her gaze, and he tilted her chin up so he could see her eyes. "Tell me what else I must do?"

"Really, there is nothing—"

"Tell me, Lenora."

She pulled a face. "'Tis only that he would like to parade his son-in-law at court," she admitted. "Which is a thing I told him you will never tolerate."

"Why?" He shrugged. "I can stand that and plenty more if it makes you happy."

Lenora stared. "What? But—"

"I wasn't planning on attending court until the royal tournament, but if he wants me there before that—?"

"No, he suggested that himself," Lenora assured him. "It was only that I did not think you would find such a thing congenial."

He shrugged again. "Now tell me how can I worm my way into your grandmother's graces?"

She marveled at his willingness to even try. "No grand gesture would win her over," she admitted. "But rather the test of time."

He was silent a moment. "I can pass that test, given time, Lenora." She nodded. "You're going to give me that chance, my love?" he asked in a gravelly voice.

"Yes," she whispered, and he was kissing her again.

"Thank the gods," he said devoutly as she wound her arms around his neck. "Are you too tired—?"

"No," she assured him. "Not too tired."

"I love you, Lenora," he repeated as his hand slid up her thigh, hitching up her shift. "I've missed you everywhere, but in my bed the most. Not just for this," he said hastily. "But because I could not be sure you slept soundly without me. I feared you might return to that accursed crypt in your dreams. That thought tormented me—"

Lenora opened her legs and he caught his breath. "I did not have bad dreams," she said. "For I could not allow myself to believe you would not come."

"I don't deserve you," he said shakily as he eased himself between her legs. "But I swear, I'll work at being the man who does."

Lenora clasped him to her, and they affirmed their love through broken murmurs as their bodies welcomed each other's embrace.

"Ah gods, I've missed this," he groaned. "You have no idea how much."

"I might have *some* idea," Lenora teased, but he only shook his head.

"You can't have," he insisted, trailing kisses down her jaw as was his custom. "I've been a soul in torment."

"That bad?" she choked out.

"Worse." Then he started to tremble. "I won't last long."

Lenora wrapped her legs around his hips. "If we stop talking, you might last longer," she suggested.

He gave an uneven laugh. "Don't tease me when I'm this close. You know I can't withstand you."

Lenora bit her lip and arched up into him. "Don't you want to change the position?"

He groaned. "No, I want it this way, so I can look at your face."

Lenora swallowed. "My face?" she asked in a deceptively light voice.

"Aye, wife, your face." His voice was thick with emotion and lust, but he held her gaze as he started to thrust in earnest. "For it's the face I love best in all the world."

Lenora felt the tears rolling down her cheeks at her release, but he kissed them away and then noisily followed her into his own blissful oblivion. Long before Lenora had even resurfaced from her own torpor, he rolled off her, still panting, and tucked her into his side. Sleepily, Lenora placed a hand on his chest and felt the rise and fall as his breathing recovered to a normal pace. At some point her own eyes drifted shut, and she felt him lightly kiss their lids. Comforted, she fell into a deep, unbroken sleep.

When next she woke it was to the gray light of dawn. Turning her head, she was greatly relieved to see Garman lying on his back next to her, one hand resting under his head. He gave her a grin that set her heart fluttering before leaning over and dropping a kiss on her lips.

"Morning, wife."

"For a moment, I was scared it had all been a dream," she admitted drowsily.

His arm closed around her. "You slept like the dead. I've been lying here waiting for you to wake."

"Did you not sleep at all?" she asked, startled.

"Aye, on and off." He looked evasive before admitting, "I wanted to watch over you."

"I told you there were no nightmares."

He snorted. "You also told me I was the best of husbands."

She smiled as memories from the day before flitted into her head. He had come to her; he loved her and could not live without her. Then her eyes widened as she remembered the agreement she had wrung out of him. "Did you really meant what you said about living here at Twyford Castle?" she blurted.

He nodded, looking relaxed. "Of course."

"To change your plans so swiftly—" she marveled, but he cut her short.

"Let's not rehash it," he said with a frown. "I meant every word. In truth, there is no condition you could have set that I would not have agreed to." He gave a wry smile. "You held all the cards."

504

"But I—"

"My love," he said, pulling her firmly against him. "You want to live here, and I want to keep you happy."

"Yes, but please let me explain," Lenora said, trying to slide out of his grip and face him. "You don't have to—"

"Yes, I do," he said, retaining his hold on her with ease. "I want to make you my countess. That means I have certain responsibilities to face up to. My grandfather has been giving me hell," he admitted, "pointing out just that fact." He frowned. "He's never shouted or railed at me before this, you know."

"Grandfather Sutton shouted at you?"

"He called me a bloody-minded young fool," Garman said dryly. "And said he would wash his hands of me altogether if I did not set things to rights with you." He gave a short laugh. "It was by far the most natural conversation we've ever had. I cursed at him and he swore back at me, quite purple in the face." He looked thoughtful. "I didn't even know he knew such words."

"He must have been a good deal upset!" Lenora exclaimed. "He's always so unfailingly polite!"

"That always bothered me." Garman frowned. "I always felt that he saw me as his master and not his grandson."

"He loves you very much, and you really need to work at your relationship," Lenora said sternly.

Garman's frown relaxed. "Yes, I know," he said, running a fingertip between her breasts.

Lenora caught his hand in hers. "Stop trying to distract me, for I have several things to clarify."

He laughed. "Do your worst."

She took a deep breath. "What did you mean when you asked last night if I knew what kind of person I was?"

A shadow stole over his face. "I meant you are the best kind," he answered promptly. "It bothered me a great deal at Kellingford when you said you were nothing and it did not signify what became of you." He gave her a piercing look. "That it did not matter what manner of man you married."

Lenora flushed. "Oh, that." She plucked at the bedcovers. "My opinion of my self-worth has risen a good deal since then."

"Good."

She peeped up at him. "And my opinion of you, naturally."

"Naturally," he agreed dryly, and when he went to reach for her, she stayed his arm.

"I do like the person I am now," she said earnestly. "Becoming this person is what made me whole. Does that make sense? I mean, it was *worth* losing my beauty to become someone both capable of love and worthy of loving."

He frowned over this a moment. "I like your looks, Lenora." He reached out and ran his thumb down the skin of her jaw. "These marks show how you suffered and overcame. They are far more interesting than mere perfection."

She swallowed. "I would like to know when you fell in love with me," she admitted wistfully.

There was a heavy pause before he spoke with a groan. "I think it was when you showed me your eyelids."

"My eyelids?"

He gave a short nod. "Aye," he said gruffly. Then his frown deepened. "Then you flirted with that guard and I wanted to punch him in the face."

Lenora felt she was losing track of the conversation. "I don't think I—?"

"Then you were just so fucking distracting and unexpected. I didn't know what the hell to think," he said, shaking his head. "I already knew by the time we were married that I was in big trouble. But it was too late. I was already in over my head."

Lenora stared at him. "You mean when I showed you my eyelids after I proposed to you?"

"Of course." He sounded slightly impatient.

"*Of course*?" Lenora echoed. "But that was from the very outset. You can't possibly have—"

"Yes, from the outset," he insisted. "I just didn't realize what was happening."

Lenora thought this over in stupefied silence.

"I never wanted to call a woman my own. Not before you."

Lenora held her breath. "Oh."

"But with you, I wanted that almost from the start." He sent a troubled look her way. "You remember how I made that priest bind us? I should have known then."

Gently, she stroked the back of his neck. "You're not in trouble, Garman, because I'm going to be a very good wife to you."

He smiled grimly. "You'd better be…otherwise I'll be disgracing us both."

"Nonsense," she said lightly. "You just require careful handling on my part."

"Lots of handling," he corrected her, sliding his own hands over her hips and around to cup her bottom. "Lots and lots of handling. Even then, I'll likely show you up now and again."

She had smiled at the literal mention of handling, but that faded now. "I don't know what you mean," she said with some spirit. "I would never be ashamed of you."

"You would if you'd seen how I've been carrying on this last week." He winced. "My grandfather pulling out his hair. All his servants muttering and disapproving of the way I drove you away with my sullen ways."

"That wouldn't drive me away."

"Even Huw told me I was a damn fool to let you go. Ivo said I would end up bitter and lonely."

"Really?"

He nodded, shamefaced.

"And they both agree to marrying your cousins?" Lenora pressed.

His eyes slid to hers. "Aye, but don't ask me for details of their decision, as that's all a blur to me. A miserable, wretched blur."

"They told me you spent some of it drunk as a lord."

"Mmm," he agreed. "I don't want to talk about them, Lenora. They can figure things out for themselves."

"But you'll be civil to your cousins," she said anxiously. "They have been very welcoming to me and—"

"Aye, I know that," he growled. "Magda was singing your praises to me last night."

"I want to be good to them, Garman," she said softly. "They have not had an easy life."

That seemed to give him pause for thought. "Very well," he agreed. "If that's what you want."

Lenora gave a happy sigh. "I'm not sure when precisely I fell in love with you," she admitted dreamily. "I only know that I felt so put out when you kept scurrying off to the Hainfroys' that I realized I was actually jealous for the first time in my life!"

"Jealous of the Hainfroys?" He looked startled and disbelieving.

"Yes, for I feared you preferred their company to mine."

"Never."

"I suppose that means I must have fallen for you at Kellingford," she mused. "But you kept confusing me by backing off in horror whenever we grew close, so I did not realize it as I should."

He winced. "I was a damned jealous mess at Kellingford. Next time we attend a tournament, I'll handle it better. At least," he added scrupulously, "I'll try."

She smiled up at him and felt her own eyes shining.

"Gods, Lenora," he said. "I'll do anything to keep you looking at me like that."

"Who do you think put this expression on my face in the first place?" she murmured as she reached up to bring his face down level to hers. "It was you," she whispered and kissed him.

Epilogue

One Month Later

Garman walked down from the stables in the direction of the Grange. He had meant every word when he said his cousins and the Hainfroys would have to work things out for themselves. Still, after spending four weeks at Twyford Castle, occasionally, very occasionally during a quiet moment, he would feel a twinge of unease about his hasty action in marrying them off so precipitately to each other. Lenora said he was at last growing a conscience, but he wasn't so sure about that.

As he reached the door, he steeled himself for a flood of complaints—half of which would no doubt come from Berta, who he was starting to suspect was habitually foul-tempered. Certainly, he had noticed no sweetening of her nature since she had been transplanted from Matchings Farm. Lenora met with her every market day and implored Berta to join them at Twyford Castle if she was truly unhappy, but the old woman refused to budge another inch. *I been hassled from pillar to post already*, she would grumble. *And shall be worried into an early grave at this rate!*

Garman was hard-pressed to retain a sympathetic look on his face while Lenora updated him about Berta's woes, though he just about managed it in the main. He certainly was not keen for the old crone to get her feet back under his table. Hawise and most of the farm staff had accompanied his grandfather to Twyford Castle and were rubbing along tolerably well with Oates and the other retainers. The last thing he wanted was Berta coming along and upsetting the delicate balance.

As for the Hainfroys, they had been invited to the castle many a time since their marriages, but so far had failed to make even one appearance. Lenora had sent him along this morning to make sure all was well with them.

510

To his surprise, he did not see Berta in the low-beamed kitchen, but instead Magda and Ivo sat opposite each other at the kitchen table. Garman checked on the threshold, unsure whether to intrude. Magda was cutting vegetables to pieces and nervously chattering in a manner which seemed very uncharacteristic of her haughty character. She looked skittish in the extreme, and small wonder Garman thought a moment later when he noticed Ivo, for his friend's gaze was trained on her with a single-minded intensity that even a stout-hearted person would find unnerving.

Ivo, he realized, was watching his bride like she was his prey. Brows raised, Garman turned back to his cousin who was making a right hash of preparing their food, though Ivo clearly did not care. Magda's face was red as a beet and she kept stealing glances at her husband like some shy village girl at her swain.

All of a sudden, she let out a yell and dropped her knife. Ivo was on her in a trice, binding her wounded finger in a cloth. Even from his spot at the door, Garman could see it was just a trifling nick. For some reason, Ivo, who had his own face sliced open on the battlefield, was fussing over it more than if it were a war wound. Garman cleared his throat, and both turned toward him guiltily, Magda looking embarrassed and Ivo resentful of the interruption.

"Morning. Where is Huw?" Garman asked with a frown.

"Out in the barn." Ivo did not even trouble to take his gaze from his wife as he spoke.

Garman backed out of the kitchen as fast as his legs could carry him. Still, to his surprise he saw Ivo drop a kiss on the top of her injured finger. Magda turned crimson and held her breath. Garman turned away hurriedly. What the fuck was this about? He'd find Huw and ask him.

Huw had not been as keen as Ivo to go through with the handfasting ceremony and had looked surly on the occasion, getting very drunk in the aftermath. No doubt, it would take him far longer for him to smooth things over with his bride.

He had only got halfway to the stables when he heard the rumble of Huw's deep-timbred voice. It wasn't coming from the barn where they kept the horses, but a smaller one where Berta did the laundry. Garman made his way warily in that direction.

As he approached, he could hear Agnes's voice, raised and belligerent. "What do you do here and what do you want with me?" she asked crossly. "I thought I would at least find some peace in this quiet corner, but you come and persecute me with your company even here!"

"I'm bored," Garman heard Huw rumble back at her. "Your sister and my brother are acting like a pair of lovebirds and frankly, I find it hard to stomach. Come and bear me company at least."

"I will not!" Agnes flung back at him. "I've no more stomach for it than you have!"

Huw gave an amused chuckle. "Well, you're not dull in any event."

"Were you expecting me to be?" Agnes asked sharply.

"I was expecting you to be a damn useless invalid," he admitted bluntly. "But I have heard from other sources that you're not lame, just lazy."

Garman heard Agnes's indignant splutter and braced himself to intervene if Agnes let fly, but instead all he heard was the rustle of something.

"What are you doing?" he heard Agnes ask with a muffled squeak.

"Determining how much sensation you have in your legs. You feel that?"

"Of course!"

Garman frowned. Instead of blundering in, he applied his eye to a crack in the barn door. Huw was knelt next to Agnes's chair, his hands encircling her ankles. Agnes looked stunned to find her ankles being touched in such a fashion. She blinked down at her husband in astonishment. After a moment, Huw slid his hands up her calves to Agnes's knees.

"And this?"

"I—yes! S-stop that!" Agnes gasped, sitting upright, her face flushing bright red.

"Shhh, keep quiet now or your little dog will come running, yapping his head off, and then we'll be interrupted," Huw advised her, glancing swiftly at the door. "And neither of us wants that now, do we, love?" His hands were still under Agnes's skirts and from the slight rustling sound, Garman suspected he was stroking her calves. Huw's voice lowered. "How about you let me go higher still, Agnes?"

Agnes clamped her mouth shut, looking scandalized, but not, Garman noted, telling him to stop. He straightened up hastily. He didn't need to see any more. If his cousin had cried out or objected, he would have made it his business to interrupt them. But clearly, that was not the case, so he swiftly made his way back toward the stables where he had left Bria'ag and started back home. He was halfway to Twyford Castle before he even realized he had not seen Berta or the cats. Damn it, he would

513

have to call out again the next day or Lenora would be setting a flea in his ear.

*

"Things are even more chaotic at the Grange," he announced, entering the great hall where Lenora sat poring over some ledger. He had paused only to hand Bria'ag to Kit and give him his list of exhaustive duties for the day. So far, Lenora's cousin was proving to be an apt learner, though sometimes his high spirits needed ruthlessly suppressing.

Fendrel had taken to following Kit around the courtyard, watching his training with great interest. The little gray cat mewed a greeting to him from a window ledge and Garman reached up his hand to absently scratch his ears as he passed by him.

Lenora looked up with interest at his greeting and returned the swift kiss he pressed to her cheek. "Why, husband? What's happening now?"

He shot a glance in the opposite direction where Oates and his grandfather Sutton were stood conferring over some household matter. "If I didn't know better, wife," he said slowly, "I would suspect you had been trying to thwart my revenge from the very start."

She smiled at that. "I can't think what you mean," she said, closing her book. "What's amiss?"

"Depends on your viewpoint."

A look of concern crossed Lenora's face. "Not Agnes? Her leg—?"

"Does not seem to be troubling her," Garman cut her off, reaching for a cup and the jug of ale. "Or slowing down Huw's seduction."

Lenora's mouth fell open. "Huw's seduction—?" she spluttered.

"Aye." He poured a drink. "It's just as well you did not accompany me. It was not fit viewing for a modest woman."

A question trembled on Lenora's lips. He could see discretion was struggling with blatant curiosity. "What happened?" she blurted as curiosity came out the victor.

He smirked. "Well, first I was treated to a display of Magda mangling the vegetables for their dinner." He took a deep drink of ale.

"Was Ivo around?"

"Aye and watching her like a hawk."

Lenora's eyes were round with wonder. She sat up straighter. "Go on," she urged. "How did they seem?"

"She's a rotten hand in the kitchen, I can tell that much. Ended up bleeding all over the leeks."

"Oh dear!"

He regarded her a moment with narrowed eyes. "This is your doing, wife."

"What is?" She colored at his words and touched the hair coiled at her nape lightly. "I don't know what you mean. Tell me about Magda," she insisted. "Was Ivo concerned when she cut herself?"

He snorted. "He acted like she'd suffered a mortal wound." He watched the small smile play around Lenora's lips. At one time, he would have been annoyed by this turn of events, he reflected wryly. All his plans had come to naught, but for some reason, he didn't give a damn. Even now, he could feel the flicker of a pulse in his groin that had kicked into life at the sight of his wife's curving lips.

"Why do you say Huw is seducing Agnes?" she demanded.

He rolled his eyes. "Because I walked in on them playing farmhand and country maiden in the barn."

Lenora looked intrigued. "How does one play that?" Then she seemed to collect herself, catching sight of his expression. "Never mind," she said hastily. "But relations seem to be going well between them?"

He grunted a reluctant affirmative. "You anticipated this turn of events, wife, and you won't convince me otherwise. It always seemed odd to me that you insisted the elder Hainfroy was married to the younger of the sisters," he added suspiciously. "You had some reason for it, I have no doubt."

"You said you did not wish to know anything about my nefarious plots," Lenora reminded him virtuously. "You were quite firm on the matter as I recall."

"True," he growled, regarding her with a gleaming eye. "Shall I show you how one plays that game, Lenora? There are plenty of barns and outhouses on our own property."

Lenora looked evasive. "I'm not sure," she said. "Is it a proper thing for a countess to know?"

"It depends."

She lifted a brow. "On what?"

"If the farmhand is also an earl."

She laughed at that. "I've got far too much work to do," she scolded as he rounded the table and scooped her up in his arms. "Garman!" Grizelda, who had been sleeping on the bench next to her, opened sleepy eyes in reproach. The white cat yawned and rolled onto her other side.

Garman nodded to his grandfather, who was watching them exit the room with benign approval.

"You can't keep carrying me off to our bedchamber like this whenever the fancy takes you!" Lenora reproached him.

"I think you'll find I can, my love."

"Not without repercussions," she warned him direly.

"Such as?" he asked idly as he mounted the first few stairs.

"You realize you'll likely put a baby in my belly?"

His step never even faltered. "Oh yes," he agreed richly. "I'll do that, alright. Probably several, you'd like that, would you, wife?"

She gazed at him speechlessly. "Do you know," she said, "I rather think I would?"

A wolfish smile greeted this. "Just as well," he said. "Because it turns out I have absolutely no control when I'm with you."

She fell silent a moment. "If we have daughters…" She hesitated. "They may be beautiful."

He almost laughed at how troubled she sounded at the notion. "Bound to be, if they follow their mother," he acknowledged calmly.

"That could bring attendant difficulties," she said. "How should you handle suitors lurking around every corner?" she asked, biting her lip.

"How do you think?" he growled.

Lenora laughed. "I think you might be equal to the problem."

"As do I," he agreed. "If we have a son, he may be very stubborn and strong-willed. What say you to that?"

"Honestly, that's the only kind of male I have experience in handling," Lenora pointed out.

Just for an instant, his elusive smile flashed out again. "Never a truer word was spoken."

"Of course," she started as they reached the top of the staircase. "It will mean expanding the tiny cache of people you permit yourself to care about."

He halted, looking down at her. "People keep sneaking into that category now," he complained.

Lenora perked up excitedly. "Such as?"

He glowered at her. "We'll discuss it later."

Lenora beamed. "I look forward to it."

"You will be exhausted, and I will be brief."

"I will rouse myself from my lethargy to pay attention," she said smugly. "And then remind you of it at inopportune times."

"I don't doubt that, wife," he said, swinging open the door to their bedchamber. "So long as you remember who heads the list, I don't mind."

"Who heads your list, husband?" she asked softly.

"You do," he replied promptly, heading for the bed. "You know I love you with all my heart."

It still took her breath away when he said it. Glancing down at the enameled ring she now wore on her finger depicting the black Twyford heart shedding its three drops of red blood, Lenora nodded. "Yes," she agreed. "The same way that I love you."

THE END

If you want to read more about Karadok, then the next book in the series is Princess Una's story:

The Consulation Prize

Princess Una harbors no illusions about her claims to Karadok's throne. The days of the royal house of Blechmarsh are done. The last of that ill-fated line, she is just grateful she emerged from the dark days of war with her head still on her shoulders. Now if only she could stop these rebellious northern lords from plotting to overthrow the King and set her up in his stead!

When her royal cousin bids her to join him at court, Una is eager for the opportunity to publicly renounce her rights. After three years languishing under house arrest, she is keen to start her own life afresh, hopefully in relative obscurity.

Little does she realize what manner of husband fate has in store for her…

If you enjoyed this book, please consider leaving me a rating on Goodreads, Amazon, Bookbub or wherever else you leave your reviews. I would be very grateful.

You can find my website at: www.alicecoldbreath.com where you can sign up for my monthly newsletter and find out what I am up to.

Also, please do check out some of my other stories!
Many thanks, Alice